James H. Graff, James Grant

Jane Seton

The king's Advocate

James H. Graff, James Grant

Jane Seton
The king's Advocate

ISBN/EAN: 9783337348908

Printed in Europe, USA, Canada, Australia, Japan

Cover: Foto ©Andreas Hilbeck / pixelio.de

More available books at **www.hansebooks.com**

JANE SETON:

OR,

THE KING'S ADVOCATE.

A Scottish Historical Romance.

By JAMES GRANT,

AUTHOR OF

"THE ROMANCE OF WAR," "THE AIDE-DE-CAMP," ETC. ETC.

NEW EDITION.

LONDON:

GEORGE ROUTLEDGE AND SONS,

BROADWAY, LUDGATE HILL.

NEW YORK: 129, GRAND STREET.

1865.

LONDON:
SAVILL AND EDWARDS, PRINTERS,
CHANDOS-STREET.

PREFACE.

THE genius of a monarch is said to stamp a character upon his time; but this can scarcely be said to have been the good fortune of the sovereign in whose reign I have laid the following romance.

Like all the princes of his house, James V. was far in advance of the age in which he lived; for to all his forefathers' valour and passionate love of their native Scotland (for whose soil so many of them had shed their blood in battle), to their elegant taste in all the arts, their patronage of science and commerce, he united a love for romantic adventure, which, like James IV., made him the idol of the people. But the Scottish nobles, though affording us many bright and glorious examples of high valour and pure patriotism, have generally been a race of men too ready to sacrifice the dearest interests of their country for lucre or ambition; and were really, in all ages, a curse alike to our kings and the nation.

In the following pages I have endeavoured to portray something of their savage pride and unscrupulous spirit; and to give a picture of those dark days of violence when danger was the pastime and arms the occupation of our people; when it was sadly but truly said, that grey hairs were seldom seen under a Scotsman's bonnet, and that a Scottish mother had seldom a son left to lay her head in the grave, for in civil strife or foreign war they had all gone before her to the land of the leal.

There is much that is veritable history, and much that is old tradition, woven up with my fiction; and though the reader may be able to distinguish these passages, I shall mention, that the king's adventure in the cavern, the *three* trees of Dysart, and John of Clatto, are ancient legends of Fife; while the point on which the whole story turns—the strange and frantic love of Otterburn—is taken partly from an incident which is mentioned in the annals of the House of Angus, and bears a conspicuous place in the early criminal records of Scotland. It will be found related at further length in the notes.

The King's Advocate was so named, to distinguish him from the Crown Prince's Advocate, an office which existed before the abolition of many of those more important public institutions of which Scotland has permitted herself to be deprived.

The King's Advocate, with whose name I have made so free in these volumes, was the son of Thomas Otterburn of Edinburgh, who was slain at the battle of Flodden, and of Katharine Brown. He was Lord Provost of Edinburgh from 1524 to 1535, and was our ambassador to England between the same years. He was knighted in 1534, but was imprisoned in the castle of Dumbarton for being too partial to Englishmen. He was highly esteemed by Buchanan, who has embalmed his memory in beautiful Latin verse.

Vipont, the hero, bears an old Scottish surname, which was famous in the middle ages, though it has now almost disappeared. Andro Wyntown, the Prior of St. Serf, mentions that *Alan ye Vipownt* was keeper of Lochlevin, and defended that fortress valiantly in the wars of the Scottish succession. Another, Sir William Vipont, was one of the two Scottish knights slain on the glorious 24th of June, 1314. They were barons of Aberdour on the northern shore of the Forth, where their ruined castle, a massive pile indicative of great strength and ancient grandeur, is yet to be seen. Roland Vipont is meant to represent the last of that old race, whose arms are still recorded to have been six annulets *or*, with a swan's head rising from a coronet.

Let it not be thought that I have made James V. or his minister speak too harshly of Henry VIII.'s moral character, when we bear in mind that Dr. Bayley, in his "Life of Bishop Fisher," has plainly asserted and proved, that the English king married Anne Boleyn, knowing her to be his *own* daughter. So much for the "Bluff King Hal" of romance.

If, on one hand, I have omitted to portray the Cardinal Primate as the monster we have been taught to believe him, I do not, on the *other*, wish it to be thought that I consider the good Father St. Bernard as a type of the Scottish clergy in 1537. Very far from it; they were the reverse of all I have made that meek old priest. But, doubtless, there must have been exceptions; and it must be remembered, that all our accounts of them and the Cardinal have come down to us from their enemies.

A Scottish novelist labours under a great disadvantage, when endeavouring to introduce effectively for English readers old national characters who speak their own language, which, to a modern Englishman, would be as unintelligible as Choctaw; hence the conventional half-dialect usually adopted. It is a curious fact, that in the days of Alexander I. or

Robert I., the dialects of the two nations were more alike than they are *to-day*. Since then, the language of South Britain has gradually been changing, and becoming what is strictly termed *English;* while the Gothic dialect of the North has remained pretty much the same; hence the Scot can read with ease, and fully understand, the obsolete phrases and idioms of Chaucer, Spenser, Shakespeare, &c., many parts of the old editions of whose works are now almost unintelligible to the mass of their own countrymen.

EDINBURGH,
1*st January*, 1853.

CONTENTS.

JANE SETON:

OR,

THE KING'S ADVOCATE.

CHAPTER I.

JANE SETON.

" I prithee mark
His countenance; unlike bold calumny,
Which sometime dare not speak the thing it looks,
He dare not look the thing he speaks, but bends
His gaze on the blind earth."—*The Cenci.*

On the 19th of May, 1537, the bells of Edinburgh rang joyously. It was a day of loyalty and merriment such as never more may gladden Scotland's ancient capital.

After a nine months' absence, James V.—"the good king James, the commons' king, the father of the poor," the patron of the infant arts and sciences, the mirror of chivalry and romance, as he was affectionately named by a people who idolized him—had arrived in the Firth of Forth with his young queen Magdalene of Valois, whom for her dazzling beauty he had chosen from among three princesses, all possessed of unusual charms, and whom he had espoused in the great cathedral of Notre Dame de Paris, in presence of her father, the magnificent and magnanimous Francis I., seven cardinals, and all the noblesse and beauty of France. After spending the honeymoon at the Hôtel de Cluny, a beautiful old gothic house belonging to the family of Lorraine, they had sailed for Scotland.

All the capital was on tiptoe, and its streets were crowded to excess by the retinues of the nobles and lesser barons, who had come thither to gratify their curiosity and evince their loyalty on the auspicious occasion.

The day was one of the most beautiful of all that sunny

month; and the summer air was laden with the perfume of flowers, for garlands and bouquets were festooned from window to window across the main street leading to the palace, a thoroughfare six-and-twenty yards in breadth; while the stone columns of the girth-cross of the holy sanctuary, the Jerusalem-cross of St. John, the great market-cross of the city, bearing aloft the unicorn rearing on a tressured shield, and the famous stone statue of Our Lady which then stood at the east end of St. Giles's church, were all wreathed and hidden under the spoil of a hundred blooming gardens.

Scaffolds and balconies hung with tapestry and rare carpets of foreign manufacture, or painted with azure, starred with shining gold, occupied the sides of the streets in many places, and were crowded with the families of the surrounding land-holders, the better classes of citizens, and the baronial dwellers of the Blackfriars' Wynd and the Canongate; a great part of the latter street consisted then of turreted villas and strongly-built but detached mansion-houses surrounded by spacious gardens. Banners innumerable, bearing the heraldic cognizances of the proud, the noble, and the brave of Scotland's ancient days, waved from window, turret, and bartizan; the city fountains poured forth purple wine and nut-brown ale alternately (for the Scots had the former duty-free before the Union), and the stalwart deacon convener of the gallant craftsmen, sheathed in complete armour, with the famous Blue Blanket, or banner of the Holy Ghost, displayed, mustered the Baxters, the Websters, Cordiners, Dagger and Bonnet makers, and other ancient corporations, each under their several standards, to line the High-street, on either side, from the Butter Tron to the Netherbow, keeping clear a lane of some forty feet in breadth. These stout craftsmen, who mustered to the number of several thousands, were all arrayed in green gaberdines, red hose, and blue bonnets, and were armed as archers, with a steel gorget, a short but strong Scottish bow, a sheaf of arrows, a battle-axe, and long dagger.

With the city sword and mace, and his own helmet and banner borne before him, the Lord Provost, Sir James Lawson, of the Highrigs, with all the baillies and burgesses clad in gowns of scarlet, furred with miniver, and wearing chains of gold; the heralds and pursuivants in their plumed bonnets and gorgeous tabards, with standards and trumpets, musicians, minstrels, and macers, waited at the western entrance of the city to receive the king and queen with all due loyalty and splendour of pageantry; while the priests of rank, the knights, nobles, and senators of the College of Justice, had all ridden to Leith to conduct the royal pair in procession to Holyrood.

It is said that the beautiful Magdalene, on landing from the high-pooped and gaily-bannered ship of Sir Robert Barton, the king's admiral, knelt gracefully down on the sands of Leith, and lifting a handful to her lips, kissed it ere she threw it away crosswise, and raising her large dark eyes to heaven, prayed with deep pathos "to God, the blessed Virgin, and all the saints, for the happiness of Scotland, the land of her adoption, and its people."

The bright sunshine of the glorious May morning poured aslant its flaky radiance between the breaks and openings in those irregular masses of building, that tower up to such a giddy height on both sides of the central street of the ancient city; the south was sombre and grey, but the north was glowing in warmth, as the sunlight played along its far-stretching vista. Many of these houses were flat-roofed, flagged with large stones, like ancient towers, or covered with thatch; but few that overlooked the pageant about to be described are standing now, as the city was fired by the English in eight places seven years after, in the war with Henry VIII.

By the skill of a certain cunning craftsman, the High-street, even at that early period, was well paved; and the monks of Holyrood kept the Canongate (which is but a further continuation of the same thoroughfare) well cause-wayed, for which the reverend Lord Abbot levied a duty upon every cart, laden or unladen, which entered the eastern barrier of the burgh. All the open windows of that great street, the tall edifices of which rise to the height of eight and ten stories, exciting still the astonishment of every tra-veller, were filled with glad faces; every bartizan, outshot, and projection bore its load of shouting urchins; even the leads and parapets of the great cathedral, with its hideously grotesque stone-gutters, carved into devils and dragons, wyverns and other monsters, bore a freight of spectators, the buzz of whose voices, above and below, imparted a liveliness to the scene, and relieved the tedium of long expectation and waiting for the approach of the royal party.

The utmost good-humour pervaded these expectant crowds, though sometimes a brawl seemed likely to ensue, when a gentleman of pride and pedigree, with velvet cloak, a long rapier, and tall feather, despising the authority of the convener and his bands of mechanical craftsmen, marched down the centre of the street, with a few well-armed serving-men following doggedly at his heels, with brows bent, their swords girt up, and that expression on their faces which seemed so much as to say, "We are Humes, Douglases, or Scotts, or Setons, and who will dare to meddle with us!"

With these, such was the patent of gentle blood, the burgher archers dared not interfere; but their unstrung bows and gauntleted hands pommelled without mercy any luckless countryman or denizen of Leith or St. Ninian's Row who encroached on the causeway, which by order of the knightly provost was to be kept clear by all. Such incidental brawls were generally quelled by the interference of some passing grey friar or Dominican.

Those cavaliers who assumed the right of perambulating the open street were, as I have said, almost invariably attended by bands of followers, armed with swords and round targets, steel caps and corslets. Several of these were invariably greeted by a yell of hostility and epithets of opprobrium from those who occupied the windows, and who found this a more safe experiment than it could have proved to those who stood in the street below.

These obnoxious personages were generally lesser barons and gentlemen of the house of Douglas, a clan which, from its numerical force, pride, power, and turbulence, had long been inimical to the house of Stuart, and more especially to James V., who after many efforts had completely broken its strength, reduced its numerous strongholds, and driven the chief, Archibald sixth Earl of Angus, and Knight of St. Michael, from his high offices of Lord Chancellor and Lieutenant of the East and Middle Marches, with all the noblesse of his surname and faction, to exile in England; where, like all Scottish rebels and malcontents, according to the ancient line of southern policy, they were fostered and protected by Henry VIII.

By the knights and gentlemen of the proscribed name those marks of hostility from the vulgar herd were treated with silent scorn; but their followers scowled about them with clenched weapons and kindling eyes, that showed how intensely they longed to react the great High-street conflict of 1520, and revenge on the rabble of Edinburgh the insults they now endured. These evidences of hostility and political disgust were soon lost amid the general spirit of rejoicing that pervaded the entire body of the people; for loyalty and devotion to their old hereditary line of princes was then an inborn sentiment in the Scots, who were devout believers in the divine right of kings, and had not yet been taught by their preachers to view their old regal race as tyrants and oppressors.

Among all this mirth and festivity there were two persons whose sobriety and staidness of demeanour were very remarkable.

One was a young man about six-and-twenty, who had, apparently, just entered the city, for his boots and leathern gambadoes were covered with dust. He wore a plain gaberdine, or frock, of white Galloway frieze, with horn buttons; but beneath it appeared a doublet of escaupil to protect him from sword thrusts, an unusual garment for one of his class, for his grey maud, or plaid, blue bonnet, backsword, and hunting-knife announced him a yeomen or agriculturist. He carried a great knotty walking-staff, recently cut from some wayside thicket; but to a close observer it would have seemed perfectly evident that the profusion of his beard and moustache was worn rather for disguise than adornment. He was reading a paper affixed to the cross of St. John of Jerusalem which stood in the centre of the Canongate, immediately opposite the arch which now gives admittance to St. John's-street, the ground of which was then closely built upon.

It was a proclamation, issued by the nobles who governed in the king's absence, offering a thousand merks of Scottish money for " ye heid of Archibald Seton, umquhile Earle of Ashkirk," accused of leaguing with that false traitor, Archibald Douglas, sometime Earl of Angus, who had recently been on the borders, at the head of some English mosstroopers, infesting the bounds of the knight, Sir Mark Kerr, of Cessford.

With a brow that loured, and fierce eye that kindled, the young man read, from beginning to end, this proclamation (which was obnoxious to so many), and his hand gradually tightened on the handle of his poniard as he proceeded. Sud denly remembering that he might be observed, a smile of scorn, such a lordly smile as never clown could have given, spread over his dark features; he gave a glance of peculiar import at a group of ladies who occupied a balcony imme-diately opposite St. John's Cross, and, drawing his bonnet well over his brows, looked round for some obscure nook from whence to see, in security, the progress of the royal pageant.

" How little can they imagine that *I* am so near them," said the Earl of Ashkirk (for the stranger was no other than he), as he dived among the crowd and disappeared.

The other personage to whom reference has been made, was a tall and finely-formed man, of a noble presence and commanding stature, possessing a remarkably handsome face, with a loftiness of bearing that never failed to strike the beholder with interest. His complexion was dark, his nose slightly aquiline, his eyes black, and sparkling beneath two brows that were almost joined together. At times, a fierce and restless expression lit up these fiery and penetrating eyes, and knit his smooth expansive forehead, while his mous-tached lip curled with pride and severity; and then a languor and sadness stole over them, as other and softer emotions subdued the bitter thoughts some passing incidents had roused. He was dressed in a doublet and trunk hose of black velvet, laced and buttoned with silver, and trimmed with miniver : a black velvet bonnet, adorned by a single diamond and one tail white ostrich feather, shaded his dark, short, curly hair. He wore a short poniard and long rapier in an embroidered belt, and had spurs, heavily gilded and embossed, on the heels of his maroquin boots.

This man was Sir Adam Otterburn, of Redhall, the King's Advocate in the recently-instituted College of Justice, a great favourite with his royal master, and one who, for his learning, probity, courage, and office, was loved by some, respected by many, and feared by all. His features were pale and hollow, for he was recovering from a late illness, brought on by a wound received in a conflict with the Douglases, a circum-stance which alone, on this auspicious day, confined him to a cushioned chair at the window of his house, which over-looked the High-street, where all the beauty and bravery of Edinburgh had thronged to welcome home King James.

Oblivious of the bustle pervading that long and stately

thoroughfare, the streaming pennons, the waving banners, the
gaudy tapestries and garlands that festooned every balcony
and decorated every window, the Knight of Redhall continued
to gaze upon the fair occupants of the temporary gallery
which we have before mentioned as standing near St. John's
Cross.

It was hung and canopied with scarlet cloth and festoons of
flowers; the front was painted with gold and azure, and
thereon lay a banner, bearing under an earl's coronet, and
within a widow's lozenge, the three crescents of Seton, within
a double tressure, flowered and counter-flowered with golden
fleurs-de-lis, quartered with "the bloody heart," the dreaded
cognizance of the obnoxious Douglases—a badge which,
though it seldom gained love, never failed to inspire fear.
An old lady and several fair young belles, whose beauty alone
saved them from the insults which popular hatred levelled at
all in alliance with the exiled Earl of Angus, occupied this
balcony, and reclined beneath its shady canopy, chatting
gaily, and expectant of the royal approach.

The elder lady was Margaret Douglas, of the house of Kilspindie, dowager of John Earl of Ashkirk, and mother of
Archibald, the present earl, who was then under doom of
exile with Lord Angus, his kinsman and ally. The younger
ladies were Jane Seton, her daughter, Marion Logan of
Restalrig, Alison Hume of Fastcastle, and Sybil Douglas of
Kilspindie, all noble damsels, who had come to Edinburgh to
witness the splendid entrée of Queen Magdalene.

Tall in stature and dark in complexion, with deep black
eyes, and a hauteur of brow which the sweet expression of
her mouth alone relieved, the Countess Dowager of Ashkirk,
though all but unable to read or write (for letters were then
held in low repute), was a woman of a shrewd and masculine
turn of mind; for the inborn dignity of noble birth, the
martial spirit of her race, the stormy life she had led since
childhood among feudal brawls and intestine battles, had imparted an emphatic decision, if not a fierceness, at times, to
her manner and modes of expression. A stiff suit of the
richest Genoese brocade lent additional stateliness to her
figure, while the diamond-shaped head-dress, then in fashion
for noble matrons, added greatly to her stature, which was
far above the middle height. The inner folds of this angular
coif were of white linen, the outer of purple silk edged with

yellow fringe, and it formed a corner at each ear with an apex at the top, while the folds lay close to her cheeks, scarcely permitting her hair to be visible, and where it was so its raven hue seemed turning fast to silver-grey.

A little negro boy, black as Lucifer, but dressed entirely in a rich suit of white satin, puffed and slashed at the trunks and shoulders, held up her train. Ugly as a fiend, with a broad nose, capacious mouth, and long pendent cars adorned with massive silver rings, Master Sabrino, being the first or the second person of his colour ever seen in Scotland, was an object of fear to some, disgust to others, and wonder to all. The vulgar viewed him as an imp or devil incarnate, and studiously avoided the glance of his shining black eyeballs; but *the creature*, as they termed him, was affectionately devoted to his mistress, and to all who used him kindly. Though the fashion of being attended by a black page or dwarf was not uncommon at continental courts, and had been first introduced into Scotland by Anne de la Tour of Vendôme, Duchess of Albany, it did not tend to increase the popularity of the proud and distant Dowager of Ashkirk, whom, as a Douglas, the people were generally disposed to view with hostility and mistrust.

Lady Jane Seton was, in many respects, the reverse of her mother; for she had neither her lofty stature, her keenness of eye, nor her haughty decision of manner; for her figure, though full and round, was, by turns, light, graceful, and yielding. Neither her youth, for she was barely twenty, nor her beauty, though it was of the first class, were her chief characteristics. There was a depth of expression in her dark blue eye, which, by turns, was dreamy and thoughtful, or bright and laughing, a charm in her radiant complexion and a fascination in her manner, which drew all instinctively towards her. When silent, she seemed full of intense thought; when speaking, all vivacity and animation. Her hair was of the darkest and glossiest brown, and her neck arched and slender. Simple and pleasing, sinless in soul and pure in heart, her goodness and gentleness were her greatest charms; and though she appeared *petite* beside her towering mother, there was a grace in all her movements, and a bewitching piquancy in every expression, that made Jane Seton adorable to her lovers, and she had many.

Her companions were worthy the association, all fair and handsome girls.

Alison of Fastcastle was a beautiful blonde ; she carried a falcon on her wrist, and from time to time pressed its smooth pinions against her dimpled cheek. Marion of Restalrig was a tall, flaxen-haired, and blue-eyed beauty, ever laughing and ever gay; while Sybil Douglas of Kilspindie was a brunette, like all the beauties of her house. Her deep black eyes and sable tresses would have lost nothing by comparison with those of Andalucia ; and though generally quiet, and, as some deemed her, insipid, her silence concealed a world of sentiment and thoughts that were exquisitely feminine : but, though silent and retiring, there were times when this fair daughter of the house of Douglas could manifest a fire and spirit becoming Black Liddlesdale himself.

They were all dressed nearly alike, in white satin, slashed at the breast and shoulders with variously coloured silk, and all had coifs of velvet squared above their temples, and falling in lappets on their cheeks. They were all talking at once, laughing at everything, like Sabrino the page, whose wide mouth was expanded in an endless grin; but the old countess was buried in thought, and with her forehead resting on her hand, and her elbow on the edge of the balcony, continued to gaze abstractedly on the long and bustling vista of the sunlit Canongate.

CHAPTER II.

MAGDALENE OF FRANCE.

> " Saw'st thou not the great preparatives
>   Of Edinburgh, that famous noble town;
> Thou saw'st the people labouring for their lives,
>   To make triumph with trump and clarion :
> Thou saw'st full well many a fresh galland,
>   Well ordered for receiving of their queen,
> Each craftsman with his bent bow in his hand,
>   Right gallantlie in clothing short of green."
>   LINDESAY OF THE MOUNT.

" THEIR graces tarry long," said the countess, glancing impatiently up the street; " it is almost midday by the sun. Jane, child, hast got thy pocket-dial about thee ?"

Lady Jane took from her embroidered girdle a little silver dial, and placing it duly east and west, found the hour to be twelve by the shadow of the gnomon, for the sur, shone brightly,

"I warrant me," said the countess, "that his eminence the cardinal will be relieving himself of some prosy oration at the foot of the Broad Wynd, for the benefit of the king's grace."

"Of the queen's, you mean, Lady Ashkirk," said Alison Home, "for his lordship is a great admirer of beauty. Thou knowest, cousin Jane, how often he hath admired thee."

Jane coloured with something of displeasure at this remark, for, by the rumour of his gallantries, to be admired by this great prelate was no high honour.

"I would the king were come, for my patience is wearing fast away," said she, raising her bright eyes from the silver index to her mother's thoughtful face.

"Is it for the king alone thou art so impatient, child?" said the old lady, with a keen but smiling glance.

"Nay, for one who accompanies him—for the queen," said Jane, growing pale, for she always turned pale where others grew red. "Is not James the avowed enemy of our house?"

"But is there no other for whom ye long, silly lassie?" asked Marion Logan, throwing an arm round Jane.

"My sweet friend—yes; for one who is dearer to me almost than thee; he who sent me this dial from Paris. Oh, Marion! to think that he hath been there for nine weary months!"

"Marry come up, bairn, what matters it?" said the countess, who overheard them, though the two fair friends spoke in low tones; "he will be so changed, and improved in gallantry and grace, that you will scarcely recognise him."

"I cry you mercy, mother," said Jane, pouting; "I knew not that he required improvement in either."

"By my troth, lady countess," said Alison Home, "if you mean Sir Rowland Vipont, the Master of the King's Ordnance, I think him so finished a cavalier that no court in Europe could improve him more."

"Save the court of King Cupid," said Marion.

"And where does he reign?" asked Jane.

"In thine own heart, cousin," said little Sybil, quietly; and then all the girls laughed aloud.

"I thank you, sweet Alison," said Jane, in a low voice, kissing her friend, for her heart danced lightly to hear her lover praised; "but dost thou know that, though I am full of joy, I would give the world to shed a shower of quiet tears just now."

"Heaven give thee happiness to-day, dear Jane," replied her friend, in the same soft, earnest voice, "and may it send thy lover back to thee in love and truth, and health and comeliness, as when he left thee these nine long months ago."

"Sabrino," said the countess, suddenly; "prick up those long ears of thine! dost thou not hear the sound of trumpets?"

"Ees, madame—me tink so," grinned the sable page, whose efforts at articulation cost him a fearful grimace.

"Then, James must be ascending the West Bow," replied the countess, as a commotion and murmur became apparent among the mighty masses that crowded the whole street.

At that moment the roar of the castle artillery pealed over the city, and announced the entrance of the king by its western barrier, along the Highrigs, past the tilting-ground and the chapel of the Virgin Mary. Deeply and hoarsely carthoun and culverin thundered from the towers of St. Margaret and King David, and a deafening shout of welcome and acclamation resounded from the crowded streets.

"Though the enemy and oppressor of the Douglases and the Homes," continued the countess, standing up in front of the balcony, "I cannot forget that he is our anointed king—that he has long been absent, and has endured great perils by sea and land; and so this day I bid him hail and welcome home in the name of Heaven."

"'Tis said the queen will ride behind him on a pillion," said Alison Home.

"Nay, child," replied the countess; "the Master of the Horse passed up street with a beautiful palfrey of spotless white, having a golden footcloth that swept the ground, for her grace's especial behoof. Ha! bairns, the mention of pillions remindeth me of the days of our good King James IV. I was but a lassie then, in my teens, like yourselves; and when James espoused the younger sister of Henry Tudor, though liking not the English match, I was appointed a lady of honour to Queen Margaret, for then—(and the countess spoke bitterly)—then to be a Douglas was different from what it is to-day! Like his son, James IV was then a winsome youth, and fair to look upon. Few matched him for courage and hardiment in the field, and none surpassed him in grace and courtly devoir. Amid a gallant band of spears, with ladies, lords and knights, all clad in silk and taffety, laced and

furred with miniver, with many a waving plume, and many a
golden chain, they issued forth from Saint Mary of New-
battle, beneath the old oak trees, and James had his fair
young English bride behind him on a pillion, riding just like
any douce farmer and his gudewife, and, certes! a bonnie
young pair they were as ever had holy water sprinkled on their
bended heads! James was bravely attired—a doublet of
velvet bordered with cloth-of-gold, and his bride was blazing
with diamonds. As we rode townward, by the wayside, near
Our Lady's Well at Kirk Liberton, we saw a fair pavilion
pitched on the green brae side, and at the door thereof stood
a lance fixed in the earth, with a shield hung upon it. A lady,
holding a siller bugle horn, came forth to greet the royal
pair, when suddenly, a savage knight, mounted, and clad in a
lion's skin, dashed out of a neighbouring coppice and bore her
away. Then, lo! another knight, armed at all points, spurred
his fleet horse from the gay pavilion, and assailed him with
uplifted sword. Bravely they fell on, with the captive dame
between them, and the keen-edged blades made ilka tempered
casque and corselet ring like kirk bells on a festival. The
rescuer struck the sword from the hand of his enemy, the
king cried, 'Redd ye, sirs!' and so the combat was closed,
and the lady released."

" And who was this fair dame ?" asked Alison, with assumed
curiosity, for she had heard the same story, in the same words,
a hundred times before.

" Whom think ye, but *I;* and my leal Lord Archibald was
the errant knight who saved me from the savage warrior, and
he was no other than thy father, dear Alison, Sir Cuthbert
Home of Fastcastle, who died by King James's side at Flodden; for you must know, maidens, that it was all a fair
masque prepared to suit the warlike taste of the king, who
loved well to see his knights under harness, and proving their
hardiment on each other's coats of mail. All that and mickle
mair I remember as if 'twere yesterday, and now 'tis three
and thirty years ago. Three and thirty!" continued the
garrulous old lady, " how the false traitors Death and Time
have changed my cheer since then."

" True, madam," said little Sybil, thoughtfully ; " the best
part of our life is made up of the anticipations of hope, and
the pleasures, the sad pleasures, of memory."

" Thy thoughts are running on my son, Lord Archibald,"

said the countess, with a fond smile, as she smoothed the thick tresses of Sybil. "The first is for the young like you, and the last to solace the auld like me. St. Mary keep us! how year runs after year. My fair bairns, I hope a time may come when ye will all look back to *this* day as I do to that; but not with a sigh, to think such things have been, but can never be again!"

The countess sighed, and a tear stole into her eye; but a cry from the girls of—

"Oh! here they come—the king and queen!" followed by a clapping of hands, and a burst of acclamation from the populace, amid which the old cry, which the Scots had lately borrowed from their allies, the French—"Vive la Royne! Vive la Royne!" was conspicuous. It was a shout that rang from the crowded streets below, the windows and bartizans above, loud enough to rend the summer welkin, and heralded the approach of James and his French bride.

The occasional flourish of trumpets, mingled with the sound of the drum, the shalm, the cymbal, the clarion, and the clang of hoofs, rang in the lofty street. Spears glittered, banners waved, and silken pennons streamed in the sunlight at a distance, above the sea of heads; while armour flashed, and embroidery sparkled, as the superb procession, conveying the royal pair to Holyrood, approached.

Under the high sheriff of Lothian and Sir Andrew Preston of Gourtoun, a strong body of mounted spearmen, sheathed in dark armour, cleared and lined the streets, while the provost, Sir James Lawson of the Highrigs, chequered them with several thousands of the burgher archers and craftsmen, for each armed corporation was arrayed under its own pennon; and the great consecrated standard of the city, bearing the image of Saint Giles, floated near the battlements of the Cross—as tradition avers it floated over Salem. A volume would be required to describe the magnificence of the romantic pageant that now approached; for James, as I have said, was the idol of his people, and a nine months' absence had endeared him to them more; and all their loyalty and enthusiasm now blazed forth at his return. First came three hundred of his royal guard, clad in blue bonnets and scarlet doublets, armed with long partizans and poniards. These were all men of Edinburgh, given by the city to attend James "on all occasions, especially against his auld and auncient

enemies of England." Then came a long train of that fierce
and proud nobility whose turbulence and intrigues ultimately
broke the good king's heart. They wore robes of state over
their rich armour; their jewelled coronets were borne before,
and their gallant banners behind them; each was attended
by a knight, a page, an esquire, or other gentleman, in accordance with his rank. Then came the lesser barons, each riding
with his pennon displayed; and then the honourable commis-
sioners of burghs, clad in gowns of scarlet, with gold chains;
the twelve heralds and pursuivants, with six bannered trumpets, sounding before them a triumphal march, to which the
kettle-drums and cymbals of the horsemen lent additional
animation.

But the shouts which greeted this part of the procession
became subdued; for now came a single horseman, riding
alone, with a page on each side supporting his footcloth,
which was composed entirely of cloth-of-gold. He was a
man of a singularly noble presence and commanding stature;
his deep dark eyes were full of fire and expression, yet
his face was calm and placid, and his gaze was fixed on the
flowing mane of his beautiful roan horse; and though every
head bowed at his approach, he seemed abstracted and oblivious of all; his cope and stockings were scarlet, and a very
broad hat of the same sanguine hue cast a pleasant shadow
over his sombre features.

"Rise, my bairns," said the Countess of Ashkirk; "it is his
eminence the cardinal!"

And chancing to raise his head at that moment, he waved
a benediction towards the balcony. He was David Beaton,
cardinal of St. Stephen, the lord high chancellor of Scotland,
legate of Paul III., and the terror of those who, in their
secret hearts, had begun to nourish the doctrines of the reformed church. A young cavalier, in a half suit of magnificently gilded armour, attended him, and spent his time
between caressing a falcon which sat upon his dexter wrist,
and bowing to the ladies on either side of the street. He
was Sir Norman Leslie of Rothes, who, a few years after,
slew the cardinal in his archiepiscopal palace. Immediately
behind him came a crowd of ecclesiastics, and the eight
bishops—Stewart of Aberdeen, Hepburn of Brechin, Chis-
holm, the worthless holder of the see of Dunblane, Dunkeld,
Moray, Ross, Orkney, and Ferquhard of the Isles, all riding

on led horses, with their mitres, crosiers, and magnificent vestments, glittering in the sunlight.

Then came the black abbot of Cambus Kenneth (the lord president of the New College of Justice), attended by his fourteen senators, the *ten* sworn advocates, the clerks to the signet, notaries and macers of court, all of whom were greeted with lowering brows and murmurs of ill-repressed hatred and dislike; for the introduction of the courts of session and justiciary had been a very unpalateable measure to the factious and turbulent Scots.

Surrounded by the chief ladies of the kingdom, and by the damsels of honour all richly attired in hoods of velvet tied with strings of pearl, with kirtles of brocade and cloth-of-gold, Magdalene of France approached on a palfrey white as the new fallen snow, with six young knights (each the son of an earl) supporting on their lances a silken canopy above her head. The splendour of her dress, which was shining with costly jewels, enhanced the greatness of her beauty, which outshone the charms of all around her, even the fair girls to whom the reader has been so lately introduced. Sprung from a royal line long famous for the charms of its princesses, Magdalene was only in her sixteenth year; but over her girlish loveliness the pallor of consumption was then spreading a veil more tender and enchanting. The novelty and excitement of the scene around lent additional animation to her lively French features, and heightened the brilliancy of her complexion, which was exquisitely fair; her eyes were light blue, and her braided hair was of the most beautiful blonde. She was rather small in stature, but beautifully formed; and the sweetness of her happy smile, and the grace with which she bowed and kissed both her hands alternately to the subjects of her husband, filled them with a storm of enthusiasm; and the respectful silence which had greeted her at first, expanded into a burst of rapture and congratulation. The ambassadors of England, Spain, France, and Savoy, wearing the collars of various knightly orders, rode near her.

With the sword, sceptre, and crown, borne, each by an earl, before him, James appeared, attended by the leading nobles of the realm. A cuirass of steel, polished like a mirror and inlaid with gold, showed to advantage his bold breast and taper waist. His doublet and trunk breeches were of white satin slashed with yellow and buttoned with diamonds, and

his short mantle of azure velvet was tied over his breast with
golden tassels.   The collars of the Thistle, the Garter, the
Golden Fleece, and the escallops of St. Michael, were hanging
on his breast, and flashed in one broad blaze to the noon-day
sun.   His dark eyes were full of animation, and the ringlets
of his rich brown hair fluttered in the breeze as he waved his
plumed cap to the people who loved him well, for he was
better pleased to be thought the king of the *poor* than king
of the peers of Scotland.   He was surrounded by all the
great officers of state and household; Robert, abbot of Holyrood, bearing his high treasurer's mace with its beryl ball,
rode beside Colville of Culross, the great chamberlain of Scotland.   Then came the lord high constable and the great
marischal, the former with a naked sword, and the latter with
an axe, borne before him; Colville of Ochiltrie, the comp-
troller; the dean of Glasgow, the secretary of state; Argyle,
the lord justice-general, and Colinton, the lord clerk registrar;
Lord Evandale, director of the chancery, the preceptor of the
Knights of St. John, the high admiral, the royal standard-
bearer, the grand carver, the great cup-bearer, the masters of
the horse, the hounds, and the falcons, the marshal of the
household, and though last, not least, Jock Macilree, the
king's jester, who has been immortalized by the Knight of
the Mount; and though ignobly bestriding a sleek donkey,
his parti-coloured garb, his longeared cap, jingling bells,
hanging bladder, and resounding laugh, attracted more attention than the mailed chivalry and sumptuously-attired
noblesse who encircled the king.

   James, who bowed affably to the people on every side, was
scrupulous in recognising all ladies, especially if handsome,
and consequently the bright group clustered round the
Countess of Ashkirk could not escape his observation.   Waving his bonnet, he was about to bow to his horse's mane,
when his eye caught the quarterings of Douglas, and an
ominous flash of undisguised anger immediately crimsoned
his fine features; he was turning away, when a rose was
thrown upon his breast, and a pleasant voice cried,

   "Heaven save your grace, and bless our fair lady the
queen!"

   It was Jane Seton's voice, and the richness of its tone with
the sweetness of her smile subdued James at once; and
placing the rose in the diamond George that hung from the

splendid collar of the garter, this gallant young king bowed low, and kissed his hand.

"Hark you, Vipont," said he, to a handsome young man about his own age, who rode by his side; "what dame and damoiselles are these? You vailed your bonnet with more than usual reverence to them."

The cavalier hesitated.

"Faith," continued James, "there was a most undeniable scowl in the dark eyes of the elder lady in that outrageous English coif. Who is she, and why, i' the devil's name, does she wear *that*?"

"I trust your majesty is mistaken," replied the young man, hurriedly, and with confusion; "she is the countess dowager of Ashkirk, with her daughter the Lady Jane."

"Ashkirk!" reiterated James, knitting his brows; "is she not a daughter of old Greysteel, and hath more than a spark of old Bell-the-cat in her spirit? By St. Anne, this accounts for her English coif, when, out of compliment to our royal consort, the French fashions are all in vogue!"

"Please your majesty," urged Vipont——

"I remember the dame of old, in the days of the Douglases' tyranny, when they kept me a close captive in the old tower of Falkland. God's malison on the whole tribe; I would it had but one neck, and that it lay under my heel!"

"Amen, say I;" "and I," "and I," added several courtiers, who enjoyed gifts from the forfeited estates of the banished barons.

The young man sighed and bit his lips as he checked his horse a little, and permitted Sir David Lindesay of the Mount, another favourite, to assume his place by the side of the king.

Tall, and finely formed, with an erect bearing and athletic figure, Sir Roland Vipont was the very model of a graceful cavalier. His features, though not strictly handsome, were pleasing, manly, and expressive of health, good humour, and the utmost frankness. His heavy moustaches were pointed sharply upwards, and his hair was shorn close (*à la* Philip II.), to permit his wearing a helmet with ease, for, as master of the royal ordnance, a week seldom passed in those turbulent times without his being engaged on the king's service. A smart bonnet of blue velvet, adorned by a single feather, by its elegant slouch gave a grace to the contour of his head;

while a short mantle of the same material, lined with white satin, and furred, as usual, with miniver, waved from his left shoulder. His trunk breeches were also of white satin, and slashed with red; his doublet was cloth-of-gold, and, blazing in the sunlight, rivalled his magnificent baldrick, which, like his bugle-horn, sword, and dagger, was studded with precious stones. No knight present, not even the king himself, surpassed the master of the ordnance in the splendour of attire, the caparisons of his horse, or the grace with which he managed it; and yet poor Sir Roland, though the last representative of the Viponts of Fifeshire (the Scoto-Norman barons of Aberdour), possessed not one acre of land, and, soldier-like, carried all his riches about him.

His whole features beamed with joy and ardour, as he raised his eyes to the Ashkirk balcony; his sunburned cheek grew crimson, and his heart bounded with delight. Jane trembled as she smiled, and grew pale (for, as I have said elsewhere, she grew pale when other girls would have blushed). Many months had elapsed since they had looked on each other's beaming faces, and a volume of happiness and recognition was exchanged in their mutual glances.

"Brave Vipont!" exclaimed the old countess, with something of a mother's ardour, as she looked after him, "of a verity, there are few more noble among our Scottish knights. How unfortunate that he is such a minion to the will of a pampered king!"

"Minion, good mother!" said Jane, faintly.

"I said minion, child; and I now say slave! Didst thou not see how covertly he bowed to us, and then only when the king looked another 'way? A proper squire, by our Lady! and didst thou not mark how James frowned when first he saw us, nor bowed——"

"Until I smiled on him," said Jane, playfully.

"Naughty little varlet, methought 'twas when _I_ smiled," said Alison Home, gaily, as she kissed her beautiful friend.

"Poor Vipont!" continued the countess, "he dreads the loss of thy love, Jane, on one hand, and of the king's favour on the other. But for this paltry manœuvring, child, thou hadst been the lady of his heart a year ago."

"Mother, I have been the lady of his heart these _three_ years; but poor Roland hath no more to give me than a heart in return. His estate——"

" Consists of old Mons Meg and her marrows," said Marion Logan.

" A lucrative estate he hath found them sometimes," said the countess, coldly, " when he bent their cannon-balls against the castles of the Douglases. But for this paltry fear, I repeat, thou hadst been his wedded wife a year ago, and he had been now a true man to the Earls of Ashkirk and Angus, instead of being the silken slave of James Stuart, whose poor ambition is to grind beneath his heel that Red Heart which my husband hath often bore, amid crashing spears, in the van of Scotland's battles—and ever bore victoriously!" And as she spoke, the countess struck her clenched hand upon the banner which was spread over the balcony before her.

" Thou sayest well, dearest madam!" said little Sybil Douglas, whose dark eyes sparkled as she imbibed some of the countess's fiery spirit ; " and again that Red Heart shall be a terror to the Lowlands, and a scourge for past injuries.

At that moment Lady Jane Seton raised her eyes to a window opposite, and encountered the fixed gaze of a sickly and ghastly face ; the features were rigid, the lips firmly compressed, the dark eyes were fiery and red. There was a basilisk or rattlesnake expression in them that riveted her attention. They were those of Sir Adam Otterburn of Red-hall, who had been attentively observing the greeting which passed between her and Vipont—a greeting that wrung his heart with agony and jealousy ; but he bowed with studied politeness, and hurriedly withdrew.

Jane felt relieved by his absence, and again drew breath more freely ; but her colour came and went, and her heart for a moment became filled (she knew not why) with vague apprehensions. She knew all Sir Adam's glance conveyed, and trembled for her lover ; for the King's Advocate of the New Court was then vested with such powers and terrors as a romancer would alone endow a grand inquisitor.

The pageant passed on to Holyrood accompanied by loud and incessant bursts of acclamation ; by songs and carols of welcome and of triumph ; for the people, already predisposed to loyalty and jollity, were enraptured by the return of the king, by the gallantry of his bearing, and the beauty of his young French bride. Thus the wells continued to pour forth wine and ale alternately, the castle to fire its ordnance, and the people to shout until St. Marie (a great bell with a very

sweet tone, which then hung in the rood tower of St. Giles)
rung the citizens to vespers and to rest.

CHAPTER III.

THE MASTER OF THE ORDNANCE.

" The bride into her bower is sent,
  The ribald rhyme and jesting spent ;
  The lover's whispered words and few,
  Have bade the bashful maid adieu ;
  The dancing floor is silent quite,
  No foot bounds there—Good night ! good night !"
                        JOANNA BAILLIE.

EVENING was closing, when a brilliantly-attired cavalier
caracoled his horse from the palace porch, past the high
Flemish gables of an ancient edifice, which was then the
Mint of Scotland, past the strong round archway known
as the Water Gate, because it led to the great horsepond of
the palace, and throwing a handful of groats (twenty to king
James's golden penny) among the poor dyvours who clustered
round the girth cross of the Holy Sanctuary, rode up the
Canongate. It was Sir Roland Vipont, the master of the
king's ordnance.

Compared to the bustle it had exhibited at noon, the
street, though many still thronged it, seemed lifeless and
empty. The windows were closed, the balconies deserted,
the banners, pennons, and tapestry hung pendant and motionless, and the gay garlands were withering on the stone cross
of St. John of Jerusalem. Casting a hasty glance around
him to discover whether he was observed (for the political,
feudal, and court intrigues of the time made it necessary that
his visit to the family of Ashkirk should be as little noted as
possible), he dismounted.

A low-browed pend, or archway, opening from the street,
and surmounted by a massive coat of arms within a deep
square panel, gave admittance to the paved court of the
mansion. He led his horse through, and was buckling the
bridle to one of the numerous rings with which, for the
convenience of mounted visitors, the walls of the court were
furnished, when a man, who for some time before had been
standing in the shadow of the archway, roughly jostled him.

" How now, sirrah ?" exclaimed Vipont, feeling for his poniard, " what mean you by this ?"

" Pardon me—my foot tripped," replied the other, in a husky voice.

" Who are you," asked Vipont, suspiciously, " and what make you here, sir ?"

" In the first place, I am no friend of yours ; in the second, my purpose matters nothing to any man—so, keep your way, in Heaven's name, and let me keep mine, or it may fare the worse with you."

" This is language rarely addressed to me."

" Thou !" said the other, scornfully, " and who art *thou ?*"

" Devil choke thee, rascal !" exclaimed the soldier, angrily ; " I am master of the king's ordnance."

" To be master of your own temper would be better ; but, like your brass culverins, it seems apt to go off upon occasions."

" Hark you, sir ; if you deem this witty, you are labouring under a delusion ; and, had I not matters of more importance in hand, by the holy mass ! I would break every bone in your body."

The other made no immediate reply, but his eyes gleamed like two red coals beneath the black bonnet, which he wore drawn over his brows ; but he was so well muffled up by the cape of his large mantle, that Sir Roland strove in vain to discover some clue as to whom he might be, that was prowling by night near the mansion of the Setons ; and there was something so startling and cat-like in the aspect of his eyes, that the soldier recoiled a pace.

" Sir Roland," continued the stranger, sarcastically, " you had acted a wiser part in staying by James's side at Holyrood to-night, than in forfeiting his fickle favour by visiting those who are his avowed enemies."

"Thou liest, sirrah !" said Vipont, striking him on the shoulder with his clenched hand. " The Setons of Ashkirk are loyal as any in the land, and I will meet hand to hand, and body for body, any false traitor that gainsays me. But keep your own way, in the devil's name, and trouble me no more—so, a good even, sir."

" I bid thee joy of thy wooing, fair sir," replied the other, scornfully, as the master of the ordnance entered, and closed the gate behind him. It was Redhall who spoke, and a sigh

of rage and bitterness escaped him as Vipont approached the
turnpike tower of the mansion. "Painted wasp!" he exclaimed, as he walked hurriedly away, " by Him who died
upon the rood, that blow shall cost thee dear!"

Within an apartment which was completely hung with the
richest arras, though the floor was bare, the Countess of
Ashkirk, her daughter, and the ladies, were seated at various
occupations. The old lady was slowly and laboriously endeavouring to decipher, word by word, one of those curious old
tomes which, at times, issued from the shop of Chepman and
Millar, two ancient bibliopoles, who established, in the Cowgate, the first printing-press in Scotland, in the time of
James IV., who granted them the privilege of "imprenting
all bukes" within the realm.

Alison Hume and the black page were playing at chess,
the fair young girl looking almost like a divinity when contrasted with the frightful African boy; while Jane Seton and
her dark-eyed kinswoman, Sybil Douglas, influenced by that
spirit of industry which then pervaded all ranks, were plying
their busy hands in embroidering a velvet cover for a large
vellum missal, which they were working in flowers of gold
and silk, and which was to be a donation from Jane to her
friend Josina Henrison, the lady superior of St. Catherine's
Convent, near the Burghloch.

The light of the setting sun streamed through the windows,
and fell upon their dark hair, as it mingled together, and
edged their white necks and nimble fingers with dazzling
whiteness. A bell tolled at a distance; they paused, and
looked up.

" Eight o'clock," said the countess; " the bell is ringing
for the *compline*, at St. Marie of Placentia."

" And *he* tarries yet," said Jane, in a low voice, to Sybil.

" Do not speak reproachfully, cousin," replied Sybil,
gently; " he is not always master of his own actions, and
thou knowest well——"

The black page touched her arm, laid a finger on his great
nether lip, and pointed towards the street.

" Dear Sabrino," said Jane, " what dost thou hear?"

" Horse!" replied the page, briefly.

" Sabrino, thou hast the very ears of a bratch hound,"
said the countess. " Now spurs are jingling under the pend
—'tis he," continued the old lady, whose cheek flushed, and

eyes filled with joyous expectation. A manly step, and the clear ringing of silver spurs, were heard ascending the stone staircase of the mansion; a hand covered with a steel gauntlet drew back the heavy arras, and the lights flashed on the glittering doublet and jewelled baldrick of Sir Roland Vipont as he sprang blithely in.

"Heaven keep you, Lady Ashkirk, and you, my dear Jane, and all fair ladies!" said he, bowing, and kissing all their hands. "Hail to thee, merry Alison, and thou, my sad little Sybil! why, I have not been long absent, and yet thou seemest quite a woman, now!"

"Welcome home— a thousand welcomes to thee, Roland, and a thousand more!" said the countess, forgetting her starched dignity in her native kindliness of heart, and kissing him on the forehead—for though he was tall, they were nearly of a height—while Jane grew pale with excitement, and then blushed with pleasure to see her suitor looking so handsome in his rich attire—browned by nine months' exposure to a continental sun, and appearing, if possible, more graceful and athletic than ever. "Welcome, Roland," continued the countess, passing her hand fondly over his broad, clear, open forehead, his arched eyebrows, and his thick glossy hair; "we have all heard how thou hast been proving thy prowess on the crests of King Francis and his knights, and letting the gay tilters of Paris and Versailles feel the weight of a tough Lowland spear in a true Scottish hand."

"True, madam," replied the young man, laughing, and showing a set of teeth which any of the fair belles present might have envied; "it would have gladdened your haughty Douglas spirit, Lady Ashkirk, to have seen King Francis with twenty Scottish knights keeping the old wooden bridge of St. Michael at Paris for three days against our own King James, with the best chivalry of Burgundy, Brabant, and Alsace, and with all comers who chose to try their hardiment against us. By my faith, sweet Jane, the knot of ribbands your dear hands wove in my helmet were the mark of many a sword and many a spear during these three brawling days; but they seemed to possess a charm, for thrust of lance and blow of blade were levelled at them in vain. But what think ye of the new queen we have brought you home? Is not the fair Magdalene a mirror of beauty? and may not France and Scotland too be proud of her? Jane, what sayest thou?"

c 2

"Hum!" said Jane, a little piqued at her lover's excessive admiration for the queen; "methinks she is very passable."

"Passable! Ah, surely *you* can afford to praise her more than that. I think she is like *la belle Isonde*, in Sir Thomas Malory's 'Romance of King Arthur,'" replied Vipont, drawing near Jane, while, as if instinctively, the other persons present withdrew to the extreme end of the apartment, and conversed with the countess. "Now tell me, thou merry wag, thy opinion of her."

"I do not think her by one half so charming as my own little self," replied Jane, archly; "and thou, who oughtest to have only eyes for me, should see in her an exceedingly plain woman. When thou seemest so much pleased with her, what surety have I that I was not forgotten by her admirer, amid all the gaieties, the fêtes, and splendour of King Francis' court?"

"Forgotten, Jane!" responded the young man, tenderly, while his dark eyes filled with a soft expression. "Those who see and love thee will never forget! Have not our hearts been entwined for years, and am I not thy gallant brother's oldest and earliest friend? Have we not grown together from infancy to childhood, from childhood to maturity? and now, in the full flush of our love and joy, you hint that I might forget you!"

"I cry you mercy! what an exordium; I spoke but in pure raillery and jest, dear Roland."

"But why jest thus? Ah no, my gentle Jane, never for an instant were your fair face and sunny smiles absent from my mind, and their memory spurred me on to encounter a thousand difficulties, and enabled me to surmount a thousand dire temptations that beset the path of others; and thus I am come back to you more loving if possible, more true, and more impassioned than ever!"

"Oh, Roland, I can believe it well!" sighed the girl, as her lover, borne away by the depth of his passion (though speaking in a low voice), pressed both her hands to his heart, regardless that the eyes of others saw them.

"Behold what I have brought you from this far-famed city of Paris," said he, as he clasped around her delicate throat a circlet of magnificent diamonds.

"Ah! my poor Vipont," exclaimed Jane; "you must have ruined yourself to bring me this. What a sum it must have cost!"

" Eleonora of Austria, the Queen of France and sister of the great Charles V., took it from her own fair neck and bestowed it on me as a gift for my Scottish bride ; and joyously I thought of you, Jane, when I knelt to receive it from her hands. It was at a passage of arms held near the Porte Papale, just without the walls of Paris, and on the festival of St. Denis, when with a single lance I kept the barrier for an hour, successively prostrating in the dust six Italian knights who had come to France in the train of the Milanese ambassador. By my faith, sweet flower, I covered myself with glory and popularity that day; for it so happened that Sforza, duke of Milan, is the sworn foe of Francis I., and the hearts of the people were all with the victorious Scottish knight."

"And did King James see thee, Sir Roland ?" asked the young ladies, who crowded round the delighted girl to observe her splendid gift.

" He sat by the side of Queen Eleonora, and when the sixth cavalier was unhorsed, sprang up from his seat, and throwing his blue bonnet into the air, exclaimed, ' Now, God be with thee, my valiant Vipont, thou hast well sustained our Scottish name to-day, and I will never forget it.' But his rewards are yet to come, fair ladies," added Vipont, as he sighed secretly and glanced at Jane Seton.

" Roland," said the countess, who was beginning to reflect that she had been too long silent ; " believe me, those who put their trust in princes are ever deceived. I heard our good King James IV say so when I was but a girl."

" He referred then to his brother-in-law of England, whom the laws of neither God nor man could bind ; but judge not so of James V., lady. As yet I am but the captain of his ordnance, with the pittance doled out to me monthly by the clerk of his exchequer. Many a fair promise he hath made me of some small portion of those solid gifts—the towers and acres of wold and woodland, which he lavishes on Hamilton the Inquisitor, on Abbot Robert the Treasurer, his eminence the cardinal, and others, but, to our sad experience, Jane, we find them as yet unperformed."

" Better it is that they are so," said the countess, "for then, as Beaton and the abbot do, ye should brook the patrimonies of the proscribed and banished knights and nobles of my father's name."

" True, lady countess; but J-mes is so winning and cour-
teous in manner, so generous and heroic in disposition, that
no true Scottish man can behold him without feeling a glow
of admiration and loyalty, and at times methinks I could lay
down my life for him (ah! I see thou holdest up thy finger),
were it not, Jane, dedicated to thee. I could cheerfully
battle to the death against all that are his enemies."

" Even the Douglases and the Setons of Ashkirk," said
the countess, coldly. "Oh, thou hast become an apt bravo of
this commons' king, I fear me!"

" Noble lady," replied Roland, bitterly, "there, as I take
God to witness, thou tasketh me sorely. I could not bend
a weapon against the house of Douglas, for this dear being,"
and he took Jane's hand in his, " is the inheritor of their
blood; and yet to fail the king even in that particular would
be to prove me a mansworn knight and false traitor!"

" Thou art ever by his side, Roland," said Jane, "and can
say how he is affected towards us—the Setons of Ashkirk."

" Implacable as ever! Thou rememberest, mine own ladyekin,
of the solemn vow he swore, when, by the troopers of Angus,
Sir David Falconer was slain by his side, under the ramparts of
Tantallon—that solemn vow made above a crucifix and dagger,
*never while he lived to forgive a Douglas, or one of the Douglas'
blood.* There is no hope, for that oath I know the king will
keep, even though his holiness Paul III. should offer to absolve
him from it."

" And let him keep it!" said the countess, with bitterness
and scorn; "it matters little. There are spears by the Liddle
and archers in Douglasdale who may one day absolve him, as
his grandsire was absolved on the field of Sauchieburn. Let us
remember the deeds of that day, and the old prophecy that a
lion should be killed by its whelps. The Master of Angus, the
knights of Glenbernie, Drumlanrig, Lochlevin, and Kinross,"
continued the countess, reckoning them on her fingers, " with
two hundred gentlemen of the surname of Douglas, all died at
Flodden, beneath the banner of King James IV., and thus it is
his son rewards us!"

" Oh, lady countess, hush! and pardon me, but there seems
something hateful in your hostility to James V"

" By the Holy Rood, and the blessed St. Bryde to boot! I
have no patience with thee, friend Roland. I warrant thee in
secret a sworn foe to Angus."

" On my honour, no!"

" And my mind misgives me sorely anent ye and my daughter, having both had the misfortune to be born on a Friday."

" I pray you hear me," said Roland, with a secret smile. " So happy was James on beholding the Scottish shore, that, in a burst of gratitude to heaven and love for his people, he was not disinclined to relax those severe statutes under which the exiled peers and barons of the house of Douglas writhe and languish——"

" Say writhe, Sir Roland, for I warrant me they will never languish!" said the tall countess, folding her hands, sitting very upright, and looking disdainfully.

" Something might have been achieved by his eminence the Cardinal Beaton, whom I know to be my friend—for I am come, like himself, of an old Fifeshire family—when lo! the first barge from the shore brought a packet from Sir Adam Otterburn of Redhall, containing a woeful relation of raid, hership, and hamesucken, committed on the Knight of Cessford by the Earl of Ashkirk and a band of Northumbrian troopers whom he has taken into pay. Alas! lady, is this the verity?"

" Not less so than just!" responded the countess, who shook every fold of her lofty head-dress with *hauteur*. " Is not Cessford the hereditary foe of my son; and God's blood! Rowland Vipont, why should his sword rest? Nay, my gallant Archibald, the moths will never eat the silk of that banner which these old hands wove thee!"

Roland made no immediate reply to this outburst of the old Scottish spirit, but pressed the hand of Jane, and sighed.

" This event, however, is most unfortunate, Lady Ashkirk," he said, after a pause, addressing the countess, and looking with a sad smile at Jane. " It will have a most serious effect upon our fortunes and our happiness. On reading the letter of his advocate, James never spoke, but struck his sword upon the deck and turned sharply away from us. His look was dark as midnight."

" Redhall was over-officious," said the ladies.

" The unmitigated fool!" exclaimed the countess, shaking her clenched hand. " I would my son were here."

" Mother of God—nay, at such a time as this?" said little Sybil, with her dark eyes full of tears. " And think you, Sir Roland, that James is really so much incensed?"

"So much, that I came this night to visit you by—by stealth."

"Stealth!" reiterated the fiery countess, rising to the full height of her five feet ten inches, exclusive of red-heeled shoes. "Now, marry, come up and away with us! Sir Roland Vipont, what will you have the assurance to tell me next?"

"Forgive me, dear and nobly lady; thou knowest well how poor I am—how dependent on my sword and the precarious favour of a king, surrounded by a host of needy and rival competitors. Had I lands and vassals, as I have not; were I the son of a lord or baron instead of a poor gentleman archer of the Scottish Guard, it might have been otherwise with me—and thou, Jane, had long ere this"—he paused and pressed her hand. "Oh, lady countess, my fate is not in my own keeping; and too often have I felt bitterly how abject a thing it is to be dependent on the will of another, even though that other be a prince."

"Thou hast thy rapier, Roland, and with the blood of that brave Vipont who brooked the appanage of Aberdour in the days of King David, dost inherit the spirit thy gallant father gave up to God from the battle field of Ravenno, when the Scottish Guard stood like a rampart around Gaston de Foix. Thou hast thy sword, Roland, and all the realms of Europe are before thee."

"Yes," replied Roland, mournfully; "but then Jane Seton would be left behind."

"Gallant Vipont, thou art indeed my other son!" said the countess, as she kissed his cheek and became quite pacified, while Jane's bright face became radiant with pleasure.

The countess and her niece, Sybil, with Alison Home and Marian Logan, knowing that they could now be spared, retired to prepare for that early supper of which our late dinners have now usurped the place, and the lovers were left alone, seated together hand in hand, for the first time during nine long months.

They were all eye and ear for each other, as they conversed in voices that were soft and low, and love carried them back to those days of gaiety and simplicity before the cold hand of etiquette had interposed between them. Little Sybil closed the arras as she went out, and we have no wish, by raising it, to break the spell that love and pleasure threw around them.

CHAPTER IV.

REDHALL.

" The will is free; why must it then be curbed
I would be happy, gain what I desire,
Or feel each pulse throb pleasure in the chase—
Yet this new teacher tells such pleasure is
A fruit I must untasted shun."—*Nimrod.* *Act III.*

THE apartment, which was half darkened, was partly tapestried and partly wainscoted. A stone fireplace, on grotesque columns covered with carved roses, destitute of grate (for grates were not then in fashion) and of fire, for the season was summer, by its emptiness lent a somewhat dreary aspect to the chamber. The floor was without carpet, for carpets were almost unknown in Scotland till 1560 (three and twenty years after); the furniture was of massive oak. The wellgrated windows, which looked to the Friar Wynd, were concealed by thick curtains, and gaudily-flowered tapestries, framed in richly-carved oak, covered most part of the walls. A brilliant suit of armour, hanging upon a nail or steel hook, and a few shelves of gigantic folios bound in vellum, edged with red, and clasped with brass, were the leading features in this chamber. A sandglass stood upon the table, for one was usually carried by fellows of colleges and other learned men about this period in lieu of a watch, as we may read in Aubrey's Memoirs.

A folio lay on the black oak table, and on its closely-written leaves the light fell from a great iron lamp of grotesque form, covered by a circular shade. With his head reclined on one hand, and the other thrust into the breast of his black velvet doublet, the King's Advocate sat dreamily and moodily immersed in deep thought. His grave and classic face was of a clear olive complexion. His nose was perfectly straight, his eyes large, black, and sparkling, and his knit eyebrows now formed one complete arch above them. His smooth and lofty brow was expressive of deep thought, of watching and study, and even of tranquillity, though there were times when it could assume a terrible expression, and his keen dark orbs would fill with fire, and every hair of his short moustaches bristle with passion. His mouth was decidedly his worst feature; but his short beard concealed those thin lips which Lavater considered the infallible sign of a mind pregnant with evil. His aspect was lofty and severe, and his eye was so penetrating that few could sustain the fire and inquiry of its glance.

The pages of the *Forest Laws*, written by King William the Lion, lay before him, but his eyes were fixed on his jewelled poniard that lay on the table close by, showing how his mind wandered from the subject he had sat down to study to the irate promptings of jealousy and revenge.

For Jane Seton, Sir Adam Otterburn and Ronald Vipont had long been rivals; at least so the former had viewed the latter, who had neither dreaded him nor feared his attentions, for such was his confidence in the love and truth of Jane; yet he had nothing to rely on but his sword and the somewhat precarious favour of James V., while Redhall was the proprietor of a strong baronial fortalice, a noble domain situated a few miles south of the city, and as lord advocate of Scotland was a powerful officer of state, then armed with more powers and terrors than any ten inquisitors of the Holy Office. His position was most honourable, and in virtue of it he was always addressed "My Lord." His knowledge of law was little, but his privileges were great; he was permitted to sit covered within the bar of the Court of Session like a peer of the realm, and he had the power of issuing warrants for searching, apprehending, imprisoning and putting to the torture any person in Scotland—his warrants being valid as those of the king. Such was Roland's formidable competitor for the hand of Jane Seton, to whom the young cavalier would have been wedded fully two years before the time in which this history opens, but for the fear of forfeiting king James's favour, and the implacable hostility of that prince to the house of Douglas, which formed an insuperable barrier to any of the court favourites who might be disposed (which few of them were) to form alliances with any noble family of that obnoxious surname.

Aware of this, Otterburn, whose landed possessions rendered him happily independent of James's frowns or favour, had redoubled his assiduity and attentions, never once permitting the hope to die, that Jane might ultimately regard him with favour. During the nine months' absence of the master of the ordnance in France with King James, the addresses of Otterburn had been as unmistakeable as they were obnoxious to the young lady; who seeing in him only the great public prosecutor of her own and her mother's family, viewed him with horror and hostility, though she dismissed him with a cold but cautious politeness, that, strange to say, while it eclipsed his hopes, in no way extinguished his ardour.

From that time forward he could visit her no more; but his inborn obstinacy of spirit and indomitable vanity would not admit of his totally resigning her—especially during the absence of Vipont, against whose safe return there were many chances, during the escapades and broils, the midnight rambles and madcap adventures, in which he and the king were constantly involved. For a time, Otterburn had again given way to the illusions of hope and the impulses of his heart; but now the safe and sudden return of his brilliant rival had swept them all away, together with a thousand bright day-dreams, as a breeze does the gossamer webs; and the strong mind of the statesman and judge became a prey to anxious jealousy and furious hatred.

"As a rainbow fades from the sky, so has this bright vision passed from before me!" he exclaimed, as he struck his hands together, and looked upward with something of despair. In his better moments he felt only grief, when his more generous impulses would prompt him to resign Jane Seton in peace to her more favoured lover.

"Were she mine," he mused, with a face that became alternately sad and mournful, or dark and saturnine, "her happiness would be my only object; then why should I seek to mar it because she is *not?* By what glamour can this mere girl, who never once thought of me otherwise than as the persecutor of the Douglases, fascinate me thus, swaying my heart, my soul, my every purpose—being the object of every effort —the inspirer of every thought? How cometh it that her coldness, her disdain, her hate (nay, she is too gentle for *that*), all serve but to increase my love? Oh! 'tis sorcery! 'tis sorcery! . . . . Oh! in how many a long and weary night I have pressed a pillow sleeplessly, and courted slumber, but in vain? How often have I tried to rend her image from my heart, to supplant it by another, and in vain? I have recoiled from that other with disgust, as the more winning image of Jane came before me; and yet she loves me not. How often have I fruitlessly striven to crush this mad and besotting passion, and to nourish only hatred, indifference, or revenge? . . . . . God help me! I am very miserable. And shall I resign her to the arms of this upstart favourite, this cut-throat cannoneer, and gilded hireling of King James—resign her without a struggle—I, who am so immeasurably his superior in fortune, mind, and purpose?—Never! . . . How strong this passion of love is! How noble, and for how glorious a purpose has God implanted it in our hearts; but oh, may few endure like me to love an object that loves another, and yieldeth no return! Let dotard monks and deceived misanthropes, let stoics and philosophers say what they will, there is more magic and power in the single smile of a woman than in all the impulses of the human heart put together. Ambition dazzles, hatred sways, and revenge impels us—they are powerful incentives, and their triumph is delicious—but love is greater than all. Generosity urges me to leave her to the fool she loves—to avoid her path, her presence, and her spells for ever; but passion, obstinacy, and infatuation, lead me on, and, overwhelming every gentler sentiment, impel me to the pursuit. Shall I, then, be baffled and foiled by this poor caterpillar, whose wings have expanded in the brief sunshine of royal favour—this silken slave—this Roland Vipont, who, not six years since, wore an iron hongreline and brass plate, as a mere French cannoneer, under Vaudmont and Marshal Lautreque? Never! And, by the holy arm of St. Giles! this night shall end our rivalry for ever!"

Thus said, or rather thought, Redhall; and, suddenly pausing, he snatched up a long metal whistle, that lay always at hand, and blew a shrill call.

Almost immediately afterwards the arras was lifted, a man entered, and, making a respectful obeisance, stood at a little distance.

CHAPTER V.

THE WITCH-PRICKER.

"*Flam.* Malicious fortune!
Ænob. Now thou seest my meaning!"—*Boadicea.*

THE personage who appeared was a short, thickset, and bandy-legged man, whose malformation his chocolate-coloured stockings and white cloth breeches displayed to the utmost advantage. He had a neck and chest like a bullock, with the sinister visage of a thorough-paced ruffian. In size, his head and hands were altogether disproportioned to his body; his hair, beard, and moustaches, which appeared to have been preserved sacred from comb and scissors, were all woven into one matted mass, which was of the deepest black; while drinking and exposure to the weather had bronzed his skin to an almost oriental blackness. He wore a plain frock or gaberdine of white Galloway cloth, confined at the girdle by a broad calfskin belt and steel buckle, in which he carried a long dirk or knife. He wore rough brogues of brown leather on his broad splay feet, and a small rosary of oak beads which dangled at his left wrist evinced his wish to be deemed a respectable member of society; but arrogance, cunning, and brutality, were powerfully depicted on his otherwise stolid visage, which had a very repulsive squareness of aspect, two enormous ears, and a great mastiff mouth.

This worthy was Nichol Birrel, the brodder or witch-pricker of the newly-established high court of justiciary, one of the most unscrupulous and atrocious ruffians that ever occupied this important, and, in after years, lucrative situation.

Born and bred a vassal on the estate of the lord advocate, to whom he was intensely devoted, he had obtained the place of prover or witchfinder, as it peculiarly suited his ruffianly and sanguinary disposition. Several other minor officials of the new court were, like him, the immediate and devoted dependents of Redhall, for whom they acted as bravos on a hundred occasions. Nichol, though cruel, false, bitter, and treacherous to all the rest of mankind, was true, faithful, and sincerely a friend to his lord and benefactor; for he seemed to be possessed by the same instinct which attaches a ferocious hound to the hand that feeds him.

"Od save us, my lord, ye look ill! Is there aught the matter wi' ye?" he asked, gruffly.

"Nichol, is there none in attendance on me but thee?" asked the advocate, without regarding his inquiry; "where are all the servitors?"

"At the palace, seeing the merry masquers."

"Mass! where I should have been but for this accursed sickness, which, to-night, hath fallen so heavily upon me. It

matters not; I am invited by the lord chamberlain to the
fête to-morrow."

"Ye look worse to-night, Redhall, than I have seen ye
since Lententime."

"I am sick at heart, Nichol."

"I have been so at the stomach many a time and oft, when
I mixed my ale with usquebaugh, but as for the heart ——"

"Psha!" exclaimed the advocate, starting abruptly, "either
my brain is under the influence of insanity, or there is a spell
of sorcery upon me."

"Dost suspect any ill-woman of being the cause thereof,
Sir Adam?" asked the brodder, whose eyes began to twinkle
in anticipation of a pricking fee, while his square mouth expanded into a grin.

"No, no; I spoke but in metaphor, and suspect none."
He paused. "Thou sawest the procession to-day?"

Nichol nodded his vast head affirmatively.

"Didst mark any man there whom ye knew to be my enemy?"

"I marked his eminence the cardinal, who confined a damosel
of yours, among his other ladies, in the auld tower of Creich."

"Tush!"

"I observed the lord abbot of the Holy Cross, who won his
plea against thee anent the duty on every cart entering the
barriers of the town."

"Thou triflest! didst mark no one else?"

"Well, then, I marked the master of the king's ordnance,
shining in cloth of gold and crammasie."

"Good!—anything more?"

"I saw him smile as he curveted, in his bravery, past the
ladies of Ashkirk," replied Nichol, with a cunning leer, while
the advocate gnashed his teeth; "and sweetly the lady Jane
smiled on him again. It was a braw sight and a brave; and
a gude ransom the master's doublet and foot-cloth would
have been to any bold fellow that met him in the gloaming
by Leith Loan or the Burghmuir; for they were pure cloth-
of-gold, and champit with pearls, so that I marvel not the
Lady Seton smiled so brightly; for, if love maketh a woman's
eye bright, gold will make it brighter."

"Thou art a mercenary slave!" said the advocate, bitterly;
"and never felt the passion of which thou talkest so glibly.
Nichol, have I not been to thee ever a friend rather than a
lord and master—kind, indulgent, and liberal ——"

" When service was to be performed," said Nichol, paren-
thetically, closing one of his yellow eyes with another hideous
leer.

" At all times, Nichol," continued the king's advocate,
striking his heel sharply on the ground. " Thou knowest
that the master of the ordnance and I have long been at
deadly feud about—but it recks not thee about what."

" Say Jane Seton of Ashkirk, my lord, and you will shoot
near the mark."

Redhall's eyes flashed, and he made a fierce gesture of impatience, for he disliked to hear her name in the mouth of
this ruffian, whom he despised while he fed and fostered him.

" It is enough, Nichol Birrel—thou understandest me—the
master of the ordnance bars my way ; this must not be, and
shall not be."

There was a pause.

" Well, Sir Adam ?" growled the pricker.

" Thou hast thy poniard," said the knight, hoarsely.

" Ay," replied the ruffian, as a broad grin expanded his
mastiff mouth, and his great teeth appeared like a row of
fangs through his matted beard ; " ay, the same gude knife
with which I slew Maclellan, the Knight of Bombie, at the
north door of St. Giles's kirk. By one backhanded stroke I
dashed it into his heart, and he fell with his rosary in his
uplifted hand, the name of God on his lips, and the half-
signed cross on his brow, yet they saved him not."

There was a pause, for Birrel, who had commenced, in a
tone of ruffian irony, ended in a dismal quaver, and grew pale.

" Wretch and fool !" cried the lord advocate, " why remind
me of that ?"

He gave his dependent a terrible glance.

" I crave pardon, Sir Adam ; but when I bethink me that
this Sir Thomas of Bombie had the lairds of Achlanc, Glen-
shannoch, and Bourg, with nine other knights of his surname
to avenge him, I surely ran some risk."

" The Lords of Drumlanrig and Lochinvar were said, by
common rumour, to have slain him, and so let it be ; he was
a foe of the house of Otterburn," hissed the advocate through
his teeth, " and of the faction to which that house adhered ;
a foe to me in particular, and as such must Vipont, the
accursed Vipont, die."

Nichol uttered a sound between a growl and a laugh.

" Are Dobbie the doomster, and Sanders the torturer below ? I warrant they will be snoring, like gorged hounds, by the kitchen ingle."

" No, they are birling their cans in the buttery.

" Then see to this affair; but dost think we can rely on them ?"

" Like myself, Sir Adam, they and their forbears have been leal men and true to the house of Redhall, and wherefore would they fail it now ? We are the servants of the law, and what matters it whether we string this soldier of the king in a tow at the cross, or pink him in the dark ? 'tis death, any way;" and here the fellow uttered a ferocious laugh again.

" For your own sakes and mine be secret, sincere, and sure."

The pricker touched his knife, bowed, and raising the arras, dropped it again, and shaking his matted head, paused irresolutely.

" What is it now ?" asked Redhall, taking the purse from his girdle. " Money ?"

" No, no, Sir Adam, I never served ye for siller, but as my bounden duty ; so I crave leave to remind ye that the place of forester up at Kinleith and Bonallie is vacant, and my sister's son, Tom Trotter, a deadly shot with bow and hackbut——"

" Enough; thy sister's son shall have the place of forester; and, for thee, methinks that the master's cloth-of-gold and diamond baldrick might serve for that, and to procure absolution to boot for the three of ye."

" We care not for that, Sir Adam," replied the pricker, " for we are among those who have seen the new light."

" And believe not in the delegated power of the priesthood ; eh, is it so ?"

Birrel nodded.

" Then why carriest thou that great rosary. I vow it looks like a fetter on thy wrist."

" As a blind."

" Lollards, Wickliffites—ha! ha! these new preachers of schism and heresy have made three creditable proselytes; yet, for thy soul's sake, Nichol (and there was a very perceptible sneer in the advocate's face as he said this), I hope thou art a true Catholic at heart ; but away to thy comrades, for the night wears on, and Vipont hath not yet left the house of the Setons, for I have not heard the hoofs of his horse. To-morrow," continued Redhall, with a ghastly expression of ferocity, " to-morrow——"

" He shall be either in Catholic purgatory or Protestant hell," grinned the pricker, as he raised the arras and retired.

The ghastly smile yet played upon the thin lips of Redhall. " To-morrow I shall be freed of these fears, and for ever," he mused; " but at no distant period I must rid me of those three bloodhounds, who have stuck like burs to my skirts since first I took upon me this unhappy office of advocate to the king. Ha, and so they are heretics! Let them serve my purpose in this, and ere another week hath passed the cardinal shall have them under his inquisitorial eyes, and the stake will rid me and society of them for ever. Vipont, beware thee, now, for this night shall be the darkest in the calendar for thee and for thine!"

———

CHAPTER VI.

THE ILLUMINATED SPIRE.

" Our pathway leads but to a precipice;
And all must follow, fearful as it is!
From the first step 'tis known; but—no delay!
On, 'tis decreed. We tremble and obey."
ROGERS, *Human Life*.

TWELVE had tolled from the spire of the Netherbow Port ere Vipont came forth from the Ashkirk Lodging, as the mansion was named (like other hotels of the Scottish noblesse), and taking his horse, rode through the archway. His heart was beating lightly, for the gentle pressure of a soft hand yet seemed to linger in his, and the kiss of a warm little lip was on his cheek. His breast was filled with joy, and his mind with the happiest anticipations of the future.

There was to be a grand masque or fête given by Queen Magdalene to the ladies of the nobility on the night of the morrow, and Roland had resolved that an invitation should be sent to the ladies of Ashkirk, even should he beg it in person of the fair young sovereign; and full of pleasure at the contemplation of how his beautiful Jane would outshine all her compeers, and how surely James, when he saw her, would recal all his edicts against the Setons of Ashkirk, he

D

put spurs to his horse, and, stooping low, made him clear the
archway with one bound.

The moon was up, and it rolled through a clear and starry
sky. A few light and fleecy clouds that slept afar off in the
bright radiance, seemed to float above the grim dark summits
of the city, whose clusters of close-piled mansions, turreted,
gableted and crow-stepped, tall and fantastic, stark and
strong, started up ghost-like out of the depths of street and
wynd, and stood in bold outline against the clear cold blue of
the midnight sky.

As Roland left the archway, three dark figures, which he
had not observed, shrunk close together; and when he issued
forth, followed him with stealthy steps. They wore short
black mantles, and had their bonnets pulled well over their
faces; but though they lurked on the shadowy side of the
street (which the bright light above rendered yet darker),
the haft of a poniard, or knife, glittered at times under
their upper garments, as they followed the master of the
ordnance cautiously and softly, like cats about to spring on a
mouse, and as noiselessly, for they were shod with felt, or
some such material, that muffled their footsteps.

Vipont was about to descend towards the palace, near which
he lived, in St. Anne's-yard, when a column of light in the
west made him pause, and turn towards the centre of the
town. A ball of fire was burning on the summit of St. Giles's
steeple, and having heard that it was to be illuminated in
honour of the queen's arrival and king's return, he resolved
to see this unusual display; and riding up the Canongate to
the strong barrier which separated the greater from the lesser
burgh, he gave his horse to the care of the under-warder of
the porte, and from thence walked up the High-street with
his long rapier under his arm.

The hour was late, but many persons were abroad, and the
windows were so full of faces, all gazing at the great tower
of St. Giles's, that even had Vipont known that three assassins were on his track and only seeking an opportunity to
plunge their poniards in his heart, he would not have felt
much alarm.

The airy lantern of this magnificent church is formed by
eight ribs of stone that spring from beautiful corbels, and
meeting far above the bartizan of the great rood-spire, support a spacious gallery and lofty pinnacle, forming altogether

an architectural feature of remarkable beauty, and which (save the church of St. Nicholas at Newcastle) is entirely peculiar to Scotland. It is a complete Gothic diadem of stone. The rich crockets on the arches rise tier above tier, and represent the pearls; the parapets from which they spring, with their row of quatrefoils, being in place of the circlet. The whole of this structure had been covered with variegated lamps, which had been brought from Italy, and were hung by the taste and skill of Father St. Bernard, one of the prebendaries, to the wonder and astonishment of the simple-minded citizens. As yet they were unlit, but a single light, we have said, was burning on the upper pinnacle, like a large red star, and to this every face was turned.

The stone crown of the cathedral was all in dark outline; a faint light shone through the large stained window at the east end, and the tapers flickered at the shrine of Our Lady that stood close by. Save these, all the vast church, with its rows of massive buttresses and pointed windows, was im-mersed in gloom, though the moonlight silvered the edges of the crocketed pinnacles. Suddenly a volume of light burst over the whole; the ball of fire which had been burning steadily, threw out a million of sparkles which fell like a haze of brilliance over the arches of the spire, lighting up the diminutive lamps in rapid succession, until the whole struc-ture seemed bathed in one broad sheet of coloured flame. The groined arches, the carved pinnacles, and all the airy tracery of the spire, were as plainly visible in their beautiful and grotesque detail as if the beholders had been close to them, instead of being a hundred and sixty feet below; while the lamps of variegated glass produced the most extra-ordinary variety of light and shadow.

The devils, dragons, and other stone chimeras that pro-jected from the battlements of the clerestory were all tipped with fiery red or ghastly blue light, and seemed to be vomit-ing flames; every pinnacle and tower of the cathedral stood forth in strong outline, one half being bathed in brilliant light, and the other sunk in black shadow, while a myriad prismatic hues were thrown upon the upturned and countless faces of the gaping crowds who occupied the streets below and the windows around. Into the far depths of many a close and wynd, on the square tower of St. Mary-in-the-Field, on the clustered Bastelhouses of the castle, on the spire of the Netherbow, and square belfreys of the Holy Cross, on all the countless roofs and chimneys of the town, the light fell full and redly, scaring even the coot and the swan among the sedges of the Burghloch, and the eagle and the osprey on the lofty craigs of Salisbury.

Cries of astonishment and delight were heard from time to time, mingled with the murmurs of the wondering and the fearful, who, in accordance with the taste and superstition of the age, were, as usual, inclined to attribute the taste and skill which dictated this illumination to sorcery, simply because it was beyond their comprehension.

" Ye say true,'my lord abbot," said a voice near Roland; ' I have had mine own suspicions anent the fact."

" I have always secretly suspected this Father St. Bernard was a sorcerer; he studied at Padua and Salamanca, where there is more kenned of develrie than theologie."

" He is confessor of the Countess of Ashkirk."

" Who hath a familiar, in the shape of a black page, anent whilk my lord advocate and I have had several conferences— but hush !"

Roland did not hear these last observations, which passed between the Abbot of Kinloss and one of the ten advocates of the new court.

Intent on the beauty of the illumination, Roland Vipont saw not the three muffled men who still dogged him, and from behind the grotesque columns of a stone arcade, which still stands opposite the old church (but is completely obscured by modern shops), were intently observing his motions while keeping their own concealed in shadow.

Having been long absent from his native capital, he gazed with admiration on the beautiful effect produced upon its picturesque and fantastic architecture, and he was just wishing that the ladies he had left were with him, to see this new and magnificent spectacle (which in their happiness he and Jane had completely forgotten), when several strong hands were laid violently upon his cloak and belt; he was suddenly dragged from the street, and hurried backwards nearly to the foot of one of those dark, narrow, and then solitary closes that descended abruptly towards the artificial lake, enclosing the city on the north.

So steep was the descent, and so sudden the impetus he received, that before Sir Roland could offer the least resistance, he was beaten to the earth, and the blow of more than one poniard struck sparks of fire from his tempered corslet.

Now deadly was the struggle that ensued; but the three ruffians, in their very eagerness to destroy him, impeded and wounded each other; and though prostrate on the pavement, with his poniard under him, the knees of one bent on his breast, and the hands of another pressing on his throat, which, happily, was encircled with a thick ruff, Roland resisted manfully, his great natural strength and activity being increased by despair and rage. Grasping one by the ruff, he twisted it so as nearly to strangle him, and paralyze the efforts of his right hand, which brandished a long and double-edged poniard, that gleamed ominously in the dim light of the alley.

"God defend me! he panted; "must I perish here like a child, or a woman? Release me, villains, or I will spit you all like rabbits. Ho, armour! armour! treason and rescue!"

"No help is nigh thee!" answered Nichol Birrel, with his hyæna-like laugh; "but curses choke thee, take thy hand from my throat!" and he raised his arm for the death-stroke, but Roland caught his descending hand by the wrist, while with a blow of his foot he hurled the third assailant, Sanders Screw, to the very bottom of the close. A howl from Birrel, at the same moment, announced that his companion had wounded him again, a mistake which raised his demon-spirit to a frightful pitch; and furiously he strove to free his wrist, and stab Roland between the joint of his corslet and gorget. His eyes filled with a yellow light; he panted rather than breathed; he seemed no longer a man, but a devil!

Suddenly Roland found this maddened assailant had become too strong for him; and once again, but more feebly (for he had received a wound in the shoulder), he cried—

"Armour and rescue!"

"Knight and gentleman though ye be," panted Birrel— "by hell! I will have thy blood for mine! Strike again, Dobbie, thou coward and dog! Ho, my gay cannonier, ye are as a dead man now!"

"Thou liest, villain! take *that!*" cried a voice; and he received a blow from a staff which hurled him to the earth. Roland sprang up with a heart full of fury and his sword unsheathed; but his two remaining assailants rushed down the close, and disappeared along the rough bank of the loch before his confusion and giddiness would admit of his following them.

"By St. John, my good friend," said he, adjusting his mantle and ruff, "thou comest at a critical time; a moment later had seen my corslet riddled."

"Ay, and your doublet slashed after the comely Douglas fashion," replied his preserver, whose plain coarse garb, as well as the knotty cudgel he carried, announced him a countryman or peasant.

"Good fellow, I owe thee my life," said Roland, taking his purse from his girdle, "and would gladly yield some adequate recompense. Here, I fear me, there are but few Flemish ryders, and still fewer golden lions."

"Tush!" replied the other with a laugh, as he drew himself haughtily up; "dost offer money to me? Roland Vipont, hast thou quite forgotten me? I am Archibald, Earl of Ashkirk."

"Ashkirk!" reiterated Roland, in a faint whisper, as if he feared the very stones of the street would hear him. "My rash lord and friend," he added, taking the earl's hands within his own, "you know the risk of entering the gates of Edinburgh?"

"Bah!—my head; but who will venture to take it?"

"There is a price set upon it, nevertheless."

"A thousand merks of Scottish money?"

"True: might I not be false enough to win this sum, so tempting to a soldier?"

"Nay, friend Roland, for then thou wouldst lose my sister Jane."

"Lord earl, if discovered by any other than myself thou art lost."

"Perhaps so; but I shall take particular care to prevent all discovery. In fact, I mean to live for awhile in King James's own palace, where I do not think my enemies will ever dream of looking for me. The king's lances, and the riders of the east, west, and middle Marches, have scoured the whole land for me, from Tweedmouth to Solway sands. Besides, I am resolved to see my mother the countess, and my sister Jane, and endeavour to persuade my dear little Sybil to sojourn with me awhile at the court of England; for though it boasts of dames as fair as the world can show, I long ever for the black eyes and gentle voice of my quiet little cousin. Dost comprehend?"

"Rejoiced as I am to see you, Lord Ashkirk, for the memory of our old friendship, I would rather you were a thousand miles hence than standing to-night in the streets of Edinburgh."

The young noble laughed heartily.

"Methinks, Sir Captain of the Ordnance, it was fortunate for thee that I was not even one mile from this when those ruffians had thee at such vantage; but dost know wherefore they beset thee so?"

"Nay, not I; they were some villanous cutpurses, doubtless. Mass! I gave one a rough kick in the belt that will cure him of cloak-snatching for a time!"

"Nay, I opine more shrewdly thou art indebted to the third man in Scotland for this affair."

"The third, say you? How?—the first is the king."

"The second?" said the earl.

"His eminence the cardinal; but the third—who is he?"

"Who but Redhall, whom I would have sworn I heard one of those rogues cursing for sending them on such a devil's errand."

"Redhall!"

"Ay, doubtless; the great archpriest of judicial tyranny, the very spirit of oppression, who sits brooding over the people and the peers of Scotland—he whose villanous panders are gorged and overgorged with gifts of escheat from our forfeited possessions, and are ever needy and inexorable."

"Sayest thou so? then by Heavens I will have a sure assythement of him for this."

"What other assythement is requisite than a sword-thrust?"

"But, 'fore God! I am in no way this man's enemy," replied Roland.

"All whom the king loves are his enemies."

"Still more so are those whom the king hates; witness his severe prosecution of the Douglases. But we all know, my lord, that the friendship of a Scottish king is too often a fatal gift to his subjects."

"Redhall's ambition is inordinate as that of Beaton; blood-guilty as that of Finnart; and his hatred is as that of the coiled-up snake. By St. Bride! I know not which I hate most," exclaimed the rebellious earl, " James Stuart or his minion advocate."

" Hush, hush! lord earl," said Roland, as they slowly ascended the dark street, "for these words, if ever heard, would bring you to the scaffold ere the sun sets to-morrow."

" I crave pardon," replied the earl, with angry scorn, " I forgot that I spoke to a staunch adherent of this crowned oppressor of the Douglases, and their ally, the house of Ashkirk."

" Noble earl, in this devotion to your mother's princely house you wrong our generous king, who, on his happy return to the capital of his ancestors, intended to have recalled all the lords now banished for the rebellion of Angus, and would, ere this late hour, have done so but for your recent inroad from the south, which has closed and steeled his heart against you and against them ; and I know well that his able adviser, the stern Cardinal Beaton, devoted as he is to his country, and ever hostile to the grasping and aggressive spirit of England, will leave nothing unsaid to fan the king's vengeance and prompt his retaliation."

" I need not to be told what all Europe says ; that James of Scotland allows himself to be led by the nose just as Redlegs and the old ruffs of his council please."

" *Redlegs!* soh! a ceremonious title for his eminence ; I pray God, you have not become tainted by the damning heresies of this English Henry, who has so long been your patron.   But where did your lordship intend to dispose of yourself to-night ?"

" Faith, I had not made up my mind ; for in every change-house I entered, a copy of that proclamation for my apprehension was pasted over the chimneypiece ; so, fearing recognition, as the summer night was short and warm, I had resolved to sleep like a mosstrooper on the green brae yonder by the loch, when your cry summoned me to the rescue, and I am here."

" 'Twas a bright thought, that of yours, about Holyrood," said Vipont, " so, come with me to my apartment, for I know no place where you could be safer than in the very palace. None but the devil himself would dream of looking for you *there*, under the king's very nose."

" But my disguise is somewhat unlike the finery of your court gallants."

"Come with me to-night, and to-morrow we will think of something else."

"That will be necessary, for I am going to the queen's masque."

"What, thou?"

"Yes, I," replied the madcap earl. "What scest thou in that?"

"Thy discovery, arrest, condemnation, and execution; for God's sake, my lord, be not so criminally rash."

"Fear not, I will never compromise thee."

"I have no fear of that, but——"

"Fear nought else, then, for I have resolved to go, and words are useless."

They had talked so long in the dark alley, that when they issued from its archway into the street opposite the church of St. Giles, the lights on the spire were all extinguished, and the crowd had dispersed. The whole façade of the edifice rose before them in dark outline, and the only light that tipped its pinnacles was the slanting lustre of the brilliant moon, as she seemed to sail to the westward through the pure blue of the star-studded sky.

One o'clock rang from the Netherbow spire as Roland and the earl passed it, so that the events of this chapter occupied exactly an hour.

CHAPTER VII.

TWO OFFICIALS.

> " *Pedro.* Would to God it might be so!
> Thou twin to Satan, beautiful deceit!
> I almost wish I'd never met with thee.
> Yet the scheme's good—the scheme's exceeding good."
> *Edward the Black Prince.*

THE lord advocate was sitting in his library or study, which we have already described to the reader. Reclined in a softly-cushioned easy chair, he was gazing listlessly at the mass of papers that covered his writing table, which was of grotesquely-carved oak, and all of which he had to examine; but thoughts, to him of a more vital interest, occupied his mind, and he recoiled with disgust from the every-day task of public business. More than an hour passed away, and the advocate still sat dreamily, with his docquets of inhibitions and arrestments, letters of law-burrowes, indictments, and other criminal papers, lying pell-mell among secret information sent him from his correspondents on the English borders and the Highland frontier, among the turbulent islesmen of the west, and the intriguing Douglases nearer the capital. All these he had to peruse, to consider and consign to different portfolios, making comments and memorandums thereon, so as to have them all ready for service at a moment's notice, whenever the suspected noble, baron, or burgess should be arrested and indicted before the new and obnoxious court.

The information lodged by enemies against each other was of the most diverse description.

One baron lodged a secret complaint that another was meditating an inroad into England in time of peace ; that another had been selling cattle to the English contrary to law ; while a third complained that for three weeks he had been besieged in his own castle, and battered by the cannon of a neighbouring feudatory.

One burgess reported another for "girnelling mair victual than was required for his own sustenance," against which there was then a wise law, that in these our days would have pressed heavily upon corn-factors and other oppressors of the poor ; one had lost his horses, another his cattle, another his corn, and another his wife, all by dint of sword and spear ; and there were innumerable complaints anent Highland sorners, border hamesuckers, and landless Egyptians, who forcibly quartered themselves in houses and villages, and dwelt there until everything was eaten up in girnel, byre, and barn. Among other papers were numerous informations against and warrants required for the arrest of Englishmen who had come into Scotland without the *safeconduct* demanded and rendered necessary by the twelfth parliament of James II.; for the prosecution of those who slew the king's lieges in street and roadway, and against others who slew hares in time of snow. Warrants against lairds for storming each other's castles, and thieves who broke into farm dovecots ; and countless accusations of sorcery brought by the ignorant against those whose little discoveries and inventions would now, perhaps, have won for them patents from the crown and fellowships of the Royal Society.

The whole of the last night and half of the next day had passed without his bravos having returned.

The advocate began to fear that Vipont had proved victorious, and either killed or captured his assailants. In either case Redhall knew well suspicions would fall heavily upon himself, for ever since the murder of the Knight of Bombie, at the north door of St. Giles's, he had borne a somewhat evil repute in the minds of many. He glared impatiently at a large dialstone on a house opposite; it indicated the meridian, and he was about to buckle on his sword and poniard, preparatory to issuing forth in search of news, when heavy and irregular steps were heard ascending the stair; a coarse and muscular hand made several ineffectual attempts to raise the arras, a movement which nearly caused the owner to topple over on his nose, and half scrambling in, Nichol Birrel, balancing himself on each leg alternately, and looking rather discomposed from the potations and encounter of the past night, stood before his feudal lord and judicial patron.

" How now, thou presumptuous villain !" said Redhall, looking round for his cane, " is it thus thou appearest before me ?"

" Ay, ay—just as you see," hiccupped Nichol.

" Drunk ?"

" Rather so, Sir Adam—that is—my lord."

" Sot ! I verily believe thou wert born drunk. And where, then, is this Vipont now ?"

" I neither ken nor care, for he escaped us."

" Am I then to believe, sot and slug-a-bed, that with all thy boasting thou hast failed ?"

" Even so, in part."

" Dog ! I will have your ears cut off for this."

" Bide ye there, Sir Adam," said the ruffian, deprecatingly, while he ground his teeth at his master's anger, "I have gien him a wound that he will carry to his grave; but God's plague on your feuds, Redhall, for in your service I have gotten a slash o' the knuckles that shall gar me rue lang the last night."

" Here is a pretty rascal ;" exclaimed the advocate, almost beside himself with anger.

" I would some douce damsel said as muckle," said this overgrown gnome, contemplating his visage with one of his frightful leers, in a mirror opposite.

" Peace, fellow ! And thou livest to tell me that he actually escaped from three of ye ? He must be the very devil himself, this Roland Vipont ! Have you all returned alive ?"

"All : Nichol, Dobbie, and Sanders Screw—safe and sound, like the three kings o' Cologne in the Black Friary up bye there."

"Silence! 'tis blasphemy, this."

"Murder at night, and blasphemy in the morning! Ewhow, sirs, but that d—d mum-beer was strong yesternight."

"Thou gavest him a wound, thou sayest?" resumed Redhall, whose strong and relentless mind was of that description which, when once it conceived an idea, would pursue its accomplishment to the very verge of the earth ; and, moreover, feeling confident that those laws which he meted out so severely to others, could never recoil upon or entangle himself, he did whatever he pleased. "Was this wound a deep one?"

"So Dobbie swears, but he's a gomeral body in these respects. Yet, if ye will it, Sir Adam, as monk or apothegar, or something else, I may find my way to his chamber ere he is awake some morning, and probe the scar anew wi' my poniard. Even gif I were ta'en in his chamber 'twouldna matter muckle, as no *new* scar would be seen, and blood flowing would be attributed to the auld gash."

"'Tis not a bad scheme, then see to it as you please; but now I mistrust ye all, and think that, were I to fight him with my own more legal weapons, the pen and the parchment, he would assuredly be vanquished. We shall see," mused the advocate; "I may have him one day before the lords on some desperate charge (he loves a lady of the Douglas faction). Proofs of conspiracy could soon be foisted up, and if we once had him under the hands of Sanders Screw——"

Birrel mechanically felt for his steel needle.

"Nay," said Redhall, with a grim smile, as he observed this motion, "Vipont is a mere soldier, and thou knowest that a soldier is seldom deep or designing enough to be a conjuror. Now prythee, rascal, act soberly, and assist me to dress and truss my points with care; for I am to dine with his eminence the cardinal and the lord bishop of Limoges to-day, and thereafter we are all going to the queen's masque at Holyrood. Bring me the last taffety dress that was sent me from that French stallanger at the Tron, with my silver walking-sword —and the little poniard—hath Hew the dalmascar sent it from his booth in the Bow? Oh, here it is," added Redhall, stepping into an apartment that opened off the library, and to

which (as we may still see in old houses) there was an ascent
of two or three steps. This was his dressing-room, and
formed a square turret which projected on heavy stone corbels
over the pavement of the Canongate.

An antique mirror, imbedded in an oak frame, stood on one
side; a basin stand furnished with a pewter basin and ewer
(such as the Leith traders then brought out of Flanders)
stood on the other; and between them was a large cabinet,
one door of which was open, showing the various laced dresses,
doublets, gowns, ruffs and collars, mantles, tags, tassels and
aiguilettes, which made up the wardrobe of this official, whose
ample judicial robe was carelessly thrown over a large high-
backed chair, against which and on which were piled pieces of
armour, swords, gloves, gauntlets, files, poniards, and wheelock-
pistols; showing that, though a civil officer of state, Redhall
could assume the offensive as well as any swashbuckler or
cavalier of his day; and not many weeks had elapsed since, at
the head of three hundred men-at-arms, he had been severely
repulsed in an attempt to sack and burn the tower of his
neighbour, Sir James Foulis of Colinton, the lord clerk
register.

A jerkin of black velvet, with open sleeves of dark purple
satin, embroidered all over with silver, black trunk breeches
slashed with purple silk, and black hose, with shoes round-
toed and slashed, formed his principal attire. Over the close
jerkin he threw a loose "cassock coate" of black silk, the
collar of which was tied by silver cords under his thick close
ruff, and from thence it was open, though furnished with
twenty-four buttons of Bruges silver.

Over this he hung his shoulder-belt, which sustained a long
and slender walking-sword, having a hilt of curiously-cut steel
and silver net-work; thus, everything about him was either
dark or silver, save the solitary white feather which adorned
his black velvet bonnet, and gave a smart and lofty bearing to
his noble head, which a grave dark visage, piercing eyes, and
fierce moustache completed.

His ruffian dependent, who to his public official duties
united the private one of valet, had scarcely given the last
finishing-touch to his elaborate costume when the clatter of
hoofs drew Redhall to the window, and he saw the master of
the ordnance, with his plumes waving, his polished corselet,
his embroidered dress, and rich gold aiguilettes glittering in

the sunshine, ride up the street. A tall, stout serving-man, clad in a half suit of ribbed armour, wearing that kind of close helmet which was then called a coursing-hat, and carrying over his shoulder a mighty two-handed wall-sword, nearly as long as himself, followed close at his heels, running as if for his life.

(This armed valet was no other than the Earl of Ashkirk.)

Almost at the same moment, as if she had been watching for the sound of the hoofs, Jane Seton appeared at an opposite window, which she threw open. There was a radiant smile on her bright face as she kissed her hand to the handsome cavalier, who uncovered and bowed to his horse's mane; and there was a happy expression in his eyes, a gallant and adventurous air about him, that, with the splendour of his attire, failed not to impress even Redhall; for, as Vipont saluted his charming mistress, the spirited animal he rode approached her sideways, keeping his front to the windows, curveting, prancing, and shaking his flowing mane and the silver ornaments of the embossed bridle.

"St. Mary!" muttered the advocate, while he bit his thin lips, and a fierce smile twinkled in his eyes, "how she welcomes him!—an empty fool, who hath no thought beyond his ruffs and his aiguilettes, and who, though he hath scarcely a cross in his pouch, is doubtless ready to cut the throat of any man who doubts him rich as Crœsus, and able to purchase the three Lothians."

Charged with an invitation, secretly obtained from the queen, for the ladies of Ashkirk, Roland was in high spirits, for he had procured it through the influence of Madame de Montreuil, the governess of Magdalene; and, with his face all smiles, he sprung from his horse and entered the mansion.

Lady Jane disappeared from the window.

Then Redhall ground his teeth, and turned furiously away, for then he knew the happy lovers had met, and were together.

He hurriedly left his house, and descending the Blackfriars Wynd to the Archiepiscopal Palace, a fragment of which is still prominent by its large octagon tower which overhangs the Cowgate, he was admitted by the cardinal's armed vassals, or guards, at a low-browed doorway, surmounted by the coat armorial of Bethune and Balfour, over which was the broad-tasselled hat, which indicates a prince of the holy Roman empire.

There, at dinner, Redhall heard from his friend, the Abbot of Kinloss, the rumour which was then current in the city, that " the master of the king's ordnance had been most inalapertly beset upon the Hiegait by a party of the Douglas traitors," from whom he had been only saved by a miraculous exertion of valour; for (as Buchanan relates) whatever happened in those days was invariably placed to the score of the Douglases.

CHAPTER VIII.

THE QUEEN'S MASQUE.

" Old Holyrood rung merrily
    That night with wassail, mirth, and glee:
    King James, within her princely towers,
    Feasted the chiefs of Scotland's powers."—*Marmion.*

ATTENDED by Ashkirk, who carried the tremendous sword before mentioned, and was arrayed in clothes somewhat sad-coloured, but in fashion between those of a valet and esquire, Roland, agitated by no ordinary fear and exultation, approached the illuminated hall of the palace—fear, because, despite every warning, the madcap noble insisted on accompanying him—and exultation, because Jane Seton and her companions were all to be there; though the haughty old countess had coldly declined, on the plea of age and ill health, which, in reality, was caused by dread of the risk so foolishly run by her son, whom she had implored, with tears, to seek shelter among his own vassals in Forfarshire, if he could not regain the court of England; for the frontiers were said to be closely watched.

With his doublet of cloth-of-gold, all dotted with seed pearls, a short purple velvet mantle, lined with yellow satin, dangling from his left shoulder, his gold aiguilettes, ruff, and sword, Roland had donned his best bravery, curled his dark locks, and pointed his moustaches with particular care on this auspicious evening. He carried his bonnet in his hand, as they traversed the crowded courts of the palace; and every minute he turned to look anxiously at Ashkirk; but his peculiar helmet, with its low peak, and the thick beard, which he had permitted to grow long for disguise, together with his bombastic doublet, completely transformed him, and he marched behind, bearing his six-foot rapier with imperturbable gravity.

The gloomy and antique courts, overlooked by grated windows and heavy roofs of stone, the cloistered passages and vast stone stairs of this ancient palace (which was burnt by the English), were lighted with numerous coloured lamps. The king's guard, wearing their blue bonnets, stockings and doublets of scarlet, slashed and faced with black, and armed with pike, poniard, and arquebuse, formed two glittering lines from the palace gate to the main entrance, and from thence along the passages to the head of the grand staircase, where stood their captain, Sir John Forrester of Corstorphine, a handsome and reckless-looking young gallant, clad in the uniform colours of the guard (a jerkin of scarlet velvet, richly lined with Venetian gold), and having twelve short aiguilettes on each shoulder of his trunk sleeves, which terminated in steel gauntlets, for he wore his gorget, and, being on duty, had an esquire near him, who carried his helmet.

His lieutenant, Louis Leslie of Balquhan, in the Garioch, was similarly arrayed; and both were remarkably elegant and military-looking young men.

" Holy mass!" said Forrester, looking down the long staircase, "here cometh Vipont, and his new valet with the outrageous sword!"

" 'Fore God! he looks like one of the twelve peers of Charlemagne," said Leslie, with a loud laugh.

" Ho! Vipont, where the devil didst steal that ancient paladine?"

" 'Tis the excalibur of King Arthur he carries," said Leslie.

" 'Tis the lance of Urganda the Unknown!"

And the young men laughed aloud as their friend ascended the stair with his tall valet three paces behind. When he drew near, Forrester playfully made a pass with his sword at Roland's face, a second at his breast, and a third at his ruff, keeping him down the stair. The cannonier immediately unsheathed his rapier, and simply saying—

" Guard!" attacked his assailant in the same playful manner; and they fenced for more than a minute, while Louis Leslie held his sides, and laughed boisterously on seeing that Vipont found the impossibility of ascending, and was beginning to lose his temper.

The approach of Cardinal Beaton, who was surrounded by

a large body of vassals wearing his own livery, put an end to this dangerous frolic; and though openly saluted by the king's soldiers, the cardinal's guards were secretly greeted with haughty and supercilious glances as they marched between the double ranks that led to the foot of the grand staircase, jostling as they ascended the train of Sir Thomas Clifford, the ambassador of England—a country which the cardinal abhorred, politically and religiously.

" Harkee, Forrester," said Roland, as he passed; " have the ladies of Ashkirk arrived yet ?"

" Yes, some ten minutes ago. I was thunderstruck to see them !"

" Wherefore ?"

" Hast thou not heard the rumour ?"

" Of what ?"

" That the Earl of Ashkirk is among us here, in the good town of Edinburgh."

" Twenty devils ! dost thou say so ?"

" 'Tis a fact—on some treasonable mission from English Henry—at least, so sayeth my lord advocate."

Roland's blood ran alternately hot and cold.

" This demon advocate hears of everything !" said he to the earl, as they passed along the corridor. " My God ! lord earl, if discovered——"

" Thou canst save me, perhaps," said the earl, who was himself a little alarmed.

" If not ?"

" I can die then, with my sword in my hand," replied the earl, through his teeth. " But art thou not rich in the favour of this holiday king ?"

" In that alone ; otherwise I am poor enough, God wot."

" Thy father left thee——"

" His sword, his arms, and motto—nothing more. The first is here at my side—the second, I know by heart, having nought else whereon to grave them—*gules*, six annulets *or*."

" Tush ! thou wilt build thee a castle some day, and put the crest above the gate."

" A swan's head winged, rising from a ducal coronet—ha! ha! my father was a soldier, and poor, as we soldiers always are."

" 'Tis a madcap adventure, this, I know right well," said the earl ; " but I have armed me (sans leave) with your best corslet ; and as I have a strong affection for my poor head (which is, in fact, of no use to any one save myself), they shall never possess it if my hands can keep it. If I am beset to-night—fiends! I would mow them all down with this long blade, like death with his scythe."

" St. Mary! use it warily," said Roland, laughing; " thou wilt punch a hole in the roof else."

" Thou lovest this King James well ?"

" Love him—yes. I am ready to be cut in pieces for him to-morrow."

" Still thou art poor !"

" I have quite made up my mind to be rich at some future day, but *when* that day shall come, the Lord alone knows," replied Roland, without perceiving that the earl was covertly ridiculing his loyalty to James.

Notwithstanding his disguise, the whole air and bearing of Ashkirk were eminently noble. Though brave and passionate, he veiled a promptitude to anger under an outwardly impassible equanimity of temper; thus, while he could be at one time rash to excess, at another he could affect to be doggedly cool. He had innumerable excellent qualities of head and heart, which would have rendered him of inestimable value to such a prince as James V.; but his blind devotion to the faction of Angus (a faction of which we will treat more at large elsewhere) rendered them nugatory. Though considerably above the middle height, he was strong, elegant, and graceful. His nose was almost aquiline; his eyes were dark and piercing; his mouth was like that of a Cæsar; and his well-defined chin was indicative of that obstinacy of purpose, which is a leading feature of the Scottish character; and, like every gentleman of his time, he rode, fenced, and danced to perfection.

Roland sighed when he thought on all these lost good qualities, and bestowing a parting glance on the earl, who, as his valet, was obliged to leave him at the large gothic door of the hall, he passed through with the guests, who were ushered between a double line of pages and liverymen. The chamberlain of the household waved his wand, and announced—

" Sir Roland Vipont of that ilk, master of the king's ordnance."

In one little heart only, amid all the gay throng in that magnificent hall, did the name of the king's first favourite find an echo.

Two hundred wax-lights, in branching chandeliers, illu-

minated the high arched roof and lofty walls of the vast
apartment, which was decorated with all that florid ornament and grandeur which we find in the palaces of James V
It was one of his new additions to the regal mansion which
his uncle Albany, and his father, James IV., had first
engrafted on the old monastic edifice of the Holy Cross. In
honour of the queen, the walls were hung with arras composed of resplendent cloth-of-gold and silver, impaled with
velvet, and the floors were covered with Persian carpets,
which were among the gifts received by James V from
Francis I.*

On one side the arras was festooned to reveal the refresh-
ment-rooms which lay beyond, and the long tables, whereon
lay every continental delicacy, with the richest wines of
France and Italy, all of which the poorest Scottish artizan
could procure duty free before the union. There, too, lay one
of the queen's cupboards of silver plate, which was valued at
more than a hundred thousand crowns, and watched by four
of the royal guard, with their arquebuses loaded. Chairs
covered with white velvet, brocaded with gold, and surmounted by imperial crowns, with sofas or settles of purple
velvet, were ranged along the sides of these rooms; but the
great hall was cleared of all obstruction for the dancers. The
king's musicians, among whom were the four drummers, the
four trumpeters, and three flute-players of the queen's French
band, all clad in yellow satin, occupied the music gallery,
and were just striking up king James's favourite march,
The Battle of Harlaw, which was then very popular in
Scotland, and remained so down to the time of Drummond
of Hawthornden.

Amid the crowd of ladies, nobles, and splendidly-attired
cavaliers, who thronged the vast length of that great apartment, seeming as one mass of velvet, silk, satin, and waving
plumage of every hue, mingled with jewels that sparkled and
lace that glittered, aiguilettes, swords and mantles, poniards
and spurs, trains, ruffs, and knightly orders—surrounded by
a sea of light, for the gleaming cloth-of-gold that covered the

* " *Item.* Foure suitts of rich arras hangings of 8 pices a suitt, wroght with
gold and silke.

" *Item.* Foure suitts of hangings of cloth-of-gold-silver, impaled with
velvett.

" *Item.* 20 Persian carpets, faire and large."—See list of " gifts and pro-
pynes," *Balfour's Annales,* vol. i. pp. 266-7.

walls seemed nothing else—Roland looked anxiously, but in vain, for Lady Seton, as he walked straight towards the upper end, to present himself to the king and queen.

James leaned on the side of Magdalene's chair, conversing with her and the six privileged ladies of honour, who sat near her, three being on each side, occupying little stools, which were covered with blue velvet, and called tabourettes. Among this group were Madame de Montreuil, Mademoiselle de Brissac, and several noble Frenchwomen, who had known Vipont in France, and greeted with a smile of welcome.

James was magnificently clad in his favourite dress of white brocaded satin, slashed with rose-coloured silk. His four orders (the first in Europe) sparkled on his neck, and the band of his slouched blue bonnet shone like a zone with diamonds. His rich brown hair fell in ringlets on his ruff, and his dark hazel eyes were bright with gaiety and pride. He wore a short mantle, a long sword, sheathed in blue velvet, buff boots, and gold spurs. His white silk stockings were the first seen in Scotland, and the motto of the Garter encircled his left leg.

With that frankness which made him so charming to all, this handsome young monarch immediately approached Sir Roland, and met him half way.

" Here comes my Vipont!" said he; "ah! thou art a fine fellow, Roland. I would know thee for a noble, or a soldier, at a league's distance, by that inimitable bearing of thine."

Roland bowed profoundly; but the king took his hand, while many a fierce glance was exchanged between the various nobles who beheld the warm reception of this rising favourite.

" And so, my poor Vipont, thou wert attacked last night?"

" A mere joke, your majesty."

" Three daggers are no joke; but you were wounded?"

" Oh, a mere scratch with a pin."

" Dost suspect any one as having caused it?"

" Your majesty alone," replied Roland, with a peculiar smile at the group around the king; "for your favour is ever fatal to your friends."

" Doubtless," said James, with a darkening brow, " it hath been some of those accursed——" (Douglases he was about to say, but on seeing how quickly the colour mounted to Vipont's brow he said) " cloak-snatchers and cutpurses, who make their lair in the Burghmuir-woods, and elsewhere;

but this must be looked to, sirs! such doings cannot be permitted in our burghs and landward towns."

They conversed in the old-court Scots, then "the language of a whole country" (says Lord Jeffrey in one of his able essays), "an independent kingdom, still separate in laws, character, and manners; a language by no means common to the vulgar, but the common speech of the whole nation in early life, and connected in their imagination, not only with that olden time which is uniformly conceived as being more simple, pure, and lofty than the present, but also with all the soft bright colours of remembered childhood and domestic affection."

Roland advanced at once towards the young queen, who gave him her hand to kiss, and received him with her brightest smile; for his face had become familiar to her in the king's train at her father's court.

"Ah! Monsieur le Maître d'Artillerie," she said, in a very sweet voice, "thou seemest quite like an old friend, and remindest me so much of my father's house at St. Germain-en-Laye—that pretty little hunting-lodge, near the Seine, where I was so happy—though not so happy as I am here—*O Dieu me pardonne*, no," she added, with covert glance at the king full of the utmost affection.

"My dear Madame de Montreuil," said Roland, in a low voice; "express for me to her majesty the thousand thanks I owe you and her for the favour shown to my friends."

This charming daughter of Queen Claud the Good was (as we have elsewhere said) only in her sixteenth year. Her fair brown hair, of which she had a great profusion, was most becomingly arranged in plaits and curls; her eyes were of the most beautiful blue; her small velvet cap, squared at the temples, and falling straight down each cheek, was blue, lined with satin, and edged with little pearls; her skirt was all of frosted cloth-of-gold, with a body of violet-coloured satin, embroidered also with gold, and having hanging sleeves of the richest lace lined with latticed ribbons; her gloves were highly perfumed; and around her neck was a gift of the Countess of Arran—a string of those large and snow-white pearls, that in the olden time were found in the burn of Cluny. She frequently sighed, as if with pain and weariness, and pressed a hand at times upon her breast.

Having now paid his devoirs to the young queen, Roland

scrutinized the glittering throng for the fair form of her who, though perhaps less beautiful than the gentle Magdalene, was to him the queen indeed of all the ladies there.

"Vipont," said the king, coldly, as he drew Roland aside, "I know for whom thou art looking—for one whose brother is under sentence of forfeiture, the price of his head being at this moment written on the palace gates; for one who, I can assure thee, Sir Roland, should not have been under the roof-tree of Holyrood to-night, but for the kind wishes of her majesty and Madame de Montreuil, whose weak side I see thou hast attained, as any handsome gallant may easily do."

Roland's heart sank at these words.

"Alas! your majesty," he replied, in the same low voice, "are the houses of Douglas and Seton fallen so low, that a fair young being, who unites the blood of both in her pure and sinless heart is merely tolerated in Holyrood? Your royal sire, around whom so many brave men of both these names fell on that dark day at Flodden, foresaw not a time like this."

"There is truth in this, though I have the deepest cause for enmity to these families that ever king had to a subject," replied James, frankly. "The mere rebellion of Earl John of Ashkirk I might have forgotten, and that of his son I could have forgiven, but his leaguing with Englishmen never! And yonder stands my little rebel, Jane of Ashkirk; faith, she *is* beautiful—yea, as love herself!"

"I think her inferior to the queen."

"With all thy partiality? Rogue, thou flatterest me! A true lover should deem his lady-love inferior to none under God!"

"I have heard that she is as much famed for her beauty as her mother is for her salves and recipes," said a Hamilton, with a very unmistakeable sneer.

"Nay, Sir John of Kincavil," said the king, "thou art too severe to be gallant. I will swear that her hair is the finest I ever saw."

"And her teeth," said young Leslie of Balquhan.

"And her skin, which is like the finest velvet!" said Roland, simply.

"Ah, the devil! thou hast discovered *that!*" said the king—and several courtiers and soldiers laughed. "I must really see this fair one," he whispered; she looks at you,

Sir Roland.   Ah ! I see—'tis the unmistakeable glance of a woman at the man she loves.   I find I am about to lose my master of the ordnance."

" Sir John of Kincavil," said Roland, in a low voice, as he passed that tall and brilliantly attired knight ; " at noon to-morrow I will be waiting you at the Water Gate."

" I shall bring my best rapier," replied the other, with a bow.

" And a pot of the countess's salve," said Roland, with a dark smile, as they mutually bit their gloves in defiance, and passed on.

During the presentation of Roland to the queen and this colloquy with the king, Lady Jane Seton, who had not yet been presented to Magdalene, felt herself somewhat unpleasantly situated.   Her companions, Marion Logan, and Alison Hume, had both disappeared in the crowd, the first with the well-known Norman Leslie, Master of Rothes, and the second with Sir John Forrester, of the king's guard ; while, quite oblivious of the many hostile eyes around, the beautiful Sybil, with a large fan outspread before her, had thrown aside her usual sadness, and, exhilirated with the gaiety of the scene, was coquetting and smiling to a gay crowd of young cavaliers, to whose jests and gallantries she was replying, however, with the words alone, for her thoughts were concentrated on the tall valet, whom she had seen more than once at the opposite doorway, armed with his portentous rapier.

The hostile eyes were those of the Hamilton faction, which was always in the ascendant when the power of the Douglases were at a low ebb ; and thus, marvelling how the sister of the exiled earl had found her way into their privileged and exclusive circle, cold, haughty, and inquiring glances met those of the timid Jane, whose cheeks began to crimson with anger. She had now lost the thoughtless Sybil ; she saw not her lover ; and amid that vast crowd found herself utterly alone. Margaret Countess of Arran, the ladies of Barncleugh and Evandale, Dalserf, and Drumrye, of Raploch, and others, all wives and daughters of knights and gentlemen of the hostile surname, were gazing stolidly upon her.

Cardinal Beaton, clad in his scarlet cope and baretta, with a gold cross upon his breast, was standing near her, conversing with a prelate in purple.   This was the French Bishop of Limoges, in the Vienne, to whom, with his right forefinger

laid on the palm of his left hand, he was impressively holding
forth on "the damnable persuasions of the English heretics,
whose perverse doctrines were spreading schisms and scandals
in the holy church in Scotland." His large, dark, and
thoughtful eyes, which were (inadvertently however) fixed on
Jane, completed her confusion. The great and terrible cardinal was evidently speaking of her; she felt almost sinking
when the crowd around fell back, and the king, with her
lover, approached to her relief.

CHAPTER IX.

LA VOLTA.

" Yet is there one, the most delightful kind,
  A lofty jumping, or a leaping round,
  Where, arm in arm, two dancers are entwined,
  And whirl themselves, with strict embracements bound,
  And still their feet an anapest do sound :
  An anapest is all their music's song,
  Whose first two feet are short, and third is long."
                    Orchestra, by Sir J. DAVIES, 1596.

" MAY I present to your majesty," said Roland, "the Lady
Jane Seton, the only daughter of brave Earl John of Ashkirk——"

" Who thrice saved my father's banner at Flodden—a right
royal welcome to Holyrood, madame," said James, bowing
gracefully and low, while all his hostility vanished as he
gazed on the pure open brow and clear eyes of Jane ; " but
how is this, Sir Roland? thou oughtest to have introduced
me to the lady, not the lady to *me*—the knight to the dame
—the inferior to the superior. But hark ! the music is striking ' Kinge Willyiam's Notte ;' 'tis a ϕound we are to dance—
Lady Jane, wilt favour me—your hand for this measure ; see,
my Lord Arran is leading forth the queen."

And thus, almost before she had time for reflection, Jane
found herself led to the head of that shining hall, the part-
ner of King James, who had seen the hostile eyes that were
bent upon her, had seen how their cold glances thawed into
smiles at his approach, and resolved, by a striking example, to
rebuke the malicious spirit he despised.

Roland finding himself anticipated, had now no desire to
dance, and wishing to follow Jane with his eyes, retired

among the spectators, whose hostile remarks more than once made him bite his glove and grasp the pommel of his poniard.

The dancers were performing the round, a species of country-dance, which continued in fashion while quadrilles were in futurity, and until the time of Charles I.

The king's principal favourite, James Hamilton, Earl of Arran (afterwards the Regent Duke of Chatelherault, knight of St. Michael), a stately noble, arrayed in dark violet-coloured velvet, becoming his years and grave diplomatic character, led forth the bright young queen. There were about thirty couples on the floor, all the gentlemen wearing high ruffs, short mantles, and immense long swords. The captain of the guards, and Leslie, his lieutenant, were with Alison Hume and Marion Logan. At a given signal, a burst of music came from the balcony, and the dancers began with that spirit and grace which belonged to the olden time, and then the whole hall vibrated with joy and happiness, brilliancy and praise; for if the king was the most finished cavalier in Scotland, Magdalene was assuredly the fairest young being that had ever worn its diadem.

The great Earl of Arran acquitted himself, however, very much to the queen's dissatisfaction; for this thoughtful statesman and favourite minister was confounded to find Lady Seton dancing with the king, and knew not what to think of this sudden and dangerous change in his sentiments towards the Douglas party.

Above the well-bred hum of modulated voices in the hall, a loud uproar of tongues in one of the courts below drew Roland to the windows more than once.

" By Heaven, they have discovered Ashkirk !" was his first thought. But the noise was occasioned by the king's jester, Jock Macilree, frolicking among the pages, lacqueys, and yeomen of the guard, with his cap-and-bells, bladder, and fantastic dress, exercising on the poor black page, Sabrino, that wit which, for the present, was excluded from the royal circle, as his rough jests, boisterous laughter, and grotesque aspect terrified and agitated the timid young queen.

" God keep you, Sir Roland Vipont," said a flute-like voice (with the usual greeting for which our more homely " How are you?" is now substituted). Roland turned, and bowed on encountering the grave face and keen dark eyes of the lord advocate.

"God keep you, Sir Adam," he replied, rather coldly, as may be easily supposed. "Understanding that you laboured under a severe illness, I did not expect the pleasure of meeting you here."

"As little did I expect the honour of meeting *you*, having heard that you had received an unfortunate wound."

"Ah! a scratch, as your lordship heard me tell the king," replied Roland, colouring with indignation; but the face of Redhall was impassible as that of a statue.

"Courtiers must expect such scratches at times."

"Under favour, my lord, I am no courtier."

"No, excuse me—better than a thousand courtiers—thou art a brave soldier."

Roland bowed.

"He flatters me for some end," thought he. There was a mixture of politeness and disdain in the manner of Redhall that was fast provoking Roland, for they had never spoken before, save once, more than a year ago, on the king's service. "Can this really be the villain who attempted to slay me," he reflected, "or hath the hostility of Ashkirk led his ears into error? I think not; for, strange to say, my wound *smarted* the moment he addressed me. Doubtless, had I been dead, it would have bled at his touch."

"You know, Sir Roland, 'tis my peculiar province to have the laws enforced. Have you any suspicions of who your assailant was?"

"Yes, the instigator of the assault is here to-night—yea, in this very hall!"

"His name?"

"Is written on the blade of my sword, where I am wont to keep such memorandums," replied Roland, with a glance which made the official start, change colour, and raise his eyebrows with an expression of surprise, as he turned away; for at that moment the king came up, the dance having ended, and the blood mounted to the temples of Redhall, for Lady Jane Seton was leaning on his arm.

"How now, lord advocate?" said the frank monarch, "why so grave and so grim? Thou art a sorely changed man now! Dost thou remember when we two were but halfling callants at our tasks together, in the barred chambers of David's tower, trembling under terror of old Gavin's ferrule—Gavin Dunbar, the poor prisoner of my uncle Albany?"

"And how oft we played truanderie together," replied the advocate, with a faint smile.

"To seek birds'-nests in the woods of Coates, throw kail-castocks down the wide lums of the Grassmarket, and fish for powowets in the Nor'loch, By St. Paul! those were indeed the happy days of guileless hearts; for, if we quarreled, we beat each other until we were weary, and thenceforward became better friends than ever. But how cometh it that thou, my gay cannonier, hast not had a measure to-night, and when no dance seems perfect without thee? Madame de Montreuil and some of our French demoiselles are anxious to dance *la volta*, which was all the rage at the fêtes of King Francis; but not one of our Scottish gallants knoweth the least about it save thyself."

"I am sure the Lady Jane does, and if she will favour me with her hand, and your majesty will spare her ——"

"To thee only will I, for I long now to speak with mine own true love," and, with a graceful smile, James retired to the group that remained around the young queen and her dames of the tabourette.

The feeble health of Magdalene was apparent to all by the languor and alternate flushing and pallor of her face, after the trifling exercise of *la ronde*.

As Vipont led away Lady Jane, Redhall turned to conceal his sudden emotion. He faced a mirror and was startled at his own expression. Swollen like cords, the veins rose on his forehead like lines painted there. Jane had gone off without even bestowing on him a smile or a bow. She had quite forgotten his presence. He felt painfully that in her mind there would, doubtless, be a mighty gulf between himself and this gay young soldier, whose light spirit and chivalric heart were so entirely strangers to that burning jealousy and passionate desire of vengeance that struggled for supremacy with love. He passed a hand over his pale brow, as if to efface the emotion written there, and turned again with his wonted smile of coldness and placidity to address the person nearest him. This chanced to be no other than his gossip, the abbot of Kinloss, a peep-eyed little churchman, whose head and face, as they peered from his ample cope, so strongly resembled those of a rat looking forth from a hole, that no other description is required.

The ambassador of the great Charles V., a richly-dressed

cavalier in black, on whose breast shone the gold cross of
Calatrava and the silver dove of Castile, and whose scarf of
scarlet and gold sustained a long spada of the pure Toledo
steel, now appeared on the Persian-carpeted floor, leading
Madame de Montreuil, a gay little Frenchwoman in white
brocade, which stuck out all round her nearly six feet in
diameter; Roland and Lady Seton were their *vis-à-vis*. All
eyes were upon them, for the dance was so completely new,
that none in Scotland had ever seen it, and the expectations
were great as the music which floated through the oak-carved
screen of the gallery seemed divine. The right arm of each
cavalier was placed round the waist of his lady, while her
right hand rested in his left, and was pressed against his
heart; in short, *la volta*, which had thus made its appearance
in old Holyrood on the night of the 20th May, in the year
of grace 1537, was nothing more than the vault step, now
known, in modern times, as the waltz.

There was a pause; the music again burst forth, rising and
falling in regular time, and away went the dancers, round and
round, in a succession of whirls, the little red-heeled and white
velvet shoes of the ladies seeming to chase the buff boots and
gold spurs of the gentlemen; round and round they went,
rapidly, lightly, and gracefully. The tall Spanish ambassador
and little Madame de Montreuil acquitted themselves to perfection; but Roland and Jane, to whom he had only given
a few lessons during the preceding forenoon, perhaps less so;
but none there observed it, and a burst of acclamation welcomed this graceful dance, which was now for the first time
seen in Scotland, but which the prejudices of after years
abolished till the beginning of the present century.

"What thinkest thou of this new spring, father abbot?"
said Redhall, with a cold smile in his keen eyes.

"There is sorcery in it, by my faith there is!" whispered
the abbot, lowering his voice and his bushy eyebrows; "there
is sorcery in it, my lord advocate, or my name is not Robin
Reid, abbot of Kinloss."

"Ha! dost thou think so?"

"Think so? Ken ye not that it hath been partly condemned by the parliament of Paris (whom we take for our
model in all matters of justiciary), for it originated in Italy,
from whence it was taken into France by the witches, who
dance it with the devil on the Sabbath. Ah, 'tis well worth

making a memorandum of," continued this meagre little senator, perceiving that Redhall was writing something in his
note-book or tablets, behind the shadow of a window-curtain.

" But the Spaniard is a knight of a religious order," urged
Redhall, pausing.

" A religious order!" repeated the testy abbot; " 'tis such
a cloister of religieux as our knights of Torphichen, who spend
night and day in drinking and dicing, fighting anent their
prerogatives, and debauching the country maidens on their
fiefs and baronies.   Were he not ambassador of Charles V.,
I would vote for having him under the nippers of Nichol
Birrel; for if ever a sorcerer trod on Scottish ground, 'tis he.
He dabbles in charms and philtres, and every night 'tis said
his chimney in St. John's Close emitteth blue sparks, which
are those of hell, as sure as I am Robin Reid, abbot of Kinloss.   He and father St. Bernard are ever searching among
the baser minerals for the spirit of the gold; at least so say
the prebendaries of St. Giles's."

" Um! he is confessor of the Lady Ashkirk," muttered
Redhall, making another memorandum.

" As we were talking of sorcery, what hath the high sheriff
of Lothian done with your vassal, the forester of Kinleith,
who buried a living cat under his hearthstone, as a charm
against evil?"

" Ah," said Redhall, with a smile, " Birrel soon found such
proofs against him, that he is sent to the justiciary court."

" Ho! ho!" said the little abbot, rubbing his hands;
" Sanders Screw and his concurrents will bring mickle to
light, or my name is not Robin ——"

But here the advocate hurried abruptly away, for at that
moment the dance ended; and flushed, heated, and fatigued,
the two ladies were led away—De Montreuil, by her cavalier,
into the adjoining apartment, and Lady Jane towards a staircase which descended from the hall to the level and grassy
lawn, that lay between the palace and the foot of the craigs
of Salisbury.

The green sides of the silent hills and rocky brows of those
basaltic cliffs, which seem but the half of some vast mountain
which volcanic throes have rent and torn asunder, were bathed
in the splendour of the broad and cloudless moon ; the palace
towers and vanes stood forth in strong white light, while the
curtain walls and cloistered courts were steeped in sable

shadow. On the right were a cluster of small antique houses where some of the royal retainers dwelt, and where Roland had his temporary domicile. This was called St. Anne's Yard; on the left, apparently among the hills, two red lights were shining. One was from an ancient mansion at the foot of Salisbury craigs, where Robert, abbot of the Holy Cross, dwelt; the other was from the illuminated shrine of St. Antony's Hermitage.

Several revellers were lounging on the green sward in the moonlight, or sitting on the carved stone benches that were placed against the palace wall, and the lovers took possession of the most remote, where the south garden of the king bordered the burial-ground of the abbey.

"Jane," said Roland, as he gazed fondly on her pure brow and snowy skin, which seemed so dazzlingly white in the clear moonlight; "your smiles to-night have done more to raise the Douglas cause than twenty thousand lances. How my heart leaps! I seem to tread on air! I knew well that James had but to see you, to appreciate your worth and beauty. He has done so; and now old dame Margaret of Arran, and all the Hamiltons of Cadyow and Clydesdale, will be ready to burst their boddices and die of sheer vexation."

"But if Archibald should be discovered ——"

"Chut! dost think that James would dance with the sister over-night and decapitate the brother in the morning?"

"The king never once referred to the frightful position in which he is placed."

"He is much too courtly to do so. But say, art thou not happy, dearest?"

"Happy? with a proclamation on this palace-gate offering a thousand merks for my brother's head! Oh, Roland, Roland! I would justly merit contempt to be so. I came not hither to rejoice, or with any other intention than to beg his life and pardon from the king. The figures of a dance were certainly not the place to prefer such a solemn request —Mother of God! no; and, as my mother says, but with a different meaning, I am yet biding my time. My heart sickens at the splendour of that glittering hall, when I bethink me that the gallant earl, my brother, whose plume should have waved among the loftiest there, is now the companion of lacqueys and liverymen—the retainers of our actual enemies and oppressors—the butt, perhaps, of their coarse

mirth and ribald jests, and fearing to repel them with the
spirit he possesses, lest he should be discovered and unmasked
by those whose innate hatred of the Seton and the Douglas
require not the additional incentive of King James's gold."

"It was, I own, a madcap adventure, his coming here to-
night; but thou knowest that he is headstrong as a Highland
bull. However, Lintstock, my servant, a wary old gunner of
King James IV., is with him, and will see he is neither insulted nor discovered."

"Anything is better than suspense," said Jane, sobbing.
"Would that the king were here."

"I will bring him if you wish it," said Roland, rising and
taking both her hands in his; "he would come in a moment,
for to him a lady's message is paramount to one from the
parliament. But would you say that the carl is in Scotland
—here among us in Edinburgh?"

"I would, Roland—yes, for such is my confidence in the
honour and generosity of the king."

"'Tis not misplaced, for James is alike good and merciful;
but 'twere better to ask his French bride, whom he loves too
well to refuse her anything—even to become the ally of his
uncle, English Henry; and certes! the pardon of a gallant
Scottish noble is no great boon to crave of a generous Scottish king."

Roland started, for at that moment the voice of James was
heard at one of the open windows of the hall just above them.

"Vipont! Sir Roland Vipont!" he said.

"I am here, at your grace's service," replied Sir Roland,
raising his bonnet.

"Wilt thou favour us a moment? here, my lord the bishop
of Limoges and I have a dispute as to whether our old gun
of Galloway, Mollance Meg, or the Devil of Bois le Duc,
carry the largest ball. I say Meg; the bishop says the
Devil; and as 'tis thy office to know all points of gunner-
craft, come hither, if that fair dame will do us the honour to
spare thee for one moment, for we have laid a hundred lions
Scots on the matter."

Loth to leave Jane, and anxious to please the king, Roland
hesitated, till she said—

"Obey the king, and I will wait your return; luckily, yonder
is my cousin Sybil and Louis Leslie of the king's guard."

Roland pressed her hand, sprang up the flight of steps, and

the moment he was gone Lady Jane found some one standing at her side.

She turned, and encountered the sombre figure of Redhall, the sad glance of whose piercing eyes ran like lightning through her veins; and she trembled at the double reflection that she was almost alone, and that he might have overheard their dangerous conversation concerning her brother.

CHAPTER X.

LOVE AND ABHORRENCE.

> " Ah! who can e'er forget so fair a being?
> Who can forget her half retiring sweets?
> God! she is like a milk-white lamb that bleats
> For man's protection."

WHEN Jane thought for a moment of how long this great political inquisitor and public prosecutor had been the feudal foe and legal oppressor of her mother's kinsman and her father's house, and that he had but recently (as she had gathered from her brother) meditated or attempted the assassination of her lover,—as he had previously done the chief of the Maclellans,—she felt her whole heart recoil from him as from a serpent, with terror and abhorrence. Nevertheless, finding that Sybil and her cavalier had disappeared among the groups of revellers who dotted the moonlit lawn, she had sufficient tact to veil her inward repugnance and suspicions under an outward politeness, and to incline her head slightly when he bowed and assumed a position for conversing by leaning his handsome and stately figure against the stone arm of the sofa, which was formed of a wyvern with its wings outspread.

He was dazzled by the splendour of her beauty, which the unwonted magnificence of her attire had so much enhanced; and remained silent and embarrassed, till Jane said—

" I did not imagine that so grave a man as Sir Adam Otterburn would have much to amuse him among these gay frivolities."

" Nor have I, madam, for my mind is usually filled with thoughts of deeper and more vital import than the comely fashion of a ruff or mantle, or the curling of a pretty ringlet. I came but to steal a few moments from my unhappy destiny;

and I swear by my faith, that to see you dancing with the
king was the only tranquil joy I have had for many a day.
Ah! madame, you excelled yourself; you outshone them all,
as yonder moon outshines the stars around it!"

Lady Jane bowed again, and glanced uneasily at the staircase; there was no appearance of Roland, and knowing intui-
tively the dangerous topic to which the speaker was inclining,
she trembled for what he might say next, for Redhall was
not a man to dally much when he had any end in view.

He had seen her dancing with Roland Vipont; he had
heard those whispers by which the whole court linked their
names together as lovers, yet an incontrollable folly or fatality
led him blindly on.

"Notwithstanding that we were such good friends when
last we met," said he, in his soft and flute-like voice, while
bending his fine dark eyes on the green sward, "you have
shunned me so much of late, Lady Jane, that I have had no
opportunity of begging your permission to renew that conversation in which I presumed first to say—that—that——"

"What?——"

"That I loved you"—his voice sank to a whisper at the
abruptness of the declaration.

"Oh! Sir Adam; thou followest a phantom."

Redhall sighed sadly and bitterly.

"There was a time, dearest madam, when I did not think
so," he continued slowly and earnestly—"a time when I
almost flattered myself that you loved me in return."

"I!" said Jane, faintly.

"*Thou*," he replied, impressively, fixing upon her his piercing eyes with an expression which fascinated her. "It was
in the garden of my lord the abbot of Holyrood, at his mansion near yonder craigs, some nine or ten months ago, about
the vesper time; it was a glorious evening, and a broad yellow
harvest-moon was shining in the blue heavens, among golden-
coloured clouds; the air was pure, and laden with perfume
and with the fragrance of yonder orchards, and these fields
covered with the grain of a ripe harvest. Abbot Robert had
given a supper to Henrico Godscallo, the ambassador who
came to offer as a bride Mary of Austria or Mary of Portugal
to King James. Oh! thou canst not have forgotten it. We
walked together in the garden, and you did me the honour
to lean upon my arm. I bent my head towards you, and

F

your beautiful hair touched my forehead. My heart beat
like lightning—every vein trembled! Oh! I have never
forgotten that night—that hour—the place—the time!
You seemed good and kind, merry and gentle with me. I
was on the point of declaring myself then—of saying how I
loved you—how I worshipped you; and your charming em-
barrassment seemed to expect the avowal; when the countess's
page—yonder black devil with the rings in his ears—approached, and the spell was broken. My God! the same
moment, the same soft influences and adorable opportunity
have never come again!"

"My lord advocate, you can plead ably for yourself," replied Jane, coldly.

"My soul is in the cause at issue," said he, looking at her
anxiously; "'tis very true, I am very miserable. I am as
one in a dream. I love the air she breathes—the ground she
treads on." He was speaking to himself. In the very depth
of his thoughts he forgot that she was beside him.

"My lord, my lord, 'tis the rhapsody, this, of Sir David
Lindesay, or some such balladier."

"Nay, nay; oh! do not mock me. It seemeth as if my
love for you is not the common love of this cold and utili-
tarian world; for if ten ages rolled over our heads, I feel sure
that my love would be the same; nor time, nor circumstance,
not even despair, can overcome it. Oh! lady, believe me,
there is no other man loves thee as I do."

Jane thought of Roland, but either the fury or the profundity of the speaker's passion awed her into silence, for she
made no reply; and thereby encouraged, he continued—

"Pride and ambition are strong within me; but, believe
me, my breast never had a passion so deep, so pure, as my
love for thee. There is a silent strength in it that grows out
of its very hopelessness. Canst thou conceive this? Every
glance, and smile, and word of thine I have treasured up for
years, and in solitude I gloat over them, even as a miser
would over his gold and silver."

Covered with confusion, and trembling excessively, Jane
made an effort to withdraw.

"Beautiful tyrant!" said he, haughtily and firmly, as he
stepped before her, "thou knowest thy power, and findest a
cruel pleasure in its exercise; thy lips are full of pride as
thine eyes are full of light, and with the very smile of a god-

dess thou repayest the homage of all but me. Yet with all these charms I can conceive that no passion can dwell within thee, for thou art cold and impassible as the marble of that fountain which sparkles in the moonlight—vain as vanity herself, and selfish as Circe. While weaving thy spells thou thinkest not of me, or the fatal power of thy beauty, which is destroying me."

"Holy Mary!" said Jane, in terror at his growing excitement; "did I tell thee to love me? Am I to blame for this unruly frenzy?"

"Oh! my passion is very deep," he continued, clasping his hands, and fixing his dark eyes on the stars. "My God! my God! It besets me—it transfixes and transforms me into the object I love—our existence seems the same."

"What!" cried Jane, laughing, "hast thou transformed thyself into me?"

Redhall did not anticipate having his high-sounding sophistry so acutely criticized; he started as if a viper was beside him, and fixing upon her his eyes, which were fired with a strange mixture of sternness and ardour, he said in his slow calm voice—

"Strong and serene in thy boasted purity and pride, thou laughest at me; and by that laugh," he continued, in a hoarse and bitter voice, "I know that all is over with me; but beware thee, proud woman—for love and illusion may die fast together."

"Sir Adam Otterburn," replied Jane, haughtily, attempting again to retire, "for the last time I tell thee, that death were a thousand times preferable to thy love! Art thou not the sworn foe of my brother?"

"But not *thine*," replied the advocate, with a lowering brow; "make me not *that*, I pray thee." His heart glowed alternately with love and fury at her unmoved aspect. His self-importance was wounded by her apathy; and his galled pride was fast kindling a sentiment of hatred in his heart—a hate that grew side by side with his love—if such a state of heart can be conceived. "Thy brother's enemy?" he repeated, with a bitter laugh; "if I were indeed so much his enemy, I might astonish the Lord Arran and his Hamiltons to-night."

"My God!" thought Jane, as her heart sank within her; "he has overheard us, and learned our terrible secret!"

Alarmed by the ghastly expression of his face, which was

F 2

white as marble, all save the jetty moustaches and the eyebrows that met over his finely-formed nose, Jane glanced
anxiously towards the stair which ascended to the hall, and
Sir Adam observed it. A smile curled his pale lips, but the
fire of the most ferocious jealousy kindled in his dark and
deep-set eyes.

"I know for whom thou art looking," said he, grasping
her by the arm; "for yonder brainless fop, who thinks of
nothing but his ruff and his plume and the glory of being
master of the king's ordnance—a wretched worm, whom the
heat of our Scottish wars hath nourished into a gilded butterfly, and who dares to cock his bonnet in our faces with the
bearing of a landed baron."

"Gramercy!" said Jane, waggishly; "I knew not that a
butterfly wore a bonnet."

"Hah!" he muttered, fiercely, "the lover who is once
laughed at *is lost!*"

The grasp of his strong hand compressed her slender arm
like a vice; there was an oath trembling on his lips, and fury
flashing in his eye, for love and hatred, as they struggled in
his heart, made him both selfish and savage.

"Oh Mother of Mercy!" murmured Jane; "away ruffian!
or I will shriek that thou art a vampire!"

At that moment the shadow of a tall figure, armed with a
prodigious sword, was thrown by the moon along the velvet
sward; and Redhall was prostrated by a blow on the ear,
dealt by a ponderous and unsparing hand. Jane turned with
terror, and saw her brother, the earl, spring back and disap-
pear under the cloister arches of the abbey; while, at the
same moment, Roland Vipont leaped down stairs from the
hall, taking four steps at once.

"A thousand pardons, dearest Jane, and a thousand more,"
he exclaimed, drawing her arm through his, and leading her
away; "but this tiresome argument concerning old Mollance
Meg and the Devil of Bois le Duc (plague take them both!)
occupied more time than I had the least idea of; and my
lord the bishop of Limoges hath lost on the matter a hundred silver livres, which the king means to give the Franciscans to-morrow. But thou art not angry with me?"

"Angry? oh, no! I know thou art sufficiently punished,
minutes being ages when absent from me."

"Ah, thou art right, for my sojourn in Paris was a very
eternity."

"Then let us join the dancers, and be merry while we may," said she, with a gaiety which was scarcely assumed, for she was but too happy to hurry him into the hall, without observing the lord advocate, who, stunned by the effects of the blow, lay for a second or two unseen, and somewhat ignominiously, upon a parterre of rose-bushes, from whence he arose with fury in his heart, and his sword in his hand, but to find himself alone—a fortunate circumstance, as he would infallibly have slain the first man near him. He adjusted his ruff and doublet, brushed a speck or two from his trunk breeches, and shaking his clenched hand, said hoarsely, under his moustaches—

"Either Roland Vipont or the Earl of Ashkirk dishonoured me by that blow. Be it so—I have them all in my grasp! Revenge is a joy for gods and demons, and, by the Holy Rood, I will be avenged, and fearfully, too!"

By this time the ball was nearly over, for the good people of those days had not yet conceived the idea of turning day into night; and as the king and court were to depart on a grand hawking expedition on the morrow, and, as usual, had to be all up with the lark and the eagle, the bell-clock of the neighbouring abbey church had barely tolled twelve when the dancing concluded, and the guests began to retire in rapid succession, each paying their adieux to the king and queen as they departed, and paying them with a solemnity and parade such as one may see nowhere now, save in Old Castile.

"Take courage, my sweet flower, Jane, for now is your most fortunate time to prefer to Magdalene your request that Ashkirk may be pardoned. She will never, by refusal, send away her principal guest ungraciously," said Roland, as, hurrying through the festooned arras from the refreshment-room, where they had been tarrying for a time, they joined the stream of departing revellers who promenaded round the hall, and approached their royal host and hostess somewhat like a glittering procession. James and Magdalene were standing at the head of the hall, just as when the entertainment began. His bonnet was in his right hand, his left rested on his sword, and was hidden by his short mantle; the queen leant on his arm, and he bowed low to each of the nobles, and lower still to their brocaded ladies. The Scottish and French ladies of honour were grouped a little behind, all beautiful, young, nobly born, and brilliantly attired.

"If she procures me this boon," said Jane, "I will say nine

prayers for her at the altar of St. Magdalene to-morrow, when
we go to St. Giles's. Of course you go with us to hear father
St. Bernard's oration on the patron saint of the city ?"

"Wherever you go I shall go; but the hour ?"

"One o'clock; but you will come at noon and see me ?"

"Plague on it, I have a meeting."

"A meeting ?" said Jane, anxiously.

"Oh, a duty, dearest—an indispensable duty to perform,"
said Roland, remembering his brief challenge to Kincavil.

"What duty is this, of which I hear now for the first time ?"

"To see those fifty-six pieces of cannon which King Francis
hath sent to King James; they are to be landed from Sir
Robert Barton's ships, and conveyed to the Gun-house to-
morrow. A most important duty, Jane; they are all beautiful brass culverins, royal and demi; 'twould do your heart
good to see them !"

"Ah, if James and the queen should refuse me this !—we
are close to them now."

"Refuse you ? they will refuse nothing that is asked in a
voice so soft and so gentle."

As they drew near the royal group, Jane felt her heart
almost failing her; she clung to Roland's arm, and watched
the expression in the face of Magdalene. She seemed now
very pale; her eyes were humid and downcast; gentleness
and languor pervaded her beautiful features; she was overcome with lassitude and sinking with fatigue—the weakness
incident to that hereditary disease which fast and surely was
preying upon her fragile form. The proud nobles, to whom
the king spoke occasionally as he bade them adieu, received
his courtly attentions as a tribute due to their patriotic and
lofty ancestry, and their proud bearing seemed to say, plainly,
"I am George Earl of Errol, Constable of Scotland," or "I
am William Earl of Montrose, and come of that Græme whom
King David knighted when the Stuarts were but thanes of
Kyle and Strathgryfe;" for it was an age when the king was
only a great baron, and every baron or laird was a king and a
kaiser to boot.

As they approached, Roland could perceive that cold glances
welcomed Jane Seton from the ladies of honour, who were all
enemies of her house, and whose fathers and brothers enjoyed
many fiefs of the Douglas lands and fortresses, defacing the
crowned heart on their battlements and substituting the three

cinque-foils of Hamilton; but, to crown all and increase the poor girl's perturbation, she perceived Redhall standing near the king, seeming, with his dark figure and pallid visage, like her evil genius, cold, impassible, and dignified as if the startling episode we have just related had never taken place.

"*Ah ma bonne!*" they heard Magdalene say to Mademoiselle de Brissac, "how tired I am, and excessively sick of all this parade!"

"Now be of good heart, my sweet Jane," said Roland, pressing her arm, "and prefer your request firmly; for Madame de Montreuil has explained to the queen all that we wish."

When she drew near the beautiful young girl that leaned on James's arm, instead of bowing and passing on, Jane sunk on one knee, and said—

"I beseech your grace to crave my brother's pardon from our sovereign lord."

"I know that he cannot refuse me anything," said the young queen, with girlish simplicity, as she looked up lovingly and trustingly in the king's face, while stretching out her hand to Jane. The latter pressed to her beautiful lips that fair little hand which was dimpled like that of a child, and the king was about to speak (and benignly, too, for every feature of his fine face said so), when Magdalene, overcome by her recent illness, by the close atmosphere of the hall, which was perfumed to excess, and by the glitter of innumerable wax-lights, uttered a faint cry, and fell backwards into the arms of Mademoiselle de Brissac.

Consternation and concern were visible in every face; the queen was borne away senseless, and James hastily followed her almost inanimate figure; the crowd behind pressed on, and Roland and Jane were carried before it. Redhall smiled, and said to the abbot of Kinloss, in James's hearing—

"Did I not tell you, my lord, how rash it was to have the Lady Seton here?"

"Agnus Dei! yea, verily, for her mother deals in salves and philtres; and there was sorcery at work just now, Sir Adam, or my name is not Robin Reid."

These words made a deep impression on the few who were meant to hear them, but chiefly on the king, who darted an angry glance after Jane Seton, and turned on his heel.

At the palace gate the discomfited pair met Marion Logan,

Alison Hume, and Sybil Douglas, who were all muffled in their hoods and mantles, and surrounded by an escort of serving-men, armed with steel caps and bucklers, swords, and wheel-lock dagues, and who bore lighted links. A few cavaliers with whom they had danced (Roland among them, of course) accompanied them, and in this order they hurried home on foot, for wheeled vehicles were as yet unknown in the kingdom.

Terrified by the practical jokes of the king's jester and the din of his bladder and bells, Sabrino had long since fled the precincts of the court, and taken refuge in his usual sleeping-place (a small alcove near the door of the countess's apartment), which he shared in common with a large black stag-hound.

"Come early to-morrow, dear Roland, and we will talk over the adventures of the last few hours," whispered Jane, as she bade adieu to her lover; "alas! father St. Bernard warned me against going to-night; but I have gone, and what has been the result?"

CHAPTER XI.

SWORDBLADES AND SALVE.

" Quhen Marche with variand windis wes past,
And Apryll had with her silver shouris
Tane leif of Nature with an orient blast;
And lusty May, that mother is of flouris,
Had maid the birdis to begyn their houris,
Amang the tender odouris red and quhyt,
Quhais harmony to heir it was delyt."
DUNBAR'S *Thrissal and the Rois*, 1503.

THE next morning was bright and beautiful; the birds sang merrily in the old orchards of the palace and the older oak trees of the abbey of Sancte Crucis. The sunlight, as it poured over the dark craigs of Salisbury, and through chasms and fissures in their rocks, shone upon the green valleys below like a golden haze, and tipped with yellow light the grey masses of the strong old city. The fresh grass and the open flowers loaded the soft west wind perfume, and glad-dened the hearts of the happy hawking party, which left the palace an hour after sunrise, and all gaily mounted, with bugles sounding, horses prancing, plumes waving, and accompanied by a dozen of falconers in the royal livery, running on foot, with perches of hawks slung on their shoulders.

As they rode eastward, by the base of Arthur's Seat, and past the green and mossy bank where, among the clambering wild roses, stood the little pillared well, dedicated in the old time "to the good Saint Margaret, queen of Scotland, and mother of the poor," and pursued thence their merry route towards the Loch of Restalrig, which lay amongst its rocks and sedges, like a lake of blue and gold, Roland was compelled, by the cold manner of the king, to retire from his side. He saw with pain that the clear and benevolent eye of the monarch was clouded—that anger, unmistakeable anger, lowered upon his open brow. The inquiries of Roland for the health of the queen were received so haughtily, and replied to so briefly, that, with a heart full of wrath and pride, before the first heron had been raised from among the rushes and water-lilies to do battle in the air, he turned abruptly away, and resigned his place to Sir Adam Otterburn of Redhall, whose face was lighted with an indescribable smile, as he pressed forward to the side of the young king.

The bells of the Carmelites, on the north side of the city, of the Dominicans on the south, of the Franciscans in the Grassmarket, and other large establishments, were all ringing for morning mass, when the cavalcade returned; and Roland, sick at heart, and dispirited, without bidding adieu to the king (who with his company passed on to prayer in the abbey church), dismounted at the door of his own lodgings, and throwing the bridle of his horse to his servant, demanded breakfast, for he was in too furious a mood to attend mass. He was anxious to see Lord Ashkirk, but, encouraged by his disguise, and trusting implicitly in the old domestics of the house, that rash noble had gone to visit his family.

Breakfast was prepared and laid on the table by Roland's servant, Linton Stock, whose name had been professionally shortened into Lintstock. He was an old, iron-visaged culvernier, of King James IV's days (as the countess would say), hard-featured, wiry-haired, weather-beaten, and empurpled with hard drinking. It was his constant boast that he had levelled one of Borthwick's Brass Sisters on the field of Flodden, and thrawn Mow at the siege of Tantallan. Like Hannibal, this veteran had only one eye, for Mow (a famous cannon of Scottish antiquity) lost a piece of her muzzle every

time she was discharged; and one of the said pieces deprived
Lintstock of his dexter eye, which, as he said, ever after saved
him the trouble of closing it when taking aim, or adjusting
the quoins under the breach of a culverin. For wages he had
all his master's cast cloaks, doublets, and breeches; and being
borne on the muster-roll of the king's gunners, his pay, which
was somewhere about three-halfpence Scots *per diem* made
him independent of all mankind.

On the anniversary of a Scottish victory this one-eyed
patriot invariably got himself uproariously drunk, and broke
the windows of the English ambassador: on the anniversary
of any of our defeats he was invariably ditto from vexation;
and as these alternate sources of joy and grief occurred pretty
often, the ancient warrior was seldom long sober.

Neither Roland's anger at the king, nor his intended combat with Kincavil, prevented him from making an excellent
breakfast on broiled fish, cold meat, and bright brown ale.
Before setting down he selected the strongest and longest of
some half-dozen swords that hung in a corner. It was a large
double-edged weapon, with an ample hilt of steel; the blade,
being inlaid, was one of those called damasquinée, from the
Asiatic art just then introduced into Europe by the famous
Benvenuto Cellini. It was a beautiful rapier, which he had
taken in battle from an Italian cavalier when serving under
John Stuart Duke of Albany, when, at the head of ten thousand French men-at-arms, that gallant prince invaded the
kingdom of Naples. Roland never used it save on important
and desperate occasions, and remembering that Kincavil was
an able swordsman, he took it down and handed it to Lintstock
to polish; a duty which he performed in silent precision,
with the aid of an old buff belt. Thereafter, with true military coolness, he tore a shirt into bandages, and prepared
some lint against his master's return.

" How many pots hast thou of that rubbish Lady Ashkirk
sent me ?—the salve, I mean," asked Roland, with his
moustaches whitened over by ale froth.

" Three, sir."

" Dost thou know the laird of Kincavil's lodging ?"

" Aboon the Tron—yes."

" Then leave the pots there to-day, with my best commendations; for, by my faith, he will need them all."

Lintstock continued to rub, and watched the polish of the

"Thou knowest I expect two friends to supper, and must trust to thy ingenuity, for, 'fore God! I have not a testoon in the world."

"Be easy, Sir Roland, I'll provide supper for the king himself, if he come, and plenty Bordeaux to boot, forbye and attour the Rochelle," replied Lintstock, with a nod and a knowing wink of his solitary eye.

The moment breakfast was over, Roland crossed himself and wiped his moustaches. Receiving his sword, he placed it in his belt on the left side, hung a long armpit dagger on the right, stuck his bonnet rather over the right eye, clasped his doublet carefully to the throat, and giving his curls a last adjust, for he was somewhat of a beau, whistled the "March to Harlaw," as he issued forth, with the fullest intention of perforating the laird of Kincavil like a pepperbox.

He passed the long and irregular façade of the palace, the strongly-grated windows of which were glittering in the bright sunshine that bathed the varied architecture of its courts and towers. Clad in their red doublets slashed with black, and wearing caps and gorgets of steel, the sentinels of the king's guard were leaning on their heavy arquebuses, the rests or forks of which were slung in their sword-belts; and they stood in the bright blaze of the sun, as listlessly and still as the banner of the red lion that waved above the gate. Beyond the precincts of the palace, the street, which is overlooked by gable-ended houses, in the old Flemish taste, becomes much wider. He turned to the right, and passed through the Watergate, the most eastern barrier of Edinburgh. This strong and venerable porte obtained its name because the king's horses were led out that way every morning to water, in a large pond near it. On quitting this ivied and grass-tufted archway, Roland found the open space allotted for tennis-players lying on his right hand, the horsepond lay on his left, and before him the verdant Calton reared up its lonely ridge.

The whole place was then quite solitary enough for such a meeting, though now the site of the pond, the tennis court, and even the hill itself, are covered with houses.

Roland's anger was somewhat increased by perceiving that his adversary was already on the ground, and whiling away the time by skimming flat stones across the pond.

"Ah! thou villanous Hamilton," thought he, "how I long to be at thee! My sword is like a razor, my wrist is like steel, this morning, and I will curry thee in such fashion, that thou shalt tremble at the name of Jane Seton or a salve-pot ever after."

"God be with you, Sir Roland; you have not kept me waiting long," said Kincavil, bowing with cold politeness.

"I am glad of it."

"You have been at mass this morning with the king, I think?"

"No, faith!" said Roland, knitting his brows as he thought of the hawking party "I feared there would be no room for me among so many Hamiltons, panders, and parasites."

"Then I hope you said prayers at home," replied Kincavil, whose eyes flashed as he unsheathed his sword.

"As usual; but I forgot to bring for your use a pot of that notable salve of which you made a jest last night."

"Keep it for yourself, Sir Roland—guard."

"Come on, then—you *will* have it."

They saluted each other, the bright blades clashed, and they both engaged with great address and skill. Clad in blue velvet and gold, Kincavil was both strong and handsome; but as a swordsman considerably inferior to Roland, who had studied his thrusts at the court of Francis I.; and thus, three passes had scarcely been exchanged on the right, when he made a sudden *appel* on the left, and quickly disengaging to the right again, passed his sword completely through the body of his adversary, who bent forward over it, and sank upon his knees. He made a futile effort to rise, but the moment Roland's blade was withdrawn, sank prostrate on the grass, with the blood gushing from his wound.

"Ask me not to beg my life, Sir Roland," said Hamilton in a broken voice, "for I will rather die than condescend so far."

"Thou art a gallant man, Sir John Hamilton; and may the devil take me if I make any such request; but methinks I have taught you the danger of jesting with the names of noble ladies."

"My Heaven! yes. I am bleeding fast; and yet, if the Lady Ashkirk doth really make that precious salve," said Kincavil, with true Scottish obstinacy, "tell her, for God's love to send me a pot thereof, for I am enduring the torments of hell!" and he reclined against a stone, pale and motionless, with his beautiful doublet of blue velvet drenched in blood.

Roland carefully wiped and sheathed his favourite Italian sword with the air of a man who was used to such encounters; and after vainly endeavouring to staunch the crimson torrent, he hastened to the Watergate, from whence he sent the under-warders to look after the wounded man, and then walked up the street towards the house of the countess, as if nothing had happened.

A thrust or so through the body was a mere nothing in those days.

CHAPTER XII.

EDINBURGH IN 1537.

" Installed on hills, her head near starry bowers,
Edina shines amid protecting powers;
Religious temples guard her on the east,
And Mar's strong towers defend her on the west;
For sceptres nowhere stands a town more fit,
Nor where a queen of all the world might sit;
Be this thy praise, above all be most brave,
No man did e'er defame thee but *a slave*."
ARTHUR JOHNSTONE, 1630.

THE Countess Margaret was attired in her great capuchon of James the Fourth's days; it was turned back above the apex of her stupendous coif, and flowed over her shoulders. Her lofty figure and towering head-dress completely dwarfed Jane and her companions, whose triangular velvet hoods were of a less imposing form. The whole family and household were about to set forth for St. Giles's, and Ronald met the procession in the archway. The old lady was looking unusually grave, for that morning she had put on her stockings with the wrong side outwards—an infallible omen of misfortune. We have said the whole household, for in addition to several female attendants and the black page, there were Gilzean Seton, the countess's esquire, or seneschal, and six or eight tall fellows in steel bonnets or corslets, armed with Jedwood axes and wheel-lock pistols—a new weapon, which had just been introduced from Italy, and was esteemed one of the wonders of mechanism. These were all of iron, butted like the pommel of a poniard, and were fired by the rapid revolution of a wheel against a piece of sulphuret of iron, which was secured like the flint of a modern musket, but had the cock on that side where of late we have seen the pan.

Gilzean and his companions were all clad in the countess's livery (rather worn-looking certainly), but all having on their sleeves the coronet and the green dragon of the Setons, spouting fire.

The earl, still disguised, and bearing his long sword, marched among them; but by their whispers and subdued manner in his presence, it was evident to Roland that the secret identity of his new valet was known to them all.

"Rash lord!" thought he; "if one of these should prove a traitor."

"I see reproach in your eye," said the earl, in a low tone, and with an acuteness that somewhat startled Roland. "But think you that my father's roof ever sheltered a slipper-helmet so pitiful that he would betray his son? I trow not. Nay, nay, Sir Roland, the vassals of our house are all good men and true."

"And such my husband ever found them," said the countess, looking with a proud smile from her tall son to his stately followers; "for the fathers of mair than one of these my buirdly lads died by his bridle-rein under King James the Fourth, of gude and gallant memorie."

"Now, Sir Roland," said Lady Jane, as she took his proffered arm, with a smile on her coral lip; "you come not by stealth to visit us to-day. The king and his displeasure——"

"May go to the ——"

"Fie! I hope thy debarcation of cannon is over, and that thou art free to bask in my smiles for the rest of the day?"

"It is over," replied Roland, avoiding the eye of the earl, who perceived a sword-thrust in his doublet, and a rent in his velvet mantle, where none had been visible the day before; "and to-morrow I am to show them all to the queen, and must, with my own hands, fire off the great gun Meg for her behoof. By Jove! I will carry off the cock from St. Anthony's spire at Leith!"

"And what of this dainty dame," said the countess, as they proceeded up the street; "hast heard how her health is this morning?"

"I have not; but if I am to judge from the unwonted reserve of the king, I should deem her poorly enough."

"His reserve?" said the earl, scornfully; "and thus he vents his petulance on a gallant knight, as he would upon his pimps of the house of Arran—those rascally Hamiltons," he added, with eyes flashing fire, "who, gorged to their full with the plunder of our kinsmen, and building unto themselves strengths from which even our valour can never drive them—castles and towers, to which the palaces of Lochmaben and Linlithgow are but huts and sheilings."

" Oh ! hush, ye unwise bairn," said the countess; " hush, and take your place among the serving-men, lest we be seen conversing, and so excite suspicion. Let us not talk harshly of this puir French stranger, whom, father St. Bernard tells me, hath a deadly disease, which preyeth upon her vitals, and will, ere long, bear her to the grave."

" Disease !" exclaimed Jane and her companions, with surprise; "and what is this disease ?"

" 'Tis a catarrh, which descendeth daily into her stomach, and must, sooner or later, cause death, for it hath defied the most skilful physicians and apothegars of France and Italy. Yet, were she mine ain bairn, or had I the place o' that fashionless body, Madame de Montreuil, I would soon make her whole and well."

" How, how, Lady Ashkirk ?" asked Sybil and the others, who put great faith in the countess's skill as a leech; and really, at salving a slash from a sword, or staunching a thrust from a poniard, few in Edinburgh equalled her; and it was a time when she found plenty of patients.

" 'Tis a great secret, and yet withal a simple one; for with it my mother, the Lady Jane Gordon of Glenbucket (quhom God assoilzie), made a whole man of her sister's son, the abbot of Pluscardine, who hath now departed to the company of the saints. 'Tis the first egg that a pullet hath laid (and mark, ye damsels, it must be laid upon a Friday), beat up widdershins with the first dew of the morning, and with thirteen drops of holy water, for ye ken there is a charm in that number; and this simple, if taken as the first food for nine successive mornings, would cure her. Gif it failed, there is one other mode—by applying a stone called a *magnet*, of potent and miraculous power, to the pit of the stomach, and repeating the word *Abrodætia* three times; whilk failing, we must trust to God, for then it can be no other than the demon *Archeus*, who, at times, takes possession of the stomach, as the learned Paracelsus told father St. Bernard, when he dwelt with him at the Scottish cloister of Wurtzburg, in the year 1528."

" Mother of God !" exclaimed all the girls, looking at each

other with fear, for the countess's manner was so serious, and she quoted such imposing names, that even Roland put his hand to his waist-belt, as if to assure himself that there was no such tenant as the said *Archeus* under it.

" I shall die with fear if ever I feel ill after this," said Sybil; " I shall be sure to think I am possessed of a demon. Wouldst thou not, cousin Archibald ?"

" Mass!" replied the earl, " I would drown the demon in good wine, and if that failed, should exorcise him in warm usquebaugh."

Roland could not restrain a sensation of uneasiness during this conversation ; for though deeply imbued with superstition, like every man at that time, and as a soldier believing a little in suits of charmed mail, that rendered the wearer invulnerable, he knew that the vulgar regarded the countess (like the lady of Buccleugh in the next age) with some terror for her abstruse knowledge; and at the present crisis he had no wish, certainly, that this suspicion should be increased.

The High-street, which had just been paved for the first time, was gay and crowded, for all the *élite* of the court and city, with their attendants, were thronging towards the church of St. Giles. All the balconies erected for the queen's entrance had been taken down, the banners were long since removed, but the garlands yet displayed their faded flowers around the various crosses which then encumbered the central street—though less so, certainly, than the innumerable outshots and projections, outside stairs, turnpike towers, round, square, and octagon; wooden balconies and stone arcades, which imparted an aspect so picturesque to the High-street and Canongate. The total absence of all manner of vehicles, or other obstruction (save watermen with their barrels, or a few equestrians), made the middle of the street—or, as it was popularly named, "the crown of the causeway," the most convenient place for walking, as well as the most honourable. Thus the possession of it was frequently disputed at point of sword, for in these good old times no man of equal rank would yield to another the breadth of a hair unless he was of the same *name*—for clanship was the great bond of brotherhood—the second religion of the Scottish people, by which the humblest in the land can yet count kindred with their nobles.

As a lady, there was little chance of the countess being obstructed, unless some noble dame of the opposite faction was descending with *her* train towards the palace; and now, as she had reached the more crowded thoroughfare, she took the arm of Sir Roland Vipont; her daughter, with the ladies Alison, Logan, and Sybil, followed; while the armed servants marched before and behind, with axes shouldered.

Crowds attired in velvet cloaks and plumed bonnets, satin hoods and silk mantles; Dominicans in black robes, and Carmelites in white; Hospitallers of St. Anthony, and Franciscans in grey, were seen pouring like a living flood into the various doors of St. Giles; and, though it was then apparently destitute of shops, the vast High-street seemed to glitter with gaudy dresses in the gay sunshine. The places where the merchants sold their wares were mere dens, to which stairs descended abruptly from the pavement; the goods were thus exposed for sale in those stone vaults which formed the superstructure of every Scottish edifice. All the principal markets were kept in other parts of the town, for, in the year of grace 1477, when the potent and valiant knight Sir James Crichton of Ruthven was lord provost of our good city, it had been ordained that hay and corn should be sold in the Cowgate, and salt in Niddry's Wynd; that the craimes, or booths, for the retail of goods, should be ranged from the Bellhouse to the Tron; that wood and timber should be sold westward of the Grey Friary. The shoemakers' stalls stood between Forrester's Wynd and the dyke of Dalrymple's yard; and the nolt-market, where also " partrickes, pluvars, capones, and conyngs " were sold, occupied Blackfriars Wynd; the cloth-merchants and bonnet-makers dwelt in the Upper Bow; while the dealers in all manner of irongraith, dagger, and bow-makers, dalmascars of swords, armourers, lorimers, and lock-makers, were domiciled under the shadow of that strong and stately barrier, the Netherbow.

There, immediately below the arcades of a tenement bearing the arms of the Lord Abbot of Kinloss, stood a shop, the small deep windows of which were secured by gratings, that were each like an iron harrow, built into the ponderous masonry. In the good town, we still build our walls three feet thick; but in the days of James V., they built them six, and even seven feet thick. A board over the door announced it to be the shop of *John Mossman, Jeweller, and Makkar of Silverwork to ye King's Majestie;* and here the countess and her party tarried a moment to see the new crown of Queen

G

Magdalene, whose coronation was to take place in a month
or so.

Master Mossman, a short and pursy, but well-fed burgess,
clad in a cassocke-coat of Galloway cloth, was just in the act
of giving the finishing touches to a silver maizer, or drinking-
cup. He rose up with all his workmen and apprentices on
the entrance of the countess, and welcomed her to his shop
with studious politeness, though his chief patrons were the
Hamiltons. His premises were vaulted with stone, and
painted with various ornamental designs between the glazed
cupboards of oak, which contained chased and elaborate
vessels of silver, sword and dagger-hilts, buckles, and falcon-
bells of every pattern and device. A small statue of St. Eloi,
the patron of his craft, occupied a gothic niche above the
fireplace, so that the silversmith might warm himself when
saying his prayers in winter, which was a saving of time ; and
on each side thereof hung the steel bonnets, swords, and axes
with which he and his men armed them for weekly duty, as
municipal guards within the eight Portes of the city.

" Good Master Mossman," said Roland, on seeing that the
wealthy artificer looked somewhat uneasily at the jackmen,
whose swords and axes made such a terrible clatter on his
stone floor, " our lady the Countess of Ashkirk would be
favoured with a view of the queen's new crown, that she may
judge of thy handiwork, anent which we hear so much
daily."

The jeweller, who had feared that the countess (whose circumstances he knew were the reverse of flourishing) had come to
order a quantity of plate, breathed more freely, and bowed almost
to his red garters; whereupon the countess curtseyed, for he was
known to be one of the richest burgesses and freeholders in
Edinburgh, and his voice bore all before it at the council-board.
From a round box, strongly bound with brass and lined with
purple velvet, he drew forth the glittering diadem for the
queen consort—the same crown which James VI. took to
London in 1603, and which the government ought in honour
to restore to the Castle of Edinburgh. It is composed of
pure gold from Crawfordmuir, and is enriched with many
precious stones and curious embossings.

" It is a fair gaud," said the countess, sighing ; " but my
mind misgives me sorely that the puir bairn for whom it is
intended may never live to wear it."

" Poor little queen !" said Jane, with moistened eyes, " if all be as thou sayest, her days are indeed numbered."

The silversmith seemed surprised, and his men raised their heads to listen ; but the delight expressed by the ladies at the jewels and workmanship of this new addition to the regalia gratified the artificer, a smile spread over his jovial visage, and he gallantly held it over the head of Lady Jane, saying—

" My fair lady, it would become thee as well as her for whom it is intended."

" By my soul, Master Mossman, thou hast more the air of a gallant than a mere worker of metals," said Vipont, pleased with the compliments of the silversmith, but, like every soldier, unable to conceal how lightly he valued the mere mechanic ; " and I marvel much that thou didst not in thy youth re-nounce the hammer and pincers for the helmet and partisan, as being better suited to one who could so compliment a fair demoiselle."

" You wrong me, noble sir," said the silversmith, calmly ; " I *have* borne arms in my youth——"

" Under our gude King James IV.?" interposed the countess.

" Yea, madame," replied the burgess, with a kindling eye ; " three hundred of us marched to Flodden under the banner of Provost Lauder; but few, unco few, ever again heard the ding o' the Tron-bell. But, as deacon of the honourable cor-poration of hammermen, I deem myself nowise inferior, Sir Roland, to what I was in my youth."

" Assuredly not, good Master Mossman," said the countess, " for I have ever esteemed thee an honest and worthy citizen ; and we may remember how, at the last feast of St. Eloi, our good father St. Bernard illustrated the great honour which God hath bestowed on artisans in all ages."

" True, madame ; Tubal Cain was a cunning artificer in all manner of brass and iron work ; Porus, king of the Indies, was the son of a shaver, and worked himself as a puir tinkler-body and mender of kail-pots ; Agathocles, king of Sicily, was a potter and maker of crocks, cans, and milk-luggies ; Zeno of Constantia was a puir wabster, that clothed the naked from his ain loom ; and Artagorus, lord of Cyconia, was the son of a cook ; nor must we forget Joseph the carpenter, the spouse of the blessed Virgin, whilk, as my neighbour Deacon Plane sayeth, will ever redound to the immortal honour of his craft, the wrichts."

Sir Roland, who did not expect such a volley of hard names to be opened upon him, had nothing more to urge, but bowed with a pleasant smile as they retired, leaving the king's jeweller master of the field.

At the same moment Nichol Birrel, who had been inquisitively peering through the grated window, hastened away and mingled with the crowd.

CHAPTER XIII.

SAINT GILES.

> " You might have heard a pebble fall,
> A beetle hum, a cricket sing,
> An owlet flap his boding wing,
>   On Giles's steeple tall.
> The antique buildings climbing high,
> Whose gothic frontlets sought the sky."
>
> *Marmion,* Canto V.

At the great entrance of St. Giles's church (a deep and lofty gothic doorway) the steps of which were yet stained with the gallant blood of M'Clellan of Bombie, among the gaily-attired crowd that was pressing up the flight and into that magnificent fane, the countess, with her friends and followers, encountered Redhall, with *his* friend (Kinloss), and his followers, Nichol Birrel, Dobbie, and Sanders Screw, whose official capacities did not prevent their appearance among his retinue, like whom, they wore steel bonnets, and were barbed to the teeth.

The king's advocate bowed profoundly, and, with all respect, fell back a pace or so, while the countess and her ladies swept into the church like a frigate followed by four cutters. A true gallant of the day, Roland dipped his hand into the font, and assisted Jane to holy water, scattering the rest over the poor people who knelt at the doorway, looking for alms in silence.

All the windows of this great edifice were then filled with stained glass; thus the prismatic hues of many a martyr's robe, many a blood-red cross, many a glorious halo and gaudy armorial blazon were thrown on the silent throng who crowded the choir, the nave, and the transepts of this majestic church. Now it is divided into three; then it was open, and unincumbered by galleries, stood in all the pristine glory of its gothic architecture, two hundred feet in length by one hundred and twenty in breadth, the four arms of the vast cross being open under the stupendous central arches which sprung away aloft, upholding the square tower and mural crown of its spire. There stood the great altar, the splendid canopy of which uprose from columns of burnished brass. Underneath was the pix of gold, where the host was kept; above this stood a gigantic crucifix of silver, and the solid candlesticks of the same metal, which were of great size and weight. At the Reformation, these and all other sacred utensils were seized by the provost, who ordered the brazen pillars to be cast into cannon for the ramparts of the city.

The pulpit was yet unoccupied; but round the four sides of the great altar were many persons kneeling in prayer. Five streams of brilliantly-coloured sunlight fell from the south aslant the great church, from the five vaulted chapels which Johne Skayer and Johne of Stone, two cunning masons, built during the provostry of that "good man and noble," the Laird of Netherliberton. Then the church was without other seats than those cushions and stools which were borne by servants, or by cavaliers for the use of the ladies they accompanied. Many a group in velvet cloaks and high ruffs, with satin trains and hoods of crammasie; many a moustachioed and belted man, half noble and wholly soldier, many a shaven friar, and many a sweet young girl with that fair hair so famed in Scottish song (the golden hair which Raphael loved so well), were kneeling before the lesser altars, of which that great temple, "our mother kirk of old St. Giles," boasted not less than forty.

The most magnificent were those of the Holy Blood, the Holy Cross de Lucano, Nostre Domine, St. Michael de Monte Tomba, Our Lady of Piety, and St. Eloi, the most eastern shrine, which belonged to the gallant craftsmen, as being that of their peculiar patron. Behind it they had placed a window, whereon were painted the elephant and crowned hammer of the principal corporation; and before it hung a beautiful lamp of silver, which was said to have been brought by them from the sack of Jerusalem, and the light of which was never extinguished. The most beautifully-decorated columns of the church are four, where this altar stood. Like the branches of a forest, the ribs of the groined roof

sprung away aloft into the dusky clerestory, through the
deep windows of which fell many a flake of light of every
rainbow hue, revealing many a grotesque carving and many
a grim old head.

" Many a scutcheon and banner riven "

decorated the side chapels, and many a sword and helmet
were rusting above the tombs of departed valour.   Many
marble statues of saints and warriors, of mitred abbots and
good old citizens, were standing there in niches, with their
hands clasped in one eternal prayer; for there now lie the
dead of more than seven hundred years, with the wise Moray,
and Montrose the loyal ; for many a proud peer and valiant
warrior, the faithful and the false, the just and the unjust,
the impious and the true, the beautiful and the deformed,
all blent in one common and undistinguishable dust, have
mouldered beneath the pavement of its deep vaults and
solemn aisles.

Bowing to the great altar, the countess, with all her train,
passed down the church towards the north-east pillar, which
is called *the king's*, as it bears the arms of James II., where
she usually sat, for her husband, Earl John, lay near it, before
the altar of St. John the Baptist.   The servants arranged
the kneeling cushions, and the countess received her velvet-
bound missal from Sabrino, who sat down behind her, not
on his knees, but *à la turque*, which made the people, who
viewed the poor negro with fear and hostility, mutter among
themselves.

"Gudesake! she bringeth her black devil into the very
kirk wi' her !" said Deacon Plane, under his thick beard, to
his better half.

" I could have sworn upon the gospels, gudeman, that the
holy water hissed when she dipped her hand in the font."

"Her finger, ye mean, neibour," said another, behind his
bonnet; "think ye a wizard-body would dip in mair than they
could help?"

" Wheesht, Elsie—Losh keep us, the thing is looking at ye!"

" Weel, I carena a bodle—let it look !" replied the woman
confidently, while feeling for a blessed relique of St. Roque,
which she carried in her bosom; but Sabrino grinned, and
showed all his white teeth, and, what was still more appalling,
an almost total absence of tongue—the poor being was a

mute, or nearly so—upon which the woman shrunk close to her husband, and began to cross herself with great energy; while at the same moment the Provost of St. Giles and the sixteen prebendaries, preceded by their curate and cross-bearer, the sacristan ringing a bell, the beadle, the minister of the choir bearing a standard, four choristers, and eight tapers, passed through the church, in procession, to their stalls within the sanctuary, softly and noiselessly, while all the vast congregation knelt, and when again they rose, Father St. Bernard was in the pulpit, which projected from one of the four great columns sustaining the spire.

He was a mild and benevolent-looking old priest, whom all the citizens loved for his piety, goodness, and attention to the sick and poor during the frightful pestilence of 1520. His hair was white as snow, his grey eyes were bright and gentle. Father St. Bernard was now in his sixtieth year; and, when accompanying the Scottish army as a confessor, had seen the battles of Sauchie, of Flodden, and Linlithgow.

On this day he had elaborately decorated and lighted the shrine of St. Giles, and his statue, the same which the re-formers threw into the North Loch, was encircled by a wreath of roses, made by Jane Seton and her companions; around it was hung a piece of red cloth, then known as "Sanct Geiles' coat," and before it, in a casket of chased silver, lay his skeleton arm—a relique which the Knight of Gourtoun had received from Louis XI. of France, and bequeathed to the church.

Oblivious of the oration he had come to hear, of the magnificent manner in which the church was decorated, and of the attentive crowds that filled it, Redhall leaned against a column not far from the king's, and watched attentively the group which knelt beside the countess. When Father St. Bernard prayed, Jane and Vipont read from the same missal, and their heads were so close that her forehead touched his ear. Redhall ground his teeth; and when they turned to each other and smiled (for they could sympathize without speaking), he felt his heart swell with suppressed passion. His attention, however, soon became divided between Jane and her lover's attendant, who had placed his long sword against the king's pillar, and while affecting to be listening to the panegyric on St. Giles, was in reality studying intently the vast assemblage, and dealing covert glances of hostility,

for everywhere he recognised the colours, the crests, and
badges of the Hamiltons.

"Despite that voluminous beard, and these painted eyebrows, yonder fellow is either the Earl of Ashkirk or the
devil!" thought Redhall; "but let me be wary, for he is
slippery as an eel. So, so! our good Sir Roland Vipont, the
king's favourite minion, is a resetter of rebels—hah! I have
it *now*."

He almost said this aloud, so bright, or rather so dark and
so devilish, was the thought that flashed upon his mind.
Beckoning to his henchman and factotum—

"Nichol," said he, "thou seest that valet in the livery of
Sir Roland Vipont?"

"He wi' that beard like a colt's tail?"

"The same. I would fain have him committed to sure
ward—privately though; not in the castle, for there every
one would hear of it an hour after, but quietly, in the vault
of my own house here. Dost thou understand me?"

"Wi' ease can we do so, my lord," replied Nichol, with a
grin on his mastiff mouth, "for by the use o' my long lugs I
have just learned that he is to attend the Lady Seton on a
visit to St. Katherine's convent to-night."

"'Slife! dost thou say so? And that captain of the ordnance, doth he go too?"

"No."

"Ah! and wherefore?"

"Because it seems that the captain of the king's guard
and that gay buckie, Leslie of Balquhan, are to sup with
him to-night."

"Thou art sure of this?" said Redhall, whose heart
glowed, and whose eyes sparkled.

"Sure as I am a born man."

"Watch well, then, and learn more, if you can. Oh,
Nichol Birrel, thou art worth thy weight in gold to me—yea,
gold trebly refined! Continue to watch them strictly while
I go to his eminence the cardinal concerning a raid against
the Douglases; for, mark me, both the Lady Seton and
yonder valet of her squire must be safe within our bolts and
bars to-night. I have suspected that long beard concealed
something for these some days past."

"And so have I, your lordship."

"Indeed—remarkable! and you think——"

" As your lordship doth."

" That he is no other than the Earl of Ashkirk ?"

The brodder—who, in fact, had never bestowed a thought upon the matter—now opened his eyes wide with astonishment.

" Deil gae owre us ! *he* is worth a bushel o' silver merks."

" Which I will pay thee privately, for thy secrecy and istance."

" And by-and-bye, I may get the other thousand from the council—eh ? "

" Of course."

" And Sir Roland ?"

" Is about to be sent on a fool's errand into Douglasdale."

" Disguised as a black friar, I sought admittance to his lodging at St. Anne's-yard while he was yet a-bed ; for I was bent on probing his wound anew," whispered this bloodhound, with a terrible smile ; " but his servitor, a wary auld birkie, that hath served in the border wars, said, ' Na, na, my master needs na ghostly counsel, gude father ; indeed he seldom confesses, save now and then to Father St. Bernard.' ' But I am a notable apothgar,' said I, under my cowl, ' and cure a' manner o' sword wounds, forbye and attour shot-holes.' ' Ouaye,' he replied, ' but my master hath got from the Lady Ashkirk a notable red salve, that cures a' thing, frae a prick wi' a pin to a slash wi' a Jethart axe. He had but a clean stab frae a poniard, and the salve hath made him whole :' and so, my lord, I came away like a hound that loses the scent."

" Good !" muttered the advocate, opening his note-book. " Vipont seldom goes to confession (that will be information for the cardinal and Fynnard the grand inquisitor), save to the Father St. Bernard (*that* looketh like conspiracy); and he hath actually received a pot of salve from the Countess of Ashkirk, which savoureth of sorcery and working by damnable charms. By my soul, Nichol Birrel," said he, closing his tablets, " thou art an invaluable fellow. The cardinal would give his best benefice for such a spy. I will find military service for the master of the ordnance, and can also dispose of the countess. I have them all in my grasp ! Oh, how subtly the web is weaving, and how tangled are the meshes of the plot that will lay them all at my mercy !"

Redhall unwittingly thought *aloud*, and his fierce whisper

was heard by Birrel. Under the tufted masses of his shock-head, the ruffian gave a leer of delight and intelligence, at least so much as his yellow bilious visage could express, and drew nearer the countess, while Redhall, softly and on tiptoe, lest the jingle of his silver spurs might be heard, hastened from the church, to seek the lord chancellor (to whom James intrusted everything) concerning the proposed raid to Douglasdale and other projects, of which the reader will soon learn more.

During this conversation, Father St. Bernard had proceeded far with his oration on St. Giles, the abbot and confessor, with a pathos and power of oratory that enchained the attention of his hearers while it fired and enchanted them. Unacquainted with care, and long separated from the world, the aspect of this venerable prebendary was singularly saintly and winning; his eye was alternately mild and penetrating, and his voice was soft and persuasive. All were irresistibly drawn towards him; and while he spoke, the most profound silence reigned throughout the long dim aisles and misty perspective of that vast and crowded church. With all that filial love and respect which of old a Catholic girl felt for her confessor, Lady Jane Seton kept her bright eyes fixed on St. Bernard's face. She was proud of his oratory, his clear and beautiful language, his fervid enthusiasm, and deep research into abstruse writing and the lore of ancient days.

We can give but an outline of how the good father traced the earthly pilgrimage of the city's patron saint, from the day when his eyes first opened to the light in ancient Athens. "It was towards the close of the seventh century," he continued, "and his birth was noble as any in old Cecropia. The dwelling of his father stood near the temple of the Eumenides, and under the brow of that very platform from whence the blessed apostle Paul had preached to the Athenians."

He described his extraordinary learning, his deep and solemn piety, which won for him the admiration of Greece, and other countries far beyond his native province of Achaia; so much so that it soon became impossible for him to enjoy in his splendid home the retirement and meditation for which he longed. Shrinking alike from the applause of men and the dangerous temptations of wealth and prosperity, he gave all he possessed to the poor, and bade farewell for ever to Athens and Achaia the beautiful. Sailing towards France, he landed on the open and desert shore near the Rhone, from whence, with a cross on his staff, he travelled into wild places, teaching the blessed gospels to the pagan Gauls, until he reached a forest in the district of Nismes, where then stood a city built by the Roman warriors of Augustus; and there still men and beasts fought like demons in the amphitheatre of Arennes, and the poor pagans worshipped their graven idols in the temple of Diana—for the savage Goths then held the city and all the land around it.

"There, in the vast forest which had been growing since the deluge, St. Giles built him a hermitage, and there," continued, the preacher, "subsisting on the berries and other wild fruits of the desert, with water only for his drink, he passed many years in the voiceless solitude, till, purified by prayer, disengaged from earth, and filled with the ardour of his holy meditations, he became as an angel rather than a man." He related, too, how the saint planted his cross-staff before the door of his hermitage, and watered it daily, until it took root, sprouted, and grew into a stately orange-tree; and how (like the holy St. Aicard), having once in forgetfulness shaved his bald crown so late on a Saturday night that he encroached on the Sunday morning, when turning about he saw the devil —and here every one crossed themselves—yea, the devil, busily picking up every atom of hair, to produce the whole against him at the divine tribunal: and how severely he was punished thereafter; for a savage Gothic chief had him seized, scourged, and thrown into one of the Roman towers of Nismes, where he prayed to his Maker in great agony of spirit.

Lo! in the night a halo shone around him, his fetters fell off, the doors of his dungeon revolved, and the clear light of the stars beamed upon him. A deep slumber fell upon his guards, and St. Giles walked forth in peace, to seek once more the shade of his miraculous orange-tree and his beloved hermitage near the dark green woods and bright blue waters of the Rhone.

Now, spreading fast in Gaul, the Goths had made themselves lords of the two Narbonensis and the three Acquitani: in their wild ravages they destroyed even the forests, and by these and their cruelty brought so sore a famine upon the land, that even the saint, in his extreme old age, would have perished, but for the fruit of his orange-tree, and the milk of a doe, which visited him daily, sent doubtless by the Lord, and which became his sole companion and sustenance; and it chanced that when Wamba, king of the Goths, was hunting one day in the forest of Nismes, he was about to slay the doe, but spared her at the saint's intercession; upon which Ionie, his queen, who was almost dying of a grievous sickness, became straightway restored to her former strength and beauty.

St. Giles outlived the famine, and by the miracles he wrought became famous throughout all the land of Gaul, and died at a wondrous old age in that year when the infidel Saracens sacked Nismes; the recapture of which by Charles Martel, mayor of the palace, and the great victory of the Christian knights between Tours and Poictiers, in the year of our redemption 728, he foretold, with his last breath; and so, in the full odour of sanctity, he passed away to heaven.

"The doe, the companion of his solitude, was found lying dead by his side; but to this day," continued the venerable priest, in conclusion, "in memory of the saint, we may yet see her retained in the banner of this good city, upon which the blessed St. Giles is now looking down, as upon that of his chosen children, through the dim vista of eight long centuries!"*

He then blessed the people, and descending into one of the side aisles, disappeared.

The vast multitudes who thronged the church now poured from all its doorways like a flood upon the streets, and down the steep old burial-ground that descended on the south towards the Cowgate (a place of interment coeval with the *first huts* of the city), and where a little doorway in the wall, at the bottom, gave egress to that thoroughfare, then so fashionable. It stood just beside the little chapel of the Holyrood, which survived till the end of the sixteenth century.

As closely as they dared, Nichol Birrel and his friend Dobbie, with their poniards in their belts and wooden rosaries dangling at their better wrists, followed the countess and her party home to her residence, near the court end of the town; and thereafter stationed themselves at the *Cross and Gill-stoup*, a small change-house, the low grated windows of which commanded a view of the archway, whereon were carved the coronet and arms of the Setons of Ashkirk; and there the two worthy followers of Redhall sat down to drink and watch for the remainder of the afternoon.

* St. Giles was the crest of Edinburgh until 1560, when an anchor was substituted by the Reformers; but the doe still remains as a supporter.

At six o'clock, Sir Roland Vipont, with his bonnet on one side, his feather erect, and his rapier tilting up a corner of his mantle, like a true dandy of the sixteenth century, came forth alone, and descended the street towards Holyrood.

"Brawly!" muttered Dobbie, rubbing his large misshapen paws with exultation; "the dare-devil's awa, but the valet is yet there."

"Yea; and the visit to the sister of the Sheens yet holdeth gude. But have ye any money?" asked the pricker.

"Nocht but a Flemish rydar, and three of old King James's gowden pennies."

"Ho there, gudewife!" cried Birrel, with a grin of delight on his mastiff mouth, while he clattered on the hard table with his rosary; "fetch us twa mair mutchkins of your wine —that red wine, which I ken right well ye get smuggled contrary to the act, straight frae the Flemmings o' the Dam —quick!"

And while their slipshod attendant was bringing the fresh supply, these worthies proceeded to examine their poniards, in case they should be required, and tried whether the guards were true, the points sharp, the hilts fitting well to the blades, and the blades to the hilts; for to them deeds of outrage and cruelty were the business of life; and we may add that, by the loose lives of the clergy prior to the Reformation—a measure which that very laxity of discipline brought about—religion and morality were fast sinking to a low ebb in Scotland.

CHAPTER XIV.

THE CHANCELLOR OF SCOTLAND.

"I made such service to our Sovereign King,
   He did promote me still to high estate;
A prince above all priestis for to reign,
   Archbishop of St. Andrew's consecrate.
   To that honour when I was elevate,
My prideful heart was not content withal,
Till that I was created cardinal."
                    Sir D. LINDESAY'S *Tragedie of the Cardinal.*

WITH his long rapier under his arm, and his bonnet drawn well over his face, the lord advocate, with all the air of a man who has found a clue to something, or is mentally pursuing a distant object, hurried, as we have said, from the

church, and threaded his way between the fleshers' stalls,
which encumbered both sides of the street about the Netherbow and arch of the Blackfriars Wynd.

Descending the latter, he reached the residence of Cardinal
Beaton, where, through the medium of several pages, esquires,
and pikemen, he sent up his name, requesting an audience,
and was immediately admitted.

David Beaton was then in the prime of life; his stature
was commanding, his air was dignified, his bearing noble. As
we may see by the portraits of him, still preserved at Edinburgh, his face was grave, dark, and eminently handsome;
his eyes were bright and piercing, and he wore his beard and
moustaches pointed *à la cavalier*, rather than shaven off like
a priest. He was seated in an easy-chair, and wore his red
baretta, black cassock, and gold cross. His large scarlet hat
lay upon a side table, near the two-handed sword of his
grandfather, old Sir David of Pitmilly.

Our Scottish Wolsey was seated near a table covered with
books and papers; there were several portfolios marked with
the fleur-de-lys, the rose, the eagle, &c., containing the memorandums of correspondence with France, England, the
Empire, and so forth. The apartment, which was little and
elegant, was hung with green damask flowered with leaves of
red and gold; his patrimonial arms, the blazon of " Bethune's
line of Picardie," appeared above the mantelpiece. There was
no fire, for the season was summer, and the andirons were
burnished bright as silver. A book was half open in his
hand, but his eyes were thoughtfully fixed on a window,
through which he saw the antique buildings of the opposite
street, a steep wynd, that led towards the Dominican monastery, the square tower and slated spire of which shone in the
light of the western sun, and terminated the view. His
daughter, the Lady Margaret Beaton, a charming young
girl with blue eyes and dark brown hair—the same who, five
years after, became the bride of the young Lord Lindesay—
was sitting on a little tabourette by his side, decorating a
little kitten with ribbons.

As she had been born prior to his taking vows of celibacy,
the cardinal had no reason to conceal her; but as soon as Sir
Adam Otterburn entered, at a sign from her father, she kissed
his hand, snatched the kitten, which she considered her peculiar property, placed a chair for the visitor, and withdrew.

"God be with your eminence!" said Redhall, half kneeling, as he saluted the cardinal.

"And peace with you," replied Beaton, with a gracious wave of the hand, which, while it pointed to a seat, passed also for a priestly benediction. He closed his book "La Légende de Monseigneur Saint Dominique,"&c., an old black-letter quarto, "*Imprimé à Paris*, 1495," and continued— "Have I the pleasure of seeing Sir Adam as a friend, or in his official capacity?"

"I trust your eminence will never consider my visits the less friendly because I come so frequently on the service of the state; but now mine errand closely concerns the latter."

"I think that thou, as lord advocate, and I, as lord chancellor, ought to be collared together, like a couple of questing dogs. Well, what in God's name is astir now?"

"Treason!"

"That is nothing new."

"Trafficking with the English—and it may be sorcery!"

"My God! dost thou say so? Those accursed Douglases, I warrant me?"

Redhall gave an emphatic nod, and put one leg over the other. The cardinal let fall his book, grasped the knobs of his chair, and reclined his head back as if he expected to hear something momentous. "Well, my lord, and what now of this turbulent tribe?"

"I seek a *carte blanche* warrant of arrest and committal to ward—or rather, concurrence with it—does your eminence understand?"

"Agnus Dei!" said the cardinal, crossing, and speaking with great bitterness and energy; "how sad it is that, from being the bulwark and buckler of Scotland, the house of Angus and its allies have become her sworn foes! Too blindly the enemies of Arran, they never rest while a Hamilton lives, and are too much in Henry's interest ever again to be true to Scotland. How was it when James assumed the government, and, by the intercession of Wolsey and myself, so unwisely permitted the ambitious Earls of Ashkirk and of Angus to return home? No sooner were their feet on Scottish ground, than, ever restless, they raised a faction to expel the queen-mother and the minister Arran, and came at once to blows about where the Parliament should meet. 'I will hold it here,' said the determined Arran. 'Thou shalt hold it *there*,' said the imperious Angus. Then were banners displayed and lances lifted; and Angus and Ashkirk feared not to bend their cannon against the royal castle of Edinburgh, where the young king, the queen-mother, and their prime minister were residing. Then came trooping and hosting, and castles were stormed, and garrisoned, and stormed again; towns were burned and tenants plundered. The high-sheriff of Ayr slew the Earl of Cassilis; the islesmen of Orkney expelled and slew the Lord Caithness; the knight of Tulliallan slew the Abbot of Culrosse; and some ruffian of hell murdered my steadfast friend and true, Sir Thomas Maclellan of Bombie, at the door of St. Giles. (Redhall felt himself grow pale.) The Douglases pillaged the castle of St. Andrews and the abbey of Dunfermline; they fought the battles of Melrose and Linlithgow, where the good Earl of Lennox was so cruelly run through the body after he had surrendered. The whole country seemed to be hastening to destruction, for the swords of the Douglases bore all before them, and every post, place, and perquisite under the crown, every royal castle and office of state, was held by a Douglas. The royal guards were all Douglases; and the young king was their prisoner, while his people were reduced to slavery. Well! I then thought the time had come to bestir me," continued the cardinal, with a smile of satisfaction. " I did so; and the king escaped from the tower of Falkland. He summoned the nobles in arms at Stirling; the wheel of fate revolved again, and, deprived of place and power, the Douglases were proscribed, forfeited, and driven into England—England, whose kings have ever rejoiced in fanning the flame of Scottish civil war—the policy of hell, which none have adopted more than the present atrocious tyrant, their eighth Henry."

"All this I know well," said Redhall, endeavouring to repress his impatience at this retrospective reverie.

" There, fostered by this heretic prince, they have become the enemies of their fatherland, the believers of a false doctrine, the rebels of their king and the accursed of their God. None has done more than the Lord Ashkirk to further a marriage between King James and a daughter of the mansworn Tudor; but happily, I have ever been victorious; for the honour and policy of Scotland and France require that they must league together against the grasping ambition and centralizing greed of England. Thou knowest that I have ever been for France, and bear about as much love for England as a tiger doth to a panther. When Henry offered his daughter to James, with the office of lieutenant-general of all England and Ireland, happily, I warned him of the gilded snare, and dismissed the ambassador, Howard, with a remembrance of how England had treated the shipwrecked James I. When Godscallo came from the Emperor Charles to offer his sister Mary of Austria as a queen for Scotland, who defeated him, and turned his dangerous eloquence against himself?"

" Your eminence," said Redhall, putting the left leg over the right.

" When he offered Donna Maria of Portugal, the daughter of Eleonora of Austria," resumed Beaton, with a smile of gratified vanity, " and boasted of her beauty and the sixty battles of her victorious uncle, who waived all his sophistry by a word ?"

" Your eminence of course," sighed Redhall.

" When Christian II. of Denmark offered *his* daughter, the Princess Dorothea, though she was already contracted to the beggarly Elector Frederick, I dismissed him, and briefly too ; for my whole soul was bent on preserving the ancient league of amity, that together the banners of Scotland and France might be turned against their common enemy ; and by my own energy, assisted by God and our Blessed Lady, I had the young Queen Magdalene espoused to James ; and now let the Douglases do their worst, for, ratified before the holy altar of Notre Dame de Paris, that alliance can never be broken !"

" Death will break it," said the advocate, revengefully, for he was somewhat irritated by this long preamble. " Magdalene is dying by inches, and there are abroad such rumours of sorcery in the matter that I crave a warrant to seize——"

" Whom ?" asked Beaton, with a terrible glance.

" The Countess of Ashkirk and her daughter, the Lady Jane Seton," said Redhall, with a sinking heart.

" Margaret of Ashkirk ?" said the cardinal, with a look of blank astonishment, " the widow of the good Earl John ? Beware thee, my lord, lest zeal outrun discretion. Her husband was a stout knight and true to Scotland."

" As I tell your eminence that his widow is an ill-woman and false ! Her son, the outlawed earl, hath again re-entered Scotland by the Middle Marches."

" Thou dost not say so ?"

H

" Sure as I live and breathe."

" On what errand ?"

" Can you ask ?" said Redhall, with a smile; " treason,
civil war, and the destruction of the Hamiltons, no doubt.
And with the knowledge that he is an outlawed traitor, the
countess hath reset him."

" Natural enough, he is the poor woman's son."

" But the master of the ordnance hath likewise done so."

" Natural enough, too, for he is said to love the earl's
sister."

" Your eminence is strangely cool in this matter," said
Redhall, grinding his teeth; " but you know not all that
common rumour sayeth."

" Ah! what the devil says it now ?"

" That the young queen is dying," replied the advocate,
drawing near, sinking his voice impressively, and presuming
even to grasp his arm; " sorcery is at work; every man who
looks upon her reads death in her face, and the hopes of Henry
that James may yet marry his daughter are rising again."

" Hah !"   There was a brief pause.

" And what wouldst thou have ?" asked Beaton.

" Permission to seize and commit to sure ward the Countess
of Ashkirk and her daughter—a measure demanded by the
safety of the nation."

Beaton shook his head.

" Rumour is busy, and avers that the earl is concealed
within the ports of Edinburgh," continued the wily advocate,
who, for his own ends, did not choose to say *where;* " my
spies inform me that he has been heard to boast of being, ere
long, at Stirling bridge with an army of English borderers,
for he hath made a vow to sup——"

" Where ?"

" In thy tower of Creich."

The dark eyes of Beaton flashed fire; for in the tower of
Creich, rumour (which in those days supplied, somewhat in-
differently, however, the place of the public press) asserted
that the cardinal kept quite a seraglio.   It touched him in
the quick.

" The earl said so—ha !" he muttered, opening his portfolio; " indeed—um—um—and where dost thou wish the
countess committed to ward ?"

" Your eminence's castle of St. Andrew is a sure place."

" I send none there but heretics ; the tower of Inchkeith is a stronger fortlet."

" The Knight of Barncleugh is captain there—a Hamilton too."

" Very suitable," continued the cardinal, writing on a slip of paper a warrant to arrest and imprison, ' during the king's pleasure, Margaret Countess Dowager, and the Lady Jane, daughter of the umquhile John Earl of Ashkirk, together with Archibald Seton, sometyme designated of Ashkirk, but now under sentence of forfeiture.' " Send the Albany herald to the countess, and let him take some fifteen pikes of my guard ; one of Sir Robert Barton's boats will convey the ladies to the Inch. Of late, James has shown over much favour to this family, whose besetting sin has been their leaguing with England ; and I hope that, ere long," continued Beaton, thinking of the tower of Creich, " this troublesome young lord will pay the penalty of his insolence to me and his crimes against the state——"

" My lord the Bishop of Limoges," announced the young Lord Lindesay, the cardinal's favourite page, ushering in that reverend prelate.

" Your eminence will not omit to send the requisite troops and cannon towards Douglasdale to-morrow, for Ashkirk may be there," said the lord advocate, rising.

" Before vespers, Sir Roland Vipont shall hear from me," replied Beaton, as Redhall sank on one knee, kissed the ruby ring on his finger, and hurried away with a hasty step and a beating heart.

CHAPTER XV.

THE NOON OF LOVE.

" He looked upon her, and her humid gaze
　　Was at his look dropped instant on the ground :
　But o'er her cheek of beauty rushed a blaze,
　　Her bosom heaved within its silken bound—
　And though her voice is trembling as I sigh,
　Love triumphs in her smile and fond delicious eye."
　　　　　　　　　　　CROLY'S *Angel of the World.*

THE sun was in the west, and threw the long shadow of the Netherbow so far down the vista of the Canongate that it almost reached to the Girth-cross of the Holyrood. Save when the summer wind made strange sounds among the

H 2

peaked roofs and enormous chimneys of the narrow closes, the streets were still and quiet. A hoof rang occasionally, just as if to remind one that they were recently paved for the first time; or the distant cries were heard of those who sold curds and milk at the cross, or cockles and whelks at the Tron, as we may learn from William Dunbar's poem in the year 1500.

The countess and her family had just adjourned from the dining hall to that tapestried chamber in which we had the honour of first introducing them to the reader. With no foreboding of the mischief that was then brewing against them at that moment in the little turret-room of the cardinal's mansion, the good old Lady Margaret and all around her were very happy.

Roland instinctively drew to the side of Jane, who approached her embroidery frame, for ladies were never idle in those industrious days; Earl Archibald seated himself by the side of Sybil, where he could very well have spared the additional company of her companions, Marion and Alison, who seated themselves near, to hear her perform on the virginals; and the countess assumed her accustomed and well-cushioned bench, in the sunny corner of a window, where the shadows of the thick basket grating were thrown upon her face. Drawing her spinning-wheel towards her with one hand, she made a motion with the other to Father St. Bernard to sit near; for the confessor had that day been invited to dinner the moment his oration concluded.

"I pray Heaven I may not hear some evil tidings," said the countess, "for the wind is so high."

"Nay, fear not, madam, for this is Friday," replied the old priest, "and the festival of Queen Ellen to boot."

"And yet I remind me, father, that in the days of King James IV., I heard the wind soughing just so, and in two hours thereafter news came frae the west countrie that my kinsman, Sir John Colquhoun of Luss, who was lord chamberlain and ambassador to England in 1487, was killed at the siege of Dumbarton, by a ball from a culverin."

"In 1489—yea, madam, I mind that leaguer well, as if twere yesterday."

"Eight-and-forty years ago," said the countess. "St. Mary! I was but a wee tot at my mother's knee in the auld tower of Kilspindie then!"

"Udsdagger!" whispered the earl to Sybil, "the old lady

my mother is full tilt again at her musty recollections of James IV "

"She will soon dose poor Father St. Bernard with het salves, her charms against witchcraft, and prosy reminiscences of Flodden and Queen Margaret."

"And he will reply with scriptural texts and astounding miracles. On my honour, they are a pair of the most veritable prosers between the tower of Creich and the tower of Babel !"

"Hush! to mention that tower of Creich in the cardinal's hearing makes one his enemy for life."

"Fiend take the cardinal and his red hat to boot !" whispered the earl, "for in England I have learned to laugh both at red legs and shaven crowns. But now, my own fair cousin, sing me, I pray, the old song of Duke Albany's days, that song my father loved so well. In Holyrood it might be treason to sing of a French minion's fall, but none are here save friends; and oh, my dear Sybil, thou knowest not how blythe I am to hear thy soft low voice again. Do not refuse me," he added, seeing that she was about to object; "for in a day or two I go to exile again, and we may meet no more."

The young noble gallantly kissed a handful of Sybil's long dark hair; and in the desire to please her handsome lover, she at once commenced one of those old songs, to which something of a melancholy interest will ever cling, when we consider that they cheered or soothed our Scottish sires three hundred years ago—

> " God send that the duke had byded in France,
> And the Sieur de la Beauté had never come hame,
> With his tall men-at-arms, by banner and lance,
> The Douglas, the Home, and the Seton to tame."*

The voice of Sybil was worthy of her name; it was bewitchingly soft and low and sweet; but the sharp, wiry, and somewhat unmusical accompaniment of the virginal, rather injured than improved the effect of her performance, which was admirable; for the frank girl was at no pains to conceal the amiable wish to please her kinsman and lover. Seated very erectly upon a high-backed chair, her white hands tinkled over the keys of this old-fashioned instrument, which, perhaps, obtained its name from being played upon almost solely by young ladies. Though externally not unlike our modern

* See VEDDERBURNE'S *Complainte of Scotland*, printed at St. Andrew's, A.D. 1549.

pianoforte, the virginal was internally more like the spinet of the succeeding age, which formed, in fact, the link between the two.

That on which Sybil played had been presented to Jane Seton by Anne de la Tour, the late Duchess of Albany. The case was of cedar, covered with blue Genoese velvet, and clasped by four large gilded locks finely engraven with the arms of Scotland and France. The whole of the front was magnificently enamelled, and had forty keys provided with jacks and quills, twenty being of ebony tipped with silver, and twenty of ivory tipped with gold, to mark the semitones. Supported by two dragons of oak, it was only five feet long by twenty inches deep; but as there were but few virginals in Scotland, its splendour formed one of the topics of the day; and those evil minds were not wanting who affirmed that it was merely a box of devils who played at the command of the black page.

Thus, while singing and soft glances were the entertainment in one corner of that tall tapestried room, miracles and omens in another, a quiet little flirtation was proceeding in a third, where Lady Jane was sitting, to all appearance very intent upon her embroidery, while her lover leant over the back of her chair, conversing in low tones, looking kisses and all manner of soft things, and contriving to say a good many too, under cover of Sybil's musical performance, notwithstanding the presence of Father St. Bernard, whose apostolical aspect was sufficiently imposing.

"And so, my gentle Jeanie, thou art still bent on visiting this convent of Sienna to-night?"

"Have I not told you ten times that I have promised this book as a birthday gift to the reverend mother ever since the martyrdom of St. Victor—more than a month ago," said Jane, reckoning the time on her pretty fingers; "and she has never yet received it. By-the-bye, sir—of all the world, I think thou oughtest to accompany me to-night."

"Impossible, my own sweetheart."

"What would you say if I were to be carried off?"

"Carried off! Bah! I should like to see any one carry you off."

"It would be very unpleasant," said Jane, shrugging her shoulders; "and within a month of our marriage, too."

"Adorable Jane!"

"Hush! Father St. Bernard—you forget."

"You know well how gladly I would go; but as I have said, both the captain and lieutenant of the king's guard have sent to say, they will do themselves the pleasure of supping with me to-night, and hospitality requires that I should not decline, for we are three *bon camarados*, and have made a compact to dine and sup with each other alternately whenever our cash was low."

"Then the cash of these wild gallants is gone?"

"Sunk to the lowest ebb, Jane. I met them this morning, swearing like Turks, for they had lost all they possessed, even to their rings, at the French ambassador's. With the earl and his enormous Tizona, and these tall trenchermen, who are always lounging about the kitchen-fire and stable-yard, none will dare to molest you to-night."

"Be not too certain. Oh, I have so many lovers, that I dare scarcely look from under my hood, lest I add one to the number. Abduction is not so uncommon, surely. Did not King James carry off the lady of Lochlevin on her bridal night? Is not the Knight of Casche now a prisoner in the castle for carrying off the wife of Sir David Scott, whom he slew in the kirk of Strathmiglo? And 'tis only six days since Kincaid of Coates forcibly abducted the poor wife of master Quentin Smebard, when she was cheapening her a new hood at the Tron—yea, in the High-street, and at noon-day."

"Tush! a pitiful clerk of the chancery," said Roland, play-ing with her curls. "Believe me, my little ladykin, that none will dare meddle with thee who see the livery of thy followers, and remember thou art the affianced bride of Sir Roland Vipont. So in vain, cunning fairy, thou wouldest frighten me from performing what friendship and hospitality require. But what is this book, for which madam the prioress of St. Katherine is so anxious?"

"See, it is *The Lyf of St. Katherin of Sienna*," said Jane, opening a little volume of Wynkyn de Worde's, the velvet cover of which she had embroidered beautifully with gold upon crimson. "Thou canst read this black letter, of course?"

"Why, thanks to fortune and my good friend the father here, I learned the *Grace Buke* and *Prymar*, at the principal grammar school of this good burgh, when it was first opened by Provost Logan of Coatfield."

"In the year of grace 1519," said the countess, "just six

years after the death of the good King James, whose munificence founded it—woe's me!"

' And why doth this prioress not embroider her own books? How, i' the devil's name, do they spend the long dull day in yonder convent; for I vow 'tis a fortress all walled round like the city of Lisle—and I suppose the fair sisters are never beyond it."

"Save when sickness or sorrow, want or misery, call them into the world; for they are of inestimable service to the poor. Ah! had you seen them in time of the plague. The Prioress Josina—thou remembrest the beautiful Josina Henrison, who with me was a damoiselle of honour to madam the Duchess Anne of Albany? Ah! she is a very angel of goodness. Now, do not look in that way, as if you were just about to laugh at me?"

"Who—I? Mass! I would almost have fallen sick on purpose, to have had such a nurse as the pretty Josina—had I not——"

"What, sir?"

"Loved thee, and consequently been sure of another."

"'Tis well you say so," replied Jane, playfully, pinching his ear. "Ah! my mother is watching us!"

"God bless ye, bairns!" said the old countess, kindly and fondly; "for ye were born under the same star, ilk being destined for the other."

"*Pax Domini sit semper vobiscum*," said Father St. Bernard, with closed eyes, and waving his right hand towards them.

"Plague take thy Latin," muttered the earl.

"Which meaneth, the peace of the Lord be about you," continued the priest.

"I never tried Latin but once, good father, and then it was to curse roundly when my Scottish failed—*in nomine patris et filii*, and so forth."

"And when was this, my son?"

"Retreating up Yarrow-braes from Cessford's spearmen, with two bullets and three arrows sticking in my body."

The old priest crossed himself, and turned up his eyes; but those of the countess kindled as her son spoke, and some fiery remark was hovering on her lips, when her bower-woman, a demure looking abigail, clad in solemn black taffety, raised the arras, glided in on tiptoe, and whispered something in her ear.

Lady Ashkirk turned very pale.

"Mother dear," said Lady Jane, tenderly, "what has happened?"

"That hen hath crowed again, as Janet tells me."

"Hen—what hen?" said the earl.

"An ill-omened hen in the poultry-yard, whilk hath now crown thrice since you came amongst us. Oh! my doo Archibald! my doo Archibald!—it's a sad boding of evil, whilk the Mother o' God avert."

"Amen!" said the old priest, "*pax domini*——"

"Friend Roland," said the earl, with a smile, "did you ever know any one who dwelt in such an atmosphere of omens and predictions, salves and recipes, as the good lady my mother? 'Tis very perplexing, to say the least of it."

"Hush, lord earl!" said the countess, with some asperity; "every bairn kens that the crowing of a hen bodeth evil, and that no house can thrive where the hens are addicted to sic an ungodly and unnatural amusement. Harkee, Janet, let its neck be drawn, and bestow it as an almous on the first Franciscan who comes hither wi' his begging box."

This episode was rather "a damper" to the ladies; but Roland endeavoured to divert them, by engaging and vanquishing them all successively at the old French military game of *passe dix*, which was played with three dice, at which (as we learn from the *Complete Gamester*, 1680) "the caster throws continually till he hath thrown doublets under ten, and then he is *out*, and loseth, or doublets above ten, and then he *passeth*, and wins." At this simple game fortune favoured Roland, and he swept off the entire passbank, which was composed of little *bon-bons* of honey and flour, for sugar was then growing in the mist of futurity—at least, it was unknown in Scotland. The time stole swiftly on; at last the ringing of vespers warned him that he must retire, as his friends, who had so annoyingly invited themselves, would be awaiting him.

"Say a prayer for me at St. Katherine's to-night, my dear Jane," said Roland, as he buckled on his rapier. "I fear me I am a sad rogue, and often omit to pray for myself in these stirring times, when one's armour is so rarely off; and of all things forget not to give my very best commendations to the fair Josina."

"Sirrah! thou wantest thine other car well pinched."

"And you return?"

"To-morrow, at noon."

"Ah—the devil! and shall I not see thee till then?" said
Roland, scared at the prospect of an eighteen hours' separation.

"Thou wilt not die of despair in that time, surely?" replied Jane, archly.

"Then to-morrow, at noon, I will be at the convent
gate, or under the old lime-trees that border its pathway,
near the loch; and so till then, my sweet flower, farewell."

After paying his adieux to all with that grave formality
which French intercourse had impressed upon the manners of
the Scottish noblesse, he retired; whereupon the messieurs
Birrel and Dobbie ordered in the additional stoup of Flemish
wine, as we have related in the thirteenth chapter of this
history.

CHAPTER XVI.

VIPONT'S HOUSEHOLD.

"At length they to the house retreated,
And round the supper soon were seated;
When the time quickly passed away,
And gay good humour closed the day."
                        Dr. Syntax, Canto XIV.

HAVING lost all their money at play with the French and
Spaniards, Roland's two comrades, the captain of the arquebusiers, and Leslie, his lieutenant, had both invited themselves
to sup with him on that evening, according (as he has already
stated) to an arrangement the three friends had made—that
he whose exchequer was low should dine or sup with the
others.   But now it chanced that Roland's purse was drained
too; and though hospitality and the manners of the time
forbade the least evasion of this visit, or rather visitation, old
Lintstock had fully participated in the consternation it occasioned his master.   Lintstock, however, with the coolness of
an old soldier who was well used to foraging, begged Sir
Roland to keep his mind at ease, as he would provide an
adequate supper by the hour of the cavaliers' arrival.

Roland knew not what to make of this; but he was aware
of the fertility of his valet's resources, and that the cunning
old vender of projectiles had made love to an inn (as he
said), or rather an innkeeper's widow, whom he had been in-
tending to espouse for the last five years; thus he doubted
not Lintstock would provide the viands if Heaven did not.

Roland lodged with the widow of one of the king's falconers; but the pittance he received per month from the exchequer (for although styled master of the ordnance, he was in reality only captain of a few hundred cannoniers, who were scattered throughout the royal castles) afforded little more than what soldiers usually term comforts—*i. e.*, plain bed, board, and quarters. He was never so much in camp or garrison as to lose the polish of the courtier or relish for the society of ladies. The "rough and round" of a soldier's life never discomposed him; he wore his heavy armour as easily as Jane Seton did her gloves of Blois; and his love for her threw a poetry around all that plainness and positive discomfort which generally surrounded him, but of which she was totally ignorant. Soldiering had, of course, considerably sharpened his faculties; but Roland never forgot the gentle bearing of the perfect cavalier; and though perhaps inferior in head to such a man as Sir Adam Otterburn, he was immensely superior in heart and straightforwardness of purpose.

Roland's windows overlooked the Abbey Close, and the setting sun shone partly through them. They were strongly grated, and lighted a room which was wainscoted with Scottish fir, and furnished with six hardwood chairs and a table of oak. An almerie or corner cupboard, a boxed bed within a recess, a suit of bright armour, and a quantity of other harness for horse and man, with various weapons, hung upon pegs; a few books of old romances, and a French *Manuel de l'Artilleur*, made up its furniture.

" What the devil shall I do, if Lintstock has failed?" thought Roland, as he entered his domicile. " Hallo, old Ironhead, how goeth the supper?" (People supped then at seven o'clock.)

" Right weel, Sir Roland, as ye may see for yoursel," replied the old fellow, over whose broad visage and solitary eye there spread a brilliant smile of self-satisfaction.

A snow-white cloth covered the old oak-table; a knife, a drinking-horn, and platter were laid for each of the friends; a silver salt-cellar occupied the centre; a plate, with four roasted ducks, stood on one side thereof, a tart and stewed pigeons on the other, with a joint of veal daintily roasted; while an eel-pie and two large manchets of white flour, with other et cetera, appeared on the side buffet, with a row of wine flasks in fair battaglia, side by side, telling by their

gaudy badges that they were from France, and such wine as
was then sold by the retailers at sixpence Scots (one half-
penny sterling) the pint, under penalty of having the head of
the cask beaten out, as an edict of the provost and baillies in
1520 remains to show.

" By Jove, thou art the very fiend himself!" said Roland,
lost in astonishment at the sight of all these good things;
" how else couldst thou get these gallant bottles of Rochelle
and Bourdeaux from that old curmudgeon of the *Cross and
Gillstoup*—for I see they bear his mark. On my honour, I
am mightily tickled by thine ingenuity!"

" I said we would pay——"

" *We ?*"

"That is, your worship would pay them at eventide, the morn."

" Why, Lintstock, I have not had a cross for these three
days."

" But there is a rumour about the palace," said Lintstock,
closing his remaining eye, " that we march by daylight, the
morn, for Douglasdale, or thereawa; and sae the auld screw
of an hosteller may whistle on his thumb for the money till
we come back again."

" March! oh, impossible—for I have not heard a word of
it; and how then shouldst thou? I warrant me the old
cullion grumbled."

" Like a boar in a high wind. 'Thou false knave and
loon,' said I, with a hand on my dirk, just so; 'these twelve
flasks are for the captain, my master.' 'He owes me thirty
crowns and mair,' replied the dour carle. 'If he owed thee
ten times as muckle, 'tis all right, for he will pay thee some
day, and nobly too; so hand me over the flasks, or I will set
the house on fire, and flay thee like St. Bartholomew!' "

" But the veal and the ducks ?"

" I fished for one, and borrowed the other—but here come
our gentlemen."

Roland gave Lintstock one of the flasks to rejoice over,
and laughed. He knew well what the old forager meant, for
the royal poultry-yard was close by, and Lintstock, with a
piece of meat tied to a string, as a lure for King James's
full-fed ducks, had many a time and oft towed them in at the
back-windows, with outspread wings; and more than one
dozen of fowls had disappeared thus, to the astonishment of
the royal poulterer.

" But the pigeons?"

" I shot with my arblast at Redhall's dovecot."

" And the eels?"

" I borrowed them frae the abbot's eel-arks, at the Canon-mills loch."

" Mass! thou'st had a busy day on't. Never mind; when I have the mains of Ashkirk with—tush, I will repay all these debts and borrowings with usury."

With a towel under his arm, the old gunner drew himself up like a post, as the two cavaliers entered, attired in velvets richly laced and slashed, and looking very gay and smiling.

" Welcome, Sir John Forrester!—and thou too, my gay Leslie! Ah! where didst get that scratch on thy nose?"

" From the fan of little Sybil Douglas, at the queen's masque yesterday."

" The little firefly! Seats, gentlemen, seats! By my faith, you are in ill-luck. 'Tis quite a fast-day with me, this, and you will sup like starveling Franciscans."

" Fast!" said tall Forrester, as he threw aside his cloak and plume: " by St. Roque! if this is a fast-day, what are thy festivals? But who is thy provant master—thy *fourrier de campement?*"

" My servitor—my trusty Lintstock."

" Mass! would that I had such a valet as thou, and such noble credit with my wine-merchant. Thou seest, Leslie, what it is to be the king's favourite. Verily, Sir Roland Vipont carries a coronet on the point of his sword. Rogue! thou must pray well to have all these good things."

" Nay, nay," said young Leslie, with a burst of reckless laughter. " he pays old Father St. Bernard to do all that for him."

" Hast heard the news?"

" Nay, what news, Sir John?"

" Thou art to boune thee for the borders; for the king swore in my hearing he would find other work for thy sword than killing his most favourite courtiers."

" These rascally Hamiltons? But Kincavil is not dead, I hope?"

" Far from it," said Leslie; " but the apothegar, from whom I was purchasing some perfumes for little Sybil Douglas, averred to me that he is in a perilous bad way."

" When did these knaves of leeches ever aver a man was

otherwise?" said Roland, seating himself. "To table, gentlemen, and pray do justice to the industry of my fourrier, and the comforts of my poor den, or hermitage, which you will; but prayer or no prayer, take care the cardinal heareth not of your jesting, Leslie—about prayers, I mean."

"The cardinal, that scarlet bugbear of the heretics? Oh, I don't fear the cardinal; he is the steadfast friend and true of my kinsman Norman, the Master of Rothes."

"A slice of this veal, Leslie?"

"Nay, I thank you; this roasted duck is quite admirable."

"'Tis from my estates in the country somewhere."

"Rochelle—or Bourdeaux?"

"Thank you—what news are abroad?"

"Nothing," said Forrester, "but of the queen having fainted twice to-day—poor little woman—to the consternation of Madame de Montreuil, De Brissac, the king, and all his court."

"How pure this Bourdeaux is—spiced, too!" said Vipont. "His eminence the cardinal (whom God long preserve!)——"

"Save us, friend Roland!" said Leslie; "thou art turning very religious."

"Is about to take such measures as shall assuredly exterminate the followers of those heretics, Resby, the Englishman, and the abbot of Fearn. Master Buchanan is now in the oubliette of St. Andrew's, where he will likely pay dearly for his satire *Franciscanus*."

"His eminence should confine himself to the pretty little amusements afforded by his country-house at Creich," said Forrester.

"Didst thou see that poor devil drowned to-day?"

"Who, Leslie?"

"He whom the king's advocate discovered burying a cat alive."

"Nay, I was hawking with the king on the Figgate-muir —the more fool I! Lintstock, thou knave!" cried Vipont to that functionary—who stood erect as a pike behind his chair—"uncork me half-a-dozen of these flasks. Drain, gentlemen, and replenish again; wine is a specific for care— worth a thousand homilies!"

"Lucky dog!" said Forrester; "thou drinkest out of horns hooped with silver, while I, who am lord of Corstor-

phine and Uchtertyre, must content me with plain beech
luggies."

"Lintstock found them during our last raid into West-
moreland. Nevertheless, Sir John, thank Heaven that you
were not, like me, born with a most portentous wooden spoon
in your mouth. I was an unlucky brat, and cried, it seems,
like a pagan at my baptism; a bad omen, as the Lady Ashkirk told me. Fill again; but excuse me—my wound, you
know."

"Ah! that dainty dagger-thrust; but it is healing fast?"

"By the total absence of an apothegar—yes. Hah!
yonder is a gay dame, followed by an esquire with the argent
and gules in his bonnet, crossing the Abbey Close. My
faith! 'tis Lady Anne of Arran, whom rumour says thou
lovest, Leslie."

"How! that muirland-meg, Anne Hamilton? Ah! what
a taste I must have!" replied Leslie.

"Nay, thou wrongest him, Vipont," said Sir John of Corstorphine; "'tis Marion Logan of Restalrig, who hath thy
heart; is it not, lieutenant of mine?"

Lesie laughed, and coloured as he replied—

"'Tis Marion whom we see, and not the Lord Arran's
daughter." The three gallants hastened to the window, as a
lady, holding up her brocaded skirt in that fashion which the
witty Knight of the Mount reprehended in his satires, passed
into a door of the palace.

"Hast thou seen what Lindesay's new poem says of yonder
fashion of skirt-bearing?" said Forrester:—

> "I trow St. Bernard, nor St. Blaise,
> Caused never man bear up their claise;
> Nor Peter, Paul, nor St. Androw,
> Bore up their tails like these, I trow;
> But I laugh most to see a nun
> Cause bear her tail——"

"The rest is vile ribaldry," said Vipont.

"And by St. Bernard, and St. Blaise to boot, Sir David
deserves to be run through the body for so severely satirizing
the ladies of Holyrood. Ha! who cometh next?—the
cardinal!"

As he spoke, Beaton, with a cavalcade of horsemen, passed
through the Abbey Close on an evening ride.

"He sits on his horse like a true cavalier," said Vipont,

withdrawing a pace, as he observed the cardinal scrutinizing his windows.

"But observe the Abbot of Kinloss; he always rides faster than his horse, and hangs on the bridle like a drowning man."

"His roan nag is covered with foam, while those of the cardinal and his gentlemen are fresh as when they left their stalls."

"The daughter of his eminence and the young Lord Lindesay are riding together," said Vipont; "a love case that, I think."

Amid jesting and laughing—for their light hearts and the somewhat reckless manners of the time, when the sword was rarely out of men's hands, imparted an almost boisterous gaiety to the supper—the evening closed in, cloudy and grey; darkness approached, and candles were lighted. The clock struck half-past eight; but there were still four flasks uncorked, when Lintstock entered, with a portentous expression in his remaining eye, and laid before his master a square packet, tied with blue ribands, which, like the edicts of council, were officially sealed with green wax.

"The devil! now what doth this portend?" muttered his friends.

"If the king knows that I have harboured a rebel lord!" thought Roland, breathlessly, "my commission would be worth about as much as my head. By the faith of Vipont! 'tis in the name of the king, and countersigned by the cardinal too!"

"*To our trusty friend, Sir Roland Vipont, of that Ilk.*

"JAMES REX.

"Right trusty friend, we greet you well and heartillie.

"It is our royal will and pleasure, that with one hundred arquebussiers of our guard, under Louis Leslie of Balquhan, and two brass culverins, with their powder, shot, and cannoneers conform, you do march to-morrow at daybreak unto Douglasdale, for the capture, dead or alive, of Archibald Seton, sometime Earl of Archkirk, our rebel and traitor, who is rumoured to be resett in that district; where, without fail, you will give all to fire and sword, be it castle or be it cottage, wherein the said lord findeth shelter; for which you have this our warrant. Hoping that you will do your devoire truly and valiantly, according to the custom observit of auld, we commit you to the protection of God.

"DAVID,

"*Cardinal, Sancti Andreæ, Commendator de Arbroath,*
Chancellor of Scotland.*

" From our Palace of Holyrood,
the 20th day of May, 1537."

"There, now, was not rumour right for once?" said Forrester.

" Still the same enmity to my unfortunate friend!" said Roland, whose face became pale, and whose teeth were clenched with anger.

" So we are to search for Lord Ashkirk among the Douglases," laughed Leslie; " a right perilous expedition. Take thy tall valet with thee, Vipont. 'Fore Heaven! that fellow, with his prodigious sword, were worth a troop of lances on such a service."

Roland glanced keenly at the speaker. Had he penetrated the earl's disguise? but there was nothing to be read but pure honesty and candour in Leslie's handsome features. He suspected not that the dictators of the order he had just received knew well that the earl was much nearer than Douglasdale.

" Ha! do you not hear something?" said Roland, rising up and listening.

" The cry of a woman, as I live!" replied Leslie; "shrill and deathly, too, as of one in sore distress; and there, now, is the patter of pistolettes!"

" Look out, Lintstock—thy one eye is worth a dozen—at the back window—what scest thou?"

" 'Torches moving about on St. John's Hill, the gleam ot steel, and I hear the cries of a woman; eh, sirs, but she scraighs dreichly and eerilie!" was the reply of Lintstock, as he snatched up a partisan.

" To your swords, and away, gentlemen!" cried Roland, unhooking his rapier from the wall; " 'tis a woman in distress! Meanwhile, Lintstock, away thou to the castle, seek my firemaster and his matrosses, and desire that two pieces of cannon and sixteen men in their armour, with horses and

---

* It is thus the Cardinal signed his name to more than one document in the author's possession.

I

all in fighting order, be before the palace by daybreak to-morrow; look well to my own horses and new coat of mail too. And now, sirs, let us go, in God's name!" and with their mantles rolled round their left arms, and swords un-sheathed, they sprang down stairs, and dashed up the south back of the Canongate, towards the base of St. John's Hill.

They saw no one: the place was desolate, and perfectly silent.

The moon, which had been partially obscured, shone forth for a moment, and revealed a pool of blood on the dusty road which skirted the base of the hill. Near it lay a lady's glove, and a man's bonnet of coarse blue cloth, but no traces of a fray.

On the bonnet was a pewter badge.

" 'Tis the cognisance of Redhall," said Roland, tossing the bonnet away, and placing the glove in his belt.

After frequently hallooing, and searching long and fruit-lessly, the three friends again sought St. Ann's Yard, but not to finish the remaining flasks; for Roland and Leslie had to prepare for their march by daybreak on the morrow, and now the hour was late.

CHAPTER XVII.

A LORD ADVOCATE OF THE SIXTEENTH CENTURY.

> "*Camillo.* Thou execrable man, beware!—
> "*Cenci.* Of thee?
> Nay this is idle:—We should know each other.
> As to my character for what men call *crime*,
> Seeing I please my senses as I list,
> And vindicate that right with force of guile,
> It is a public matter, and I care not
> If I discuss it with you."—*The Cenci.*

THE young earl and Lady Sybil were loth to part, for they had met but recently; and after a long and painful separation —painful by its danger and uncertainty—and full of them-selves and their plans for the future, the hours stole swiftly past them. Thus the earl delayed so long in accompanying his impatient sister, that the dusk had almost set in before they left the house, on their promised visit to her friend at St. Katherine's, where Jane proposed remaining until the noon of the next day.

The night was cloudy, and the streets were dark and misty, so that two men, who emerged half tipsy from the *Cross and Gillstoup*, following them softly and warily, and at the gate of Redhall's house were joined by five others, were quite unobserved.

The earl was still disguised and liveried as Vipont's valet. He wore a cuirass below his doublet, and carried the conspicuous long rapier over his shoulder. Jane was muffled in a close hood, so as to be completely unknown to the few persons who were abroad in the dusk; and thus with security she accompanied him, and leant upon his arm. Two servants of their own name, from the earl's barony in Forfarshire, marched before them with lighted links. Both these men were tall, athletic and well armed, with jacks and caps of iron, swords, daggers and hacques, or small handguns, about three-quarters of a yard long. In those dangerous times every trifling visit and affair had quite the aspect of a conspiracy.

The brother and sister were chatting merrily, and each was speaking of the person whose image and interest lay nearest their hearts: thus Jane spoke of Roland, his courage and sincerity, his truth and hope; and of King James's ingratitude in neglecting to reward his valour and loyal service.

The earl spoke of his dark-eyed Sybil, and how he would one day place his father's coronet on her brow; and would do so on the morrow, if she would but fly with him to England, where they might wed without that dispensation which was yet required in Catholic Scotland, as they were both within the prohibited degrees—a dispensation which the cardinal's hostility, he feared, would withhold for ever, for Beaton was legate of Paul III., north of the English frontier.

Rendered wary by necessity, and from the nature of the times instinctively cautious, the earl looked back more than once to observe whether they were followed. The streets were almost deserted, and echoed to no other footsteps than their own. They descended the Canongate, which was then more open and less regular as a street than now; and passing down a narrow loan between hedges, having a barnyard on one side and a large " Berne-Kilne and Kobill " (the appurtenances of an ancient distillery) on the other, they found themselves on the solitary horseway which skirted the city on

the south, and led straight from the Cowgate Porte to the
Palace and St. Anne's Yard.

On one side the craigs heaved up their tremendous front;
on the other rose a lofty ridge, at the north end of which
stood a chapel of St. John, at the south end a chapel dedicated to St. Leonard, the Hermit of Orleans, and midway
between, the sharp ridgy roof of a large convent—St. Mary's
of Placentia—cut the sky. About its walls grew a number
of willows, planted by the fair recluses, in the spirit of that
beautiful old tradition which tells that our Saviour had been
scourged by willow rods, for which offence the trees had
drooped or wept in sorrow ever after. And there the migra-
ting crossbills built their nests—a bird, said by another old
legend to have taken its name from the circumstance of
having striven with its little bill to draw forth the nails from
the feet and hands of the dead Christ.

A faint and pale light in the east brought the ridge and
its triple edifices forward in strong outline, and the gigantic
willows were seen waving their graceful branches mournfully
in the rising wind. The darkness of utter obscurity veiled
the front of the craigs, and the deep hollow at their base,
then a rough and savage gorge, round the edge of which lay
the road the earl and his sister were to pursue.

A bell rang.

"Oh, Archibald, let us hasten," said Lady Jane; "the
nuns are already saying the compline at St. Mary's yonder;
see how the chapel is lighted up!"

"Faith! my good sister, I have dwelt so long under English Henry's roof, that I have well-nigh forgotten these small
items of our ancient faith. I have seen church lands turned
into fair lay baronies, and more than one stately priory become
an earl's fief, its chapel a dining-hall, its cloisters a stable-
yard, its refectory a dog's kennel. But omit not to ask the
fair Josina * to say one prayer for me, though I *am* such a
reprobate pagan. By all the furies! it seems very droll to
think that my little friend Josina hath become a prioress! I
cannot realize it! She will have quite forgotten me."

"Do not think so, for she still uses the missal you gave
her before——"

"My kinswoman Sybil came home from the convent at

* Josina Henrison was prioress of the Dominicans, at the Siennes, near
Edinburgh, in the time of James V.

Northberwick," said the earl, quickly.   " Poor Josina!—and I shall see her once more."

" To-morrow at noon, when you and Roland come for me —and yet perhaps it were better not."

" Thou art right, sister of mine.   Poor Josina! and, with a sigh that told its own little story, the earl paused.

" A religious life certainly never seemed to be her vocation ; and yet I pray God that she is happy.   How now ?" he added, on hearing his followers wind up the wheels of their hacques by the spanners (as they were named) which were attached to the locks by small chains ; " what dost thou hear, Gilzean ?"

" Footsteps, my lord."

" The echoes of our own, perhaps ; but where ?"

" Behind ; to be forewarned is to be forearmed."

Lady Jane clung to her brother's arm, and drew her hood closer over her face.   They were now in a most lonely part of the road.   Above them, about a hundred and fifty yards up the hill, towered the convent of St. Mary, with its high black walls and waving willows ; below them, on the left, the lights of Holyrood were twinkling like wildfire, in the hollow afar off, at the foot of the Craigs.   The clouds were flying in masses from west to east, and the tremulous stars looked forth at intervals like red and fiery eyes.

" Turn, my lord!" cried Gilzean, " for armed men are close behind us."

" Armed ?"

" Like oursels.   'Odslife!   I heard the clink of iron-graith !"

" Let us halt, then.   Look to your arms, and extinguish the links ; for, if friends, we may proceed together ; if foes, we must drive them back.   But Jane, in God's name, girl, do not cling to me thus—release my sword-arm ;—tush, lassie, dost forget thou art half Seton, half Douglas ?"

Over his left shoulder the earl unsheathed the long weapon, with which Roland, partly in frolic, had accoutred him ; his two followers wound up their wheel-locks, stood by his side, and peered into the gloom behind.   They counted seven dark shadows approaching in the starlight.

" I see steel bonnets and Jedwood staves," said the earl.

" And I, drawn whingers and bent pistolettes.   Their lunts are alow," replied Gilzean, meaning that their matches were lighted.   " Three to seven !"

"'Tush! Gilzean, my good man and true, what matters that? I will spit the odd four, like so many mavises, on this long rapier."

"Stand and surrender, or you are three dead men!" cried one, through the obscurity.

"Zounds!" said the earl, clenching his sword; "surely I know that voice."

"And I, too," added Jane, trembling excessively.

"'Tis either the Laird of Redhall, or auld Hornie himsel'!" muttered Gilzean Seton.

"We are right, then—I am discovered at last! and my lord advocate comes like a common messenger, the vilest of villains, to arrest me."

"Do you yield, sirs?" asked the same person, who was now within ten yards of them.

"Not to the assassins of Sir Thomas M'Clelland of Bombie!" replied the earl, his heart animated by ferocious joy, while his sister's whole form vibrated with terror. "Keep aside, close to the fauld-dyke, my good sister, and leave us freely to deal with these rascals; the first onset is everything!"

Ashkirk led his sister close to the turf wall of the field which bordered the roadway, and cried to his followers— "Fire! and fire low!"

Gilzean and his comrade levelled their hacques, the wheels revolved like lightning, producing fire by the friction of the pyrites; the combined report of these two handguns resounded at once, and one man fell on the roadway with a wild cry that sank into a hollow groan.

The red flashes of three pistolettes replied; with a thousand reverberations, their echoes died away among the cliffs, and the bullets whistled harmlessly past the ears of the earl and his vassals. With the *cri de guerre* of his family,

"Ashkirk and SET ON,"

the gallant noble and his two devoted followers fell bravely on their six adversaries, with whom a close and furious contest ensued.

The earl singled out the leader, and on engaging him, found that he had three others to deal with at the same time, and was thus compelled to act merely on the defensive, a perilous predicament with so unwieldy a weapon. He swayed it with both hands, according to the best rules then in use for handling those ponderous wall-swords, and bent low his head (which was protected by a tempered cabosset of proof), seeking to discover the faces of his adversaries, but all seemed blackness. They were *masked*. Red sparks flew in showers from their swords, and the sudden emission of more than one cry of pain acquainted the earl that the few thrusts which he ventured to give had proved successful.

"Lord earl, yield up your weapon!" cried the clear, full voice of Redhall. Jane, as she cowered by the wall, recognized it, and uttered a low cry of terror. "Yield!—yield!"

"To thee?" said Ashkirk, with a scornful laugh. "May eternal execration lie upon me if I do!"

"Traitor, thou shalt rue this dearly!" replied the other, wrathfully; "charge me your pistolettes again," he said to his followers, "and make service surely!"

Ashkirk replied by a tremendous back-handed blow, that would infallibly have cut the speaker in two; but he sprang back nimbly, and, by the fury of his stroke, the earl overstruck himself so far, that, before he could recover his guard, six vigorous hands were upon him, as many weapons gleamed darkly at his throat, and then, for the first time, he discovered that both his faithful followers were slain. Rising to his full height, and towering above his capturers, he endeavoured to throw them from him; but his vast strength failed; for, fearing to let him free, eager to avenge the wounds he had inflicted, and more passionately eager to serve their lord, whom (lawless and savage as they were) they loved better than life, and animated, no doubt, by the bribes which had purchased their secresy and services, the followers of Redhall hung upon the hands and throat of the furious earl like bloodhounds.

In a moment he was hurled to the earth, and pinioned hand and tongue, for Nichol Birrel tore off his steel cap and forced over his head one of those iron gags called in Scotland a pair of branks. Shaped not unlike a royal crown, this ignominious fetter was composed of four cross hoops, which enclosed the head by springing from an iron ring that encircled the neck, and was furnished with a steel plate for entering the mouth, and forcibly holding down the tongue. With his strong and regular teeth set firm as a vice, the unfortunate noble resisted long this last and deadly insult, but, unhappily, Sanders Screw, the torturer of the High

Court, was among his adversaries. Being well practised in
his profession, this daring ruffian thrust his thumbs behind
the ears of the earl, and thus brutally compelled him to open
his mouth. The gag was immediately forced in, and was held
there by a padlock at the back of his neck.

The moment this was accomplished, four men raised him
by the legs and arms, and bore him off towards the town;
their wounded comrade followed, while the sixth remained
with Redhall.

"Assist me to sweep away these carrion," said he, pointing
to the bodies that lay on the road, with the blood yet oozing
from their wounds; "in that field the corn is high, and they
will feed the crows as well there as hanging on the gibbet at
St. Giles's Grange."

The bodies of the two Setons were raised upon the fauld-
dyke, but the heart of Redhall was too fiercely excited to feel
even a shudder as he and Dobbie flung them far among the
ripening grain, where they lay concealed, until found reduced
to skeletons by the terrified reapers in the harvest of that
year, as an old diary of the period informs us.

"Now, away, for we have not a moment to lose, and this
traitor lord and dame must bide with me! Quick—quick!
for I hear shouts and footsteps!"

Lady Jane, who had clung for support to the turf-wall of
the road during this furious conflict, which just terrified her
(but only in the same degree that a fisticuff battle might
scare a lady of the present day, who is all unused to see the
flash of steel), uttered shriek after shriek when her brother
was beaten down, and she saw no less than six armed men
struggling above him. Believing that they were busy with
their poniards, she rushed wildly forward to interpose, to save
or to die with him; when suddenly she was seized by one
who sheathed his sword, and threw his arms around her.

"My brother! oh, my brother! Who are you that have
dared to do this, and who that dare to grasp me thus?
Cowards—cowards! I am the Lady Jane Seton! Oh,
misery! misery! My brother! my brother! Oh, thou who
wert so good, so kind, so brave—my mother—oh, my mother
—and they have slain him!"

She uttered a shrill cry, and covered her face with her
hands on seeing him borne away; she muttered to herself
faintly and incoherently; for though she did not swoon, she

was perfectly passive, for horror and grief had prostrated all her faculties, and she hung heavily in the arms of the tall masked man, who was no other than Sir Adam Otterburn.

The fury which had animated him during the conflict now passed away as he pressed her to his breast, where a glow of another kind began to kindle. Though he deemed there was contamination in the ruffian's touch, he was glad to crave the assistance of Dobbie, as he bore her away towards the town; but they had barely reached the southern or back gate of the Redhall Lodging (as his mansion was named), when the steps of men were heard rapidly approaching from the direction of the palace. Sunk deeply in the strong and fortified wall, which bounded the Canongate on the south and was overshadowed by a group of venerable chesnuts, this gate was very much concealed and secluded.

It was barely closed upon the whole party, when three men passed with drawn swords.

They were Sir Roland Vipont and his two friends, the captain and lieutenant of the King's Foot Guard.

CHAPTER XVIII.

THE CASTLE OF INCHKEITH.

" *Prometheus.* The tyrant is but young in power, and deems
His palace inaccessible to sorrow,
But bear him this defiance: I have seen
Two hated despots hurled from the same throne,
And in him I shall soon behold a third,
Flung thence to an irreparable ruin.
" *Mercury.* It was thy proud rebellion brought thee here,
Else thou hadst from calamity been free."

HALF-AN-HOUR after the earl and Lady Jane had set out for the convent of St. Katherine, old Father St. Bernard departed; and, after failing to convince the countess that her belief in omens and predictions was altogether at variance with the principles of their faith (arguments which she always silenced by reminding him, that he was one of those who had seen the spectre which appeared to James IV. in St. Katherine's aisle at Linlithgow), he departed to his dwelling among the houses of the prebendaries at St. Giles's, and bestowed his solemn and usual benediction—" Pax Domini sit semper vobiscum"—on Janet Seton, the sister of Gilzean, and all the kneeling household, as he departed.

The dark-haired Sybil, the fair Marion Logan, and the stately figure of Alison Hume, were all bent over a large embroidery frame, where they pretended to be working (for the old-fashioned industry of the countess kept all busy about her), but in reality they were conversing intently on the late ball at the palace, and all their white necks and glossy ringlets shone in the light of the candelabrum, as they were grouped like the three Graces together. Reclined in an easy chair, with her feet on a tabourette, and her face so buried in her vast coif, that her nose (which was somewhat prominent) alone was visible, the countess was spelling over the pages of " The joyeuse Historie of the great Conqueror and excellent Prince, King Arthur, sometyme King of the noble Realm of England, with the Chivalry of the Round Table."

It was one of those old black-letter emanations from William Caxton's press, which the abbot of Westminster erected for him, at the Almonry, in the parish of St. Margaret, London. Her husband, Earl John, found it when storming the English castle of Etal, and had given it to his confessor, as a book of magic; for to the unlettered warrior of the fifteenth century its strange black characters seemed the very work of hell, and he had never touched the volume, save with his gauntlets on.

However, Father St. Bernard had taught the countess that it was merely the romance of an old Welsh monk, and, deeply immersed therein, she had just reached the account of that dreadful battle fought by Arthur against Nero and King Lot of Orkney, who was so foully deceived by the wicked enchanter Merlin, and drawn into that strife around the castle Terrible, where Sir Kaye the seneschal and Sir Hervis de Revel performed such deeds as none ever achieved but knights of the Round Table; and where twelve valiant kings were slain, and buried in Stephen's church at Camelot. The countess, we say, had just reached this interesting point, and believing it all implicitly, was crossing herself at the contemplation of such a slaughter, when her favourite tabby, which was seated on the table, with its prodigious whiskers bristling, and its sleepy eyes winking at the wax candles, sneezed violently, which made her cross herself again three several times.

A dog howled mournfully in the yard.

The countess laid aside her book, took off her barnacles, and began to think.

"All the dogs in Linlithgow howled on the day James IV. was killed at Flodden!"

The good old lady was seriously discomposed, and she was just feeling for an Agnus Dei, which Father St. Bernard had given her to keep away the nightmare, when Janet her tire-woman, and Sabrino the page, with his poniard unsheathed, rushed into the room. The former looked pale as death, and was almost breathless; the visage of the latter was a ghastly blue; his eyes were glaring with alarm; he held one finger on his lips, and pointed downwards with another to the stair-case, where now a sudden uproar of voices mingling with the clash of swords was heard.

"Oh! madam! madam! my puir dear lady! it's a' a' owre—it's a' owre noo! They are coming! they are coming!" cried Janet, with a most prolonged "Oh!" of grief.

"Then my four omens this day have not been for nocht!" said the countess, rising up to the full extent of her great stature; while the three young ladies rushed to her side like startled doves; "but speak, ye foolish woman, speak! Who are coming?"

"They are coming to arrest you, and we are a' lost! lost! lost! Oh, the hands of dule and death are spread this nicht owre the Setons o' Ashkirk." And seizing the hands of her mistress, the woman kissed them, and then throwing herself on her knees, buried her face in her scarlet curtsey, rocking her body to and fro, and exclaiming with that noisy grief so common to her class, "Oh Archibald—my nursling—my son, and mair than my son (for thou art *the* head of the name)—thy curly pow will sune be on the Netherbow, wi' the gleds and the corbies croaking owre it!"

The countess trembled and grew pale; but drawing herself proudly up (and her height was as towering as her aspect was majestic), she said calmly,

"Let them come! I have seen my father hewn down before my eyes, and I have heard the clang of steel upon my hearth ere now. Let them come—they are welcome; but more welcome would they be," she added, with an almost savage flash in her eyes, "if I were among my father's race in Douglasdale!"

While she spoke, the heavy arras concealing the doorway

was raised, and a number of sturdy legs cased in red stockings, shoes garnished with enormous red rosettes, and the butt-ends of partisans, became visible. Then the Albany herald, a dark and stately man, about forty years of age, clad in his gorgeous tabard, carrying his plumed cap in one hand and a paper in the other, entered the room, bowing almost to the ribbons at his knees. The Bute pursuivant who accompanied him held back the arras, and revealed four halberdiers of the provost clad in the city livery, blue gaberdines laced upon the seams with yellow, and ten men of the cardinal's guard, wearing the colours of Bethune and the arms of the archbishopric of St. Andrew's worked upon the sleeves and breasts of their doublets. They were armed with steel caps, swords, and partisans, but remained respectfully without the apartment. One was bleeding profusely from a wound on the cheek, having had a tough encounter with the armed servants below.

" Herald," said the countess haughtily, " if you seek the earl, my son, I swear to you that he is not here !"

The herald hesitated.

" By the forty blessed altars of St. Giles, I swear to you that he is not !"

" Madam, I do not seek the earl," said the herald, with the utmost respect ; " but I have here an order from his eminence the cardinal as lord chancellor, and in the name of the king, for your arrest."

" Mine !" rejoined the countess, thanking God in her inmost heart that it was not her unwary son they sought ; " for my arrest ! on what charge, herald !"

" Treason : the resetting of rebels, and——" he paused.

" What more wouldst thou dare to say ?"

" Suspicion of sorcery, or teaching thy daughter sorcery."

" Sorcery ?" reiterated the countess, gazing at him with terrified eyes, and speaking almost with the voice of a dying person ; while the three girls, who clung to her robe, uttered a cry of alarm. " Daredst thou have said so much to my father, Sir Archibald Douglas, of Kilspindie ?"

" I would have said so to any man under God, whom the king commanded me to arrest."

" But to a helpless woman ?"

" I am in the king's service, madam."

" Thou art a Hamilton !" said the countess, scornfully.

"I *am*, madam," replied the herald, proudly; "I am John Hamilton, of Darnagaber—a gentleman of the house of Arran."

"I thought as much," said the countess, curtsying scornfully again to conceal how her knees bent under her; "the gentlemen of that house are thick as locusts now."

"Do not look on me thus, madam," said the herald, with dignity; "I am a gentleman of coat-armour, and brook my lands as my forbears won them, by captainrie and the sword."

"Allace!" said the countess, as she obtained a glimpse of the armed men; "what new dishonour is this? why am I arrested by the cardinal's guards, who are but mere kirk vassals?"

"Sir John Forrester and the lieutenant of the king's guard, could not be found: besides, madam, they are the assured friends of the master of the ordnance, who——"

"And thou, John Hamilton of Darnagaber, art thou not ashamed to execute these orders?" said the bold and beautiful Sybil, fixing her keen black eyes, with an expression of unutterable scorn, on the calm face of the herald.

"Noble damsel," he answered, quietly, "I have said that I am in the king's service, and obey but the constituted authorities of the land; yet I do so, deploring from my soul this cruel and sad necessity."

"Sorcery!" said the countess, speaking to herself; "by my father's bones! Sorcery—oh! my God!—sorcery! Woe worth the deviser of this scheme—for a scheme it is, which the swords of Ashkirk and Angus shall unravel." She added, tying on her hood and cloak of sables with trembling hands, "Alison Hume, do thou look to my jewels and other valuables; they lie in that strong cabinet; but, Sir Herald, what of these three noble ladies, my guests and kinswomen; they——"

"Are not included in the warrant."

"Then they shall remain with my daughter here."

"Your daughter, lady," said the herald, confusedly; "nay, they must be sent to their families under safe escort: my own sons, who serve in the king's guard, shall convey them with all honour to their homes. Be easy on that score, madam."

"But thou, my doo—Sybil?"

"I," sobbed Sybil, "oh, dear madam, I go with you."

"To ward?"

"To death, madam—my second mother! for such, indeed, you have been."

"My puir bairn, thou hast nowhere else to go; for thy father is in exile, and Hamilton of Dalserf holds his castle and barony of Kilspindie."

"Lady Ashkirk, where is your daughter, the Lady Jane?" said the herald, unwilling to say that his cruel warrant included her also.

"She is at the convent of Sienna, where, I pray you, to let her hear these heavy tidings gently." The herald bowed with increasing gravity. "But whither go we now—to the castle, of course?"

"Nay, madam, to the tower of Inchkeith."

"A sure place, and a strong too! The high rocks and the deep waves were not required surely to fence in a feeble auld body like mine. Be it so—I am ready! Oh, for a score of those good men and true, that my husband led to the battle of Linlithgow! Where now are all the gallant and the generous hearts of other days?"

"God hath taken them to himself, madam," replied the herald, whose eyes moistened.

"Your pardon, sir; I knew not that I spoke aloud."

"Lady Ashkirk, your husband spared my life on that unfortunate field. When the Master of Glencairn, with a thousand Douglas lances, forded the Avon, and cut the column of Bardowie to pieces, I had there been slain but for your husband's valour. I owe his memory a debt of gratitude —trust to my kindness. Horses are in waiting to convey you to Leith; and I have orders to see that your household property is every way respected. All lights and fires are to be extinguished—all bolts and bars made fast, and I place my seal upon the doorway."

"God be with thee, Alison, and thee, my bonnie Marion. Fare-ye-well, my bairns; and thou, too, Janet, my leal servitor—"

"This woman may attend your ladyship."

"Sir, I thank you," said the countess, but Janet could only weep, and she did so with great vociferation.

The herald took the hand of the countess respectfully; she leaned on the arm of Sybil, the sable page raised her long train, the guards fell back to salute her as she passed, and, amid the sound of lamentation above, below, and around her, she descended the long stone staircase of her mansion, a prisoner.

Situated three miles from Leith, in the middle of the Firth of Forth, the ancient tower of Inchkeith (which was demolished in 1567) occupied the summit of that beautiful isle, on a rock one hundred and eighty feet above the water. It was of vast strength and great antiquity, for it was the *Caer Guidi* of the venerable Bede. Well defended by cannon and a barbican wall, which bore the royal arms of Scotland, it was deemed a place of such importance that the Queen Regent, Mary of Guise, and the French ambassador, John de Montluc, the learned bishop of Valence, paid it a visit twelve years after the date of this our history. Inaccessible on all sides, save one, this island is fertile on its summit, and is watered by many springs that flow from its rocks, which are literally swarming with grey rabbits and fierce Norwegian rats.

The night was dark, but guided by a beacon of turf and tar-barrels that blazed on the summit of the tower to direct them (for the cardinal and lord advocate had provided for everything), eight mariners of the admiral Sir Robert Barton's ship pulled sturdily across the broad river towards Inchkeith. Few stars were visible, and a chill wind from the German Sea blew coldly across the broad bosom of the open estuary.

The island, with the light gleaming like a red star on its summit, loomed darkly afar off in the distance, and seemed to rise in height at every stroke of the oars. The countess was seated in the stern beside the anxious Albany herald, whose dread of a rescue made him lose no time in executing the orders of the lord advocate.

The seamen bent to their oars in sullen silence, and under their fur caps and shaggy eyebrows gave hostile glances from time to time at the countess, for the whisper of sorcery was, in those days of superstition, more than enough to steel every heart against her. Full of her own sad and bitter thoughts, she was unaware of this, and sat proudly and erect, with the cold wind blowing on her fine but pallid features. Within the last two hours she seemed to have grown much older. Her nose had become pinched, her cheeks haggard, but her unmoistened eyes were full of fire; for indignation and studied revenge

> " Had locked the source of softer woe ;
> And burning pride, and high disdain,
> Forbade the rising tear to flow."

The graceful head of Sybil reclined on her shoulder; she wept bitterly; and the countess, who thought of her absent daughter with more fear and sorrow than for her son, whose daring character she knew well, pressed the orphan heiress of Kilspindie to her breast.

She knew not the depth or the daring of Redhall's plot; that her daughter was included in the same warrant, and that with him alone lay the power of opening or closing for ever the door of the prisons which were now to enclose them.

Two torches, which were borne by two of the Cardinal Guard (for this prelate had found a band of pikemen necessary for his protection against the assassins constantly employed by Henry VIII. for his destruction), cast a lurid glare upon the boat's crew and the seething water, as they streamed in the night wind; on the steel caps and glancing weapons of the soldiers, the wiry beards and swarthy visages of the seamen; on the herald's splendid tabard; on the black, shining visage of Sabrino, and on the reddened waves of the Forth, which became crested with foam as they neared the rocks of the isle, where they were seen dashing like snow over the jagged reefs of the Long Craig.

The torchlight, the moaning breeze, the lonely water, and the dark and gloomy sky, all combined to give a wild and picturesque aspect to the whole scene; which must infallibly have impressed the countess, and still more so the romantic Sybil, had they been less occupied with their own thoughts. Yet one could not repress a shudder, or the other a faint cry, when at times the frail boat plunged down into the trough of the dark waves, or rose on their summits, with the broad blades of the weather-oars flourishing in the air.

The jarring of the boat against the rude rocks of the creek on the south-west, the only landing-place, roused the countess from her reverie, and she shuddered still more to see, frowning stupendously above her, the strong square tower of the Inch, perched on the very verge of " the Climpers," as the fishermen name those basaltic cliffs, against which the waves are ever rolling in one eternal sheet of foam.

The sheer rocks of the creek are perpendicular as a wall, and are fully sixty feet high, while those of the tower are exactly thrice that height. In this narrow fissure the troops of the queen-mother landed in 1549, to drive out the English and Germans who had lodged themselves there; when Monsieur de Biron had half his helmet driven into his head by the shot of one arquebuse; Monsieur Desbois, his standard-bearer. was slain by another, while the Cavaliere Gaspare Strozzi, captain of the Italians, and many more, fell before the English were cut to pieces.

" Oh, my winsome bairn—my daughter Jeanie—when again shall I ever behold thee ?" exclaimed the poor old countess, as she stretched her trembling hands in the direction of the city, which being then buried in the gloom and obscurity of midnight, was totally invisible. " When shall I behold again thee ? But, till *then*, may that blessed Virgin whose wondrous sanctity our Lord hath honoured with sae many miracles, keep a watch over thee !"

"Assuredly, there is no witchcraft here !" thought the Albany herald.

Rolled up in a warm cloak of couleur-du-roi, Sir James Hamilton, of Barnclough, captain of the tower, was ready at the landing-place with a few soldiers and torchbearers to receive them. Attended by these and the herald, Lady Ashkirk, leaning on the arms of Sybil and Janet, with the taciturn Sabrino following, ascended the zigzag path which leads into the beautiful and verdant little valley that lies in the centre of the island, and is sheltered from the cold wind by basaltic cliffs on the east and west.

Above them rose the dark outline of the tower, with the large red balefire sputtering on its summit to direct the homeward-bound ships of Leith.

CHAPTER XIX.

THE FORTUNATE SWORD-THRUST.

"Adew Edinburgh! that heich triumphant toun,
    Within quhose bounds richt blytheful I have been ɟ
Of trew merchants, the rout of this regioun,
    Most ready to ressave court, king, and queen.
Thy policie and justice may be seen.
    Were devotioun, wysedom, and honestie,
    With credence tint, they micht be found in thee."
                    LINDESAY OF THE MOUNT.

IN total and happy ignorance of the events of the past night. Roland awoke next morning. The dawn was struggling through an atmosphere of mist and fog. Though roused by

K

the tramp of feet and the lumbering roll of artillery wheels,
he would fain have slept a little longer, for the palace clock
was only striking four; but he sprang out of bed with the
resolution of a soldier, and found old Lintstock all accoutred
in his sleeved habergeon, with gourgerin, salade, sword, dagger, and priming-horn, ready to dress and arm him, a process
which use and wont made wonderfully short, when we consider that Roland was to be encased in a complete suit of plate
armour.   It was elaborately gilded and engraved with legends
of the Scottish saints, for such was the superstition of the
age, that such devices were deemed a protection greater even
than a coat of tempered mail.   His helmet was surmounted
by the crest of the Viponts, a swan's head rising from a ducal
coronet, all of frosted silver, and above it floated his plume.
A belt of perfumed and embroidered leather sustained his
sword and dagger, and in his hand he carried a gilt baton as
captain or master of the ordnance.   For breakfast, a slice of
beef and a pot of wine from the relics of the supper sufficed
both him and Lintstock, who said—

"Now that old bundle of roguery, who keeps the *Cross
and Gillstoup*, will be ready to curse himsel' wi' bell, book,
and candle, when he finds we're awa'; and he may whistle on
the wind for payment."

"Till I return, say, I pray you."

"Of course; we'll pick up some braw things by way o'
contribution.   The king's soldiers, gentlemen of the sword,
maun live, and live wi' honour."

"Is the earl here?"

"The earl!"

"Of course; he is going with us."

"To look for himself?"

"Surely—an excellent joke; I meant to take him, where in
reality none expect to find him; for I tell thee, Lintstock, this
march westward is all a trick of mine enemies at court, to banish
me from the king's presence and this good town of Edinburgh,
when they know I would give my ears to remain in it."

"Aha!" said Lintstock, giving under his helmet a shrewd
Scots wink with his solitary eye; "I can see into a millstone
as far as my neighbours; but, certes! I saw na this."

Roland yawned below his visor as he faced the cold breeze
that swept from the sea round Arthur's Seat, and gave a
casual glance at the hundred soldiers of the guard whom his

friend Leslie was arraying with their arquebuses, rests, and bandoliers; and another at his sixteen gunners, who were all stout men in steel bonnets and jacks, armed with swords and glove of plate, and who were tracing the horses, and preparing two very handsome French culverins for the march. These were two of those fifty-six beautiful pieces of brass cannon, presented by Francis I. to his daughter Magdalene on her becoming queen of Scotland, and which were long after known in the arsenal by his cipher, which was engraved on them.

Like all men of the old school (for they have existed in every age, and every age has had "a good old time" to regret), Lintstock was scrutizing these cannon narrowly with his one eye, and commenting from time to time in sorrow and with anger on the various innovations they exhibited, and the multitude of ornamental rings which encircled the first and second reinforce, the chase and muzzle of each; and he could not repress a groan at the trunnions with which they were supported on the carriages, and the curved dolphins, which served for mounting and dismounting them. Thrawn-mouthed Mow, which had knocked out his left eye by her splinters, had been blessedly free (as he remembered) of all such useful ornaments, and lay on her stock like one log lying on another.

"By my holy dame! but this dings Dunse!" said the old fellow, shaking his battered morion; "this world will no do now for an auld body like me; and the suner I march to my lang hame the better. Gude-sake! what have they made o' the aim frontlets?"

"Sic auld-fashioned things are no needed, ye grumbling carle," said a young cannonier; "especially when the trunnions are so placed, and the quoins are so low."

"Ye are but a bairn; trunnions! we levelled six-and-twenty pieces on Flodden field, and devil a trunnion was among them a'. We were but ten thousand that day, and the Lord Surrey had six-and-twenty thousand under his banner: but say nae mair o' Flodden, for I feel as if this corslet would burst when I think o't."

Roland paid no attention to the old soldier's complaints; he was intently observing a man who was muffled in a sad-coloured mantle, and leaned against the wall of James the Fifth's Tower, watching the preparations for the departure of this little band. The hour was so early that no other person was visible about the palace, save the arquebusiers on duty in the archways.

"Yonder is either Redhall, or his friend with the horns," thought Roland. "Now, what errand can bring my lord advocate abroad at this early hour? Ah, rascal! more than probable it is to thee I owe this untimeous march, without bidding once adieu to her who loves me so well."

Being somewhat curious to know wherefore this man, whom he knew to be his enemy, was lounging there, Roland walked slowly and deliberately towards him.

A fatality attended Redhall this morning.

Lady Jane and the earl, her brother, were both now safe in his house—a strong edifice, which, if properly garrisoned, might have stood a siege of all their faction; and there we shall, ere long, pay them a visit. The earl he valued at a thousand merks; but his sister he prized more than all the wealth of the Indies. Restless and anxious, this arch-conspirator could not feel sure of his capture, while so enterprising a pair of comrades as Vipont and Leslie were in Edinburgh; and burning with impatience to see them fairly depart (on an expedition from which he was resolved they should never return), he had never undressed or been in bed, and had now come to observe if they marched, before the tidings of the countess's arrest, and the disappearance of her daughter, spread throughout the city.

In those stirring times, the most daring outrages were esteemed but casual occurrences, and were thought little more of than a shower of rain. A day never passed in which a dozen of castles were not stormed, or petty conflicts fought, in various parts of the country; and the good folks of Edinburgh were so much accustomed to the clash of swords, and seeing men run each other through the body for no better reason than because their worthy fathers had done the same before them, that the din of steel on the Hiegait was deemed scarcely worth raising one's window for. Ten thousand clansmen might fight a battle now and then in the wilds of Ross or Argyle, and might even burn Iuverness by way of variety; and two months after, the news thereof would reach Holyrood. The energy and ability of James V and the cardinal established the Courts of Session and Justiciary for the repression of such outrages; but these tribunals did not prevent the lord high treasurer from carrying off an heiress, a ward of the crown, and marrying her, *bongré malgré*, to his son; while the next generation saw without surprise the lord high chancellor murdering the secretary of state under the very eyes of royalty; consequently, the reader must not imagine that it was any qualm of fear or conscience either that disturbed Redhall, and banished sleep from his eyes. No; restless exultation alone kept him awake. The time to visit his fair captive had not yet come; the first paroxysm of her grief and anger had to pass; and then to cool his excitement and see his rival fairly *en route* for Douglasdale, he had walked forth with the first peep of dawn.

Who that saw his grave and thoughtful face, and knew his stern and lofty character, would have imagined that amid the sea of vast political matters in which he and the cardinal were immersed, and amid the busy whirl of their tumultuous public duties, gentle love had found a passage to his iron heart? An infernal joy had now kindled a new glow within it; and there was a wild gleam in his eyes, and a feverish flush on his cheek, as Roland Vipont approached him.

Sir Adam Otterburn, of Redhall, says an old historian, was one of the handsomest men of his time; but, notwithstanding that he knew this well, the aspect of Vipont in his armour, blending the perfect ease of the cavalier with the loftiness of a true soldier, kindled in his bosom a glow of jealousy, not unmixed with envy, and anger that he had been discovered in his lurking-place.

Turning haughtily, he was about to walk slowly away towards the great doorway of the abbey church, when the voice of Roland arrested him with more hauteur than policy.

"Ho! Sir Adam! you are abroad betimes this morning."

Redhall turned and bowed with a cold smile in his eyes, the ferocious expression of which he vainly endeavoured to conceal.

"I crave pardon for interrupting your lordship's morning reveries or orisons," said Roland, with somewhat of mischief in his eye; "but, 'odzounds! you must know that I permit no man to pass or avoid me without a pretty weighty reason; and your lordship has just so served me."

"'S life, sir! dost thou think that I will give any reasons to one who queries me in such a tone?"

"I did not *thou* thee," replied Roland, with rising wrath.

"Nor did I seek thee," rejoined Redhall; and then they paused a moment, and gazed at each other with eyes of hatred: the soldier with the expression of a lion, the lawyer with that of a serpent. In his secret soul each nourished a storm of vengeance that longed to break forth; but Redhall's was almost subdued by his giddy exultation, and the reflection that Jane Seton was now, legally and illegally, so doubly in his power. "Nor did I seek thee," he continued, "and had I on mine armour, this insolence of first addressing me had assuredly been chastised."

"Mansworn dog!" exclaimed Roland, trembling with passion; "thou who cloakest thy cowardice under the wing of this new-fangled court," he added, seizing Redhall by his short-peaked beard, and almost rending it from his chin, "am I thine inferior, that *thou* shouldst acknowledge me first?"

Redhall's bonnet fell off; his dark eyes gleamed with rage; his moustaches seemed to bristle, and his black hair waved about his face like the mane of a Scottish bull. He could only utter a cry of fury, as he unsheathed his sword, regardless of the place, and that he was totally without armour; while Roland was in full mail for active service.

"Come on," he cried, hoarsely, for rage had deprived him almost of speech; "come on—thou—thou—on your guard! quick! quick! or I am through you!" Roland hesitated.

"It were a coward's deed to slay thee," he replied, unsheathing his long Italian sword in self-defence, and feeling its point with the leather palm of his gauntlet; "though perhaps it is owing to thee, and such as thee alone, that my sword now wins more blows than bonnet-pieces in the king's service."

Redhall rushed to the assault, and both their swords became engaged from point to hilt; but Roland acted strictly on the defensive. He knew that to slay Redhall would be both dangerous and dishonourable; while, if the reverse happened, Redhall would gain immortal honour at court, and run no secondary risk. Vipont was a poor soldier of fortune, who lived by knight-service and the sword; while Redhall was a powerful baron, allied to many warlike nobles, and a high officer of state.

Roland parried one *counter-en-carte* so close to his throat that it would certainly have slain him where the gorget met the cuirass; and then, finding that he had to do with no ordinary swordsman, he endeavoured to twist his own rapier in his adversary's, and lock-in ; but Redhall met his blade in time; it glided along his own like lightning, and then they both retired a step.

In the palace yard the trumpet sounded for the march ; as Roland became impatient his anger rose, and he replied to four terrible thrusts by one which pierced the shoulder-blade of his adversary, and hurled him to the earth, breaking his sword like a crystal wand as he fell.

In the sequel it will be seen how fortunate this thrust was for Jane Seton.

" Now, hold thee, Vipont !" cried Leslie, through his barred helmet, as he ran up at that moment, " by all the powers, thou hast slain the king's advocate !"

" Be easy," said Roland, smiling, as he carefully sheathed his sword; " dost think the devil dies so readily ?"

" 'S death ! art thou not mad, to be fencing here like a French sword-player when our trumpets are sounding ?" said Leslie, as he assisted Redhall to rise. " You are not wounded, my lord, I hope ?"

" 'Tis only a stab like a button-hole—pshaw ! I will make a sure account of it," said Redhall, wrapping his cloak about him, and striking the hilt of his sword into the top of the empty sheath.

" A good day to thee, thou hypocrite and assassin in black taffeta," said Roland, leaping on his caparisoned horse, which Lintstock led up at that moment.

" Farewell, thou ruffian and cut-throat in plate and cloth-of-gold," replied Redhall, in the same tone of fierce irony.

" I will remember thy politeness, Sir Adam."

" I will not forget thine, Sir Roland ;—adieu."

And thus they separated, with bent brows, and eyes and hearts full of fire and hatred.

CHAPTER XX.

THE BLACK PAGE.

" Ha ! there was a fatal evidence.
All's over now, indeed !
The morning tide shall sweep his corpse to sea,
And hide all memory of this stern night's work."—SCOTT.

LEANING on the arm of Sybil, and attended by Sir James
Hamilton of Barncleugh, the Albany herald and their followers, we left the countess ascending the little valley which
lies in the centre of Inchkeith. They proceeded in silence,
for the path was somewhat perilous ; the early morning was
yet grey, though the eastern sky and ocean were fast
brightening with the coming day. A cold wind swept over
the bosom of the waters that girdled in the isle. About the
middle of the valley a cleft in the rocks was reached, through
which the pathway passed at direct right angles with that
they had hitherto pursued ; and from thence they continued
to ascend, until they reached the summit of those precipices
which, from the water, seemed to be inaccessible, and where
the iron gate of the barbican stood, with a moss-grown
Scottish lion carved in stone above it.

The light had been rapidly increasing as they ascended,
and now behind bars of golden cloud the broad round morning sun rose red and gloriously from his bed in the German
Ocean ; and then indeed did the beautiful river, that from
Highland hills rolls down on yellow sands, seem one vast tide
of molten gold flowing to the dark blue sea ; and beautifully
in the warm sunshine were that bright blue and brighter gold
mingling afar off in the estuary.

The morning smoke and the humid vapours of the past
night yet veiled the close dense masses of the capital; but
the spire of St. Giles's, and the embattled tower of King David,
the loftiest summit of the castle, whereon the St. Andrew's
cross was waving, were visible above the gauzy mist that
veiled the glens below.

Clad in the brightest hues of summer, on one side lay Fife,
its long expanse of sand studded by busy towns and red-
tiled villages, baronial towers and ancient churches, its bold
promontories jutting into the majestic river, and its beautiful
mountains rising behind. On the other lay the three

Lothians, with all their ripening fields and dark-green woods, the lonely cone of Soltra, the lonelier Lammermuirs, and the undulating sweep of the far-stretching Pentlands, a long blue waving chain of heath-clad mountain, that dwarfed the lesser hills, and threw the wooded cliffs of Corstorphine, the Calton, the castled rock, and even proud Arthur's basaltic brow, into comparative obscurity. So deceiving is distance, that this chain of peaks seemed to start abruptly from the very margin of the river; and Leith, with all its dense old Flemish wynds and closes, its marts and shipping, St. Mary's spire and old St. Anthony's tower, seemed to nestle at their feet.

Westward of the isle lay that armed fleet which had so recently arrived from France, under the pennon of Admiral Sir Robert Barton, brother of that other gallant Admiral Sir Andrew Barton, who, when returning from fighting the Portuguese, with two solitary ships, was waylaid by Lord Howard and the whole English fleet in the Downs, where he was slain by a cannon-ball.

The dawn of day, which had displayed this magnificent panorama to the countess and Lady Sybil, had also revealed the sable visage of Sabrino to Sir James Hamilton of Barncleugh, who had never seen or heard of a black man before; so he preceded the party, in some perturbation, signing the cross as fast as if all St. Anthony's imps were behind him, and marvelling at so hideous a masque.

"Welcome to the tower of Inchkeith, ladies," said he, turning round, and raising his bonnet at the barbican gate.

The countess replied, "Heaven grant I may soon return the welcome in my own house, Sir James."

"Though I *am* a Hamilton?" replied the knight, with a smile.

"Oh, yes; for these dire feuds begin to weary me."

"Ah! old fox," muttered the castellan under his beard; "because thy nose is below the water now. Had we lost, and the Douglases won the battle of Linlithgow," said he, with a smile, "I doubt much if the feud had been tiresome to the Lady Ashkirk."

"She had not been *here* to-day," replied the countess; "but how—what does this mean?" she added, with some asperity, on seeing that two soldiers, in obedience to a sign from Barncleugh, crossed their pikes before Sabrino, to prevent his entering the tower.

"It means, madam, that this black thing, quhilk in visage so closely resembles the promoter of all evil, cannot enter here."

"Sir James of Barncleugh," said the Albany herald, interposing, "he is the countess's page."

"Page! ugh! I like not to look upon him. I would do much for thee, John of Darnagaber, who art mine own natural-born clansman, and more for the widow of gallant Earl John of Ashkirk (a Seton and Douglas man though he was), but, by my holy dame! this black devil, whom I have no order to receive, shall not enter the tower of Inchkeith, that is flat!"

"Sir James Hamilton," said the countess, with dignity, "do be merciful, and spare us the humiliation of entreaty. This poor black boy is faithful and gentle, kind and attached to me as a spaniel, and assuredly he will die if separated from me; for he is, I know, an object of abhorrence to the ignorant and the vulgar."

At this remark, which was unintentional, the commander of the island gave her a furious look, and cocked his bonnet over his right eye.

"Madame," said he, coldly, "you will excuse me; I am but a blunt knight of James III., yet I would never forgive myself if anything evil occurred."

"Kiss the hand of this gentleman, Sabrino," said Sybil, "and he will admit you."

Sabrino was a mute, or nearly so; by some law of his barbarous native land, his tongue had been cut out near the root; thus he could only utter certain terrible and apparently unintelligible sounds, and when doing so opened his wide mouth to its utmost extent, revealing two rows of sharp teeth, and the black remains of his mutilated tongue, which he lolled about within the cavity in a manner which, to say the least of it, was very appalling. The poor terrified black was beginning to mutter his thanks in this extraordinary fashion, and gradually approached the Lord of Barncleugh, when the latter sprang back, with alarm in his eyes, and his hand on his sword.

"Get thee behind me, Satan!" he exclaimed. "Away! I will not be touched by thee. My hand? nay, I will hew it off first. Hence, imp of darkness! for may I never see God, if thou abidest in this castle for a moment, or in this island for an hour!"

To overcome his prejudices, even if the countess had stooped to flatter them, seemed impossible; therefore, she gave the herald her hand to kiss, thanked him for his kind courtesy, entrusted him with messages for her daughter concerning certain necessaries they required, for she doubted not her residence on the isle would be a protracted one; and then begging that he would see the poor black page delivered safely to the care of Sir Roland Vipont, of the captain of the guard, or any other of his friends, she entered the tower with Sybil and Janet, their last solitary attendant.

Then the iron gate was closed and barred until the herald's boat should have withdrawn from the island.

A sign from the countess had been sufficient for Sabrino, and with tears and the utterance of many a strange and unearthly lamentation, he followed the herald and Hamilton of Barncleugh, who, after taking each a quaighful from a little keg of whisky that stood in the warder's lodge, descended to the boat; the disobliging castellan going thither partly from fear, and partly from courtesy, to see his friend and the page off together.

" I like this black creature as little as thee," said the herald; " but I have heard Father St. Bernard, when preaching of St. Frumentius of Ethiopia, tell us of a land, a hundred times the size of broad Scotland, where all the tribes were of this sable hue."

" True—and I have seen such a visage on a banner, ere this."

" Morrison of the Ilk carrieth three," replied the herald; " I saw them beaten down by the Stewarts of Lennox on that day, by Linlithgow brig. But, remember thee, that my lord advocate wished a strict watch to be kept over this creature."

" Then he should have inserted his name in the warrant of committal to ward. 'S life! there is an old draw-well in the barbican, where I could have lodged it very well. Though a dour carle, I know Sir Adam Otterburn to be an upright man, an abhorrer of sorcery; and there is in this Seton family much that smelleth sorely of it. Earl John found a book of the black art once when on an English foray, as I have heard, but Redhall——"

" Ah, he is a very good man," said the herald, ironically; " descended, indeed, from one of the apostles, by the father's side."

" Which ?"

"Judas."

"Beware of thy waggery—he is a severe dispenser of the laws."

"What the devil care I for him, or for the cardinal either if it cometh to that?"

"My friend, my friend!" said Barncleugh, giving a furtive glance behind; "assuredly this black thing hath infected thee, for this discourse savoureth fearfully of the new heresy; but I forget that thou art a near kinsman of Patrick Hamilton, the umquhile abbot of Fearn, and so-called martyr."

"Nay, I remember only that I am speaking to a gentleman, Hamilton, and say what I choose."

"Not always a wise proceeding. But here is the boat, cousin."

The mariners, who had been in no way pleased at having Sabrino as a passenger to the isle, and had been mutually feeding each other's fears and prejudices during the herald's absence, were very much discomposed by his returning with the same sable attendant; and on hearing from the cardinal's pikemen that Sir James Hamilton had declined to admit him within the tower, their murmurs became loud and undisguised.

The herald shook hands with the knight, and attended by his pursuivant, sprang on board; but when Sabrino attempted to follow, the coxswain, a square-visaged and sturdily-built old fellow, with a long grey beard and shaggy eyebrows, snatched up a boat-hook, and attempted to push off the pinnace; then Sabrino, with one hand on the gunnel, and the other on his poniard, gave him a dark and terrible scowl.

"Awa, awa! thou imp of Satan—hands off, or I will ribroast thee!" cried the coxswain, somewhat alarmed at his own temerity.

"Reeve a rope through his siller ear-rings and tow him overboard," cried one sailor.

"Cast off! cast off!" cried another; "I hae heard o' sic imps that abide at Cape Non, and eat of ship-broken mariners."

The coxswain raised the iron-shod boat-hook.

"Hold!" exclaimed the herald, springing forward, but he was too late; it descended like a thunderbolt on the round, woolly head of Sabrino, and he disappeared like a stone in the deep fathomless abyss of the creek. "Dolt!" added the herald, "I have pledged my word of honour for his safety, and thou hast slain him."

" Heed it not, good fellow; I will owe thee a score of bonnet-pieces for that," cried Sir James Hamilton, as he sprang up the steep winding pathway that led towards the tower, while the oars dipt into the water, and the boat shot out upon the river, whose waves were dancing brightly in the glow of a cloudless morning.

Before this, the countess and Sybil, overcome by weariness, the grief of the past night, and a total deprivation of sleep, had fallen into a deep slumber in a chamber of the tower above.

The worthy lady of Barncleugh was somewhat of a termagant, which was generally averred to be the principal reason why the good laird her spouse had solicited from the cardinal, and retained, the solitary castellany of Inchkeith. The lady never came into the island, and the laird never went out of it; but consumed the long and dreary days, revelling in the peaceful monotony he now enjoyed, playing chess with his seneschal, and drinking usquebaugh mixed with a small proportion of the brackish spring-water of the isle. A table was placed near the gate of the tower, at a sunny angle of the barbican, on the very verge of those cliffs named the Climpers; and there, with the sea rolling nearly a hundred and eighty feet below, the seagulls and the Solan geese croaking above them, they passed the summer afternoons, playing chess and drinking, with invincible resolution and impenetrable gravity, till sunset, when the knight was usually borne upstairs and put to bed, the damp air having stiffened his limbs, as he always declared next day—an assertion which the seneschal (who had his own thoughts on the matter) never dared to deny.

It may easily be supposed that such a castellan was in no way calculated to relieve the tedium, soothe the grief and mortification, or lessen the fears, of the countess and Sybil; for days rolled on and became weeks, and weeks were approaching a month; and though the opposite coast and the city, the scene of all their anxieties, were little more than three miles distant, they remained in total and blessed ignorance of all that was passing there.

They seemed to be as utterly forgotten as if they had been in the *oubliettes* of the cardinal.

The countess heard nothing of her daughter, whom she had fully expected to join her; and Sybil learned nothing of her lover; so whether, with the Douglas faction, he was

bearing all before him at sword's point, and waging a victorious though rebellious war with the king and court; or
whether they had returned to exile at the capital of England,
they knew not.   The total absence of all intelligence made
them conclude the latter, and that he had taken Lady Jane
with him to protect her.   Then the countess would weep
bitterly at the thought of such a separation; for England
was then a hostile country; and places that are now but a
day's journey distant were then deemed afar off and difficult
of access.   A chain of royal castles watched the English from
the south, and the cannon of Berwick and Carlisle, Norham
and Newcastle, frowned towards the Scottish mountains on
the north.   Safe conducts and passports were constantly required on both sides of the frontier, the jealous Scot and his
aggressive neighbour seldom saw each other, save under the
peaks of their helmets; and an exchange of cannon-balls and
sword-cuts was the only traffic in which they were permitted
to deal.   Though we can smile at such a state of matters
between the two kingdoms, experience is daily showing that
Scotland will soon require some *firmer guarantee* for her
national privileges than a British parliament can afford her,
against the march of centralization.
    A little rocky island, half a mile in length by the eighth
of a mile in breadth, could afford but few amusements.   Sybil
soon tired of watching the white seagulls and the gigantic
Solan geese that floated about the Longcraig, in the fissures
of which the waves were ever roaring with a sound of
thunder.   She tired too of watching the passing ships, the
Holland wachters, the Flemish crayers, the Rochellers and
Dunkirkers, with their high poops and great square banners:
the large brown lug-sails of the boats which then fished between the island and the town of Kinghorn, and of hearken-
ing to the hum of that song which the fishers of the Forth
yet chant to their oars, the end of each monotonous verse
being—

> " The leal gudeman of Aberdour.
> Sits in Sir Alan Vipont's tower."

    She tired of watching the endless waves as they rolled on
the rocky beach, marking every tenth billow as the largest
and most forcible, a phenomenon known since the days of
Ovid; and Sybil sighed for the city, whose lofty castle and

ridgy outline "piled deep and massy, close and high," she saw daily shining afar off in the summer sun.

More content—for the wants, the wishes, and the hopes of age are generally few—the countess wiled away the time in the perusal of her missal, and searching for the four-leaved clover which she found sometimes in the little valley, and solemnly pulled, saying, after the old Scottish fashion, "In nomine Patris, Filii, et Spiritus Sancti," to be preserved and worn as a charm against the *evil eye*, which she thought was observable in Sir James Hamilton of Barncleugh.

"Sybil, my bairn," she frequently whispered, when the besotted castellan was dosing over his wine and chessboard, "he hath indeed a most evil eye, and whatever he looks upon cannot thrive; so keep all thy blessed relics and consecrated medals about thee. Beware," she would add, smoothing the jet-like ringlets, and kissing the cheek of Sybil, which exhibited that peculiar olive tint of the brave old Douglas race, which is so much richer than the most roseate hue; "beware thee, too, of approaching yonder end of the valley, for I fear me mickle the *gude-wichts* dwell among the rocks;" and in confirmation she pointed to those bright sparry particles which frequently stud basaltic masses, and in Scotland are denominated fairy pennies. "More than once after nightfall, when sitting at my dreary chamber window in yonder tower, I have heard melodious sounds, and seen strange gleams of light emitted from yonder brae. I remember that my worthy father, Sir Archibald (quhom God assoilzie), once showed me a knowe near unto the duletree that grew beneath our Castell o' Kilspindie, the stones whereof were studded with these sparry marks, and therein dwelt the gude-wichts in such numbers as ye will find the sand on the sea-shore. Quiet gude neibours they were, but wrathful and dangerous to molest. It happened in the year 1501, as he rode thereby, in full harness with his visor up, and the red heart fluttering on his pennon behind him—lo! the whole hillock was seemingly raised, and stood on twelve pillars, each about four feet high; and below he saw crowds of wee men and wee women all dressed in grass green, wi' foxglove and blue-bells on their heads. Thousands were dancing to the hum o' fairy harps and drums, while thousands more were airing heaps of gold, and pushing to and fro great chests full of shining coins. Sorely amazed at this sight, his hair bristled up below his helmet, but he bethought him of the patron of our house.

" 'Sancta Brigida, ora pro me!' said he (being all the Latin he had ever picked up from Father St. Bernard), when down sank the hill, its grassy side became dark, for light and sound and fairies vanished; and then the gude knight, my father, thought it no shame on his manhood to gallop swiftly away.   Ah, me! this was in the time of King James IV., of gallant memorie!"

Brighter and sunnier June came on; but such and so close were the measures of the cardinal, and his able second, the king's advocate, that no tidings reached that lonely little isle of the events which were taking place so near it.

CHAPTER XXI.

JOHN OF THE SILVERMILLS.

" I never met with an adept, or saw such a medicine, though I had fervently prayed for it.   Then, I said, 'Surely you are a learned physician?' ' No,' said he, ' I am a brass-founder, and lover of chemistry.' "—BRANDE.

THE king was seated in one of the apartments of that stately tower of Holyrood, that still bears his name, which until recently was visible on the front thereof, carved and gilt in gothic letters,—

Jac . Rex . V . Scotorum.

One window opened towards the abbey hill, an eminence then covered with apple-trees and other wood in full foliage; a path ran round its base, and another crossed its summit. The first led to the castle of Restalrig and St. Margaret's gifted well: the second was the ancient Easter-road to Leith. It was then, and for long after, destitute of houses; Gordon, in his View of Edinburgh, taken in 1647, represents only eight small dwellings on this now populous eminence and the Croft-an-Righ that lay between it and the walls of the abbey church.

The other window afforded a view of the Calton with its rocks of basalt, then bare, desolate, and unfrequented, with the eagle hovering over their summits, as if to show that his prey, the ptarmigan, the red grouse, and the black cock, were not far off.

The sun was setting, and its warm light fell aslant upon the waving orchards of Holyrood; the square towers and magnificent doorway of its church, and the green coppice on which the king was gazing listlessly, with one hand resting on the neck of his favourite old hound Bash, and the other thrust among the thick curls of his auburn hair, as a support to his head. The passers were few. A mendicant friar, with his begging-box and staff, came slowly over the hill; a knight, armed nearly cap-à-pié for travelling, spurred from the Watergate, and his armour was seen flashing in the sunbeams, among the foliage as he rode towards Restalrig. The king was lost in reverie, and sat with his eyes fixed on the sparrows that twittered on the massive gratings of the large window.

The illness of that fair young bride whom he loved so passionately pressed heavy on his heart; the more painfully so, that from its perplexing and apparently mysterious nature, it seemed utterly beyond the reach of alleviation. She laboured under a rapid consumption, of the nature of which Francis I. had repeatedly warned James V; but young, ardent, and impetuous, her royal lover would listen to nothing save the dictates of his passion; and slighting the love of Mary of Lorraine (his future wife), he had wedded Magdalene. Now, despite all the skill of his physicians, and the care of her own attendants, the young queen, within twenty days after her landing in Scotland, was almost hovering on the brink of the tomb.

As day by day she sank more and more, the Countess of Arran declared that the fairies were extracting all her strength; others averred solemnly and gravely, that she was under the influence of witchcraft: for it was an age fraught with the wildest superstition. An illness such as hers, when the secret source of decay was unseen and unknown to the quack physicians and astrologers who surrounded her couch, made their restless credulity readily adopt the idea of mystic agency.

The time was full of fanciful terrors; the dispensations of God were invariably attributed to magic invocations and demoniac maledictions; to invisible shafts from the elves and fairies who peopled every rock, hill, and tree, the only antidotes to which were the prescriptions and the countercharms of impostors and self-deluded dabblers in the occult sciences. Dreams, in those days, the result doubtless of ponderous suppers and morbid constitutions, were received as visions of the future, as solemn forewarnings and divine inspirations from God—fraught sometimes with happiness, but more frequently with death and terror, war and woe.

Thus the poor young queen, whose orient eyes while they sank never lost their lustre, and whose cheek while it grew hollow still retained its rosy and transparently beautiful hue, continued to waste and grow thinner; and the king with agony saw daily how her snowy arms and infantile hands were wearing less and less, until the bones became fearfully visible at last.

He sighed, he prayed, and he wept; but still the blasting, the wasting, the terrible attenuation went on. Her skin was white as marble, but ever hot and feverish; and though a gentle smile played ever on her lips, there was a wild, sad earnestness in her large blue eyes, in the quiet depths of which two orient stars—the stars of death—were ever shining. Everything that love could prompt and quackery advise, had been done; she was bathed repeatedly in the waters of streams that ran towards the sun; and in those of blessed and sanctified wells, which the saints had consecrated of old—but unavailingly.

Barefooted, with bowed head, and candle in hand, the king had visited many a holy shrine; but still Magdalene became worse; and it was evident to all that the hand of death would soon be upon her—unless, as many added, the *spell* was broken.

Suddenly the arras (which was of green damask flowered with gold) was shaken. The king started. It was raised, and there entered a man, whom a few words will describe.

"Well, most worthy deacon and doctor." said James, springing eagerly towards him; "what thinkest thou of the queen?"

The new comer mournfully shook his head and stroked his beard.

The young king clasped his hands, and, pushing a chair towards the physician, sank into his own.

John of the Silvermills was an old man with keen grey eyes that twinkled under bushy brows; a long hooked nose; a vast white beard that flowed over his sad-coloured cassock-coat. He wore a black velvet skull-cap, on the front of which were embroidered a cross and a triangle within a circle—being the emblems of Religion, the Trinity, and Eternity. His form was bent by age; his back was almost deformed, and one of his tremulous but active hands clutched a long silver-headed cane; the other, a small sand-glass, which supplied the place of a watch with the physicians of that age.

Patronized by King James IV., who had been an eminent dabbler in alchemy, he was the first deacon of the Barber Chirurgeons of Scotland, whom that monarch had incorporated by royal charter in the year 1505; when every guild brother was obliged to pay five pounds to the altar of St. Mungo of Glasgow, and prove his knowledge of "anatomie, the nature and complexioun of everie member of the human bodie; and in lykwayis, all the vaynis of the samyn, that he may mak flewbothamea in dew tyme; and alsua that he may know in quhilk member the *Signe* has domination for the tyme;" for then astronomy, astrology, and alchemy formed the principal part of a medical education; and King James IV spent vast sums on the wild experiments of the learned John, at his laboratory, from which a district of our capital then obtained and still retains the name of *Silvermills*.

"Ah, my God! and thou,—thou hast no good tidings for me, my venerable friend?" said the young king, imploringly, as he seated himself.

"The queen's grace is assuredly in great dolour and sore pain," replied the physician, resting his chin on the top of his cane, and fixing his keen eyes on the anxious and beautiful face of the young monarch; "she complains of an aching head, of a burning heart, and of a constant weariness and lassitude which overwhelm her. There is something in all this which perplexes me, and it seemeth——"

"Beyond thy skill, in short? But oh, say not that!"

"Nay, nay," continued the mediciner, who spoke slowly, while his keen visage shook on the staff where he had perched it; "but I must give it long and deep thought. I am assured —at least I hope—there is in my pharmacopœia some simple that will restore her. That learned apothegar and worshipful clerk (though I agree with him in few things), Galen, the physician of Pergamus, possessed a manuscript which enumerated fifty thousand families of the vegetable world, with all their restorative or destructive qualities. Oh, for one glimpse of that glorious volume! In all things following strictly the rules laid down by the learned Artesius (who lived a thousand years by that very elixir, the secret of which is, at this time, enabling Paracelsus to work so many miraculous cures), in the year 1509, I compounded my *nepenthe*, a drug which driveth away all manner of pain, and my *opobalsamum*, which was powerful, even as the blessed Balm of Gilead; to the queen's grace I have administered them both for the past week, and yet, miraculous to relate, she daily groweth worse."

"My wife! my heart!" said the king, again wringing his hands; "must I see my poor dear little Magdalene perish thus? I love her too much, and perhaps God is about to take her from me. Oh! canst thou do nothing for her?"

"I was at the University of Basil in 1525, storing my mind with fresh knowledge, when Paracelsus, by the recommendation of Œcolampadius, was called to fill the chair of physic and surgery, and was present on that day when he so presumptuously burned the works of Avicenna and Galen, assuring us that the latchets of his shoes knew more of physic than both these learned doctors; and that all the universities and all the writers of the earth, past and present, knew less than the smallest hair of his beard; for he had in his brain the mighty secret which would prolong life for ever—yea, even unto the verge of eternity—the secret of Artesius."

"This was the very madness of learning and vanity," said the king. "Well?"

"Erasmus believed in him, and was cured of a grievous illness by one drop of the principal ingredient."

"What, Desiderius Erasmus, of Rotterdam, the tutor of my brother Alexander, who fell at Flodden? Well, well—and this——"

"Ingredient was a simple used of old by a king of Egypt, and it is now written in hieroglyphics on the southern side of the great pyramid."

"And those hieroglyphics?"

"None can read save sorcerers; for Paracelsus on that day, at Basil, destroyed, with the works of Avicenna, the sole existing key thereto, and which was written on a blank leaf thereof."

"May the devil confound thee, Paracelsus, and the great pyramid to boot! I fear me much, thy musty magic will never cure the queen."

"I pardon your majesty's anger, for it hath its source in grief," replied John of the Silvermills, calmly; "nature is full of mysteries. Our cradle and our coffin may be formed from the same tree, and yet we be ignorant thereof. Paracelsus——"

"I say again, Mahound take Paracelsus! but what doth this trite remark mean?"

"That, like the mass of the unlettered world, your majesty scoffs at what appears incomprehensible, and——"

The apothegar paused, for the arras was raised by a hand covered by a glove of fine scarlet leather, and Cardinal Beaton, who at all hours had the *entrée* of the king's apartments, stood before them, and both king and subject knelt to kiss his ring.

"The peace of the Lord be with thee and with thy spirit!" said the cardinal, seating himself, and looking kindly at the king, whose grief and distress were marked in every feature of his fine face. "In the ante-chamber I have heard how poorly her majesty is, and Mademoiselle Brissac has just been imploring my prayers, poor child! But proceed, my learned doctor," he added, with a slight smile; while the deacon of the surgeons again perched his chin on the top of his cane, which was half hidden by his long white beard, and thus continued—

"Your majesty rails at the learned Paracelsus; I can afford to pardon that, when I remember me that to him we are indebted for introducing to the pharmacopœia, the mercurial, the antimonial, and ferruginous preparations which act so beneficially upon the organs of our system."

"But is not this Paracelsus, of whom thou boastest, an impure pantheist," asked the cardinal, "who, while believing in the existence of pure spirits which are without souls, receives aliment from minerals and fluids, and whose physiological theories are a wild mass of the most incoherent ideas, founded almost solely upon an application of the damnable mysteries of the cabala to the natural functions of the frame which God has given us?"

"I do not quite understand your eminence," replied John of the Silvermills, turning, with as much asperity as he dared, to the cardinal, whose towering figure and magnificent dress were imposing enough, without the memory of that important position held by him; "but I understand, and, with **Para-**

celsus, believe (what certain malevolent commentators have
lenied) that the sun hath an influence upon the heart, as the
moon hath upon the brain; that Jupiter acts upon the liver,
as Saturn doth upon the spleen, Mercury on the lungs, Mars
on the bile, and Venus on the kidneys and certain other
organs. Hence the true apothegar should know the planets
of the microcosm, their meridian, and their zodiac, before he
attempteth to cure a disease. By due attention to them, he
attains the discovery of the most hidden secrets of nature;
for our human bodies are but a conglomeration of sulphur, of
mercury, and of immaterial salt, which rendereth them peculiarly liable to planetary influences; and as each of these three
elements may admit of another, we may, without knowing it,
possess within us water that is *dry*, and fire that is *cold*."

" A subtle sophist," said the cardinal, with a smile.

The king listened in silence, and, full of Paracelsus, the
doctor continued—

" Thus, please your eminence, by identifying himself with
the celestial intelligences, hath this wondrous physician so
nearly attained a knowledge of the philosopher's stone, and,
by curing all diseases, raised to his fame a monument based
on the four quarters of the earth. And doubtless if he pro-
longeth his own life, as he doth that of others, in time to
come he will attain the secret of that *other* powerful ELIXIR,
by which Adam and the patriarchs prolonged their lives before the Deluge—yea, even unto nine centuries."

" Gramercy me!" said the cardinal; " and beware thee,
John! this man whom thou upholdest glories in the fame of
his sorcery, and openly boasts of receiving from Galen letters
that are dated *from Hell*, and also of his recent disputes held
with Avicenna at the gate of that dread abode—disputes on
the transmutation of metals, the elixir of the patriarchs, and
the quintessence of the Mithridate; for I heard of all these
things when I was studying the canon law at Paris. He
blasphemously takes as his primary supports the writings of
the holy fathers; and while asserting that the blessed Gospels
lead to all manner of truth, dares to add, that magical medicine can be learned by the study of the Apocalypse alone."

" Enough of this, lord cardinal," said the king, impatiently
observing that the doctor was angrily adjusting his velvet
cap preparatory to returning to the charge; " enough of this
jargon, amid which my poor Magdalene will probably die."

" It may be so, though God avert it ; for the disease is all but beyond my skill ; and I dread to state my suspicions, now that both my *nepenthe* and *opobalsamum* have failed."

" Thy suspicions ?" reiterated the cardinal.

" I know them already," said the king, gloomily. " Like the Countess of Arran, thou wouldest say that she is under a spell ?"

" Which nothing but a counter-spell can break."

" Mother of God !" said the king, " I cannot believe in such things ! Lord cardinal, dost thou ?"

" And what manner of charm, deacon ?" asked the cardinal, affecting not to hear the king ; for he did not scoff at sorcery, though he did at Paracelsus.

" A *muild*, as our peasants call it. She may have trod upon a muild, which is a powder of potent effect, prepared from the bones of the dead, and scattered by sorcerers in the path of their enemies. We all know that, at the Sabaoth of the witches, sepulchres are violated, corpses are dismembered, and the limy particles of the bones pulverised to operate as mischiefs upon mankind. At this time the queen hath all the symptoms of one who hath trod upon an enchanted muild, or dieth of pricked images—for they are the same. A swarfing of the heart, a fluttering of the breast. When the patients will merely sicken they turn red—when they will die, they turn pale."

" And the queen is pale ?" said the cardinal.

" Yea, even as death."

" The cure—the cure ?" sighed the king.

" There are two : the first is, to find a certain reptile, forming one of the six species of salamanders which are indigenous in southern Europe, in the head whereof is a red stone, to be taken as a powder. For it is written by Paracelsus——"

" Paracelsus again !" said James, stamping his foot ; " the second cure ?"

" Is to burn the sorcerer."

" Then Sir Adam Otterburn must sift this matter to its bottom."

" Ah, that reminds me," said the doctor, rising up, and clutching his sand-glass ; " I must now retire, with your majesty's leave."

" To visit Sir Adam ? I knew not that he ailed."

"A sword-thrust."

"From whom?"

"Sir Roland Vipont."

"Vipont again!" said James V., knitting his brows; "thus it is my friends are ever slaying each other. But he, my most valiant and true friend, has been quite besotted by those Setons of Ashkirk."

"He knew not of their arrest," said the cardinal; "it was a sudden rencontre—a quarrel."

"Oh, in that case, I have nothing to do with such little amusements. The Countess of Ashkirk?"

"Is in Barncleugh's ward at Inchkeith."

"Where I will keep her as long as James I. kept Euphemia of Ross on Inchcolin. An old intriguing limmer! And the Lady Jane?"

"Hath escaped to—no one knows where."

"Poor damsel! I feel some compunction for her, and fear that she hath been sorely misled by that deep old Douglas her mother. And then the earl?"

"Hath vanished too."

"To England?"

"Most probably."

"But is Redhall's wound severe!" asked James.

The cardinal turned to the doctor.

"A fair run through the body, at the shoulder," said the physician. "'Twas well for him that Mercury, which influences the lungs, was not in Abdevinam, or the lord advocate's gown had been vacant."

"Vipont goeth from bad to worse," said the king, as the cardinal turned away to conceal his laughter. "Kincavil run through the body one day, my lord advocate the next. We must restrain his vivacity. In this spirit, Vipont will achieve little in Douglasdale; but let him bear in mind the vow I made when Sir David Falconer, the captain of my guard, was slain when covering the retreat of the artillery from Tantallan!"

"I hope your majesty will remember as well your gracious promise anent the charter, exempting our learned corporation from watching and warding, and all manner of military service within the city, save in time of siege."

"Does your eminence hear?" said James, with a smile, to the cardinal.

" It is just passing the seals," replied the chancellor ; " and I will send the Lord Lindesay with it to-morrow—so, meantime, farewell."

The cardinal, who had more sense than a thousand such as Paracelsus or John of the Silvermills, wisely recommended the king to remove his suffering bride to Balmerino (in Fifeshire), a Cistercian abbey, founded by the queen of William the Lion, Ermengarde de Beaumont, whose grave lay there, before the high altar. In this magnificent old pile, which was dedicated to St. Mary, apartments were prepared for the sickly Magdalene. In a rich and pastoral district, it occupied a beautiful situation, among fruitful orchards and the remains of an old primeval forest, sheltered on one side by verdant hills, and fanned on the other by the cool breeze from the bright blue basin of the Tay.

On a sunny morning in June, under a salute of cannon from the castle, amid which the vast report of Old Mons or rather Monce Meg of Galloway was conspicuous, the young queen, with her anxious husband riding by her litter, and attended by a select number of courtiers (forming, however, a long cavalcade of horse), was conveyed from Holyrood to Leith, where Sir Robert Barton's ship received and landed her two hours after, on the yellow sands of Fife. From thence they crossed the deep and fertile glen called the Howe, and, descending the Scurr Hill, approached Balmerino.

With many deep sighs and portentous shakes of the head, all indicative of what no one could divine, John of the Silvermills had to abandon his smoke-begrimed laboratory near the water of Leith, and accompany the court ; carrying his books of Paracelsus, Galen, and Avicenna, and the anatomical works of Hippocrates, Herophilus, and of the great modern, Vesalius (the exposer of the errors of Galen), with all his retorts, crucibles, chafing-dishes, horoscopes, and other scientific rubbish, packed on sumpter-horses, by which much irreparable damage was sustained by certain glass phials and bottles that contained—the Lord alone knew what ; but one was said to be the famous powder of *projection*, which when thrown upon heated mercury or lead, turned them into silver or gold, and the loss whereof made the patient John rend his long beard, and passionately bequeath himself to the devil a hundred times.

" If Magdalene groweth well here," said the king to the

cardinal, as they dismounted at the gate of the monastery,
"to your eminence alone will Scotland and I be indebted for
her recovery; but if she becometh worse, and our suspicions
are confirmed, then woe to the *authors* of her illness—woe!"

CHAPTER XXII.

TEN RED GRAINS.

"Yes! in an hour like this, 'twere vain to hide
The heart so long and so severely tried:
Still to thy name that heart hath fondly thrilled,
But sterner duties called and were fulfilled."
                                    MRS. HEMANS.

PRIOR to his departure for Balmerino, and immediately on
his leaving the palace, the learned apothegar visited the king's
advocate.

The town house of Sir Adam Otterburn, the Redhall
Lodging, as it was named and as we have before stated,
stood upon the south side of the Canongate, and near to the
eastern end thereof.

At the present day the south side of this venerable street,
the memories of which go back to the days of St. David I.,
and the glories of Earl Randolph and Ramsay of Dalhousie,
is still somewhat straggling, irregular, and open; in 1537 it was
much more so. The houses were then detached, surrounded
by gardens, and even parks; for there were several barn-
yards in the Canongate, some of which were destroyed by
cannonading during the siege of 1573.

The severe plagues of 1514 and 1520, which followed the
slaughter of Flodden, swept away many of the citizens, whose
houses were demolished to remove all chance of lingering in-
fection; thus the mansion of Redhall was remarkably solitary.
A ruined and desolate barn-yard lay to the westward; and a
grass park, shaded by many beautiful sycamores, extended on
the east nearly to the foot of the alley known as the Horse-
wynd.

It was a strong square five-storied house, with walls of
enormous thickness; its crow-stepped gable and one vast
chimney studded with oyster-shells faced the street; at each
corner was a square corbelled turret, from the tops of which,

in wet weather, two stone spouts disgorged the rain-water
without mercy on the passengers. To the street, the windows
were few, small, and, according to the Scottish custom, secured
with rusty iron gratings. The first and second stories were
vaulted with solid stone, and stone slabs covered the roof.
Externally the edifice was destitute of ornament; but, strong
as rock, it would have withstood a salvo of cannon-balls;
and was one of the most perfect specimens of the old Scottish
house existing, before the introduction of the more florid
French style. Studded with iron, the small door was deeply
recessed in the wall, and protected by four loopholes, splayed
without and within, to admit of a wide range for arrows or
arquebuses; while it was further secured by a tranverse beam
of oak, which superseded all necessity for locks or bolts.

A fortnight had now elapsed since the night on which the
earl and his sister had been carried off; yet in all that
time Redhall had been totally incapable of prosecuting his
schemes either of love or vengeance; for that *fortunate* sword-
thrust which he had received from the hand of Vipont, together with the fever produced by his own furious and boiling
passions, had bound him down to a sick bed, from which,
however, by the care or quackery of the learned John of
Silvermills, he was now fast recovering.

Pale, careworn, and feverish in aspect, a day in the beginning of June saw him again seated at his writing-table,
immersed in his masses of correspondence, his mysterious
portfolios, which were full of strange memorandums in ciphers
and Latin contractions, which none could read. save himself
and the cardinal. His trusty rascal, Birrel, who was always
at hand, and ready for everything, from cleaning his master's
boots to cleaving his enemies' heads with a Jethart staff, was
in attendance as usual, when our acquaintance of the preceding
chapter was announced, and Birrel, starting from Sir Adam's
chair, where he had been in close confab, drew back the arras.

"God save you, Sir Adam Otterburn," said the learned
John, stroking his long beard according to his invariable
custom; "how—again at thy pen, despite mine earnest in-
junction?"

"Business of the State—fiend take it! I must attend now,
for a mountain of matter hath accumulated here."

"Ah," said the physician, setting down his sand-glass and
fixing his keen eyes thereon, while his bony fingers were

applied to the pulse of Redhall's left hand—"Ah! thy pulse is very irregular—thy nerves are burning. Now, nothing affects the nerves so much as intense thought, and by thine eyes I see thou hast been thinking intensely. By this, the vital motions are hurt, the functions disordered, the whole frame unhinged. Thou must continue to take my potion night and morning."

"What! more of thy diabolical drench?"

"How, Sir Adam! Dost thou so defame my prescription, which I have compounded from the identical recipe left by that worshipful clerk, John of Gaddesden, the worthy author of the 'Rosa Anglica,' the possessor of that valuable necklace which when drawn tight cured all manner of fits."

"Ah, my friend, Sanders Screw hath another which doth the very same."

"Indeed! thou amazest me," said the physician, resting his bearded chin on his staff. "John of Gaddesden's collar was an anodyne necklace, and had the word *abracadabra* written thereon."

"But the collar of Carle Sanders is only a stout cord," said the advocate, with a sardonic grin.

"I blush, Sir Adam, that thou shouldst name this vile worm in the same breath with John of Gaddesden," said the physician, indignantly, as he arose and grasped his sand-glass; "a man whose virtues shone bright as the rays of Acarnan—the star of Eridanus. Ah! he was a fortunate man, that John of Gaddesden; he was born when Astroarch, queen of the planets, was shining in all her glory in Abdevinam—the head of the twelfth mansion; while I, unhappy! was born, as I have discovered by the aid of my new astrolabe, on a night of storms."

"Thou hast brought back my poniard, I hope?"

"It is here," replied the visitor, taking a dagger from his belt; "the *contents* of this cause death within two hours after they are taken."

"Two hours?"

"He who imbibes them," he continued, in a low voice, "falleth down senseless, lifeless, and dies without a groan—suddenly as if shot with a hand-gun. Sir Michael Scott had this secret of a learned clerk at Salamanca, whither he rode in one night, and ere daybreak was again at his castle of Balwearie."

"There is a powder, too—zounds! I had well nigh forgot it: 'the sleeping powder.'"

"'Tis here," replied the physician, taking a packet from the pocket that hung at his girdle; "this was first prepared for a caliph of the East, by Geber, the learned Arabian astrologer, who flourished in the eighth century, and whose three works on chemistry were published at Strasbourg seventeen years ago, that is, in 1520."

"Hand it hither: thou weariest me; for, by St. Grisel! all thy messes seem to be compounded by devils and philosophers."

"Thou still appliest my *Unguentum Armarium?*"

"Regularly," replied the advocate, resuming impatiently the writing at which he had been interrupted.

"And thy wound?"

"Is almost closed, thank God!"

"Good—good," muttered the physician to himself; "I knew well that my ointment, compounded of the ashes of that written charm, brayed with those of the dried Zusalzef of the Arabians, would cure the deadliest wound; 'tis a potent fruit, for it ripens in the sun, and the sun acts upon the heart, the source of life."

"I would fain see some of this wonderful fruit."

"I have one in my pouch—behold!"

"'S life! 'tis but a common prune!"

"The *prune* of the unlettered is the *Zusalzef* of Geber and Paracelsus; but farewell, Sir Adam, I go; and omit not to continue the potion and the *Unguentum Armarium.*"

"Devil go with thee for a plague," muttered the advocate, as he seemingly bowed with courtesy, and became again immersed in his writing.

Nichol Birrel again approached.

"And this was all thou hadst to tell me?" said Redhall; "that no tidings had arrived from Douglasdale; and that, in short, neither Vipont nor young Balquhan had come to blows with any of the Douglas faction."

"Exactly sae, my lord."

"And that they spent their time in hunting and hawking, with free inquartering for horse and man, wherever it pleased them to halt."

"Just sae," replied Birrel, with an obsequious nod.

"Thou knowest the lands of my kinsman, Fleming of the Cairntable, whose bounds they are approaching?"

"Yes, my lord."

"Then take a good horse, and ride for your life and death; and take with thee these three-hundred groats of the fleur-de-lys to pay thy way. Tell my kinsman Fleming, that I wish this viper, this Vipont I mean, should take up his last abode in Douglasdale."

"In the kirkyard thereof?"

"Yes, yes; set them by the ears if thou canst; I will see Fleming skaithless, even though he resists the royal banner; but either by fair means or foul, keep Vipont from returning here. Dost thou see this poniard which the apothegar hath just left? observe me, and observe narrowly."

He unscrewed the pommel, and showed Birrel that the steel knob, which was hollow, contained several large red grains.

"Each of these grains," said he, carefully rescrewing it, "is a human life; there are *ten*, and Sir Roland Vipont hath but one life; take it in thy belt to Douglasdale, for they may prove useful if the blade fails. One word ere thou goest: how is the Lady Seton this morning?"

"Composed and quiet, as weel she may be, after the girning and graning of a fortnight."

"Tib, thy niece, Tib Trotter, from Redhall, still attends her with care, and Dobbie keeps watch?"

"Like a deerhound, my lord; and I forewarned Tib that the lady she was to attend was a puir demented and brain-braised creature, that would tell her a' kind o' queer stories about you, Sir Adam—stories o' whilk, on peril of her life, she was to tak nae heed; and I said that death would be as nothing to her doom, if the daft lady (whom I call a kins-woman of your ain, frae the north countrie) fled; and as puir Tib is mair frightened for you than for the devil himself, she scarcely sleeps for fear that her charge escapes."

"And Dobbie?"

"Considers her a State prisoner awaiting a private precognition."

"Good—I will ere long requit this trust, and amply too; meantime, away thou for Douglasdale: remember all my instructions; and now give me thy thumb on them, that thou wilt be for ever my firm man and true."

"Sir Adam! Sir Adam!" said the pricker, presenting his thumb reproachfully, "surely this was na' needed frae me."

But the cautious baron ratified their despicable compact by that mysterious pressure of thumbs, without which no bargain in Scotland, either for good or for evil, was ever held binding.*

During this conversation, Redhall had never ceased writing with the utmost rapidity, that he might lose no time ; but the moment Birrel retired to prepare for his embassy, he closed his portfolio, and stepped into the little dressing closet which opened off the study or library.

He examined his face with scrupulous accuracy, and a foppishness at which he smiled, as if in contempt of himself. With some concern he observed, that confinement and his wound had rendered his features paler and more haggard than ever. That wound! Every time he thought of it, and of the blood, the pain, and anxiety it had cost him, he ground his teeth vengefully ; but after arranging his long dark hair, and carefully pointing and perfuming his handsome beard and moustaches, he concluded there were many worse looking men in the city. Although his nether man was cased in sad-coloured hosen, he put on a full-skirted doublet of blue velvet, with loose hanging sleeves and a broad rolling collar of ermine ; he wore diamond-studded ruffs at his wrists, a vest with sleeves of cloth-of-gold, and the collar of his shirt, which was pinched and embroidered with red silk and gold thread, was spread over the ermine. His sword was sheathed in crimson velvet, his poniard sparkled with jewels, and he was perfumed to excess, for it was the fashion of age.

Tall and stately, pale and dark, his aspect was alike magnificent and impressive ; as thus deliberately prepared with a foppery of which he could not have believed himself capable, he took his way for the first time toward the chamber of his fair prisoner.

He felt that his step was feeble as he walked ; the room swam around him ; and ever and anon an admonitory twinge shot through his wounded shoulder.

* See Note.

CHAPTER XXIII.

THE FIRST VISIT.

" Ah ! false and cruel fortune ! foul despite !
   While others triumph, I am drowned in woe.
And can it be that I such treasure slight ?
   And can I then my weary life forego ?
No ! let me die ; 'twere happiness above
   A longer life, if I must cease to love."—*Orlando Furioso.*

SUNK in an abyss of deep and gloomy thoughts, Jane Seton
sat at a window of the apartment which had been allotted to
her, until Sir Adam Otterburn could have her removed to his
house of Redhall, a strong square tower, situated on an eminence near the village of Hailes, a few miles south-west of
Edinburgh.

This he intended to have done the moment he was able to
ride ; and nothing but his wound—" that accursed wound,"
as he called it—prevented the removal of the lady and her
brother, on the very day succeeding their capture, to this
lonely fortlet, which stood among thick woodlands above the
Leith, and just where a modern mansion occupies the site of
that more ancient Redhall which the soldiers of General Monk
besieged and destroyed.

A stupid but good-natured country girl from his barony—
one who stood in dread of Sir Adam, regarding him as a
demi-god and superior being, rather than a mere man and
master—attended Jane ; and, considering her a poor deranged
lady, had been most provokingly sympathetic, and inaccessible
to bribes, to threats, and entreaties ; while Dobbie, like a
watchful bull-dog, sat always in a niche near the door, with a
small barrel of ale to solace him, and a pack of cards, with
which he practised tricks and sleight-of-hand against himself.

The walls were of enormous thickness, and the small windows were massively barred ; the apartment was hung with
rich cream-coloured arras, studded with gorgeous red flowers ;
the cornices, the chairs, the panelling of the doors and
shutters were all profusely gilded ; a gittern, an embroidery
frame, a few black-letter books of poetry and romance, and a
few vellum illuminations of Scripture, with various other
things which might serve to wile away a lady's time, were
scattered on the buffets and window-seats ; while several boxes

of the most splendid jewels which the art of Master Mossman could produce, stood most alluringly on the table, with their lids open, but all unnoticed.

The window at which Jane sat faced the south, but the line of venerable chesnut-trees obstructed the view of the Craigs and of St. Leonard's Hill. A grass park, some hundred yards in length, extended to the wall, which these trees overhung, together with a mass of ivy and wild roses. Ruined and deserted houses lay on the right and left; and thus, for four-teen days, had the poor girl sat at that window, without an hour's cessation, watching for a passenger to whom she might cry for succour; but though the chamber was lofty, the height of the surrounding wall, the thickness of the trees, and the loneliness of the path which passed under them, had prevented her from seeing a single person (though several passed that way daily), save the girl who attended her, and occasional glimpses of the indefatigable Dobbie, on guard outside; nei-ther of whom could afford, even to her most piteous entreaties, a single word concerning the fate of her brother; why she was thus confined; or what had become of Sir Roland Vipont, for whose silence and inertness she could in no way account, unless that he was in a State prison for the wound which she understood he had given Redhall, whose consequent illness had agreeably accounted to her for *his* absence.

On the table lay fourteen notes, being those he had sent every morning, containing compliments, condolences, and entreaties to be forgiven for that rash act, to which the excess of his love, and the feverish dread of losing her, his hopes that she might yet learn to esteem him, and so forth, had driven him; but of these laborious epistles not one had been read, and the fourteen lay on the table unopened.

These fourteen days had soothed the first burst of her grief and anger; intense weariness and bitter impatience had suc-ceeded: yet she could not but acknowledge that in all, save the loss of liberty, she was treated with the utmost delicacy, attention, and respect.

It was evening now—the evening of the fourteenth weary day, as she was reckoning, for the thousandth time, on her fingers; the sun was setting on the flinty brows of Salisbury; and the leaves of the trees, as they fluttered in the wind, seemed formed alternately of green and gold. A mass of verdure overhung the walls which surrounded the tall old

M

mansion, the cold dewy shadow of which fell far to the south and eastward. Haggard in aspect, wearied with weeping, and though the month was June, benumbed and cold by want of rest, Jane, who for these fourteen days and nights had never dared to undress, or to avail herself of the luxurious couch provided for her, and who had never dared to sleep, save by snatches in an arm-chair, now turned with a wild, startled, and almost fierce expression of inquiry to Sir Adam Otterburn, as he entered; for never was there a face more admirably calculated to express the two very opposite aspects of mildness and disdain than hers.

" Proud, relentless, and pitiless woman !" thought this bold abductor, as he approached, " at last I have thee completely in my power—at my mercy, utterly !"

Lady Jane had risen full of anger and defiance, but there was an expression in the eyes of her admirer that terrified her; and feeling completely (as he had thought) at his mercy, she could only cling to her chair, and falter out—

" Oh, my God ! Sir Adam Otterburn, what is the meaning of all this ?—why am I imprisoned here ?—and what seek you from me ?"

" Pardon," said he, in his gentlest voice, and with clasped hand, bending his eyes on the ground—" pardon for this wrong, which the excess of love alone has committed."

" And why hast thou dared to do me this wrong ?"

" I dare do anything, fair Jane, but excite your displeasure. For heaven's sake be composed. Oh, spare me your hatred, and look not so wildly. Think of the depth and of the ardour of my sentiments—the sincerity of my intentions towards you. Long, long have I borne this fatal love in my heart, as a secret—a secret to brood over, since those days when you so thoughtlessly permitted me to nourish it." Jane would have spoken, but he continued, sadly and energetically: " Amid the splendid pageants, the costly banquets, the stately mummeries of a court, and the dull tedium of public business, it has ever been in my heart, in my soul, and on my lips— this secret, which I would have given the world to muse over in some noiseless solitude, where nothing would dispel the bright illusions love raised within me. Ever among the crowds of the city, and the debates of the parliament, it came to me—a soft, low whisper of your name. I heard it only ; and the voices of those around me became as a drowsy hum, and sounded as if afar off, for my whole soul was with thee. Oh, Lady Jane, this secret has been a part of my very being. Night after night I have prayed for you, and have laid my head on its pillow without consolation ; day after day I have blessed you, on awaking to a world that was without hope for me, and yet I have lived, and loved, and lingered on. But pardon me—I am grieving you."

He paused on seeing that Jane, overcome either by her feelings or by exhaustion, had again sunk into a chair. Her alarm subsided at the sound of his sad, solemn, and harmonious voice ; and something of pity rose in her bosom, for she saw that he was indeed frightfully pale and careworn.

" My brother," said she ; " and what hast thou dared to do with him ?"

" Nothing, dear madam : he is safe."

" But where ?"

" Below us."

" Below ? Gracious me !" said Jane, breathlessly, as her horror and hatred revived ; for she saw the cruel game about to be played by Redhall. " Wretch ! and to coerce the miserable sister, thou holdest in thy guilty hands the life and death of the brother !"

" Nay, do not think me so base ; warrants are out for the apprehension of the earl as a traitor, and nowhere is he safe save in the secresy of this abode, which, however, both you and he will soon change for the sunnier atmosphere of my country tower at Redhall."

Lady Jane's anger at the coolness with which this was intimated, prevented her making an immediate reply ; but she looked all she felt, yet only for a time ; there was again in the black eyes of Sir Adam that magnetic—that almost superhuman glance, which terrified her. She thought of her mother's legends of the " Evil Eye ;" and unable to sustain the powerful gaze of this remarkable man, she paused, and her eyelids drooped, to be raised again with hesitation ; for the basilisk expression of his eyes was no less singular than the melodious tone of his soft and modulated voice was pleasing and subduing.

" Lady Jane Seton, you cannot have forgotten our last meeting, and the interview to which I referred at Holyrood ; that interview which occurred now nearly a long year ago, in the garden of the abbot. Do you still remember that soft

moonlight night, and the tenor of our conversation—a conversation, to me, so full of hope, of joy, of tumult, and of
giddy expectation.   Ah, you did not then repel me with eyes
of proud disdain, or words of studied scorn.   That night,
whenever I spoke, you were all earnestness, all smiles, and all
attention."

"Because, Sir Adam—and I call Heaven to be my witness,
—I knew not that your words meant more than the mere
gallantry of a well-bred man when conversing with a pretty
woman."

"This is mere coquetry," said he, emphatically; "but
since that night I have been a dotard—a fool—the moon-
gazing slave of an illusion.   My God! on that night I could
not believe in the excess of my joy, when I thought you
were permitting me to love you : nor have I since been able
to realize the full extent of my misery and suspense.   Oh, I
have been as one in a dream—a long and fearful dream ; for
in a dream we feel so much more acutely than when awake!"
He paused ; and, clasping his hands, continued again:

"Listen !   I have a high office in the kingdom ; my power
is nearly equal to that of his eminence the cardinal.   I am
the grand inquisitor of the state, and the interrogator, the
questioner, the torturer of all alleged criminals.   I may
throw the highest in the land into a dungeon, with or without
a charge, if it suits my purpose or my fancy so to do ; and I
have at all times the ear of the king and his chancellor.
Ponder over this, dear lady, for thou art the daughter of a
fallen race.   I have a noble estate, which ere long will be
erected into an earldom——"

"On the ruin of my gallant brother's—hah !"

"On the ruin of none : but won honourably."

"I despise all earldoms that are not won as my forefathers'
were, by the sword."

"There spoke thy mother's haughty spirit, lady, and I
love it well ; but if thou didst know, fully and sorrowfully
as I do, the irreparable destruction which hovers over thee
and thine—a destruction which I alone can avert—thou
wouldst listen to my sad, my earnest, my honourable pro-
posal, with more of patience, and less, perhaps, of petulance
and pride."

"And I say unto thee, Adam Otterburn of Redhall, that
if thou knewest the horror and repugnance with which a

virtuous woman—one whose heart, in all its first freshness and the first flush of its feeling, is wholly with another—listens to the accents of love from any but the chosen of that heart, thou wouldst know what I endure in hearing these laboured addresses of thine."

Stung to the very soul by this studied reply, which was alike calculated to kindle his jealousy and extinguish his hopes, the face of that dark and stern man assumed a white and ghastly expression; his basilisk eye again terrified her, and she shrunk within herself.

"Impossible!" said he, as he grasped her arm, and a deadly smile curled his thin but finely-formed lips; "it is impossible that you, so pure in mind, so high in spirit, so accomplished and refined, can love this fop, this fool—this mere soldier, of whom you know so little. Your love for him is a mere childish fantasy, of which you are the victim. Ever brawling and fighting, this hair-brained cut-throat will probably never return from Douglasdale, whither he has marched on the king's service; but doubtless you think that this gay cavalier, this Vipont, with his tall plume and gilt armour, would make a much more romantic spouse than your most humble and more matter-of-fact serviteur."

Jane heard only one part of this rude sneer—that which informed her Roland was gone to Douglasdale. She felt consoled; his absence was thus accounted for.

"Ah, my gallant Vipont!" said she, unable to resist the ardour his name kindled within her, and the temptation to sting his enemy; "hadst thou been in Edinburgh, I had long since been free, avenged, and at my mother's side."

"'Tis time to put an end to this folly," said Redhall, gnashing his teeth. "Listen! Thy mother's side? Thy mother is a prisoner in the castle of Inchkeith; there in ward, under Hamilton of Barncleugh, charged with treason, and resetting the traitor her son."

"My mother! oh, my poor mother!" faltered Jane, clasping her hands.

"The same warrant included the arrest of you, lady, and of the unfortunate earl, your brother; but the people deem that thou and he are fled. But better were thou and he in the grave, than living to encounter all that fate has in store for you on falling into the hands of that government to which I can surrender you both in an hour!"

" My brother—who will dare to touch my brave brother ?"

" Who ? " replied Redhall, with one of those cutting smiles which sometimes exasperated even his best friends; " the worthy gentlemen who handled him so roughly a few nights ago."

" And what awaits him ?"

" Can you ask me ? The dungeon of the castle—the high court of parliament—the solemn sentence—the ignominious scaffold —the spiked head—the blighted name, and the torn banner; yet each and all of these I can avert, if—if——"

" What ?"

" Thou wilt only try to love me !"

" Horrible ! love thee ? Oh, this is mere insanity !"

" I, who have done, can undo. I will restore him to his power at court, his coronet, his castles, and his baronies, to his seat in parliament, his offices of great cupbearer to the king and governor of Blackness; I will restore him to the world, to rank, to honour, yea, to life itself, I may say, for it is doubly forfeited, if thou wilt but love me. Thy mother, old, infirm, and broken in spirit by grief, by shame, and wounded pride, I will take from that lonely island prison, where she is exposed to so many severe degradations and privations, from the damp mists of the German Sea, and many other miseries that old age cannot long endure, and will restore her to her wonted place, as mistress of the household and first lady of the court, if thou wilt but love me. A hundred gallant knights of her father's house, with the great Angus himself, shall be restored to place, to power, to home, to happiness, and to honour, and the Hamiltons of Arran shall be subverted and exiled to Cadyow and Kinniel, even though I should unroll my own banner against them, if thou wilt only permit me to love thee in return. Still no reply ! Think, lady, think of all I say, for these things are well worth pondering over. All these may be done by a word, but withhold that word, and they shall remain undone. Dost thou hear me, lady ?"

" Yes; I have heard that thou who hast *done* can *undo!*"

" And thine answer ?"

" *Is*—that I despise and abhor thee, from whom my kinsmen of Seton and Douglas have endured so much;" and she turned haughtily away.

" Be it so," said he, calmly but sternly. " Then, let

banishment and proscription, the headsman's axe and the doomster's hand, hang over the lords and barons, the knights and adherents of Ashkirk and of Angus; let infamy and vengeance, destruction and death, dog them close, since thou hast abandoned them—thou who by a word could have saved them all. They are each but as puppets in my hands—puppets whose destiny I may lengthen or shorten as I choose, for the strings of their fate are in my power, and I will be merciless to them, as thou, Jane Seton, hast been this day to me!"

Jane trembled, and her heart swelled as if it would have burst; for she knew too bitterly the truth of all Sir Adam said, and she felt that, hated and bloodstained, cool, calculating, and detestable, as this man was, she could have sacrificed herself to his insane passion to save her mother, her brother, her family and kinsmen—for kindred blood was then a sacred tie in Scotland—but for Roland.

"Oh, Vipont! Vipont!" she sobbed, and buried her face in her hands; "my heart is sorely tempted to abandon thee—but in vain!"

Then Redhall, lest he might say more to widen the gulf between them, and with lover-like indecision repenting even what he had said, retired abruptly, and left her bathed in tears, and with a bosom full of the most clamorous anxiety and alarm, not for herself, but for her mother and the earl. To know that the former was a captive in the castle of the Inch, and that she, her only daughter, was not beside her to soothe and console her grief and pride; that her brother, too, was separated from her only by a stone wall; and that they were both prisoners in the midst of a dense population—but a few feet from a busy street, where so many strong hands and stout hearts might easily be summoned to their rescue—prisoners in the hands of one so deep and stern in purpose, so relentless in his vengeance, as Redhall,—caused her the most complicated emotions of agony and dread.

For the thousandth time she examined the bolted door, the tapestried walls, and the grated windows, for a means of escape, but found them all as before; and then, after once more failing by the offer of all her rings and brooches to overcome the inflexible integrity of Tib Trotter, hopeless and despairing, she knelt down to pray and to weep.

"Come hither, Tib," said Redhall to this niece of his trusty henchman, as he retired; "the young lady, my kinswoman, is I fear, seriously indisposed; put this powder in her milk posset to-night; but on peril of thy life neither allow her to see or know aught of it."

With a low curtsey, and a downcast glance of the deepest respect, Tib received the little packet, and Redhall hurried back to his writing chamber and his portfolios.

CHAPTER XXIV.

THE KNIFE.

*" Cunning is a crooked weapon; and nothing is more hurtful than when cunning men pass for wise."—*Bacon.

THE Earl of Ashkirk occupied an apartment immediately below that of his sister; but one which was certainly of a very different aspect and description.

After their capture, it was not until daylight broke that he discovered he was only in the strong house of Redhall, scarcely a hundred yards from his own gate, and *not* (as he had first supposed) either in the towers of the castle or the Tolbooth of the city. In the scuffle preceding his capture he had been so severely handled, as to become insensible; thus, on sense returning, he found that, though the infamous gag (the thought of which made his fierce blood boil with wrath and shame) had been removed, as well as the cords which had secured his hands, his mouth had been severely cut by the iron tongue of the former, and his wrists were swollen and livid by the merciless application of the latter.

The capture of his sister by Redhall, and the certainty that she too was confined in the same mansion among the trained minions and obsequious vassals of this arch conspirator, sufficiently informed him that his ancient enemy had some ulterior motive, which he could not at that time fathom. Daring as he was, and courageous to a fault, the first thoughts of the young earl were those of terror for his sister, and some little concern for himself. He now saw and regretted, unavailingly regretted, his rashness and folly, in venturing within the walls of Edinburgh at such a time, when the tidings of his recent raid on the borders were fresh in the minds of the people; and still more did he deplore his second folly, in continuing to abide there, as if in defiance of suspicion and of fate : thus selfishly compromising the safety of his dearest friends as well as his own.

"I must have been mad, and Vipont was worse than mad to permit me! Let me sleep if I can," thought he, "fresh energies will come with slumber; and I, who have escaped from English Norham, and from the castle of Stirling, too, where once old Barncleugh had me fast in the Douglas chamber, will surely find a passage from this house—or the devil's in it!—and adieu my plans of vengeance for a time."

And thus, acting upon principle, the light-hearted young noble, whose bold heart had never known either fear or despair, lay down on the stone floor of his prison, closed his eyes, and courted sleep as if nothing had happened; and sleep came; but his slumbers were a mere nightmare, so full were they of hideous dreams, buffets, and combats ; and, more than once, he started with the certainty that he had heard his sister's cry.

"Bah!" said he, "let me sleep. She is her mother's daughter, and hath too much of Black Douglas and the devil in her, to endure insult from such a poor hang-dog as Redhall! Besides, if he dared to——" and he felt a gleam pass over his eyes in the dark, at the idea that occurred to him.

At an early hour Lord Ashkirk awoke, and proceeded at once to the examination of his prison. The walls and arched roof were of massive and unplastered stone; the floor was paved ; the window and the chimney were grated ; while the door, which he sounded with his hand, seemed a mass as solid as could be formed of oak planks and iron bolts.

"Ten devils!" thought he ; "at Norham I had the tongue of a waist buckle, and at Stirling a spur of steel ; but here are neither buckle nor spur, knife nor nail, to loosen a stone or saw a stanchel."

Between the trees he could see the rising sun gilding the top of Arthur's Seat. The solitary window, which was little more than ten inches square, was crossed by three bars built into the stone ; he saw with satisfaction that it was only about fifteen feet from the ground, for his chamber was on the second vaulted story.

"Good!" said he ; "this wall is not like the rock of Stirling; but there I stole the cord of the flagstaff."

He heard all the bells of the city ringing for morning prayer : and these sounds of life without made him feel, for the first time, some anger and impatience at the vigorous restraint imposed upon him. An hour after this, although he had not heard the approach of footsteps (so thick and so closely-jointed were the walls that encompassed him), the door of his vault was unlocked, and a sturdy fellow with a Jethart axe, secured to his wrist by a thong, in case of accidents, entered, bearing a pewter basin of water, a towel, &c., for the performance of the morning ablutions. The moment he entered, a door at the further end of the passage was closed and locked; thus securing him, as well as the prisoner, of whose name and rank he appeared ignorant; for with these the politic Redhall had acquainted only his favourite, Birrel, and one or two more on whom he could implicitly rely.

Prolonging his toilet to the utmost extent, the earl scrutinized the visage of his attendant, who was a strongly-built fellow, about five-and-twenty years of age, with a rough red beard, and whiskers that grew up to his high cheek bones, on each of which a bright red spot was visible. He wore his bonnet drawn over his shaggy brows, and his eyes, though of a pale grey, betokened a native sharpness over which the earl saw at once he would be able to achieve very little.

"Well, fellow," said he, "art thou appointed to attend me?"

"Ay, sir."

"Then what is thy name, for I must know it?"

"What would ye be the better of knowing?" he asked, cautiously.

"Very much; as we may see each other often; but, doubtless, thou art ashamed of it."

"Ashamed o' my name? Deil choke sic impudence. No, faith! It is as gude as your ain, and better, maybe. My name is Tam Trotter, and I am forester up bye at Kinleith, where my father (God rest him!) was forester before me, though folk did ca' him uncanny."

"Well, friend Tam, couldst get me a razor, in addition to this splendid toilet apparatus? I have a fancy for shaving off my beard this morning."

"Aha!" laughed Tam, with a knowing Scots wink, as he seated himself on the table, with his Jedwood axe under his arm; "I can see as far into a millstone as you, my quick gentleman; so keep on your beard, it will be a warm ruff for you in the winter nights."

" Winter nights ! What the devil dust thou tell me ? Thy master cannot think of keeping me here till the winter nights come on."

" No here, maybe, but out at Redhall. This morning I rode in with ten braw fellows, with axe and spear, to take ye out there to the auld tower ; but lo ! his lordship, our master, came home not an hour syne, wi' his doublet drookit in bluid, and his body run through by——"

" By whom ?—by whom ?" cried the earl.

" The master of the king's ordnance, who (everybody says) is a fast friend of the Lord Ashkirk ; but, God's death ! if ever the one or the other come under my hands—if I can just get one canny cloure at them—neither will ever need another !" and, setting his teeth, the fellow assumed an aspect of ferocity, and hewed a large piece off the table with his sharp-bladed axe.

" Friend Tam, thou seemest very savage and blood-thirsty," said the earl, in his bantering tone ; " but I must request thee to restrain thy troublesome vivacity, and not so damage my furniture, the stock of which is somewhat limited. Ha! ha! and so Vipont hath pinked thy master ?—and where ?"

" Here—just in the shoulder ; but it seems braw news for you," replied Trotter, sulkily.

" The thrust is not near the heart, I hope ?" said the earl, almost leaping with joy ; " not near his amiable heart—oh, do not say so—I shall quite expire if thou tellest me that !"

" Devil take me, if I ken what to make o' you," said Tam, with a face half comical and half angry ; " for, by my faith, you *are* a queer chield !"

" And thou art a good-hearted fellow ?"

" My mother aye says sae, though she bangs me wi' the beetle, for being fonder o' porridge than plowing in the morning."

" So his mother beats him ?" muttered the earl ; " good! —the fellow is a mere simpleton."

" Is he ?" rejoined Trotter, closing one eye, with his tongue in his cheek, and kicking his iron heels together ; " try me, and you will see if I am sic a simpleton ?"

" Excuse me, friend Trotter ; by simpleton, I merely mean one who is neither subtle nor abstruse—nor steeped in guilt, like the rascal, thy master."

" The rascal, my master, hath *you* nicely under his thumb,

however," grinned Trotter; "and a civil tongue, sir, would be baith advisable and becoming—a' things considered."

"Well, let us not quarrel. Thou seest this ring—'tis worth three hundred gold crowns of James III.; and it will be thine, if thou tellest me all thou knowest about the lady who was brought here last night."

"Weel—give me the ring, sir."

"'Tis a carbuncle, my friend, that once gleamed on the hand of a gallant earl."

"And it is mine, for all I ken—eh?" said Thomas, contemplating the jewel on the top of one of his great fingers with a leer of satisfaction; "the carbumple wad be a bonny die for Else' Gair; and 'tis mine, for a' I ken?"

"Yes—yes."

"Then a' I ken just amounts to nothing," said Tam, with a laugh; "so I might cheat you if I chose; but, though a puir chield (and a simpleton too), I would despise mysel' if I took your ring—so tak' it back, sir——"

"Nay, nay, fellow, I cannot accept it again."

"Weel, it may lie there on the table, for I winna touch it. Men would say, if I took it, that I had betrayed my master."

"True," said the earl, as he replaced the jewel; but I will be in thy debt three hundred Scottish crowns. And now let me have breakfast; for no vexation was ever so great that it deprived me of my appetite."

Cold beef, bread, cheese, eggs, fish, and spiced ale formed a repast which greatly comforted the earl, who saw with regret, however, how scrupulously the single knife that was allowed him was watched and removed by the careful Trotter. But the moment this meal was over, and his attendant had withdrawn, he recommenced a most minute examination of his prison, and was gradually forced to acknowledge, with a sigh of bitterness, that though neither so strong as Norham, nor so loftily situated as Stirling, its capabilities for escape were very limited indeed.

Several days passed monotonously away.

The earl became horribly impatient; he had shaken every window-bar for the hundredth time; and for the hundredth time also, with the heel of his boot, had sounded every slab of the pavement, and every stone of the walls, but all were solid as a mass of rock.

"Friend Thomas," said he, half banteringly and half

savagely, on the thirteenth day of his confinement, "how long does that prince of villains, thy master, mean to keep me here?"

"As long as he pleases, I suppose."

"A vague term, that—most unpleasantly so. I should like much to have been a little consulted in the matter; but as he omitted this politeness, I mean to escape on the first opportunity, and without formality."

"Escape?" reiterated Trotter, with a grin.

"The walls——"

"Are six feet thick, and the window hath three bars, ilk ane like the shaft of my Jethart staff."

"Yes; but some day I may pull out the stones of the wall, or saw through the bars of the window. Have you never heard of such things?"

"Ay have I, when a man had saws or files, or hammers, but never when he had only his bare hands and nails."

"I will steal a knife from you."

"Will you?" said Trotter, with his knowing wink.

"Thou shalt see; and once through the window, I will drop——"

"Into the draw-well! Ha! ha! my bauld buckie, the draw-well, forty feet deep, is just below it."

"What? Just under my window?"

"Right doon, as a plummet would sink."

"Ah, the devil! What a judicious villain thy master is!"

"You see, sir, that unless you could change yoursel' into a spider or a bumbee, here you maun just bide," replied Tam, with a loud laugh, which galled the earl to the soul; but seeing the futility of anger or hauteur, he controlled his rising temper, and said, in his usual manner—

"Well, let me have dinner; for assuredly I am weary of having nothing to look forward to, but from breakfast to dinner, at mid-day; from dinner to supper, at even; and from supper to bed—and so on. I assure you, friend Trotter, it would tire even a Carthusian."

"And tiresome I find it, too! Cocksnails! I would gie my very lugs to be again kicking my heels owre Currie Brig, or Kinleith Craig, for I am wearied o' holding watch and ward here, like the javellour of a tolbooth or the warder of a tower."

As Trotter returned with the dinner upon a broad wooden tray, which usually held the platters, covers, and one small knife, the earl contrived to place his chair in such a manner, that the attendant was tripped by it, and stumbled forward, by which the manchet, or small loaf (in those days the invariable substitute for potatoes), slipped from the tray, and fell upon the floor. While Trotter, after depositing the tray, stooped to pick up the manchet, the earl, like lightning, possessed himself of the knife, and thrust it up his sleeve.

" Look again, friend Trotter," said he, removing the first cover, " thou hast dropped the knife, I think ?"

" Have I ?" said Trotter, searching all round the table. " Surely no !"

" You must have done so, for I vow 'tis not here."

" I could have sworn it was on the trencherboard when I brought it in," said the fellow, gaping with alarm.

" If you think so, look again."

" By St. Giles ! there is nae knife here !"

" Then quick, call for another, or these dainty pullets will be cold as pebble stones."

Trotter turned to call for another knife ; and the moment he did so, the earl stepped back, and concealed that which he had secured in a nook of the chimney, which had been discovered during a previous inspection.

A second knife was brought by Dobbie, who had heard Trotter call for it.

The earl made an unusually good repast, and as he picked the pullet's bones, and drank his pint of Bordeaux, he jested merrily with his attendant, who leant against the door, from whence he cast ever and anon furtive and uneasy glances below the table, in search of the missing article, for he had his own suspicions.

" Take care, my trusty Tam, take care ; for now I have got that knife, and I mean to make a good use of it on the first opportunity. Truly thou art a simple fellow, and will be beetled by Redhall, in such wise as thy mother never beetled thee ! ha ! ha ! Zounds ! dost thou think this paltry house would hold me, who escaped from the Douglas room at Stirling, where the cardinal confined me after the battle of Linlithgow ? I trow not ! Be easy ; compose thyself, friend Thomas, for I assure thee I have got the knife, and will be-gone to-morrow "

" In your pockets ?" said Tam, advancing.

" Pockets ! Nay, dost thou think a gentleman has pockets

in his breeches and doublet to hold bread and cheese, like a rascally clown; but come hither, thou mayst feel my garments."

Trotter passed his hands over the breeches and doublet of the prisoner.

" The devil a knife is here," said he, perfectly reassured.

" Nevertheless, I have it."

" Where ?"

" In my stomach. Bring me a sword, or lend me thy poniard, and I will swallow them both also. It runs in the family. I had an uncle who could digest cannon balls."

Tam uttered another of his hoarse laughs, and, bearing away the wooden tray, retired, and secured the double doors as usual.   *   *   *   *   *

Next morning, at the early but accustomed hour, he undid the accumulated bolts and locks of the inner doorway (while Dobbie secured the outer, and entered, with breakfast on the trencher.

A cry burst from him, and he started back aghast on finding the place void, for one glance sufficed to show that it was empty.

The earl was indeed gone!

" Ah, the *knife !*" thought Trotter, as he rushed to the window. Every bar was in its place, and the undisturbed cobwebs of years were still woven between them. Not a flag of the floor, not a stone of the wall, appeared to have been displaced; and, terrified by such a phenomenon, Tam Trotter uttered a stentorian howl of dismay, and fled from the empty chamber.

CHAPTER XXV.

DOUGLASDALE.

" But you, dear scenes! that far away
    Expand beneath these mountains blue,
Where fancy sheds a purer ray,
    And robes the fields in richer hue,—
A softer voice in every gale,
  I 'mid your woodlands wild should hear;
And Death's unbreathing shades would fail
    To sigh their murmurs in mine ear."   LEYDEN.

THE sun of a morning in June shone brightly upon Douglasdale, as a valley of the middle ward of Lanarkshire is named---

the country of the puissant Douglases. The pure air, the
bright sunshine, the fresh meadows, the fragrant wind that
stole along the uplands, were all indicative of that delightful
season when the trees are heavy with their richest foliage,
and the voices of the mavis, the merle, and the wood-pigeon
are heard within their deep recesses. Under golden masses
of the dark green broom, the white hawthorn, and the wild
rose, the Douglas water stole, over its pebbled bed, towards
the west.

Hot and cloudless, the rays of the glorious summer sun
poured over the giant summit of the Cairntable, and played
along the pastoral glens below, to be reflected by the gleam
of arms and the glitter of armour descending from those
heights which overlook the towers of the Douglases—the
" Castle Dangerous " of chivalry and romance.

The lairds and warders of the various towers which overhung the valley, were all on the alert, and had barred their
gates, drawn up their bridges, and prepared their armour, with
not the less care, because they could perceive the royal
standard with the red lion waving above the copsewood below.

With their swords sheathed and visors up, Roland Vipont
and Louis Leslie rode together at the head of their little
column, which had passed a peaceful campaign of nearly three
weeks in Lanarkshire, without being molested by any one;
and, of course without hearing tidings of the Earl of Ashkirk,
for whom, as in duty bound, they made the most minute
inquiries—Roland being the more rigid in his search, because
he believed him to be in safe concealment at Edinburgh. The
horses of the artillery looked sleek and well fed; and the
cannoniers, with Leslie's hundred men of the guard, had all
their harness and arquebuses as bright as on that day when
they marched from Holyrood.

" 'S life! but we spend our time wearily ! Will nobody fight
with us ?" said Roland, with a yawn, as they wound down the
valley, by the banks of the Douglas. " St. Mary ! I feel a violent inclination to maul some of those towers, that from every
rock and hill-top look down so saucily on our line of march."

" What ?—the houses of thy Douglas friends ?"

" Assuredly."

" And why ?"

" Just to keep us in practice and because they are held by
Hamiltons."

"Lucky it is, for us, that they are so. Long before this, had the Douglases possessed the same power in Lanarkshire that they did ten years ago, we had been eaten up."

"True, in 1527, a hundred men, with two pieces of cannon, if they had once ventured into the middle ward on such an errand as ours, had never come out of it again."

"Yet 'tis very hard that no one will just fire one little shot at us, just to afford an excuse——"

"For blowing the house about their ears. A most amiable wish!"

"Thy nag looks weary, Leslie."

"Ah, 'tis a bay I picked up during our raid against the Annandale thieves last year. My blockhead of a groom lost me a beautiful roan horse at Leith, last Lammastide, where I sent it to be bathed, at sunset, in the sea."*

"Where dost think we will dine, for my stomach crieth cupboard already?"

"At the Barmkyn of Cairntable. I have heard that the gudeman there keepeth open house and free; besides, he is a kinsman of Redhall, and if we empty his girnels and broach his casks, what matter? Is it not for the king's service? and all Scotland knows," added Roland, with a smile, "how zealous the advocate is for the public weal."

"Let us halt here for one moment," said Leslie, reining up his horse beside a little rustic well, which flowed near a cottage wall; "this water looks fresh and pure; 'tis south-running, too, and I am thirsty as a sack of flour."

"Lintstock, bring hither the flask of French brandy."

From a gun-carriage, Lintstock unslung a large leathern bottle, and brought it to his master, ogling it by the way with all the ardour of which his solitary eye was capable; and thereafter, from his havresack, he produced a beechwood luggie.

"Gudewife," said Leslie, to a woman, who was grinding corn in a wooden quern at the cottage door, and who wore one of those pointed Flemish caps which had been introduced into Scotland by Mary of Gueldres, "how name you this well?"

"Sanct Bryde's of Dowglass," replied the woman, briefly and sulkily, for she was one of that hostile race.

* A superstitious custom, suppressed, by order of St. Cuthbert's kirk session, in 1647.

N

"A consecrated well! I thought so—'tis fortunate you asked," said Roland; and, after first dipping their fingers in the fountain, they crossed themselves, and then mixing the blessed water with the brandy, took each a draught, and gave a third to Lintstock.

"Hallo!" cried Roland, to a horseman who came up at a rough trot, and whose grey plaid, blue bonnet, and white Galloway doublet, as well as his gambadoes, or riding boots of rough calf-skin, declared him a plain countryman; "a good day, friend. Wilt thou have a tass of brandy?"

"God keep you, my captain—wi' mony gude thanks," replied the horseman, pulling up his nag, which was a strong Flanders mare. "Health to ye baith, sirs," said he, pulling his bonnet well forward, instead of raising it, as he nodded to each knight, and drained the vessel. "By my faith, but that's braw stuff!"

"Ay, I daresay. 'Tis not often the burnt wine of Languedoc runs over thy Lanarkshire throat," said Roland, laughing; "dost thou travel our way?"

"Sir knicht, that just depends upon which way yours may be," replied the fellow, dryly, drawing his plaid well over his face.

"We are going to the Barmkyn Cairntable," said Roland, looking keenly at him under his helmet.

"And so am I, sir."

"Well, thy nag seems fresh, and thou art not, as we are, cased in armour; so ride fast, I pray you, and inform the gudeman of the Barmkyn that a party of the king's soldiers will halt there about dinner-time—say a hundred men or so —and that we will thank the gudewife to look well to her larder and kitchen——"

"To kill the fatted calf, and set her best casks a-broach," said Leslie, laughing.

"To select the hens that roost next the cock—the most delicate pullets——"

"To examine her eel-arks—ha! ha!"

"To prepare the most dainty pasties, and highly-seasoned patties—ha! ha! ha!" continued Roland, in the same merry tone; "for as both gudewife and gudeman are friends of the good and amiable lord advocate, they cannot but rejoice to make welcome those who come among them on the king's service."

'And in whose name shall I give the message?"

"In the name of Sir Roland Vipont, master of the ordnance."

"Without fail," replied the horseman, putting spurs to his nag and galloping off; "but may the devil ryve the saul out of thee (and me too), if thou gettest not a reception as warm as auld Bauldy Fleming can give thee!" added Nichol the brodder, for the stranger was no other than he."

"That fellow's laugh bespeaks him a rascal," said Leslie, who had been narrowly observing all that could be seen of Birrel's face; "how different it was from the broad grin of an honest yeoman."

"Dost think so?" said Roland, looking after him as he galloped over an adjacent brae, and disappeared; "dost thou think he will play us false after our kindness?"

"No, perhaps—but the committal of thy message to a stranger in these times, and in this place, is, to say the least of it, rather unwary. We might be entrapped and cut off."

"A hundred chosen soldiers, with two pieces of cannon— bah! I should like to see any one attempt it, Leslie. We should sell our lives dearly; and yet my mind misgives me sorely, that it was for no other purpose that subtle villain Redhall sent so small a force into this wild and hostile district."

"Eh, gentle sirs! Gude guide us, your horses are eating a' my corn!" cried the cottager, running to her quern, which she had left for a moment; "shoo! shoo! awa' wi' ye!"

"Well, thou old devil," said Leslie, "may not soldiers' horses eat what they like?"

Roland threw a few pence into the quern; and then, both putting spurs to their horses, hurried after their soldiers, who were now some distance in advance.

CHAPTER XXVI.

THE BARMKYN OF CAIRNTABLE.

"Dark grew the sky, the wind was still,
　The sun in blood arose;
　But oh! how many a gallant man
　Ne'er saw that evening close!"—HOGG.

A FEW hours' march among the knolls and hollows, which exhibited here and there a solitary square tower, or an old thatched sheep farm, shaded by ash trees, and nestling on

the holm land of the strath through which the Douglas
winds, brought the soldiers of Vipont to the base of the Cairntable, a beautiful green mountain, sixteen hundred feet in
height.   One half was darkly rounded into shadow, on the
other shone the bright splendour of the meridian sun, which
lit up all the windings of the various little pastoral glens,
through which the Peniel, the Glespin, the Kinnox, and other
mountain tributaries, flowed to feed the Douglas at its base.

On a small spot of table-land, a shoulder of the hill, and
sheltered by its giant ridge from the south-west wind, which
usually prevails there, stood the fortified grange, or barmkyn,
of Baldwin Fleming.

Boasting of his lineal descent from Theobald le Fleming,
who is said to have possessed all that country before the rise
of the Douglases, and their gradual acquisition of the whole
district, this sturdy retainer of the encroaching Lords of
Angus, though neither laird nor lesser baron, but merely a
goodman, who held his feu of a feudal chief, and followed his
banner in battle, had procured (through the good offices of
his kinsman Redhall) a crown charter, empowering him to
fortify his farm, which he had done with a strength that
made it second only to Castle Douglas, and the envy of all
the fierce barons in that warlike district.

This vast building formed an exact square, and had four
square towers on each of its four faces.   These were all
strongly vaulted for holding grain, while the great yard within
served for securing cattle.   The twelve towers, and the curtain walls between them, were battlemented on the top,
studded with loopholes below, and all strongly, though
roughly, built with stone quarried from the adjacent rocks.

The most perfect example of a similar edifice now in Scotland, is the fortified grange of Sir John Seton of Barns, which
crowns a height southward of Haddington, where its ruined
towers resemble the remains of an ancient city, from their
strength and extent.

Within the barmkyn, on one side, stood the strong and
substantial, but thatched, dwelling of the farmer; along the
other three sides were barns, stables, and houses for his men.
At a certain distance round the whole, a deep ditch was
drawn; the margin was used as a kitchen garden, and was
stocked with common potherbs, and a few small fruit trees,
sheltered by boor-tree hedges and stockades.

The bridge was up; and opposite the gate stood a clump of large oak trees; and on a branch of one, which was conspicuous for its size and foliage, the dead body of a man was hanging by the neck, with the gleds flying about it.

"Oho!" said Roland, as a turn of the glen brought him suddenly in view of this goodly farm; "so the goodman of this grange hath a power of pit and gallows! His oaks bear other fruit than acorns."

"A peasant rascal!" replied Leslie; "and yet he tieth a tassel to his tree, like the best feudal lord in the land."

While approaching this formidable edifice, they had heard the distant blowing of bugle-horns, the springing of wooden rattles, and the incessant jangle of a large bell. These notes of alarm, together with the appearance of armed horsemen, galloping in various directions over the green hill sides, lessened the surprise of Vipont and his soldiers, when, on coming in view of the grange of Cairntable, they saw the whole line of its walls glistening with pike-heads and glittering with steel caps; while a scarlet banner, bearing the chevron of the Flemings within its flowering and counterflowering fleurs-de-lys, was unfurled in defiance; for (thanks to the cunning and amiable intentions of Nichol Birrel) such was the dinner prepared by the sturdy proprietor for his unwelcome visitors.

What the tenor of Birrel's falsehoods and misinformation may have been, we have now no means of ascertaining; but they were such, that the gudeman had all his horses secured in stall; his vast herds of cattle in their pens, his stacks of grain stowed away in vault and barn; while all the men over whom he had authority, to the number of three hundred, with their families, were in garrison, and stood to their arms, with the intention of resolutely obeying his orders, whatever they might be.

A brownie, in the shape of a little rough man, with a broad bonnet and long beard, attended the family of Fleming. He rocked the cradles of the infants, and performed various other kind and domestic services; especially foddering the horses and cattle, sweeping the kitchen floor, and filling the waterstoups for the servant girls; all of which self-imposed duties were performed by this goodnatured imp in the night, for the brownie was a being unseen by day; and to propitiate him, a libation of milk and wort were nightly poured into a rude font in the yard, called the *broonie's stane*—for in those days every thrifty housewife set apart a portion of food for the brownie, that his favour and protection, as well as his future services, might be thereby ensured. If a piece of money were left, an eldritch yell announced that the insulted brownie had found it, and fled in resentment—for from that moment he invariably abandoned the family and for ever. This familiar and usually amiable spirit, with which Scottish superstition furnished the household of every old race, was pacific, generous, and unwarying in his services; but if once offended, implacable in his revenge.

On the night preceding this eventful day, the brownie of Cairntable had been heard to utter the most doleful lamentations, and " the wee manikin with his lang beard and braid bannet," had been seen (as several of the servitors averred) to pass round the towers of the barmkyn, wringing his hands and weeping piteously, which had caused the gudeman to look well to his defences, and to his horses and armour. Thus in two hours after the arrival of his kinsman's follower, Nichol Birrel, everything was in fighting order within the grange when the king's troops approached it.

"Halt!" cried Roland Vipont.

"By my faith!" said Leslie, "we shall have no dinner here to-day, which I regret exceedingly, as this hath all the aspect and reputation of being an exceedingly well-stocked grange."

"There is some mistake here. They surely have not seen the royal standard," said Vipont, angrily, as he shaded his eyes with his hand, which was cased in a glove of steel.

"Ah! you wished for some fighting!"

"Just now I wish most for dinner; and so, Balquhan, ride thou forward with a white flag, and make open door for us."

"Dost think I am another St. Colm, to make bolts unbar and doors open by simply signing the cross?"

"No; but by threatening them with cannon shot."

Leslie tied a white handkerchief to the point of his long sword, and galloped fearlessly forward to the edge of the ditch, from whence he could distinctly see the grim faces that, from under battered morions, peered at him between the embrasures of the wall above; while from the deep-mouthed loopholes below peeped forth the keen pike-heads and the iron muzzle of many an arquebuse and pistol.

"Art thou the gudeman of the Cairntable?" asked Leslie of a stout man of great stature, whose polished coat of mail betokened a superiority over the others around him.

"At your service, my braw gallant," he replied, bending over the tower; "but what may your errand be here?"

"To learn wherefore ye receive the king's soldiers in this fashion, with closed gates, and your helmets on?"

"Gif gaff makes gude friends," replied the other, surlily; "but I trow, gif gaff shall make you none here; so, in God's name, pass on in peace. Here ilka man must just ride the ford as he finds it."

"Dost think we will burn thy house after it hath lodged us, poor devil!" said Leslie, with a lofty and patronizing air.

The buirdly farmer laughed hoarsely, as he looked to the right and left along the strong walls, which were lined by so many tall fellows in helmets and breast-plates.

"Away, away!" said he, waving his gauntleted hand; "what brings ye frae Holyrood to this puir sheep country? It's a gay place, that Holyrood! Ah, there are plenty of vacant priories, lay abbacies, captainries of castles, and other braw perquisites to be picked up there; so I marvel mickle that you left so pleasant a climate, to come here among the spirit-broken and impoverished Douglases, and the fogs o' the Cairntable, where there's nothing but rocks, whinstones, and cold iron to be had."

"Then you will not lower your bridge, and afford free entrance to the king's soldiers."

"If a' the fiends of hell came, I carena a brass bodle; so away wi' ye, or ye may fare the worse. Tell thy captain my name is Baldwin the Fleming—as good a man as he."

"Peasant hound, thou shalt rue this dearly!" replied Leslie, who was about to turn away, when he perceived the rascal whom they had met at St. Bryde's Well levelling an arquebuse full at him, from a loophole; and he had just time to make his horse rear, so that the ball, which would have pierced his own breast, entered that of the poor animal, which snorted and plunged wildly. Escaping, however, several other balls which whistled past him, Leslie forced it back at full speed to the side of Roland, where it fell down, and was dead almost ere the rider could disengage himself from the stirrups.

"To your arquebuses, Leslie," exclaimed Roland, "while I shall unbend my cannon. Ah, white-livered cowards!" he

added, shaking his clenched hand towards the hostil · grange,
"I will maul you sorely for this defiance! Soldiers! they
are all traitors to the king, for they have fired on his royal
standard. To your guns my brave cannoniers—to your lin-
stocks, and unlimber! Quick! and make me good service
against this contumacious villain and his foolish knaves."

While the cannon were wheeled round, the tumbrils cast
off, the magazines opened, and powder and shot taken there-
from; and while the cannoniers commenced pointing and
charging them home, Leslie formed his hundred arquebusiers
behind a knoll, where they fixed their rests into the turf, and
opened a fire as close and rapid as it was possible for soldiers
to maintain with these cumbrous fire-arms, which carried
balls of two, and even three ounces; which were loaded by
means of a powder-horn; were levelled over forks. and were
fired by means of a matchlock. The reports were loud and
deep, and the rocks of the Cairntable repeated them with a
thousand reverberations. White as snow, the smoke of
arquebuse and pistolette broke (but at long intervals) from
the strong dark walls of the grange, and their balls tore up
the soft turf, as they fell among the little band of besiegers,
or whistled over their heads; for so well were they posted,
that during two hours of incessant firing not one was ever
touched.

"Batter me down the entrance-gate!" cried Roland to
his gunners; " 'Tis easier to punch holes in an oak plank than
a stone rampart; so down with it, my brave cannoniers—
for this night we will carry the place by assault or die in its
ditches!"

"Art thou quite prepared for that?" asked Leslie.

"A true soldier is prepared for everything," replied the
elated Vipont; "let us only have yonder gate beaten down
by daylight, and, with my sword for a wand, I will act your
gentleman usher when night falls."

The cannon were carefully levelled and pointed; fire flashed
from their muzzles; smoke curled up in the sunshine; and
their reports rang like thunder among the windings of the
Douglas. One shot crashed through the massive gate, beating
a large hole in it; the other struck the battlements, and
threw down a heap of masonry, which fell, amid a cloud of
dust, into the ditch below. Hereupon high words ensued
between old Lintstock and the lance-spesade, whose thumb was
placed upon the vent of the culverin, which he was reloading.

"It ill becomes a gle'ed gunner like you," Roland heard him say, "to heed me less than an auld pair o' boots; but lang enough before you saw the blessed light o' day I had levelled everything like a cannon, frae a quarter Moyenne up to auld Monce Meg herself; and here now, I will wager you a stoup o' Bourdeaux, that my next shot will go straight to the keyhole."

"Done!" replied the lance-spesade; "twa stoups if you like—and here is my thumb on't."

"The lance-spesade levelled the culverin; applied his right eye to three sides of the breech, carefully adjusted the quoins, and fired. The ball struck a coat of arms above the gate, and threw a cloud of splinters around it in every direction.

"She throws high," said the soldier, throwing down his match, discomfited.

Lintstock grinned as he reloaded, and thereafter applied his single orb to the breach and quoins, looking carefully along the polished brass gun. At that moment the ball of a falconet came whizz from the barmkyn, and was splintered on its muzzle; but the cool old soldier, whose brains had so narrowly escaped being dashed out by it, neither winced nor appeared the least disturbed in his aim; but took one pace to the left, stretched out his right hand with the match, and in his turn fired. Then, where the dark keyhole of the ponderous gate had been but a moment before, a large round breach was visible, with the sunshine streaming through it. Upon this, a shout arose within the barmkyn, and the shrill cries of women and children were distinctly heard.

"Well done, my true cannonier!" said Roland. "A few more of these bitter almonds, and the gudeman of the Cairntable will be forced to afford us open house, whether he will or not. To thy cannon again, my old Lintstock: for thou hast but one eye—Saint Mary! 'tis the eye of a gaze-hound. Aim well with your cannon and arquebuses, my gallant comrades—aim well, and level low! There are many good things in yonder walls, all of which are yours by the law of war. How now, my bold Balquhan—art thou shot?" he asked, on seeing Leslie reel.

"As surely as if with an elf-arrow," replied the lieutenant, whose left arm had been wounded by the ball of a hand-gun, which had beaten his armour into the orifice, and caused him excessive pain; "but it matters not—four of my best men are lying still enough, among the broom, now."

"Zounds! this night's lodgings is likely to cost us dear!
—but, 'fore God, I will make it dearer to the rascal who holds
yonder barmkyn against us."

With his scarf, Roland bound up Leslie's arm; and having
decided on his tactics, commanded the arquebusiers to cease
firing; to lie down close under the brow of a knoll, and to
reserve their arms and matches for service at night. Meanwhile, the culverins incessantly battered the barmkyn, the
gate of which, by the time that the setting sun reddened the
wild summit of Cairntable, was beaten down, with a great
part of the wall, thus affording an open passage into the
heart of the place.

"Thank Heaven, the night will be cloudy and dark!" said
Roland, looking at the sky; "so, by day-dawn, I will show
thee, Balquhan, the Red Lion waving where the chevron of
Fleming floats upon yonder barmkyn. A thousand thanks,
my brave cannoniers—and chiefly thou, old Lintstock, for
a troop of knights might ride abreast through yonder breach."

"True; but thou forgettest the ditch," said Leslie.

"Nay; I have bethought me of that, too."

Black and gloomy the night came on; a high wind growled
along the valley; and with the deepening obscurity, it seemed
as if the brawl of the Douglas over its stony bed became
louder, for its rush was heard distinctly amid the dark and
dewy hills, from which it descended into that lonely and
pastoral strath through which it winds.

Pale and sharp as a spear-head, a horn of the new moon
appeared at times above the black outline of the Craintable;
and when old Lintstock saw it, he carefully took out his purse
(which, however, contained only four of James the Third's
black farthings), and having turned it over thrice, wished
himself good luck, according to a Scottish superstition existing
unto the present day.

When the gloom had deepened, so that nothing could be
discerned of the barmkyn but its bold outline and sable
towers, standing on a shoulder of the mountain, Roland
ordered the arquebusiers to pile their arms, and to tear down
the roof and planking of an old barn that stood near; and
thereafter to bind some ten or fifteen of the rafters together
with ropes of straw, so that, being laid close together, they
should (with the assistance of a few planks) form a temporary
bridge, or passage, across the fossé of the barmkyn, the

breadth of which, with military exactness, he had measured
with his eye.

Two hours sufficed for this, and, about midnight, he prepared to assault the place, resolving to chastise the gudeman
severely for his resistance. Notwithstanding his wound, the
gallant Leslie insisted on accompanying him, and, armed with
a Jethart staff, Lintstock left the cannoniers to follow his
master.

As the arquebusiers approached in close order, the glow of
their lighted matches must have announced their approach,
for although all was still in the barmkyn (save the incessant
lowing of the cattle in their pens), the moment they were
within range, a storm of missiles was poured upon them.
Arquebuse and pistolette, hacque, dague, and iron-drake,
flashed redly upon the darkness of the night, and many an
arrow, and many a bullet, whistled among the close ranks of
the Guard. Several fell, killed or wounded; but the rest
pressed forward bravely, and Roland, with his helmet closed,
and sword in hand, led them on.

Thick and fast fell bolt and bullet, and the hearty shouts
of the little band of stormers were soon lost in the roar of
tumultuous sounds that arose within the barmkyn; for the
cries of Fleming's followers and kinsmen, as they animated
each other at loophole and battlement, the shrieks of their
wives and daughters, the lowing of the cattle, the barking of
dogs, and the ceaseless ringing of a large alarum bell, added
to the incessant explosion of fire-arms, made a united din, that
gave a strange horror to a scene which had no other lamps to
light its dangers than the flashes of those deadly weapons,
which shot forth their contents from every nook and angle of
the strong dark walls.

" Down with the posts and planks ! Quick—Quick !" cried
Roland, through his helmet. " Close your ranks, and now
again to your arquebuses ! Fire, and club them ! Club them,
and on—on, for Vipont and the King !"

This rude substitute for a bridge was laid, and the ditch
crossed, in less time than we have taken to relate it. Shoulder
to shoulder, in the gap of the gate and drawbridge, stood a
close array of pikemen ; but, being somewhat less accustomed
to arms than the soldiers of the Guard, they were thrown into
immediate confusion by a volley from the arquebuses, which
were instantly clubbed against them for close combat.

"Forward! forward!" cried Roland, hewing a passage with
his sword, and shredding down the pike heads like ears of
wheat; his strength, stature, weight of arm, and admirable
coat of mail, rendering him invulnerable, like a knight of
romance.

In the court of the barmkyn, and just within the gate, a
close and terrible conflict ensued in the dark; for there the
sturdy farmer met the assailants in person, at the head of his
hynds and followers, all cased in iron, cuirassed and barbed to
the teeth.

A powerful man, of vast bulk and height, Fleming was
sufficiently formidable, without his other accessories of a coat
of mail of the fifteenth century, jagged with twelve iron
beaks, and one of those enormous iron-studded mauls, which
were used in Scotland until the battle of Pinkey, where they
proved perfectly futile against the Spanish and German hack-
buttiers, who were the main means of winning that battle for
the English. The giant was giving all around him to death
and destruction; three soldiers, the best men of the Guard,
had fallen before him; for, by three separate blows, their
brains and casques had been crushed like ripe pumpkins,
before Roland could reach him through the press; and, with
no other sentiments in his heart than those of rage, the
blind and clamorous longing to avenge and to destroy that
is sure to arise in one's heart at such a time, he fell furiously
upon him.

At this crisis, Roland could perceive a man in a close
helmet, who, armed with an arquebuse, kept close behind
Fleming, and more than once fired in the most cowardly
manner over his shoulder. One ball tore the cone of Roland's
helmet, and another grazed his shoulder.

"Notch me the head of that rascal with thine axe, Lintstock," cried he; "and leave me to deal alone with this rough
tilter."

Swaying his enormous maul like a giant warrior of the
dark ages, Fleming made many a feint, before pouring forth
all his strength and fury, by swinging his club from the back
of his head in one sheer downward blow, that in a moment
would have annihilated Vipont, had he not sprung nimbly
back, and escaped it as well as another shot from the fellow
with the arquebuse, who killed the lance-spesade, and so deprived Lintstock of his stoup of Bordeaux. But ere Fleming

could recover his guard, Roland darted forward, and by one tremendous lunge drove his long keen rapier through his body, just one inch below the corselet. Fleming fell instantly to the ground, and the soldiers pressed forward over him; but as Roland passed, the tremendous grasp of the dying man was fastened on his foot, and he was dragged to the earth, where a furious struggle ensued between them.

In the dark, Roland's fall was unseen by his soldiers, who advanced fighting hand to hand into the heart of the barmkyn, driving before them the retainers of Baldwin Fleming. Groaning with rage and pain, and wallowing in his blood, the latter rolled over Roland, and retained him in a grasp which gathered fresh energy from the pangs of death, till it seemed to possess the power of an iron vice. One hand encircled his throat; the other grasped a poniard, with which he made many a fruitless effort to stab him to the heart. Five times he struck, and, glancing from the tempered corselet, five times the dagger sunk harmlessly into the ground.

During this struggle there suddenly burst upon the darkness a broad and lurid gleam of light, that illuminated the whole arena of the barmkyn, its battered gate and ruined wall, its corpse-strewn court and striking architecture; and then Roland could perceive the ghastly visage of that powerful foe who grasped him—powerful even in death, for sight had all but left his glazed and sunken eyes; yet the vengeance of a demon seemed to burn in his despairing heart, and to add strength to his muscular gripe. In confusion and agony he had dropped his poniard, and now with both hands he clutched Roland's throat, and frantically endeavoured, by compressing his steel gorget, to strangle, since he had failed to stab him; and with every futile effort, the hot fierce blood welled forth from his gaping wound and clammy mouth.

Tighter and tighter grew that deadly clutch; the yielding steel compressed at last, and Roland felt his eyes starting and his brain whirling, while a thousand lights began to dance before him. An icy terror, such as never had been there before, now thrilled through his heart; he thought of Jane; and made one superhuman effort to free himself and to shout for succour; but both failed, and he thought that all was now over and for ever, when the gleam of light which shot through the barmkyn saved him. For a moment, attracted by this strange glow that flashed upon his sightless orbs, strong Fleming relaxed his iron grasp, and, fatally for himself, permitted Roland to respire.

Bearing in mind his master's injunctions, Nichol Birrel had thrice taken a deadly aim at Roland, and thrice had failed, for his bullets slew other men, when his arquebuse was dashed aside by Lintstock's Jethart axe. Then, finding that he was not likely to achieve much by dint of arms, on observing the strange combat between Roland and Fleming in the gateway—a struggle which he alone had observed, a new idea occurred to him; and, rushing to the summit of the walls, he cried:

"The kye! the kye! save your kye! or they will all become the prize and spulzie of the soldiers!" From the parapets he threw down several enormous bundles of blazing straw among the close-packed herds: already excited and terrified by the din of the combat and the report of the fire-arms, they were at once driven mad and furious by the descent of this burning shower.

Like a living torrent they poured into the court and rushed through the gateway, in their flight and terror plunging and galloping, jostling, crushing, and goring each other with their horns, as they irresistibly swept all before them, trampling the dead and the wounded in the mire of their track.

"St. Mary's knot!" cried Lintstock, hewing at their heels with his Jethart axe; "hough and hamstring! tie their legs with St. Mary's knot!"

Five hundred head of infuriated cattle poured from the barmkyn into the dark glen below, where they spread over the mountains in all directions.

Practised to such tactics in the Border war, the blaze of the straw and the wild lowing of the cattle instantly acquainted Roland with what was to ensue; but unable to free himself from the Herculean grasp of Fleming, he suddenly clasped him in his arms. Then by one tremendous effort he dragged his body over himself, and there retained it as a shield from the forest of legs and hoofs that, rushing from the pen, like a living whirlwind swept over them in hundreds for the space of five minutes; but long before the fifth of these minutes had passed, the nervous grasp of Fleming had relaxed, and his fierce spirit had fled. Breathless, panting, and infuriated by the whole encounter, Roland Vipont rose from the gory mud and mire, regained his sword, and with a tottering gait and swimming head looked around him for his followers.

By this time the conflict was over, and his little band of brave soldiers had gained complete possession of the barmkyn, the whole surviving defenders of which had effected their escape by one of those subterranean sally-ports with which every fortified house in Scotland was furnished, as a means of secret egress in the last extremity.

The lance-spesade of the cannoniers and fifteen soldiers of the Guard are said to have been slain in the assault.

CHAPTER XXVII.

THE POMMEL OF THE PONIARD.

" He gained—he gained (why stops my story ?) then,
A deadly opiate from the convent men.
And bore it to his cave."—*Marcian Colonna.*

" Now, blessed be Heaven and our own stout hands, we have made our quarters good here at last !" said Leslie, at that moment approaching Vipont. " How is this ? Zounds! thou cuttest a rare figure, all smeared in mud and mire. Art thou wounded ? No reply ? Vipont, Vipont, dost hear me ? Why, thou art mute as a fish. But come with me to the hall, for I have discovered my way there, and, what is better, a gallant demi-john of Rochelle, that would gladden the hearts of ten friars ; one cup of it will set thee all right ; so, come along, my friend."

Confused and stunned by his protracted struggle with Fleming, and the whirlwind that had swept over them, Roland could scarcely articulate a word, and when he did speak, his voice was lost in the hollow of his helmet.

Assisted by Leslie's arm, he ascended a stair to the hall of the barmkyn, where their entrance stilled, for a moment, the uproar and rejoicing of their plundering and half-famished soldiers.

Built in an age when the sole idea on which a Scottish house was constructed was the resistance of armed assault, the walls of the barmkyn were of enormous thickness, and,

in the recesses of the deeply-embayed windows were little
square cupboards for holding household utensils. The vast
fireplace contained two tall andirons, which, together with
the great dinner-table, and a number of clumsy chairs and
buffet-stools, formed the sole furniture of the farmer's hall.
The strong and bare stone walls were as destitute of ornament as the roof, which rested on twenty-four round stone
corbels, and was composed of twelve beams of oak, plainly
boarded over, to form the flooring of a vast hay-loft above.

A fox's face and horse-shoe were nailed above the door, to
exclude witches; while a cross of elder-tree twigs was fastened
above the lintel as a charm against fascination, for the age
was full of the wildest superstition.

Torches had been lighted in the tin sconces which hung on
the walls; bread, beef, cheese, and every edible on which the
soldiers could lay their hands, had been piled on the long
table; and, with their helmets off, some were crowding round
the demi-john of Rochelle which Leslie had mounted on a
binn in the centre of the floor, while others hewed down
doors and window-shutters with their swords, and lighting a
fire, began to cook with all the eagerness of hungry men.
Meantime, a guard and sentinels had been posted on the
walls without, in case of a rally or surprise.

On removing his helmet, and imbibing a draught of wine,
Sir Roland was completely restored; but he was too much
exasperated by the resistance of Fleming and the loss of life
he had occasioned, to care a jot for the manner in which his
goods and gear were going to rack and ruin.

" Drink, my soldiers!" he exclaimed, as he seated himself
on the table, that he might the more easily overlook the
frolics and revelry, "to your hearts' content; drink deep, for
this is the wine of a false traitor; but let drunkards beware
of the truncheon that awaits them on the morrow.   Lintstock!
allo, Lintstock! where are you, old ironhead?"

" Here, Sir Roland," replied the veteran, who at that
moment entered the hall, dragging in a man whose head he
was menacing at every step with his Jethart axe, and at whom
he darted such scowls of wrath as he could concentrate into
his solitary eye.

" A prisoner!"

" Whom I found skulking there without, and whom I am
ready to vow on the blessed Gospels, is the loon that thrice

levelled his arquebuse at you; and by shooting puir Laurie, our lance-spesade, hath cheated me of a stoup of wine whilk I won lawfully," he added, savagely shaking Nichol Birrel, who gave him a deep glance of hatred from his sullen eyes.

" It would seem to me, fellow," said Roland, who still occupied his elevated seat on the edge of the table, and before whom the soldiers dragged Birrel, " that I have seen thy face before. In the streets of Edinburgh, perhaps?" he added, sternly scrutinizing that worthy, who, having been deprived of arms offensive and defensive, save a small-sword, appeared before them in the attire of a peasant.

" Nay, I am but a puir sheep-farmer of Galloway, and you never set eyes on me before, Sir Roland."

" A lying varlet !" said Lintstock : " we wasted a gude tass o' brandy on ye at St. Bryde's Well."

" Oho! I remember thee, now," said Roland, with a terrible frown.

"And so thou art the villain who shot my poor horse," said Leslie.

" This is not the case," replied the dogged ruffian, in some perturbation; " but even if it were so, should a brave soldier commit such acts to memory, Laird of Balquhan?"

" Now, by the devil, my Galloway Scot, how camest thou to know my name?"

Birrel saw his mistake, and remained silent.

" Harkye!" said Lintstock again, " are ye not the runion who drove all the cattle mad, and hounded them out upon the hills? where all the collies and dogs in Lanarkshire will never collect them again; for mony a gude score hae tummelled owre the craigs of the Cairntable, and are drowned in the Douglas burn."

" Oho, my friend," said Roland, setting down his wine-cup, and gazing sternly on the brutal and bilious visage of his prisoner, every twitch of whose square mouth, and every glance of whose twinkling eyes indicated the mass of bad thoughts that festered in his heart, " the charges are coming thick and fast against thee; so 'tis to thee we owe the loss of our lawful prize—those prime herds and fattened hirsels ?"

" Say rather to witchcraft; for ken ye, sir, that when I arrived here, three were found to be elfshot, and the rest were

o

under spell; for the gudeman Fleming was dropping upon their horns the blessed wax of a paschal candle, the half whereof is yet remaining——"

"In the pen; he speaks the truth," said Lintstock, "for I saw it there mysel; but sure as I am a living man, it was you who threw the blazing straw-wisps owre the parapets of the bartizan."

"Well, rascal, and didst thou give my message to the bull-headed proprietor of this dwelling?"

"Yea, Sir Roland Vipont, by Heaven I did, word for word."

"So thou knowest *my* name too, eh? (hold him fast, Lintstock)—well?"

"And he made me prisoner."

"I verily believe, peasant, thou liest; for the Laird of Balquhan avers that he saw thee on the walls in armour."

"True, for I armed me in my own defence."

"But thou didst thrice try to shoot me with an arquebuse, as Lintstock here is ready to swear."

"Lintstock hath but one eye."

"'Tis gude as a dozen, d--n ye," growled the old soldier."

"How the devil is it this fellow wears a sword like a French barber?" said Leslie.

"Ay, how is this, thou, who art not a gentleman?"

"I am travelling, and wear it for mine own security."

"A cudgel would better become such a clown as thee; but take it away, Lintstock, and keep it for thy pains. Now, fellow, my mind misgiveth me sorely that thou art playing us a false trick; but as for thy attempts upon my own life, I say let them pass; being done under armour, and in close fray, it would ill become Roland Vipont to bear malice for such trifles—for trifles they are, to a man who feels himself as I do—with the blade of his sword. Though, as thou knowest, man, I might hang thee from one of those beams, for resisting the king's troops, who are empowered" (he added, with a covert smile at Leslie), "to search every stronghold in Douglasdale for the traitor, Ashkirk; I forgive thee, instead; and, as lord and master of this barmkyn, for one night at least, by the laws of conquest and appropriation, I say thou art welcome to a cup of wine, a slice from yon savoury roast, and a seat by the fire till dawn, when may God speed thee to thy native Galloway, and keep us from again meeting under harness. I never bore malice to living man, for blow struck, or bullet shot, after the fray was over, and so bear none to thee. Now, fellow, what is thy name ?"

" John—John Dargavel," replied Birrel, cautiously.

" Then give me thy hand, John Dargavel, and here is mine," replied Roland.

Each kissed his right hand, and presented it to the other.

" This is the generous frankness of a gallant soldier," said Leslie, as Birrel slunk away; " but, I doubt me, 'tis sorely misplaced, for that fellow hath the eye of a very ruffian. St. Mary! I could not have believed my haughty Vipont would have condescended thus—even though a friar had sworn it."

" The faggots of hell encompass thee!" muttered Birrel (uttering the favourite curse of those days), as he overheard Leslie; " but I may, ere the morning, serve my lord and myself by avenging all this! Praise God, I have still my poniard, with ten lives in its pommel !"

He drew near the great fire, and mingled with the soldiers, who were busy spitting strings of pullets, broiling eggs, basting a lordly roast, toasting cheese, and mulling wine, amid such jesting and revelling as none but soldiers can indulge in after danger dared and slaughter past. There were several among them who no doubt would have recognised him as the witch-pricker of Edinburgh, had they been less occupied with the pleasant task of satisfying their appetite, or had they more closely examined his face, the vile expression of which was considerably increased by the manner in which he had smeared it with dust and mud for concealment; but Lintstock, who had some undefinable suspicions concerning him, kept a strict watch over all his movements, and never once lost sight of him, even for a moment, during the whole night.

The feasting was over, the demi-john had been drained, fresh guards had been posted, and the soldiers lay down to sleep, for Roland had announced they were to march by sunrise, and desired Lintstock to prepare a spiced posset of wine for his friend Leslie and himself, against the time when the morning trumpet should sound.

Two box beds opened off the hall, and each officer, without removing his armour, occupied one of them; while their soldiers slept on the floor, lying close together, with their swords and arquebuses beside them; and as the pavement was somewhat cold (even though the month was June), the

staves of the demi-john, a few sturdy oak chairs, and several
other articles of furniture, had been heaped in the chimney,
where they were all blazing in a sheet of flame, like a yule-
nicht fire.

Rolled up in his grey maud, Nichol Birrel reclined in a
corner of the ingle, with his bonnet drawn over his eyes; but
instead of being asleep, as he pretended, he was intently
watching the groups that slept around him. In a more remote
corner lay Lintstock, partly under the hall table, with his
axe and sword under his head as a pillow, and his keen bright
eye fixed on the shaggy-headed brodder, who had not the
least idea that he was either watched or suspected.

And thus the two men lay, for nearly two hours. The
brodder watching the sleeping soldiers, and Lintstock watching him. The one-eyed veteran had conceived an invincible
mistrust and repugnance of their new acquaintance, and lay
awake like a lynx.

The fire began to sink and smoulder; and the objects in
the hall, its great and sturdily-legged table, the sleeping
groups in their conical corslets and red doublets, the yawning
fire-place and the rough arch of the mantelpiece, the ponderous beams of the ceiling and the deep embrasures of the
windows, assumed various shapes to the half-closed eye of
Lintstock. The shadows became black, while a fainter red
began to flicker on the walls as the embers died, and everything became grotesquely indistinct.

Sleep was fast overpowering the drowsy veteran; but before
yielding to it, he gave one last glance at the witch-brodder,
and, starting, grasped the shaft of his Jethart axe.

Birrel had arisen and thrown off his plaid. The last glow
of the sinking embers shone full on his strong squat figure,
his bilious visage, matted beard, and muscular hands, giving
him the aspect of an enormous gnome in their uncertain light.

" Ha! what now, sir ?" muttered Lintstock, quietly.

Birrel unsheathed his dagger; the blade gleamed redly in
the flame; but instead of grasping the hilt in the usual way,
he unscrewed the pommel; and then fortunately a current of
wind which streamed down the wide chimney and fanned the
embers into a sudden flame, showed Lintstock how he took
from the hollow ball a few red grains, and shook them into
the posset-cup which had been prepared for Sir Roland and
his friend, and which stood near the fire upon the warm hearth.

Lintstock grasped his axe tighter.

For a moment the wine-posset frothed and foamed in the light; then the fermentation subsided, and with the last gleam of the exhausted fire Lintstock saw the brodder envelop himself once more in his plaid, and, after stretching his limbs upon the warm ingle-seat, go composedly to sleep.

The firelight had expired, and then Lintstock could perceive the first faint grey of the morning, brightening coldly and steadily beyond the strong iron gratings of the hall windows; and being well aware that the sentinels would permit none to pass without Sir Roland's order or permission, and thus that the captive prisoner could not escape, Lintstock also addressed himself to sleep for the short two hours that intervened before the usual time of marching.

CHAPTER XXVIII.

A DRAUGHT OF WATER.

"How light is my song, as I journey along,
   Now my perilous service is o'er ;
I think on sweet home, and I carol a song,
   In remembrance of her I adore."—TANNAHILL.

WITH the first peep of the sun's red disc above the Cairn-table, the trumpet sounded in the court of the barmkyn ; and starting at once to their arms, the arquebusiers, with the ready resolution of soldiers accustomed to be roused on a moment's warning at all hours and in all seasons, hastened from the hall, and began to fall into their ranks in the yard.

Many dead bodies, and that of the stalwart Fleming among them, were lying among the mire, where the fugitive cattle had trod them ; a lance-spesade proceeded to call the roll, while the fourrier broached a cask of ale, from which every man took a long horn before marching.

Roland Vipont was the first who started at the sound of the trumpet.

" Hollo, Lintstock," cried he ; " my sword and helmet, and bring hither the wine-pot. Come forth, my light Leslie ; the trumpet hath blown."

Lintstock brought the posset to his master, who was about to divide it, by pouring a portion into another cup for Leslie ;

when the wakeful servant whispered into his ear, while lacing
on his helmet—

"Hold ye, Sir Roland, and invite our new friend in the
border maud to taste of it first."

"Methinks muddy ale, or ditch-water, would better suit
his knave's throat; but why this request?"

"There hath been foul play in the night."

"Oho!" said Roland, changing colour and setting down
the cup; "do you say so?"

"Poisoned?" asked Leslie, in a low, fierce voice.

Lintstock winked, and nodded towards Birrel, who, at that
moment, for the third or fourth time, was endeavouring
stealthily to leave the hall, with the last of the soldiers.

"Come hither, friend Dargavel,—for so I believe thou
callest thyself,"—said Roland, filling a wooden bicker from
the large pot of mulled wine; "is it thus thou stealest away
without bidding adieu to me, who am thy host; for thou
knowest that I command all here while within the walls.
Come, drink with us, friend; 'tis a bad maxim to ride with a
fasting stomach, so thou art welcome to a share of this posset,
which has simmered overnight by the fire. Dost thou hear
me, fellow? Art thou deaf?"

Birrel's visage turned deadly pale, and a perspiration suf-
fused the roots of his hair and matted beard.

"I never drink aught that is stronger than water—never,
at any time," said he, with a quavering voice.

"This is false," said Leslie; "for I saw thee dipping thy
moustaches, yea, and thy whole beard, in the demi-john last
night."

"True—but in the morning I never drink either ale, wine, or
usquebaugh—never, sir knights—wi' mony gude thanks for
your courtesie?"

"Tarry with us, friend; be not in a hurry," said Roland—
at a sign from whom Lintstock placed himself in the doorway
—"of what, in the devil's name, does thy morning draught
usually consist?"

"Milk," replied Birrel, becoming blanched with fear, and
looking round for some friendly hole wherein to hide himself.

"A very hermit in temperance! I regret that, in conse-
quence of all the cattle having escaped, we cannot accommo-
date you, my pretty man, with a draught of your favourite
beverage. But hark you, sir," said Roland, unsheathing his

formidable sword; "thou seest this blade?"—well, if thou
dost not drain this cup of wine to the bottom, I will pass
this weapon to the hilt—yea, sirrah, to the very hilt, through
thy body!"

"Of all the sights of horror and disgust," says a popular
writer, "villany transformed at the death-hour into its natural
character and original of cowardice, is among the most appalling." The witch-finder trembled in every limb, and seemed
frozen to stone by this command.

"Ha! thou unfanged reptile, so we have thee by the
throat?" cried Roland, withdrawing his keen, sharp weapon
for the death-thrust; "off with it, to the dregs—yea, to the
very dregs?"

The tongue of Birrel clove to his palate, for the fear of
death and love of life were strong in his breast; he had
dropped ten grains into the goblet—and he remembered the
words of his master, that *each grain* was the life of a man.
He gasped for breath, but could only utter inarticulate murmurs. He turned towards the doorway, and there stood
Lintstock with his eye full of ferocity and his axe uplifted.

"Harkee, hound! dost thou hear me?" said Vipont, spurn-
ing him with his foot.

"Oh, Sir Roland, have mercy, have mercy! The servant
is not responsible for what he does by the orders of his
master?"

"A pleasant rascal this!" said Leslie. "So thou hast a
master, eh?"

Birrel stammered, and paused; for, villain as he was, he
meant not to betray Redhall.

"Think not that, by divulging his name, thou wilt save
thy hang-dog life!" said Roland—who mistook his delay—
"for I swear by the God that is in heaven! if thou drainest
not this draught to the very bottom, I will run thee through
the heart without more preamble. So quick! quick! swallow,
swallow! dost think we have time to trifle about crushing a
reptile so despicable as thee!"

The villain sank upon his knees, for they refused to sustain
his weight; fear froze the very pulses of his heart, and palsied
his tongue; his countenance became livid and clayey; his
eyes sank, and his lips became blue.

"How frightful this villain is!" said Leslie. "Did ever a
brave man look thus in the face of death?"

"Mercy, sirs! mercy! I will sin no more; I will be a gudeman and true—I will tell ye all—my master's name—but mercy, sirs! mercy!"

"Thy master's name! we seek it not," said Roland, as he smote him on the mouth with his gauntleted hand; "we seek it not; for then our honour would compel us to slay him wherever we met him, by holm or hillside, at kirk or in market; and I wish not to stain my father's sword with the blood of villains."

"A priest! then let me have a priest! but five minutes wi' a priest! for, oh, I have mickle to say, and muckle to repent o'!"

"Dog! thou art a Protestant, I believe, and requirest not a priest. No, go down to thy grave with the curse of the God of the living and the God of the dead on thy brow—that dogged front where the mark of hell is written! Drink! drink! dost thou hear me, Cain?"

Roland held the dreadful cup before his eyes by one hand, while, with the other, he gave him a violent prick in the breast with the point of his sword.

Birrel uttered a shriek like a fiend; and, draining the cup to the bottom, flung it full at the face of Roland, who stooped his head, and the wooden vessel was dashed to a thousand shreds on the opposite wall.

"Now I have but two hours to live!" he cried, with the voice of a damned one; "two hours! two hours! two hours!" and, darting through the doorway, he hurled Lintstock from his path as he would a child, and, with one bound sprang down stairs into the courtyard, where he passed through the startled soldiers like a whirlwind, with his visage overspread by the blue pallor of death, his mouth covered with foam, and his matted hair streaming in elf-locks behind him.

Snatching up a cord that lay in his path, he cleared the fossé with one bound, like an evil spirit; and, uttering a succession of frightful cries, plunged down the steep bank, towards the rough rocky bed of the Douglas.

"How now! is the fellow going to hang himself?" said Roland.

"Faith, poisoning might surely satisfy him," replied Leslie.

Master Birrel certainly was about to hang himself, but *not* by the neck.

" I must live—I must live—oh, yes, I must, for venge-ance !" he yelled; for, coward as he was, he felt that he could have died happy, if, by so doing, he could destroy Roland Vipont and Jane Seton—yea, and his master too, who had sent him on an errand so fatal in its termination.

While some of the soldiers were burying the dead, and others were tracing the horses to the artillery, the poisoned ruffian ran wildly to a solitary part of the river, where he threw himself on his face, and imbibed an inordinate draught of cold water—drinking, drinking, drinking—as if he was a mere hollow pipe. Loosening his waist-belt, and untying the points of his doublet, he stooped and drank deeply again, burying his face in the water until his distended stomach felt swollen as if to bursting, and when he arose the whole landscape swam around him. Then, selecting the branch of a tree, he clambered up to it with the utmost difficulty, for he had turned himself into a mere water barrel.

Then, in a horror of anxiety—for every moment wasted seemed an eternity—he tied his ankles to the branch, and lowering his body perpendicularly till his hands rested on the turf, he remained suspended, head downwards, in the hope that, with the ocean of water he had drunk, he might dis-gorge the frightful poison he had been compelled to swallow. But long before this hideous operation was over, Roland Vipont, Leslie, and their soldiers, with the royal banners dis-played, and their bright armour gleaming in the sun, were marching down the pastoral valley, on their route to Edin-burgh, having now traversed the whole dale of the Douglas *without* discovering the Earl of Ashkirk.

" Now, fare ye well, Lanarkshire, and welcome the dun summit of Arthur's Seat," thought Roland ; as, full of the most brilliant anticipations of happiness, he spurred his gallant horse and patted its arching neck. " In three days I will be with my dear Jeanie ; and, in a month from this, whether the king sayeth yea or nay, she shall be my winsome bride !"

CHAPTER XXIX.

THE SECOND VISIT.

" Give me again my innocence of soul;
Give me my forfeit honour blanched anew;
Cancel my treasons to my royal master;
Restore me to my country's lost esteem,
To the sweet hope of mercy from above,
And the calm comforts of a virtuous heart."
Edward the Black Prince.

THE soothing or sleeping draught had been duly administered by Tib Trotter, and Jane Seton slept.

Everything of late had happened most favourably for the intriguing lord advocate. The queen's delicate health, the king's anxiety, his fear and suspicion of the Douglases; the imprisonment of the countess of Inchkeith, and the retirement of the court to the Abbey of Balmerino; but chiefly the young earl's proscription, the banishment of all his retainers from the city, and the protracted absence of Roland Vipont in Douglasdale, from whence it was to be hoped Birrel would never permit him to return alive, left Archibald Seton and his sister utterly at the mercy of Redhall, the chambers of whose mansion were as secret and secure as those of the recently-established Holy Office at St. Andrew's.

Animated by no new evil intention, but solely by his clamorous desire to see her, to be near her, that he might touch her hands or kiss her cheek unrepelled, Redhall had administered the narcotic to his fair captive, whom he now prepared to visit.

It was midnight; his whole household was buried in slumber; and as the moment approached when he had proposed to pay this somewhat equivocal visit, a tremor took possession of his heart, a dimness came over his eyes, and he imbibed more than one glass of wine, to string his nerves and still his agitation.

" Poh!" said he, as his cheek reddened; " all this excitement about visiting a girl—a girl who is asleep, too."

Like many other Scottish houses where the walls were strong, Redhall's mansion was furnished with several narrow wheel-staircases, which, like gimlet-holes, perforated the edifice from top to bottom, communicating with the various stories. One of these descended from the door of his apart-

ment to another which gave entrance to Jane Seton's, opening just behind the arras of her bed.

Redhall laid his poniard on the table, from which he took
a candle, and treading softly in his maroquin slippers, found
himself at the door of Jane's apartment, and there he paused.
Though not a current of air swept up the narrow staircase, the
candle in his tremulous hand streamed like a pennon, while
a glow of fear and shame traversed his heart like a red-hot
iron.

Tib had informed him that Lady Jane kept candles burning
in her room all night; so, extinguishing his, he noiselessly
opened the little private door, and drew back the arras. A
sense of flowers and perfume, mingled with the closer atmosphere of the chamber, was wafted towards him, and, by the
light of two candles which, in massive square holders of
Bruges silver, burned on the toilet-table, he was enabled to
make a survey of the whole dormitory on which he was in-
truding. Though he was unconscious of any guilty intention, there was (he mentally acknowledged) something equivocal in the time and manner of his visit that appalled his
heart. He felt shame glowing on his cheek : he saw spies
in every shadow, and heard a voice in every echo of his own
footfalls.

Softly he let the arras drop, but, in his excitement, forgot
to close behind him the door which it was intended to conceal.

Unused, from the first hour she had occupied the chamber,
the magnificent bed prepared for Jane Seton had not been
disturbed, and with its cornices of carved oak, its festooned
hangings and aspiring feathers, its heraldic blazonry and grotesque devices, it towered upon its dais like a monument in
some old abbey aisle.

Placed on each side of a mirror, the two candles reflected
a bright light upon the warmly-coloured tapestry of the
apartment; the Persian carpet of its floor, the fresh flowers
that, in jars of Venetian glass, decorated the mantelpiece,
and all the innumerable little ornaments with which the taste
and policy of Redhall had furnished it, to beguile the tedium
or flatter the vanity of his unwilling prisoner.

"She sleeps!" said he, advancing on tiptoe, and shading
his eyes with his hand, "she sleeps, and soundly too. Oh,
how beautiful she is! How pure, how innocent she looks

he added, gazing upon her with eyes of adoration, for he
loved her exceedingly, and with a depth of regard which,
though not based on the same sentiments of esteem, was nowise inferior perhaps to that of the more favoured Roland
Vipont.

She was seated in a large arm-chair of the most luxurious
description. Carved like a gigantic clamshell, the back, with
its arms and sides, were of damask, stuffed with the softest
down, and the woodwork was elaborately gilt. She reclined
within it, with a hand, white as alabaster, resting on each of
the arms; her head lay somewhat on her right shoulder, over
which her unbound hair poured in a shower of ringlets,
which, from her recumbent position, reached nearly to the
ground. Her face was pale as her hands; but some vision
was rising before her, through the depth of her slumber, and
a soft smile played on her beautiful mouth.

Though feeling certain that, under the influence of what
she had imbibed, Jane would not awake, Redhall scarcely
dared to breathe; but, impelled by the delirium that was
rapidly mounting to his brain, a devouring longing to touch,
to embrace her, possessed him; and, kneeling before his
sleeping divinity, he kissed both her hands repeatedly and
affectionately. Then he became giddy, and his heart beat
furiously; pulses rang in his ears, and all his senses began to
wander wildly; he gently encircled her with his arms, pressed
her to his breast, and kissed her soft cheek again and again.
A blindness seemed to come over him.

" Oh, beautiful, indeed, thou art, and most adorable, too;
but proud and pitiless to me—to poor me, that loves thee so
well!" he murmured, becoming almost maudlin; " why hast
thou so great a horror of a poor being that would kiss the
very dust whereon thou treadest? Oh, this love is bewilder-
ing me—I am not the same man—oh, no,—'tis a torment—
a frenzy."

His hot, dry eyes became moistened, and one large tear fell
upon the cheek of Jane.

She suddenly opened her large startled eyes, and fixed
them upon him with an expression of terror and stupefaction;
while his own astonishment was so great that he forget to
release her from his embrace.

The draught had been less potent than the apothegar
intended.

" 'Tis a dream!'' she muttered, and closed her eyes; " another dream, but always that face of horror!''

Then, becoming more awake, and more alive to her situation, and feeling that the arms of some one encircled her, she shuddered, and, in great alarm, attempted to rise, but her limbs were powerless, and a strange numbness tied her to her chair. She made a superhuman effort to cry, but her tongue was powerless.

" Mother! mother! what is this? Assist me, for I am wholly at his mercy! I am in the power of a demon, who will fascinate me with his eyes.''

Laying her gently back, his first impulse was to retreat before perfect consciousness returned; but she seemed so agitated, so woe-begone, and so frightfully pale, that he dared not leave her; and, on his knees, began to chafe in his her soft and dimpled hands.

Gradually, the truth forced itself upon Jane. Her actual tormentor, and no vision, was before her. She began to weep, and covered her face with her snow-white hands, over which her hair fell like a glossy veil.

" Oh, despair! despair! am I abandoned for ever? Roland, Roland! come to me, dearest Roland!'' she exclaimed, incoherently. " Oh, man, man! why dost thou persecute me thus?''

Sir Adam Otterburn was stung to the heart by her words; but, sighing deeply, he gently parted her dishevelled hair, and said—

" Lady Jane, I am aware that I am guilty of great wrong towards you; but it is the guilt of love, and love should pardon the frenzy it has caused.''

" I can pardon your love, but can I pardon the misery it hath caused me? It is not the love of a sane man, but the fantasy of a madman. I am thy prisoner, lawlessly thy prisoner; but thou hast infamously violated the ties of honour and hospitality in breaking the privacy of a helpless woman. Fie upon thee, man! for I will raise upon thee even thine own detested household!''

She rose, staggering, and more than once passed her hand across her forehead, for her faculties were as yet obscured by the potion.

" Oh, deem me not so vile!'' said Redhall, clasping his hands, and looking upon her with the most sad and solemn earnestness. "I came but to see, to touch, to be near you, to breathe but the same air with you, to look upon you without being repulsed, to sit by and worship you; and I have done so with such adoration as I have never felt even before the altar of my God; and I call Him to witness, if in my mind there was kindled one impure or one unholy thought."

"Fool!" said Jane, bitterly, for she was full of angry alarm; "thou ravest like one of Lindesay's playmen. Thy purity of thought should have made thee respect as sacred the chamber to which I am consigned. Sir Adam, in all thy love-making there is a fustian sophistry, which shows thou art immensely inferior to my Vipont; and he, though but a rough soldier, never dared resort to blasphemy in expressing his love for me."

Jane saw the agony that Vipont's name always occasioned her tormentor, and could not forbear to sting him with it. A cold moisture studded his pale forehead with diamond-like drops; a satanic smile lit up with a gleam of undisguised jealousy his dark and homicidal eyes.

In this taunt she felt her strength; but saw not the danger of driving to despair a heart so fierce, so proud, so jealous and resentful. He approached, but she drew back with a haughty look.

"Beware, Sir Adam," said she; "for even if the king and his court forget that I am the daughter of John, Earl of Ashkirk, I have a dear brother, and a dearer *friend*, who, if they cannot at present protect, will one day surely and fearfully avenge me!"

"Proud lady," he replied, with calm fury, "if neither Heaven nor hell can protect thee, dost think that thy brother, who is my prisoner, and whose life is in my hands; or that other miserable moth—that holiday captain, in steel plates and gilded scales—will succour, save, or avenge thee?"

"They will, they will, I tell thee, false baron and craven man; thou corrupt counsellor and cowardly Otterburn! And when Vipont returns, thou and all thy kindred may tremble, for neither the Otterburns of Redhall, nor Redford of Auld-hame or Avondoune, will be able to withstand him."

He smiled sourly; and she uttered a scornful laugh.

"Woman, how pitilessly thou plantest poniards in a heart that loves thee well. Oh, beware! beware! for a single drop will make the cup that brims to overflow. My heart can

know no medium; it is capable of only two extremes. Love
the most blind, hatred the most insane; and at times I feel
that it vibrates between them. Beware of the last; and, oh!
beware of thrusting this rival in my face, for slowly, but
surely, drop by drop, as it were, a savage longing for revenge
will gather in my heart; yea, drop by drop, till it swells
into a flood—a fierce, a furious flood, that, bearing all before
it (like a mountain torrent), will drown alike the stings of
conscience and of pity, and, like a feather on its surface, will
sweep you away with it."

" Sir Roland Vipont is a gallant soldier, who will laugh
alike at thy vengeance and thy bombast. True, wretch! thou
mayst murder him, as thou didst M'Clellan of Bombie," she
continued, with eyes full of tears and fire; "but even then
we will find hearts and hands to avenge us."

Redhall remained for some moments speechless with passion
and confusion.

"Bombie!" he reiterated, turning ghastly pale; "what
leads you to suppose I ever committed a crime so frightful?
Speak! But this is the wordy anger of a woman. You talk
of an affair which happened eleven years ago, when you must
have been but little more than a child. Lady, these words
are rash and unadvised. Oh! I implore thee to beware of
exciting in my heart the hatred of which I spoke, and of
which I feel it capable."

" Then I will repeat them a thousand and a thousand times,
thou murderer of the brave Sir Thomas M'Clellan, my father's
long-loved friend. I need care little for thy *hatred*, when thy
mad love costs me so dear."

" My hatred—beware, I implore thee once again—beware
of it!"

Lady Seton laughed; and a gloomy expression gathered in
the dark solemn eyes of Redhall.

" Think, dear lady—think," said he, " of the ruin that
hangs over thee and thy house."

" Do thou rather reflect on that, and remember that, were
I to wed thee, for ever wouldst thou lose the favour of James,
the cardinal, and their obsequious parliament; destroying
thyself without lessening one iota the thousand pitiless seve-
rities to which the knights and barons of our faction are
subjected."

" Nay, lady, nay; I who have done, can *undo*. Many of

those acts of proscription and severity were enacted by my advice and by my influence.''

" Another incentive to abhor thee.''

" But I can restore the banished to their homes,—the dishonoured to honour—the unhappy to happiness—the ruined and despairing to wealth and affluence; and to do all this by a word lies with thee alone.''

" St. Mary! I know not whether to weep with vexation or laugh at thee with scorn,'' said Jane, in great distress and perplexity, for she could not but acknowledge mentally that he spoke the truth. " Oh, Vipont! Vipont!'' she added, in a low voice, " assuredly thou hast abandoned me.''

Another wild gleam passed over the eyes of Redhall.

" Rash woman, how thou bravest me! if thy heart, insensible as it is, has neither love for me, nor pity for the knights and nobles of thy race, surely at least it will tremble for thyself! Behold this warrant,'' he continued, drawing a parchment from his bosom; " from this house, Jane Seton, thou canst only pass to the castle of Edinburgh. Here are accusations of treason; of conspiring with the English; of resetting rebels; and worse, oh! worse a thousand times than all—sorcery, and compassing, by spell and charm, the life of Queen Magdalene.''

He paused, and his lowering countenance assumed a diabolical expression; for his stormy passions were wavering (as he had said) between excess of love and excess of hate.

" Ponder well upon my offer, and deeper upon my threat; respect the first, and—fear the second. Life, honour, power, and happiness are in my right hand; trial and torture, disgrace and death, the stake and the gibbet, are in my left. Here, love the most tender and most true; there, revenge revelling like an unchained fiend! Think, think, oh! for mercy's sake—for pity's sake; and for the love of God, think, ere thou dost for the last time pause or repel me.''

Trembling, and scarcely able to restrain her tears—

" Sir Adam Otterburn,'' she replied, " I despise alike these offers and those threats; for if not a villain, and a cruel one, thou art (and, Heaven protect me!) assuredly a madman.''

His countenance became livid, and his eyes sad.

" Then so be it—*a madman!* Then, as a madman, let me have but one soul, one thought, and one desire—vengeance! the deep, thirsty vengeance of madness, of jealousy and despair!''

Terrified by his aspect and his fury, Jane had withdrawn to the farthest end of the apartment, when a new gust of passion seized him, and he sprang towards her.

"There is but *one* way left me now. Am I a child, a boy, a fool, that I trifle with thee, who art pitiless as a panther, and inanimate as marble?" he exclaimed, as he seized her, and endeavoured to encircle her with his arms; "in this house thou art completely in my power as in the midst of a desert, and now—and now——"

"Mercy!" cried Jane, filled with a sudden sense of new danger, as she endeavoured to elude his wild grasp, and the gaze of his large, dark, gloating eyes, and prayed aloud for safety and protection.

"Ay, invoke and cry, and pray to God or to man, as thou pleasest; but will either hear thee?"

"Vipont! Vipont!"

"Ha! ha! the hand of Birrel is in his heart."

"Archibald!" she panted, sinking down against the wall, and overcome with terror. "Oh, Archibald, my brother, my brother!"

"*Here!*" cried a voice like a trumpet; the arras was torn aside, and a man sprang forward—there was a flash as a poniard was buried in the breast of Redhall, and the black velvet of his doublet was stained with red, a cloud of darkness descended upon his eyes; and as he fell weltering in his blood, Jane was borne away by the strong intruder.

CHAPTER XXX.

SANCTUARY! SANCTUARY!

"A strange emotion stirs within him—more
  Than mere compassion ever waked before;—
  Unconsciously he opes his arms, while she
  Springs forward, as with life's lost energy."—*Lalla Rookh.*

THE Earl of Ashkirk, on finding that he was actually possessor of a small steel knife, could scarcely repress his joy till nightfall, or refrain from indulging in a merry song; so his exuberance expended itself in whistling, and drawing on the walls a variety of caricatures of Redhall hanging upon a gallows, invariably appending to his face an enormous nose;

P

for that feature of the lord advocate, though straight and singularly handsome, was, to say the least of it, somewhat long
and dignified.

As the sun set, he employed himself in tapping with the
handle of the knife the various stones of the partition wall,
for the idea of effecting a breach through the vast solidity of
the external barrier never occurred to him.

There was one part of the inner wall which was jointed
with remarkably large and square stones, where, by the frequent sound of feet ascending and descending, he felt assured
there was a stair behind; and there he resolved to commence
operations the moment he was confident of being left undisturbed for that night.

He was singularly facetious with Tam Trotter when the
latter, as usual, left him for the last time about six o'clock,
and secured all the doors. By this time the earl had decided
upon which stone to operate, and selected one about four feet
from the floor; he marked it with a cross for good luck, and
after viewing his treasured knife for the thousandth time, repaired to his little window to watch the lagging sunset.

Never, even when longing for a meeting with Sybil, did
the moments pass so slowly.

The evening was still and calm, and not a leaf was stirring
in the venerable chestnuts and sycamores at the foot of the
little park which extended towards the south, behind the
house of Redhall. The sunlight died away on Arthur's Seat,
and the sky gradually deepened to a darker and more cerulean
blue, and one by one the stars came out of its bosom; the
hum of the city, and other sounds of life without, ceased
gradually, and nothing was heard but now and then the
striking of a friary clock, or the jangling bells in the convent
of Placentia. Night—the short but beautiful night of June
—had come on; and one might have imagined that another
and a softer day was dawning in the glorious light of the
midsummer moon, as it rose in unclouded magnificence above
the craigs of Salisbury; then, with the first ray that shone
into his chamber, the earl, whose heart beat rapidly and almost
fiercely with anxiety, and whose hands trembled, but with
eagerness, drew forth his treasured knife, and commenced the
arduous and exciting work of escape.

Fitted close as books on a shelf, squared and built with
little mortar, the task of loosening and completely disengaging

one stone occupied hours. The knife bent like a willow wand; and the earl's heart almost sunk with fear lest it should break, and that if he failed or was discovered at such a task, a stronger prison, perhaps a hopeless dungeon, might be apportioned to him. Loosened on all sides, the stone he had selected was a block a foot high by eighteen inches broad; it vibrated to the touch, but the utmost exertion and art he could put in practice failed to coax it one inch from its deep bed in the wall; the knife, his nails, his fingers, were all resorted to successively again and again, but in vain—it shook, it vibrated, but obstinately remained in its place, till in a fit of fury, and when about to abandon the task in despair, he uttered a malediction, and gave the stone a violent push with both his hands! Then, lo! it shot through the wall to the outside, and disengaging others in its passage, fell upon what Lord Ashkirk discovered in a moment to be a step of one of those narrow stairs we have described in the preceding chapter.

The echoes of its fall died away in the stony windings of the stair; and grasping his knife, the earl stood for a moment petrified, lest all his labour and anxiety were lost, and the noise should rouse the household; but fortunately (save their master) all the members of it were buried in profound repose. The earl could hear his heart beating, as the blood rushed back tumultuously upon it; but all remained still as death, and he could hear the corbies croaking as they swung in their nests among the foliage of the ancient trees without.

There was not a moment to be lost.

With some difficulty he crawled through the aperture, and found himself in a dark and narrow stair. His first thought was to replace the heavy stone, which he did with ease, for this gallant young noble was strong as a Hercules; thus, as the breach was immediately behind the door, it was concealed from those who might enter the chamber; and hence the dismay of Tam Trotter on the morrow, when he found it void, without knowing or perceiving how.

The earl was naturally about to descend, when the cry of a female arrested him; and though he knew not with certainty that his sister Jane was in the power of Sir Adam Otterburn, the voice made him experience something like an electric shock; and he sprang up the stair, taking three steps at a time.

The first apartment he entered was empty; a light burned

on the table, which bore a pyramid of letters and papers;
the walls were shelved, and covered with vellum-bound
volumes—it was the study or library of the lord advocate.
A Flemish clock, in workmanship and aspect little superior
to a common roasting-jack of modern times, hung above the
mantel-piece, and pointed to the hour of twelve.

Above him the earl heard voices, whose purport he could
not discover, but whose tones seemed familiar to his ear.

Appropriating to himself a handsome poniard that lay on
the table, just where Redhall had placed it about an hour
before, he sprang to the next story, at the door of which a
candle was burning on the floor: it streamed in a current of
air, which announced to the observant earl that there must
be an external door below.

The voices were those of his sister Jane and their enemy,
Redhall.

A storm of passion filled his heart; and at the very moment she was exclaiming—" Archibald! oh, Archibald, my
brother!" he tore aside the arras, and striking Redhall to
the floor with his own poniard, seized his sister by the hand,
and led, or rather dragged her forth, and down the steep
stair, at the bottom of which they found themselves in the
vaulted stone lobby of the mansion. Everything was yet
silent.

The flaring light of a smoky oil lamp which stood on a
grotesque stone bracket projecting from the wall, revealed its
furniture, which consisted of little more than a few sturdy
oak chairs, and a stout bin, whereon stood an ale barrel,
with a quaigh hanging on its spigot, wherewith the servants
of visitors, or whoever chose, might quench their thirst; for
such was the hospitable fashion of the olden time. At the
further end of the lobby* was an arch closed by a strong
door, which was secured by one ponderous wooden bar, that
crossed it transversely, and had a solid rest in the walls at
each side.

To shoot back this bar of oak, to open the heavy door, and
rush into the Canongate, were but the work of a moment—
and then Lord Ashkirk and his sister were free.

"Oh, Archibald! Archibald!" cried Jane, as she threw

---

* Scottish for an entrance-hall; derived, I believe, from the German *laube*:
a gallery, or walking-place.

herself into the arms of her brother in a transport of grief and excitement—" am I quite saved—and by you?"

" I have not a moment to lose, dear Jeanie, for the blood-hounds of Redhall will be upon my track. Yonder is our house. I dare not enter it; but once there, thou at least art safe."

" With my mother—oh, yes; when with my mother I will fear nothing. Our dear mother! but thou——?"

" Must hasten hence. Edinburgh will be too hot to hold me after this affair; and already I have been too rash in residing here. " Hah!" he exclaimed, half savagely, but with a shudder, as he held up his hand, " this is the blood of Redhall! There will be a vacant gown in the High Court to-morrow—one villain less in that tribunal of cowards! Here, then, thou art safe. I will cross into Fife, even should I swim the Firth, and will retire towards the Highlands, as the king will be sure to look for me on the Borders. Tell Vipont of this, and intrust yourself to him, for he alone can protect thee now. I can no more."

" But Roland is in Douglasdale, and our mother a prisoner in the castle of Inchkeith!"

The earl gnashed his teeth with passion.

" How many wheels hath this dark conspiracy!" said he. " Ha! 'tis well I struck deep to-night."

" See, Archibald, our house is dark and deserted; the gates are locked. Oh! such silence and desolation!"

" What shall we do now? If I stay with thee I shall be taken, and if taken, shall indubitably be hanged, *red hand*. See, this horrible poniard is actually glued to my fingers!"

" Away thou to the hills, and leave me. Oh, Archibald! seek shelter anywhere. Thou art the last hope of us all, Archibald! with thee our father's name, and fame, and race would perish."

" True; and, what is worth them all, our hopes of vengeance on the Hamiltons. I must live for that! This night hath commenced it; and my hand has struck one from the list of Angus's foes and Arran's friends. Jane, we are now past the Girth Cross; thou art safe now, for not even Redhall would dare to violate the holy sanctuary. Its girdle will protect thee like a magic zone. Remain in the abbey church till daybreak, and then Sir John Forrester, who is Roland's friend—a good man and a gallant knight, will see thee in safety to our mother's side. One kiss, dear Jeanie, and then a long farewell till better times."

Jane thought of the terrible warrant which Redhall had held before her eyes; but fearing to delay her brother, or to alarm him more, she tendered her soft cheek, against which he pressed his long rough beard, and there they parted, in the middle of that dark and deserted street; for the light of a pale and waning moon threw the sombre shadow of the ancient Mint far beyond the Girth Cross, which, on its shaft of stone, stood in the centre of the street. Reflected from the large masses of white clouds that were scudding over the city, the cold moonlight shone on the vanes of the palace gate, and the square towers of the abbey church, for it then had three—a great rood tower, and one on each side of the entrance.

Intimate with all the localities of the town, the earl avoided the Water-gate, where he knew a sentinel was posted; and passed down a narrow close overhung by many a "sclaited lodging" and antique " timber-land;" he reached the wall at the bottom unseen, scaled it with agility, and found himself close to the hospital of St. Thomas, which was then in the course of erection, by George Crichton, Bishop of Dunkeld, and dedicated to the Virgin and all the saints, for the health of his own soul and the souls of the kings of Scotland, for so runs the charter of its foundation. From thence he bent his steps towards Leith, hoping with the dawn to cross the Forth by the first ferry-boat that departed for Kinghorn.

Though weak, feeble, and sinking with terror, Jane Seton, instead of hurrying at once to Holyrood, the dimly-lighted shrines of which were visible through its western windows and doorway (for *then* church doors stood permanently open), lingered affectionately so long as her brother was in sight, nor turned away until he had disappeared.

At the porch, which served both as an entrance to the ancient abbey and to the new palace, was a doorway, where hung a certain bell, which was only rung by those claiming the ancient and still sacred privilege of sanctuary. Opposite was an edifice occupied as a guard-house by the king's arque-busiers.

" Mother of Mercy, be praised!" she exclaimed, with a heart full of thankfulness, as she raised her hand trembling with eagerness to the bell-rope, when, lo! swift as light, a man sprang into the archway, cut the cord, and seized her by the arm. Jane uttered a faint cry, and sank against the wall, on seeing the hateful visage of Dobbie, the doomster, and hearing his false and hollow laugh in her ear. There was a savage leer in his eyes, and he lolled out a long red tongue through his short wiry beard, as he arrested her.

On one side lay the porter-lodge of the abbey, where she would have received a sanctuary; on the other lay the guardhouse of the soldiers; and she knew that if discovered by them, after what Redhall told her, she would indeed be lost. On one hand lay life—on the other death!"

"Sanctuary!" she cried with a despairing voice, as she clung to the handle of the door; "sanctuary, father abbot —good master porter! In the name of the blessed Trinity, sanctuary! For the love of God and St. Mary, sanctuary! sanctuary! Oh, man, man!" she continued, wildly, as the wretch threw his arms around her, and forcibly dragged her away, "what wrong have I ever done thee? Oh, for my brother's dagger now!—pity, pity! I am very weak and ill. Sweet Mother of Compassion have mercy upon me, for others have none!"

Her voice failed and sense began to leave her.

"How now—what the devil!" cried a rough voice, "whose brittle ware may this lass be?"

"By St. Girzy, a fair strapping dame!" cried another.

"Let go the lass, rascal, or I will brain thee with the boll of my arquebuse!" exclaimed a third, as several soldiers of the guard came hurriedly out of the porch with their swords drawn and matches lighted.

Jane's eyes were closed, but she felt several hands laid roughly upon her, as she was dragged into the court of guard.

"Ho! ho!—blood!" said one; "hath this squeeling mudlark committed a murder? see, there are red spots on her crammasie kirtle."

"Yea, and worse," said Dobbie; "she is a sorceress of the house of Seton; and here is my lord the cardinal's warrant for her committal to ward, signed and sealed wi' his braid hat, tassels and a'"

"A sorceress!" muttered the soldiers; and Jane felt their hands withdrawn as they shrunk back; and at that moment a deadly faintness came over her. . . . . .

Meanwhile, passing under the dark brow of the Doocraig,

a rock of the Calton, and past the old street and chapel of St. Ninian, which lay on the opposite eminence, the earl hurried down the long pathway then known as the Loan, which led to Leith. St. Anthony's Gate, which closed the seaport towards Edinburgh, was shut, but with the first peep of dawn it was opened by the warders; and as the earl had bestowed the interval in cleansing himself from several spots of blood, and adjusting his toilet, he passed without question the keepers of the barrier, and several of the old hospitallers of St. Anthony, who, even at that early hour, were perambulating the Kirkgate in their long black cassocks, which had a large T and a bell shaped in blue cloth on the breasts thereof.

At the pier—an ancient erection of wood which was burned by the English during Hertford's wanton invasion seven years after—the earl found the Kinghorn sloop just about to sail, and sprang on board, descending from the pier to the deck by one of those old-fashioned *treenebrigges*, which, by an act of the legislature in 1425, all ferriers were bound to have prepared for the safe shipment of horse and man. Unchanged since the days of James I., the fare was then only twopence Scots for a man or woman, and sixpence for a horse, under pain of imprisonment in the Tolbooth, and the forfeiture of forty shillings to the crown in case of extortion; thus the earl, though his funds were low indeed, easily passed on board, among the Fifeshire cottars and Burrowtown merchants of small wares, who crowded the low waist of the little vessel, which in a short time was running past the Mussel Cape and the Beacon Rock (whereon the martello tower now stands), and bearing away for the quaint and venerable town of Kinghorn, which lies on the opposite shore.

CHAPTER XXXI.

THE PORTE OF THE SPUR.

"What! no reprieve, no least indulgence given,
No beam of hope from any point of heaven?
Ah, mercy! mercy! art thou dead above?
Is love extinguished in the source of love?"

The Last Day, Book III.

REDHALL's second wound was of the most dangerous kind. It was below that inflicted by Roland, but nearer the region of the heart; it bled profusely; and his blind passion and fury on discovering that Lady Jane had really escaped, carried him beyond all bounds. While Trotter sprang on horseback, and galloped off for John of the Silvermills, and Dobbie, armed with the warrant, was despatched to recapture the fugitive Jane and her brother the earl, and have them secured in the castle of Edinburgh, Redhall, in a paroxysm of rage and despair, so great that it rendered him supine and power-less, lay on his bed as in a swoon, until the arrival of the physician, on whom, as on all, he enjoined (under the most tremendous threats) solemn silence concerning a wound, the inflicter of which he declined to name.

The strong emotions of anger and revenge, which, with every fresh interview, rejection, and defeat, had been gradu-ally gathering in his heart, had now indeed swollen, drop by drop, to the torrent he had predicted; and, like the reed upon the current, she was about to be swept away with it.

"Harkye, Dobbie!" said he, through his clenched teeth, between which the blood was oozing, as he writhed in agony on his bed; "harkye! give me thy thumb; silence on all this—as thou livest, my good man and true—silence on this matter—I tell thee *silence!* Here is the warrant—seek the Albany herald and captain of the guard—quick! have this woman committed to ward, as it imports!"

"Should she say she has been our prisoner already?"

"Begone, fool! who would believe her? Hence—hence, my God!—go, wretch," he added, in a low, hissing voice, as Dobbie hurried away; "go, and accomplish this my work of vengeance; and, one day or other, I shall brush thee, too, from my path, like the bloated spider thou art!"

In half an hour the physician arrived; and the light of the dull grey dawn presented a figure which certainly had something very appalling in it, for, in his haste, he had come away wearing a mask which was furnished with two large, green, globular glass eyes, to protect his face from the poison-ous air and scorching heats of his laboratory. His high and wrinkled forehead lowered above it, and his long beard flowed below.

The wound was speedily bathed and salved; and lint, with a bandage, was applied.

"Thou seest, friend, that I find this new office of king's advocate no sinecure," said Redhall, with a fierce smile. "A thousand furies—how the wound smarts!"

" 'Tis the *unguentum armarium*," replied the learned John, with medical composure; "one touch is sufficient to make such a wound as this shrink to the size of a pin-thrust, and two ought to efface it."

"I feel as if the dagger was still in my heart! Two touches cure, sayest thou?"

"Yea, my lord."

"I pray they may do so."

"They must, Sir Adam, if thou followest rigidly my prescriptions, which are here," and from his pouch he produced various phials marked with those cabalistic figures which are still so much in vogue among apothecaries. These he drew up in line, with their labels hanging like shields before them. "Here is my Elixir of Life, which the care of many a long year hath yet failed to perfect, for the lack of a certain herb which groweth in Arabia Petræa, and is the real *arbor vitæ*—the tree of life of the patriarchs; but still, its restorative and strengthening properties are wondrous! Here are my mercurial balm and the essence of acorns, which last giveth to the bones the strength of the oak tree, and to the nerves and sinews the toughness and tenacity of the ivy. A spoonful of each are taken night and morning, dissolved in a little warm water; and doubt not, Sir Adam, that this day week will behold you a strong man, and well—yea, with redoubled energies, like those whom the Cassida of the pagan Romans restored to life."

And with these words the physician retired, leaving Redhall to writhe and struggle, in solitude, with his mental and bodily agonies—the former outdoing the latter by a thousand-fold.

Our learned astrologer enjoyed a great reputation in Edinburgh, and doubtless would have enjoyed a still greater in the present day, if we may judge of the success of southern quacks and quackeries; as they, like everything that is English, enjoy a vast popularity among the Scottish vulgar.

At this time Lady Jane Seton was at the porch of the palace, from whence Dobbie had dispatched one soldier for the Albany herald, and another to Sir John Forrester. On reviving, she found herself surrounded by arquebusiers in their steel caps, gorgets, and bandoliers, gazing on her with bold and scrutinizing eyes.

"What manner o' lassie is this?" said they, crowding

round her chair, and winking to each other. "A dainty bird —i'faith!" said one.

"What hands;—how white!" said another.

"What ankles!" said a third connoisseur, stooping down. "Soul o' my body! but a glisk o' these would damn St. Anthony and St. Andrew to boot!"

"I am Jane Seton of Ashkirk," said she, suddenly opening her eyes, and looking wildly and imploringly upon them; "oh, where is your captain, my good soldiers—where is Sir John of Corstorphine?"

"He will be here immediately, madam," said one, while the rest fell back respectfully and abashed, and several felt themselves constrained to uncover before her, and remove their helmets. Though every man in the ranks of the royal guard was a born vassal and kinsman of the house of Hamilton, that inborn respect for gentle blood which the Scots possess in a high degree, together with that generous frankness which the camp always teaches, impressed with silence the thirty soldiers who occupied the court-of-guard; and the noisy jests and laughter, which first greeted and surrounded Lady Jane, immediately became hushed.

Seeing that she was faint and pale, one, without being asked, filled his drinking-horn with water, and brought it to her. Her fine eyes gave him a look of thankfulness that sank deep into the honest fellow's heart, and then she drank thirstily.

Pulling a ring from her finger, she offered it to him, but he shook his head, and drew back, saying, with a smile :—

"Nay, lady; a die sae braw is useless to the like o' me, a puir soldier-lad."

"But I owe thee something for thy kindness."

"You owe me nothing, Lady Jean; my mother was a Seton."

At that moment Sir John Forrester, who had been summoned from his lodgings in the palace, and had come forth armed with soldier-like alacrity, entered. with his visor up, displaying the sad and dark cloud that hovered on his brow; for the watchful Dobbie had met him in the palace-yard, and placed in his hand the warrant for Lady Jane's arrest and "committal to ward," as they phrased it in those days.

"To your arms!" said he, waving his hand to the soldiers, who immediately took their arquebuses from the rack, where they stood in a row, and leaving the guard-house, fell into their ranks before it.

" My dear Lady Jane," said the courtly knight, taking both her hands in his, the moment they were left alone; " from what has all this frightful affair arisen ?"

Jane answered only with her tears.

" Lady—dear lady, of what are you guilty ?"

" Ask the leaders of your faction, Sir John," she replied, bitterly ; " but ask not me."

" My faction, lady ?"

" Thou servest the Court ?"

" Nay, madam, I serve the king, like Sir Roland Vipont, whose fast friend I am; and as such, I beg permission to be thine.

" I thank you, Sir John Forrester," replied Jane, with another passionate burst of tears ; " but were my father and the Lord Angus here, as of old, I had needed no other friends; but, alas! the one lieth now in his grave at St. Giles's, while the other is a poor and impoverished exile, compelled to eat the bread of Englishmen. Alas! I am now totally forsaken."

" Nay, lady ; for here stand I, John Forrester of Corstorphine, ready to be your champion ; and as such, to maintain your innocence against all men living, body for body, according to the laws of battle and of arms."

" A thousand thanks, Sir John ; but remember, Sir Roland Vipont claims priority in that.   Meanwhile, let me leave this place."

" And dost thou know for where ?"

" Oh, yes," she replied, with a bitter smile ; " for the castle of Edinburgh ; be it so ; I am not the first of my race who has paid dearly the penalty of opposing tyranny.   There were Sir John de Seton, and his kinsman Sir Christopher de Seton, captain of Lochdoon, who were so barbarously murdered after surrender by English Edward, and my grandsire, William Seton, who fell at Verneuil, fighting against the English, under Lord Buchan, the Constable of France.   Let us go—let us go! the sooner this frightful drama is ended the better.   Oh, they are good men and gallant soldiers, those courtiers of King James—those slaves and parasites of Arran.   Sir John, I await you."

" But you cannot go thus—on foot, lady   Excuse me, but for a moment."

He dispatched a messenger to the palace for a horse and a pillion, and to beg the favour of a riding-cloak from the Lady Barncleugh; both of which were brought in a few minutes.

In this interval, Jane, with great energy but incoherence, and amid frequent bursts of tears and indignation, had related the story of her abduction and retention by Redhall; but, dreading to criminate her brother, or afford, even to this friendly gentleman, the least clue to his flight, she blundered the whole episode of her escape, and became so perplexed and confused, that Sir John Forrester considered the whole affair as a mere hallucination, and listened with a face expressive only of pity and sincere sorrow; and thus she found her tale received by all to whom she afterwards ventured to relate it; for the reputation for high moral worth and sterling integrity enjoyed by Redhall, placed him as on a lofty pedestal, above the reach of ordinary calumny, though some men *did* at times shake their heads and look mysteriously at the mention of the gallant Sir Thomas of Bombie, whose blood stained the steps at the north door of St. Giles for many a year after the era of James V

The sun was up and shone joyously on the palace towers and the vanes of its ancient porch, on the battlements of the traitor's tower (which Moyse speaks of in his memoirs), and the beautiful façade designed by Hamilton of Fimart, when Lady Jane was led forth from the pointed archway.

She was mounted on the pillion behind Sir John Forrester; and thereafter followed by the Albany herald with the warrant, and a party of the guard marching with matches cocked and lighted, she proceeded at a rapid pace towards the castle; for even at that early hour the High-street was beginning to be busy. The guards and warders were un-closing the portes and barriers; the merchants were opening their booths, and displaying their wares under those long arcades which then were on both sides of the street, and remnants of which still exist in several places; farm horses laden with barrels, baskets, and boxes were pouring into the markets, and the water-carriers were crowding round the fountains at the Cross and the Mile-end.

A party of the king's guard, with a knight in full armour, and a female prisoner riding behind him, drew the burgesses from all quarters to the centre of the street.

" Jean Seton of Ashkirk," flew from mouth to mouth,

mingled with mutterings of commiseration and hatred, as the sympathies or antipathies of the rabble led them. Many there were who mourned that one so young and fair should be made another sacrifice to the animosity avowedly borne by the king and the court against that humbled faction which had triumphed over both so long, and many there were who remembered the deadly strife of 1520 :—

> " When startled burghers fled afar,
> The furies of the border war ;
> When the streets of high Dunedin,
> Saw axes gleam, and falchions redden ;"

when, sheathed in full mail, her father, at the head of a hundred barbed horsemen, had thrice hewn a passage through the barricaded streets, giving to death and defeat the spearmen of Arran. Many women, whose husbands and fathers, lovers and brothers, had fallen on that terrible 29th of April, recalled their treasured hatred as keenly as if the strife of seventeen years had been enacted but seventeen hours ago, and openly, bitterly, and unpityingly reviled her.

" A Hamilton ! a Hamilton !"

" Doon wi' the Setons ! doon wi' the Douglases ! doon wi' the star and the bluidy heart !"

" Set her up, wi' her lace and her pearlings sae braw, when an honest wife like me wears but a curstsey o' flannel !"

" Holy Virgin !" cried another crone in a grey cloak and a flanders-mutch ; " and to think I hae taen an awmous frae this Seton sorceress ! 'Twas weel I had my relique o' blessed St. Roque aboot me !"

" Fie upon thee, thou fause Seton ! Death to the witch ! bones to the fire, and soul to Satan !"

Full of horror at these frightful and opprobrious cries, this poor being, whose gentleness had never created her a personal enemy, surrounded by her guard and a vast mob that every moment grew more dense as the street narrowed, arrived at the Castle-port, an ancient and massive archway in the Spur, which then lay between the castle and the town, covering the whole of what is now called the Esplanade, and surmounted by a round bastion, displaying a flag and more than twenty pieces of brass cannon.

There the governor of the fortress—the strong towers of which were looming redly and grimly in the morning sunshine above the parapets and glacis of this hornwork—received

Lady Jane, as the king's prisoner, from the herald and captain of the guard, who drew his soldiers across the Castle-hill-street, to bear back the tumultuous crowd, whose clamour reverberated with a thousand echoes in that high and narrow thoroughfare.

Bareheaded and ungloved, the castellan, Sir James Riddel, of Cranstoun-Riddel, a gallant and courtly soldier, received her with the utmost respect, and assisted her to alight. As she did so her riding hood fell back, and her pale and beautiful face was revealed to the people, who began anew to murmur variously. Then it was (such is the power of beauty) that many pitied, though more still hated and upbraided her; for the tide of common clamour in Edinburgh was against the Angus faction, among whom, in camp and council, her father and brother had borne a prominent part, having more than once, at the point of the sword, thrust their vassals as magistrates upon the people.

Confused and terrified by a scene so unusual, Jane murmured she knew not what, as her thanks and adieux to Sir John Forrester, and gave her hand to the governor, who led her within the archway, on the battlements of which was seen the head of the Master of Forbes, who a short time before had been beheaded for raising a sedition in the Scottish camp at Fala, and attempting to shoot King James with an arquebuse. Though pale and exhausted by the terrors of the night, with eyes purple and inflamed by weeping, she gave a sad and perhaps scornful smile at that strong arch, the massive wall, and iron-jagged gate, whereon her father once had nailed his glove in defiance of Arran; but her heart sunk when she really found herself within those lofty walls, where so many had pined in hopeless captivity; nor could she repress a shudder when the rattling portcullis closed behind her, sinking slowly down with a jarring sound between its stony grooves.

The Lady of Cranstoun-Riddel, a kind, and (as the Scots term it) "motherly body," now approached her, and said,—

"Lady Jane Seton, in the name of the blessed Mary, what is the meaning of all this?"

"Dearest madam, I know as little as thee," said Jane, throwing herself upon the bosom of this kind matron, rejoicing to find that one of her own sex, who, though even an entire stranger, could sympathize with her, and who, in age, appearance, and manner so nearly resembled her beloved mother. "Indeed, madam," continued Jane, sobbing, "I swear to you that I am ignorant of the cause; but I am accused of murder, of sorcery, of treason, and I know not what more,—I, that have not the heart to kill even the smallest insect. There must indeed be sorcery in this, but not with me."

"My puir bairn! my puir bairn! thou must thole mickle ere these dark charges are cleared and refuted."

"Yea, madam; for, as my brother truly said, we are but the victims and playthings of tyranny and misrule."

"Lady," said Sir James Riddel, gravely, but respectfully, "you are here by the orders of James V. and his eminence the cardinal, who fourteen days ago sent me instructions to receive you, but you had disappeared on the very night his warrant was issued. Remember, lady, that the king *is* king; besides, my lord advocate—pardon me if my words disturb you, for I am a rough old rider of James III.'s days, and unused to speaking daintily."

Jane shuddered at the name of her persecutor; and hurriedly, but with more coherence than before, began the story of her recent abduction, and more recent escape. Again, to her infinite chagrin, she found that she was utterly disbelieved, for the knight regarded her with a kind but sad smile of commiseration, as one whom terror had slightly "demented;" she saw him elevate his eyebrows, and nod perceptibly as he exchanged a glance with his lady, who kindly smoothed Jane's glossy hair, kissed her again as a mother would have done, and led her through the Spur, and up the Castle-rock towards King David's Tower. Stung to the soul by this provoking disbelief, she became immediately silent, and resolved to explain no more.

As they proceeded through the vast hornwork, which, as we have said, covered the whole Castle-hill, between the loopholes and embrasures she obtained glimpses of the rough bank that shelved abruptly down to the loch on the north, and of the reedy loch itself, where the wild ducks and swans were floating, and of the bare ridge of pasture-land where now the modern city is built.

"So I am now a captive in the castle of Edinburgh, while my poor mother pines on Inchkeith! Where will the events of this dark drama end?" thought she; and her heart sank lower still as the gigantic gates of the Constable's Tower were closed and barred behind her.

CHAPTER XXXII.

THE THREE TREES OF DYSART.

> " I launched my spear, and with a sudden wound
> Transpierced his back, and fix'd him to the ground;
> He falls, and mourns his fate with human cries:
> Through the wide wound the vital spirit flies."
>
> *Odyssey*, Book X.

AT the time when the fugitive earl bent his course towards the county (or, as it is popularly named, *the* kingdom) of Fife, the whole length and breadth of it, from the gates of St. Andrew's in the east neuk to those of Dunfermline in the west neuk, and from the waters of the Forth on the south to those of the Tay on the north, was full of terror by the ravages of an enormous wolf, which had established his quarters in the old forest of Pittencrief; from whence he extended his visits as far as the woods of Donnibrissal and Falkland, and alone the winding coast even so far as the cave of St. Monan. He was somewhat particular in his taste, and always preferred little children, when they could be had, as being more tender than either sheep or calves. He prowled about the most populous burrow-touns, and sometimes darted through their main streets at midday, making a passing snap at whoever chanced to be in his way; thus those little ones whose occupation it was to fish for pow-wowets in the pools of water which then encumbered the streets, or made dams and dirt-pies in the gutters, were in imminent danger, for his foraging excursions extended along the whole Howe of Fife.

The wood-cutters were afraid to venture into the forests, which made firing so dear, that one or two hapless " heretics " in the castle of St. Andrew were not burnt for a whole week after the Laird of Fynnard, High Inquisitor under Paul III., had solemnly delivered them over to the devil and the devouring element. The little birds held jubilee in every hedge and hawthorn tree, for their nests were now respected by truants and harriers; while the people nailed additional horseshoes, rowan-twigs, and foxes' faces on their doors at night; and old wives pinned their stockings and garters crosswise at their pillows to keep away evil. If the wind rumbled in the chimney, as it often did (for *lums* were of enormous size in those days), gudeman and gudewife trembled together in the secrecy of

Q

their snug box-beds; for they were assured it could be nothing else than the wolf bellowing at the sailing moon.

The wise men of St. Monan's kept their kirk bell (which was thought to have miraculous powers) ringing all night to scare away the prowler; but this was soon likely to cause a rebellion among the Crail and Kinghorn fishermen, who declared that the noise would scare all the herrings from the coast.

Every night the wolf was heard roaring somewhere, and next morning the bones of children or sheep were found on the highways, picked as clean as ivory. Superstition increased the terrors of the people, who averred that it was visible in many places at once. It was said by some to be red, by others to be black; some declared that its mouth was like that of a hound, others like that of the great cannon, Meg of Threive, or, as it is erroneously named, Mons Meg. It had the claws of an eagle, by one account; a barbed tail, by another; it vomited fire; it was a griffin; the devil—everything frightful that folly and fear could make it.

The best and bravest huntsmen had failed to slay or capture it; the sharpest spears had been blunted on its side, which the hereditary forester declared to be like a coat of mail; the fleetest dogs had been outrun by it, and the fiercest torn by its fangs when brought to bay; even Bash and Bawtry, the two great hounds of James V., on which Sir David of the Mount made many a witty rhyme, failed with this terrible wolf; and the unhappy Fifers were reduced to the verge of despair.

In the days of King James II. (A.D. 1547), a law ordained that for the destruction of wolves the sheriffs of counties and bailies of towns and regalities were empowered to convene the men of their districts thrice yearly, "betwixt St. Mark's day and Lambmass, for that (saith the act) is the time of the quhelpes;" and every huntsman who slew a wolf was to receive from each parishioner one penny; and whoever brought the wolf's head to the sheriff, lord, baron, or bailie, should receive six pennies.

Conformably to this law, passed eighty years before, and led in person by the gallant king (who was compelled for one day to leave his Magdalene's couch of sickness and of suffering), the whole male population of Fife, with horse and hound, spear and horn, bow and arquebuse, had made a vengeful and simultaneous search by hill and howe, by wood and wold, for this obnoxious denizen; but their efforts proved perfectly futile; and the night descended upon a hundred hunting bands without their having had even a glimpse of the enemy —at least so far as was known of those around the burgh of Kinghorn, where the earl had landed about noon that day; for an adverse wind had long detained the little sloop which plied at that ancient ferry.

On disembarking, he repaired to an hostel house, which bore the sign of *The King's Horn*, for an old tradition asserts that as the earlier Scottish monarchs had a castle there, the frequent winding of the king's horn, as he sallied out to the chase, had given a name to the little town that nestled on the shore; but the *cean-gorm*, or blue promontory of the Celtic Scots, still frowns above it, to contradict the tale. Then, as now, Kinghorn was a steep and straggling burgh of strange and quaint old houses, piled over each other, pell-mell, on the brow of a hill, and was traversed by a brawling mountain burn, that turned the wooden wheel of many an ancient mill. It is overlooked by the lofty and rugged precipice, from the summit of which Alexander III., when riding from Inverkeithing to his castle of Kinghorn, having mistaken his path in the forest, fell and broke his neck; a catastrophe which ended the old line of the Macalpine kings, and began the long wars and woes of the Scottish succession.

After a slight repast of cheese, bran-bannocks, and a draught of mum-beer, at the hostel, the earl became alarmed on discovering a proclamation, descriptive of his person, pasted on the wall immediately above his head. The unfortunate noble became still more apprehensive of suspicion or discovery, as the thirty huntsmen who filled the burrow-toun came crowding into the hostel, and on perceiving that two or three were beginning to whisper and observe him, for his whole aspect was wild, haggard, and disordered; he resolved, if questioned, to pass for a forester like themselves, and, if attacked, to sell his life as dearly as possible.

Appropriating to himself a stout hunting-spear which stood in a corner of the kitchen, he bade adieu to the sign of *The King's Horn*, and, quitting the town, struck into the old horseway that traversed the heights overhanging the coast.

The sun was now setting.

Remembering how suspiciously he had been eyed in the

Q 2

little hostelry, he grasped the hunting-spear, looked warily about him, and walked quietly to the eastward, anxious to leave Kinghorn as far as possible behind him.

The sun set darkly and lowering as he progressed, and the last flush of its light fell with a dusky yellow upon the long expanse of Kirkaldy sands, and the gigantic castle of Ravenscraig, with its round and square towers—a stronghold of the Sinclairs—which terminated them.

" I have neither money, food, nor shelter," thought the earl ; " but, praised be fortune, I am at least free !"

The wind growled along the hollows ; the Firth grew black as ink, and its waves rolled white and frothy upon the circular sands, where more than one small vessel had dropped all her anchors, and made everything secure aloft and below, to brave the coming tempest. That vague and indescribable murmur, the sure forerunner of a rising storm, was floating over the dark-green bosom of the German Sea, and he heard it mingling with the hiss of the breakers. A tempestuous night was at hand, and the hapless earl knew not where to look for refuge ; the castle of Kirkaldy-grange, the dwelling of the lord high treasurer, crowned an eminence on his left ; the fortlet of Seafield, where dwelt the hostile race of Moultray (hostile, at least, to him), overlooked the beach on his right ; so avoiding both, and the little fane called Eglise Marie, which then occupied the hollow between them, he descended the wild and then uncultivated shore, and skirting the long straggling town of Kirkaldy, hoped to find a shelter in one of those innumerable caverns with which, in many places, the coast of Fife is completely perforated.

The scudding clouds became blacker and denser ; and their shadows darkened all the foam-flecked estuary. Night came rapidly on, and by the time when Lord Ashkirk had traversed the long and winding sands, and found himself near those stupendous cliffs which were crowned by the great castle of William Lord Sinclair, baron of Dysart and Ravenscraig, the most perfect gloom had enveloped both sea and shore, while the red and fiery glow of several salt-pans on the beach imparted a singular effect to the scenery.

As yet no rain had fallen ; but now one of those appalling gusts of wind which uproot the strongest trees, and lay bare the scalps of mountains, rushed along the bosom of the Forth, hurling its waves upon the beach, rolling them sea on sea far along the level sands, and pouring them in a whirlwind of spray against the grey and lofty summit of the Ravenscraig. Startled by the din of the encroaching waves, the earl, by a winding path, was rapidly ascending the headland, when a wild cry from the ocean—for there the river was indeed an ocean—made him pause and look back.

"Mother of Mercy!" he exclaimed, as he held his bonnet on his head, struck his spear in the earth, and turned to face the storm.

A terrific glare of lightning revealed for a moment the deep dark trough of seething water, where, in flames and fragments, as the levin brand had scorched and rent her, a strong and stately ship, with all her masts and yards, her gilded sides, and tier of cannon, sank down for ever! The vision came and went with that flash of forky light; and then no more was seen, and nothing more was heard but the thunder pealing away over the mountains, the roaring of the angry wind, and the deep boom of the angrier sea.

The earl looked wistfully at the vast and opaque outline of Ravenscraig, with its stupendous keep and flanking towers, amid whose stony depths many a warm red light twinkled, indicative of comfort within; but there an avowed foeman dwelt; and he passed the gate without knowing where other shelter might be found. He now became more anxious, for a few large and warm drops, which plashed upon his face, announced that a drenching summer thunder-shower was about to fall.

He had now attained such high ground that even the turrets of Ravenscraig were below him, and the wind swept over it with redoubled force; for then the promontory was all desolate and bare, though in the Druid days a vast forest had covered it. Beneath him lay the little town of Dysart, a closely-packed and antique burgh, nestling on the steep and straggling shore, full of quaint old-fashioned houses, roofed with stone, and built upon broad and low arcades, where the merchants exposed their wares; but, save where a ray of light shone from an open shutter or an upper window, the whole town was buried in murky obscurity.

The roaring of the winds, and the din of the breakers against the promontory, prevented the earl hearing the sound of his own footsteps; and in the gloom he paused irresolutely on the brow of this rugged eminence, for now the tall and beautiful tower of Saint Denis started up from amid the architectural masses of the Black Friary, and seemed to be immediately below his feet, yet it was fully a quarter of a mile distant.

He was about to descend and claim the shelter and sanctuary which the Dominican fathers were bound to afford him, for one night at least, when a wild and frightful cry, that was borne on the wind past his ear, made him pause once more, again grasp his hunting-spear, and gaze around him.

All was darkness and obscurity behind; no object met his eye save three large and beautiful oaks, which stood equidistant on the hill-side; and against the gloomy sky he saw their gloomier outline, twisted, torn, and shaken as if by the hand of a giant, and every moment their wet leaves were swept past him on the whirling blast.

These were *the three trees* of Dysart. The earl remembered the tradition concerning them, which, with the place, the time, and the cry, caused a clamorous terror to rise suddenly in his breast; for he was far from being free of the superstitions incident to the age and country.

When all that district was covered by an old primeval forest, three sons of Henry Lord Sinclair, who was baron of the Ravenscraig, and justiciar of Kirkwall, were said to have met on that spot unexpectedly, and at midnight. Being all in their armour, amid the obscurity of the foliage, and under a moonless and starless sky, they mistook each other for robbers, and a deadly combat ensued. Two were slain on the instant, and the third fell mortally wounded, surviving only till morning, when they were all buried at the foot of the trees below which they were found. And tradition further states, that when the forest was cleared away in course of time, these three oaks were left as a memorial, to mark the former state of the ground, and the place where the three brothers lay. Lord Sinclair fell at Flodden, fighting against the enemies of his country; prior to which he had granted many a Scottish merk to the monks of St. Denis, to say prayers and masses for the souls of the three fratricides, his sons.

The story came back to the earl's mind with all the additional impressions that the darkness of the night, the storm, and the time could lend it; and though the unearthly cry made his pulses pause and his ears tingle, he was too brave a man to shun any object of terror; and drawing his bonnet well over his eyes, to prevent its being swept away by the furious blast, he turned back, and resolutely advanced to where the three tall oaks were tossing their solemn masses of foliage against the louring sky.

A dead man lay below each, and the long rank grass which covered him was whistling in the dreary wind.

"My God!—*the wolf!*" cried the earl, as a sudden gleam of lightning revealed to him the monster which so long had been the terror of Fife and Kinross. It was of gigantic size; but, appalled by the fury of the elements, was cowering against the centre tree, gnashing its fangs and darting fire from its eyes, with all the hair of its neck and back erect like the quills of a porcupine.

Aware that unless he slew it with the first thrust of his spear all in a moment would be over with him, the brave young noble charged his weapon breast high, and rushed upon the wolf. With a ferocious howl it sprang aside; the weapon struck the trunk of the tree, broke, and the earl fell headlong among the wet grass of the grave below it. Then, with the rapidity of light, the frightful animal was upon him. There was a cloud of fire before his eyes, and a wild humming in his ears; but neither the stunning fall, nor the terror of having such an antagonist, appalled him so much as to deprive him of his usual presence of mind, for at the very moment in which it sprang upon him, and when he felt its sharp claws in his shoulders, and its hot fetid breath in his face, he buried his dagger—that long dagger, so recently wet with the blood of Redhall—in its body up to the very hilt; and then its hotter blood came like a deluge over his hand and arm.

A vital part had been struck, and the wolf rolled over, tearing the grass with its teeth, and wallowing in its blood. Then, full of rage for the temporary terror with which it had inspired him, the fierce earl sprang upon it, and buried his sharp dagger again and again to the cross-guard in its body, though he received more than one terrible laceration from its claws, as the agonies of death alternately convulsed and relaxed them. Clutching its lower jaws by the shaggy fur, with three deep gashes he completely shred off its head, and then reclined breathlessly against the tree.

"Well, and so I have conquered thee!" he exclaimed, triumphantly, as he spurned the carcase with his foot. "Devilish monster, to me thy head is worth a penny from every man in Dysart—a goodly sum for an earl, forsooth! But as I lack these pennies sorely to pay my way to England, to the Highlands, or elsewhere, I will even seek the prior of St. Denis with my prize, midnight though it be."

Tying the four corners of his mantle together, he put the head into it, and arming himself with a fragment of his spear, descended to the gate of the Black Friary; but, as the wind still blew, the rain lashed the stone walls and grated windows, while the sea boomed on the rocks below, and the worthy master-porter slept like a dormouse, the din made by the earl at the door was unheard.

" The great devil confound thee!" he muttered, turning away; " for I must even go without my pence and my supper to boot."

Remembering his first project of the caverns, he scrambled along the rocky and shingly beach for more than two miles, until a ray of light, which streamed from a fissure in the bluffs, far across the wet sands and tumbling billows, attracted his attention.

Turning to the left, he approached it—the fissure widened, and entering boldly, he found himself in one of those long and deep weems, or caverns, which are there so numerous; and immediately a band of outlaws and smugglers surrounded him.

CHAPTER XXXIII.

THE WEEM.

" Blow ye horns,
And rouse each wilder passion of the soul,
To drown the voice of Nature! He must die!
He who puts forth his hand to seize a crown
Must stake his all upon the mighty game."
KÖRNER'S *Expiation*, a Drama.

" Oⁿo! here cometh *another* guest, whom the high wind hath blown us this eerie night!" cried one of the occupants of the weem, as the whole party arose and stood around the intruder.

Tall, strong, armed with a broken spear, smeared with mud from the paws of the wolf, and covered with gouts of its blood, which hung upon his matted hair and bushy beard, the aspect of the earl was sufficiently formidable to command the respect of the desperadoes among whom he had intruded; and, at a wave of his right hand and arm—the latter being drenched in blood to the elbow—they all shrunk back instinctively and grasped their clubs and poniards.

The enormous weem he had entered was one of those caverns from which a part of the coast obtains its name—Wemyss; and though the outer part of it was brilliantly illuminated by a fire of drift wood and pine-logs that blazed on the rocky floor, on progressing, the earl was impressed with a feeling of awe by the uncertainty of the vast profundity to which it penetrated; for the inner end of this frightful chasm or fissure yawned away obscurely and horribly into the bowels of the earth. It had, doubtless, been formed, like many others along the rocky coast, by that wondrous upheaval of the Scottish shores, which geologists suppose must have taken place some two thousand years ago, or when the sea receded thirty feet from its ancient margin, which to this day is visible along the summits of all the headlands in Fifeshire and Lothian.

Though several culinary utensils, Dutch kegs and tubs were placed in little cupboard-like recesses, the cavern did not seem to have been long occupied by its tenants, who were six in number, strong and muscular men, whose long matted beards flowed nearly to their girdles; and whose attire declared them to be partly beggars, partly robbers, and wholly desperadoes. That they lived at enmity with their fellow-subjects was apparent from the multiplicity and aspect of the swords, poniards, and poleaxes with which they were armed.

The earl found, when too late, that he had made an unfortunate choice of hosts, when such a price was on his head, but grasping his broken spear with one hand, and his gory bundle by the other, he confronted them resolutely.

"Now, who are you?" asked one who seemed to be the leader.

" It matters nothing to thee, thou dour carle, so lay down thy maul, or beware!" replied the earl.

" Then, what are you?"

" A gaberlunzie—a beggar!" said Ashkirk, bitterly.

" Then, where is thy parish token?"

" I spoke but metaphorically, for I have not yet taken me

unto *that* trade; and when I do, I will see King James at Jericho, and his parliament too, before I will sew a pewter badge on my doublet, tattered though it be. I will not conform to this new law, believe me, brother rogue. But I repeat, nevertheless, that I *am* a beggar, because I seek food without having the wherewithal to pay for it; and, moreover, that I am, like thyself, an outlaw."

"Gude and better!" replied the other; "but there is blood on thy sleeve; why man, thou art *red handed!*"

"Blood! true—I shed a little in my own defence, and what then? I have committed no murder. Believe me, fellow, there is more blood on thy soul than on my fingers. But, enough of this. I seek what every man who hath them not hath a right to seek from those who hath—food, fire, and shelter."

"What is this in your cloak?"

"Something that thou hast no concern with."

"We will soon see that," cried several, laying hands on their knives and daggers.

"If thou darest!" replied the earl, raising his truncheon, and confronting the strongest and the boldest.

"Byde and haud ye! Nay, nay," cried the others, laughing; "honour among thieves. Hath he not said that, like oursels, he is an outlaw? besides, ye will waken that chield in the corner."

"Sit down again, you quarrelsome loons," said the leader; "and seat thyself, too, my bold gaberlunzie, with a welcome to bite and to bicker."

As the earl seated himself, carefully placing his bundle behind him, he now for the first time perceived a cavalier, in a rich velvet mantle, lying asleep in a nook of the weem, which sheltered him both from the night wind, that blew the smoke and brands of the fire into the recesses of the rocks, and from the damp atmosphere of the sea, which burst like thunder every moment on the adjacent beach. The boots of the sleeper were of spotless white leather, adorned with spurs of gold, polished and richly chased, with rowels of glittering steel. Beside him lay his sword, which was sheathed in blue and embroidered velvet.

"Who may this gay gallant be?" asked the earl, as he warmed his hands, and, making himself quite at home, kicked up the brands to make a blaze.

"One of our king's dainty courtiers," replied the principal ruffian; a patch over whose left eye nearly concealed the little of his frightful visage which was not overgrown with hair. "St. Mary! thou mayest see he is Falkland bred, by those cork-heeled boots and gowden spurs. There hath been a brave hunt after the wolf of Pittencrief, and all the court and countryside have driven horse and hound nearly to death, without getting even sight or scent of the monster; so either the wind, the storm, or the darkness of the night, his evil chance, or our good luck, hath brought this gay galliard hither for a shelter and supper, which," he added, sinking his voice, "both his cloak and purse——"

"Breeches and doublet," said another, in the same whispering tone.

"With his horse, which we have stabled in yonder hole——"

"Yea," chimed in the earl, "and those dainty boots and spurs, shall pay for. Is it not so?"

"Right—we'll all have a share!" and here the six uttered a brutal laugh, and all exchanged glances and winks expressive of fun and ferocity.

"Meantime," said the leader, "waken up his worship, for supper is ready."

Here one pulled the wearied cavalier by the cloak. He started up, and revealed a handsome young face, aquiline features and dark hazel eyes, close clipped beard and dark moustache. He wore (very much on the right side) a smart blue bonnet, with a white feather springing from a diamond St. Andrew's cross.

"Mercy! *the king!*" said the earl, in the inmost recesses of his heart, as he respectfully gave place at the fire to the gallant and adventurous James V., who had not the most remote idea that he was recognised by any one there, and passed for nothing more than a private gentleman; the whole adventure being one of that romantic kind in which he—our Scottish Haround Alraschid—delighted. Before seating himself on the stone which was to be his chair, he signed the cross upon his breast and said: "*Benedicite.*"

A mess of rabbits and fowls stewed together in a kailpot, another of broiled fish, with cheese and bannocks, which, like the small kegs of ale and usquebaugh, had merely cost the trouble of carrying them off (at a time when the burgh-

merchants had no other police than their own eyes and
hands), were freely shared by the thieves with their illustrious
guests, one of whom they had foredoomed to death. The
other, they deemed already as one of themselves; for the earl,
the better to conceal his real character, assumed a strange
dialect, and talked, laughed, sung and swore, till he drew
upon him the marked attention of the king; but under that
matted beard and tattered attire, disfigured by many a gout
of blood, the monarch failed to recognise the outlawed noble.

With a hunting clasp-knife, one of those made and inscribed by Jacques de Liege (whence comes our Scottish
Jockteleg), the king was carving for himself a chicken which
he had laid on a broad bannock, and was evidently enjoying
the repast like a huntsman and soldier, for he was both.

" By my faith! knave of the pot," said he to the robber
who had cooked, " thou hast done thy duty well."

" Ouaye; we fisher chields can turn our hands to anything."

" Then turn them to mending the fire; for dost thou not
see 'tis all gone to cinders?"

" As we shall when we gang to auld Clootie," replied the
cook, whose reply was greeted by a roar of laughter, the
echoes of which seemed to rumble away into the heart of
the rocks.

" Friend Bloodybeard," said the king to the earl," " hand
over that keg of usquebaugh; wilt drink with me? thy health,
friend Bloodybeard."

" Thine, my gentleman of the white feather."

" How gallantly thou drainest thy bicker!" said the king,
on seeing how the earl emptied his tass of raw spirits;
" didst thou ever taste pure water, fellow?"

" Once, when an infant; but, as it nearly choked me, I
have never tried it since. Tush! wine costs us no more than
spring water. Like James and his courtiers of Arran, we help
ourselves to our neighbours' goods and gear, whenever
we lack."

The broad brow of the king knit, but he laughed, and said—

" Have the courtiers not wealth enough and to spare,
sirrah?"

" Wealth—ah, that is the greatest and most respected
quality in man."

" But beside wealth, hath not King James many virtues?"

" Tut! these are but a silly habit of differing from such.

merry men as we; but I fear me we scare thee, my dainty
gentleman, by the din we are making."

" By my word, no; I should like to see the men who would
scare me," replied the king, fishing another pullet out of the
pot; "I am but fulfilling the injunctions of the great Plato,
who said, 'live with thine inferiors as with unfortunate friends.'
Ho! by St. Anne, Bloodybeard, knock the bottoms out of
these broiled eggs, or all the Fife witches will be sailing over
to Lothian in them; dost hear me? quick, or I shall report
thee to the cardinal and his grand inquisitor."

" The inquisitor—faugh! he is but a Hamilton," said the
earl, who could not jest with the names of his enemies; "and
as for the cardinal, I say, bah! he is a mere cannonier in
canonicals—a devil in a broad red hat."

" Beware how ye get under its shadow, my fool-hardy
knaves," said the king, laughing. " Have you looked well to
my horse ?"

" Yea, sir, as a man looketh after his *own*," replied one
fellow, whose ears bore visible marks of the nails which so
frequently had fastened them to many a burgh cross; and at
his significant reply there was uttered another of those low,
ferocious laughs, which soon served to put the unwary monarch
on his guard; for, like each of his forefathers, James V was
brave as a lion.

" My gallant grey!" said he; " 'tis a gift to me from the
Laird of Largo, who took him from the Lord Cassilis at Linlithgow Bridge, on the day of that unhappy battle. I have
ridden him forty miles to day,—not a rood less, I am sure."

" After such sore toil," said the earl; " his nostrils should
be bathed with vinegar, and his breast with warm wine."

" Oho! thou knowest something of stablecraft, my smuggler, it would seem."

" Few in broad Scotland know better."

" And now I have supped right gloriously!" said the king,
reclining back against the great cyclopean wall of the weem.
" Friend robber, thy crail capons and stewed pullets have
been done in such wise, that even King James's cook might
envy thy skill; and in England, I doubt not, Henry the king
would have made thee a belted earl; for he hath just made a
baron of his cook for the exquisite manner in which he broiled
a mackarel—at least so my friend the English ambassador
said to-day, as we rode together near the old castle of Bal-

wearie. Hand over that keg again, Bloodybeard," said the king, and, on receiving it, he began to sing a popular ditty of the day :—

> " King James rode round by the Mere-cleugh-heid,
>   Booted and spurred as we a' did see;
>   But he dined and supped at Mossfennan yett,
>   Wi' the bonny young Lass o' the Loganlee.
>
> " Her hair was like the gowd sae braw,
>   Like a lammer bead her deep dark e'e,
>   Nor Falkland tower, nor Lithgow ha',
>   Had a dame like the Lass o' the Loganlee.
>
> " ' Oh, where is the king ?' quoth all the court,
>   From the great cardinal to the fool, M·Ilree;
>   But the devil a one knew where he was gone,
>   With the bonnie young Lass o' the Loganlee."

Here the merry king lay back and laughed excessively at this hunting song, which had been composed on one of his own amorous adventures.

By this time the thieves had drunk deeply, but their hilarity began to subside, and their ferocious glances warned their guest that something unpleasant was about to terminate the noisy repast. Under his mantle the king felt secretly for his sword, and grew pale as death on discovering that, either by accident or design, when he was asleep, the blade had been broken in the sheath—leaving him defenceless, with seven armed outlaws, in a lonely cavern. He was in the very act of looking hurriedly round for some other weapon to snatch up in case of need, when lo! one of the ruffians held before him a plate, whereon (according to an ancient and barbarous custom) lay two naked poniards, as a signal that he was to be sacrificed, and might choose with which blade he was to die.

Instead, as they expected, of being appalled, with the rapidity of lightning the gallant king clutched one in each hand, and striking to the right and to the left, buried both weapons in the breasts of the ruffians next him.

" Dogs and villains !" he exclaimed, " slipper-helmetted dastards ! come on, if you dare !"

Armed with mauls and axes, the other four fell furiously upon him, and he must inevitably have been slain had not the earl, with the truncheon of his spear in one hand, and a burning brand in the other, attacked them in the rear, and with such impetuosity that, by two blows he broke the arm of one, the head of a second, and drove the whole from the cavern. Thus, in less than one minute, the king and he found themselves, with two dead bodies, the sole occupants of the place.

"Well done, friend Bloodybeard!" exclaimed the breathless king; "by my soul, I thought thee one of them; and well it is for me thou didst strike in such good time. Complete me now thy service by cutting out the tongues of these two carrion, that I may give them to my hounds," he added, kicking the dead bodies, and untying his purse from his girdle. "I have here only twenty French crowns, but if thou wilt come to Falkland to-morrow, and ask for—for——"

"His majesty the king," replied the earl, whose eye moistened, and whose heart swelled, as (instead of kneeling) he drew himself proudly up to his full height; "replace your purse, James Stuart; surely Archibald Earl of Ashkirk hath not sunk so far as to be paid thus for fighting in the service of his king."

"Ashkirk!" said King James, less astonished that he was recognised than at this rencontre and discovery. "Ashkirk, is it indeed thee, thou traitor and son of a traitress?"

"I am no traitor, neither am I the son of a traitress; but an outlaw, certainly; and why? Because I am the hereditary focman of the house of Hamilton. False king, thou wrongest me sorely by such epithets as these."

"*Thou*, Ashkirk?" it is impossible!" said James, filled with pity at the deplorable aspect of his long-dreaded rebel.

"Look at me, king! My years are not yet thirty, and my brow is wrinkled; for the hand of a tyrant, less than time, hath touched it."

"A tyrant?"

"Thou!"

"Darest thou say so to my teeth?"

"Ay, thou, James V.; for thou wagest the quarrels and the feuds of the fathers upon their children. By war and death thou dost; revengefully and remorselessly. Thou hast put a price upon my head, and hunted me, even as a wild beast, from place to place. But think not that I will ever sue for pardon; I will live as my fathers hath lived, or die, sword in hand, as my fathers have died. Never shalt thou see a Seton of Ashkirk among those fawning slaves of the house of Arran, who, watching for every passing smile, crowd round thy throne like sycophants—never! never!"

" This to me!" cried the king, snatching up a sword; "to
me from thee, thou parricide, who hast carried fire and sword
into the heart of thy fatherland! Must I tell thee, false earl,
that, in addition to thy rebellion, all assurance and friendship
with Englishmen *is treason;* that the residence of a Scot in
England *is treason;* that buying from or selling to Englishmen *is treason;* that all travelling or trafficking with Englishmen, by word or writing, *is treason;* incurring the
penalties of proscription and death! Not content with the
committal of all these crimes, and with levying war against
our wardens with lances uplifted and banner displayed, I find
thee the boon-companion of thieves and outlaws, who live
by slaughter and robbery; by stealing pikes from ponds; by
breaking dowcots and orchards; by lifting sheep and slaying
parked deer; all contraventions of the laws passed by my
father, James IV., for the security of property; and involving
the penalty of the scourge."

" The scourge!" reiterated the earl, with a bitter laugh;
" I can respect the name of James IV., for he was my father's
friend, and side by side they have often fought like two brave
comrades; but thou, his son, the ruthless oppressor of the
bravest nobles Scotland ever saw—who hast thrown the
sceptre into the scales that justice might be overborne, never!
The scourge? I am indeed degraded, when even a king dare
mention it to me. Proud and ungrateful prince, hast thou,
indeed, forgotten all that thou and thy forefathers owe to the
houses of Seton and of Douglas?"

" I have not," said the king, standing on his guard; " it
is, indeed, a debt of vengeance, so take up a sword and come
on. Here, man to man, I defy thee, and repay it."

" Nay, nay; it shall never be said that the royal blood of
Scotland stained the hand of a Seton. Ten minutes ago I
might have slain thee in the *mêlée,* and there had ended thy
Stuart line for ever."

" To place thy feudal foe of Arran on the throne—eh?
That would not have mended matters with thee and Angus, I
think. But what does royal blood signify? Art thou not
at this moment covered with the blood of my subjects? Just
now, earl, I tell thee, thou hast all the aspect of a gory
murderer."

" Then, behold the head of my victim!" said the noble, as
from his mantle he rolled at the king's feet the enormous **and**

grisly head of the wolf. " Behold that *other* head, on which, as on mine, your majesty has placed a golden price."

Admiration flashed in the eyes of James V.; he threw away his sword, and took the earl's hand in his.

"Oh, Ashkirk, Ashkirk! thou triest me sorely; oh, why art thou not my friend?—but it cannot be; for thy wrongs against thy country, its parliament and crown, are too deep to be easily forgiven. For the gallant deeds of this night, I feel that I could forgive them all; but what would my people say, and what my peers, Catheart and Lennox, Darnley, Hailes, Lyle, and Lorn,—all of whom are hostile to thy house? Besides, I have sworn—solemnly and irrevocably sworn—never to forgive the crime of man or of woman in whose veins there is one drop of the Douglas blood; and too surely, at this hour, at my own hearth and home, I feel that thy mother and thy sister are Douglases. My poor Magdalene!—Lord earl, thy crimes I might afford to forgive freely, for they are only those of a rash and headstrong Scot; but the other crimes of thy family never—never!"

And here, stung deeply by the thought of that supposed sorcery which was bringing his queen to the grave, James paused, and pressed his hands upon his brow; and the earl, who was ignorant of what he referred to, remained silent and perplexed.

" Still I could forgive thee, for the memory of my father's friend, Earl John,—that arm of steel and heart of fire—but my vow!—it cannot be. Here let us part; go on, pursue thy wandering way, unfriended and unhappy lord, and may Heaven keep thee! Here, take these thirty crowns from me,—*not* as the price of this wolf's head, which I will bear with me to Falkland, with the story of thy prowess, to shame my carpet knights, but as that gift, such as one friend, one gentleman, may freely bestow or freely accept from another. There are proclamations for thine apprehension posted on every city cross, on every burgh-barrier and tolbooth-gate, throughout the length and breadth of the land; if thou escapest, I will rejoice; and if thou art taken, I will sorrow; for, by my father's soul, I must then behead thee before the gates of Stirling. So away! to France, to Flanders, to Italy—anywhere but England, the land of our enemies; and may the blessed God grant that we shall never meet again.—Farewell!"

And leading forth his horse, for the storm had now died

B

away, and the early sun of June had risen, the king put his foot in the stirrup, saying,—

" My adventures are wild and strange; and assuredly, if ever old Scotland hath a Plutarch, James V. will live in his pages. Adieu!" and with these words, placing the wolf's head at his saddle-bow, the king put spurs to his grey horse, and galloping along the sandy beach, rode over the adjacent hill in the direction of Falkland, which lay on his road to the Cistercian abbey of Balmerino.

The earl stood near the mouth of the cavern on the desolate beach, and gazed after the king's retiring figure, with mingled feelings of sadness, hostility, and admiration. Then, after long musing and much hesitation, he took up the purse of crowns which lay at his feet, and kissing his hand towards the castle of the Inch—the prison of Sybil Douglas and his mother—walked slowly and thoughtfully along the beach.

The storm had completely lulled. The sea was mirrored around the rocks and isles; the sky was blue and cloudless. The chafing waves broke with a dreamy ripple on the yellow sands. The green headlands and bold promontories, the rustic villages and quaint old fisher-town that nestled between them, were all shining in the silvery haze of that beautiful summer morning; but the soul of the young earl was sad.

CHAPTER XXXIV.

THE DEATH OF MAGDALENE.

" Envy and calumny will destroy innocence and pleasure; the oppressed will be sacrificed to the oppressor; and, in proportion as tyranny makes kings distrustful, judicial murders will depopulate the state."

Telemachus, Book XX.

DURING these passages the young queen, Magdalene, had daily become worse, and the " catarrh, which descended into her stomach," as Madame de Montreuil says in one of her letters, had brought her to the verge of the grave.

The sorrow and alarm of James were great; and remorsefully he now remembered the warnings of Francis I., contrary to whose most urgent advice he had espoused her, instead of the blooming Mary of Lorraine. Foreign physicians were sent by their kings from distant courts and cities, even from Syria and the remote countries of the east, and daily they crowded the antechamber with their long beards and longer garments, their grave visages and solemn quackeries; but their presence had no other effect than to bring lower and lower the health of poor Magdalene, and to excite the wrath and jealousy of John of the Silvermills, who (as the king's apothecary, and deacon of the barber-chirurgeons of Edinburgh), by the presence of these strangers, felt his dignity encroached upon, and his reputation impugned.

The love of the amiable French girl for her gallant young husband was excessive; it strengthened as her strength decayed; and finding that matters of state separated them long and frequently, contrary to all advice, she left Balmerino, with its shady woods and mellow air, and, to be near her beloved James V., returned to the grey and solemn courts of Holyrood on the eighth day of June.

There, to the joy of her husband, she seemed to revive a little; and the preparations for her coronation (which was to be on a scale of magnificence hitherto unknown in Scotland) had been resumed with renewed vigour; but alas! on the tenth of July, three days after the arrest of Lady Jane Seton, she suddenly threw up her hands to heaven and expired, at a moment when, stooping over her couch, the king, her husband, was playfully caressing and conversing with her; and the great solemn bells of St. Giles's, and those of the abbey church, the Dominicans, the Cistercians, and other friaries, as slowly and sadly they tolled a knell, warning all good people to pray for the passing soul, announced that direful event which plunged the whole land in sorrow; for James V., "the king of the poor," was really a monarch who reigned in the hearts of a people who were then loyal and generous as they were brave.

She was solemnly interred by torchlight in the royal vault at Holyrood; and, in her strong prison, Jane Seton heard the deep hoarse boom of the minute guns, as they broke upon the still midnight sky from the towers of King David, St. Margaret, and the ramparts of that stately fortress which enclosed her.

So great was the grief of the nation, that this was the first occasion of a general mourning in Scotland; and in the accounts of the lord high treasurer there are still preserved numerous entries of the Scottish and Holland cloths, French blacks, white crosses upon sable velvets, and many other articles for the court, together with the expenses of Magdalene's magnificent obsequies, the dirges sung and solemn masses said on that melancholy event, which became the all-absorbing topic of the time.

The whole nation mourned with the king; and everywhere, at kirk or market, on highway or in burgh-town, black cloaks and sable feathers had replaced the gaudier colours and fashions of the age. A great funeral escutcheon hung in each of the eight cathedrals, and over the gates of all the royal palaces. Like those used in France and Germany, they were lozenge-formed, bearing the royal arms of Scotland on a black ground, surrounded by those of the sixteen families from whom the queen was descended. At the four corners were placed (as usual among us at the present day) mort-heads, and the black interstices were *semée* with powdered tears.

After the funeral, King James, with a small retinue, retired to the solitude of his beautiful country palace at Falkland.

If the hidden cause of the queen's illness had puzzled the learned physicians and astrologers who had gathered around her couch, as it were, from the four winds of heaven, it occasioned greater speculation among the superstitious people of Scotland, and a universal whisper of *sorcery*, followed by a cry for vengeance on the cause of an effect so dire, went throughout the land, from the Caledonian to the German Sea.

Fettered to a sick bed, suffering under the extremes of mental and bodily agony—the double wounds, received first from Roland Vipont, and secondly from the carl, all combined, and acting upon a frame weakened by a previous illness, had brought Sir Adam Otterburn to the brink of the grave.

His hours of delirium were full of visions either of love and delight—of Jane Scton and a successful suit, or of sanguinary horror—of conflicts, tortures, and executions; while the hours of comparative calm that succeeded—the mere result of utter exhaustion—were occupied by deep-laid schemes of avenging himself upon the authors of so many miseries.

His mind had now but two thoughts—a delirium of love and a delirium of hate; and they corroded his heart between them.

He had cast off Jane Seton; for so he strove to think, and so, unto himself, he said a thousand times; he had rent her from his heart, and abandoned her to the terrors in store for her. Then love would come again, and he strove wildly to stifle it like a rising flame; for he had given the first impulse to the ball of fate, and he resolved to let it roll on its course to destruction.

In his moments of calm agony, when every voice in his heart was still but those which whispered of jealousy and revenge, he deliberately dictated, and drew up with bitter care, certain articles of accusation, implicating Jane Seton wholly and solely in the death of the queen, by sorcery of the most malignant character; and, armed by a warrant, the town mansion of the Ashkirk family, which had not been opened since the Albany herald, John Hamilton of Darnagaber, had placed his seal on every door and lockfast place thereof, was opened and searched by that unwilling functionary and the witch-finder, Nichol Birrel.

After the dose he had been compelled to swallow at Cairntable, the latter, it may be supposed, had reached Edinburgh with considerable difficulty; and, like his master, animated by personal and implacable vengeance against Sir Roland Vipont, he entered with heart and soul into the public prosecution. Thus, when by order of his lord and patron, Redhall, he was searching the house of the Setons, he contrived most opportunely to discover in the boudoir of Lady Jane a little wooden image bearing a crown, and marked with the initials M. B. It was stuck full of pins, and was partly scorched by fire; but after being duly sprinkled with holy water, and exorcised by the late queen's French confessor, was deposited in the hands of the lord advocate, who sealed it up in a box marked with the cross, as being the most tremendous and damning proof of guilt that had ever come under the notice of the newly-constituted College of Justice.

With one voice the whole city now accused, and without a moment's hesitation condemned, Jane Seton. The preparations for her trial went on rapidly; and the king, who was absorbed in his own grief, and remained secluded among the woods of Falkland, abandoned her to her fate; but the wretched Redhall suffered more than either the hapless Jane or the bereaved king, for remorse grew side by side with his anger.

Those sentiments of generosity, of pity, and of lingering love, which ever and anon dawned in the arid desert of his heart, and impelled him to free her, to sue for pardon, or to fly his country, were invariably stifled under a torrent of

jealousy and hate when he thought of Roland Vipont; and
then his half-healed wounds would sting him anew, as if
probed by poniards; the perspiration would burst from his
temples, and he writhed on his sick bed in an agony indescribable.

"She is indeed a sorceress!" he would exclaim; upon which
his nurse and housekeeper, an old and wrinkled dame who
attended him, and who never left his bedside, would make
signs of the cross, and feel for the reliques which were sewed
in the lining of her long piked stays, which, with her ruff and
coif, made her resemble those quaint figures which still live
in the pictures of Holbein.

Credulity has existed in every age of the world; and thus
chiromancy, astrology, physiognomy, and the wildest theories
of abstruse science, have risen and flourished on the ignorance
and folly of the human mind; but there were none that
equalled the *witch-mania*, which, strange to say, grew in Scotland, and flourished side by side with religious freedom and
reform.

It is a curious fact, that before the epoch of Knox sorcery was
almost unknown among us. In our earliest record of criminal
trials, that comprehending the years 1493—1504, there is
not one prosecution for sorcery. In the days of James V it
began to be much spoken of, and rapidly became a source of
terror. Lady Jane's was nearly the first indictment; but
the earliest statute against it was passed in 1563, by the first
reformed parliament, and that portion of the law which refers
to consultations "with sorcerers and witches" was not enacted
until 1594—fully thirty years after the Reformation had been
established by the law of Scotland.

Then, indeed, from that period, kirk sessions and presby-
teries, ministers, elders, sheriffs, and justiciars, went with
heart and hand into the matter; for in the *witch-mania*, that
atrocious madness which spread over Europe, though Scotland
was the last to catch the contagion, she was in no way behind
neighbouring countries in the cruelty of her prosecutions.

According to Barrington, thirty thousand witches were
burned in England, five hundred perished in three months at
Geneva, and a thousand at Como in one year. The number
committed to the flames in Scotland is incalculable, but no
less than six hundred witches were indicted during the sitting
of one parliament at Edinburgh. Suspicion, abhorrence, accu-

sation, trial, and death followed each other with appalling rapidity.

Thus we find in history, that the savage spirit of ignorance and credulity which impelled the great Cardinal Beaton to burn six men at the stake, on the charge of heresy, was out-Heroded by the still greater ignorance and credulity of his successors, who, for each of these six, sacrificed more than thousands for the imaginary crime of witchcraft.

CHAPTER XXXV.

THE COLLEGE OF JUSTICE.

" No ! in an accursed spot—our magic tree,
  Where devils from of yore their sabbath keep—
  Has all this been contrived; there did she sell
  Her soul to the eternal fiend, to be
  With brief vain-glory bonoured in this world.
  Bid her stretch forth her arm, and ye will see
  The puncture, by which bell bath marked its own."
                          SCHILLER'S *Maid of Orleans*

THE summer solstice was passed.

Heavily and louringly the 15th of July dawned over Edinburgh; and one hour after the portes were unclosed, the Right Honourable Knight, Sir Simon Preston of Craigmillar, the new Lord Provost of the city and Admiral of the Forth, entered by the Kirk-of-field Wynd, sheathed in full armour, with a party of horse; when, conformably to the orders of his eminence the cardinal, John Muckleheid, senior bailie, joined him with three hundred archers—the same burgher-archers who had lined the streets exactly two months before, on the entrance of Queen Magdalene.

A tumult was expected; very few merchants or chapmen opened their booths on this morning; and those between the Bell-house and the Tron remained closed. Sir John Forrester's guards were doubled at the palace, the Mint, the castle-gate, and elsewhere; and after arming themselves with more than usual care, vast crowds of burghers poured towards the Exchequer Chambers, or *'Checquer Chalmers,* as they then named them. The stacks of heather, broom, whins, and of other fuel, which were then permitted to encumber the street, either as being the property of householders, or for sale, bore each on their summit a load of urchins, whose yells and outcries served to increase the general clamour.

A flag was flying on the steeple of the Tolbooth, which had been built fifty years before, by John Mercer, master mason; and thirteen shops (formed at the same period), in the vaults below the edifice, remained closed and barricaded.

The respect his garb ensured him, and the liberal manner in which he said "Pax vobiscum" to all, enabled the anxious and excited Father St. Bernard, on leaving his dormitory in the house of the prebendaries, to force a passage through the dense crowd which occupied the High-street, around the Exchequer, the Tolbooth, and Council-house, spreading even down the steep churchyard of St. Giles.

The provost's kinsman, Sir Andrew Preston, of Quhitehill and Gourtown, with a squadron of horsemen, overawed the crowd. Clad in a suit of rich armour, he rode up and down the thoroughfare with his long lance, ordering and threatening some, or courteously giving admittance to others. The priest procured a place within the large hall of the Exchequer, where, for some reason now unknown, the trial of his unhappy penitent was to take place. A strong guard of archers occupied the hall-door and the turnpike-stair below, permitting none to enter without the closest scrutiny, lest armed Setons or Douglases might penetrate into the heart of the place; for rumours of rescue were abroad in the city.

Roofed with beams of oak, painted and gilded, the hall was lighted by two rows of windows, lozenged and stained with brilliant coats of arms. Those on the east faced the dark buildings of a narrow close; those on the west overlooked the churchyard of St. Giles; thus, as the sun could not (until mid-day) penetrate its recesses, the light within the hall, at the early hour of eight, when the court began to assemble, was of the most subdued and sombre kind.

At the upper end were fifteen chairs, behind a bench, all covered with scarlet cloth, whereon sat Walter Mylne, abbot of Cambuskenneth, lord president of the recently instituted, and then eminently obnoxious court of judicature, with his fourteen lords—viz., the abbot of Kinloss, the rector of Ashkirk, the provosts of Dunglass and of the Holy Trinity; the deans of Brechin, Restalrig, and Dunbar, who sat on his right hand; while the remaining seven, who were laymen—the knights of Balwearie, Lundie, Easter-Wemyss, Oxengangs, and of the Highriggs, Sir Francis Bothwell, and Otterburn of Auldhame (a cousin of Redhall)—sat upon his left. These were the first fifteen senators of the College of Justice in Scotland; and, save the churchmen, few of them could sign their names. They were all men advanced in life; and, with their black caps and scarlet gowns, looked grimly over the half circular bench, which was raised on a dais several feet above the floor of the hall.

Headed by Lord David Hamilton (a son of the Earl of Arran), their chancellor, or, as we would now turn him, their foreman, the jury, which was principally composed of Hamiltons, occupied a recess on one side of the hall; while the ten advocates, in gowns of Paris black, with a number of sworn notaries, had the privilege of occupying the other. A tall wax candle, painted over with religious emblems, burned on the right hand of the president; and coldly its light fell upon his pinched and stern features and the gold crucifix which glittered upon his breast.

Before him, on one hand, was a table where the clerks of court sat, intrenched up to their ears in papers; on the other stood an uncouth machine, covered by a black cloth. There was something in its aspect that made the blood run cold; it was the rack, with other instruments of torture. They were then in full use by the new court, but were last applied in Edinburgh by order of William III., whom the Scottish people will ever remember as the assassin-king—the butcher of Glencoe.

Near this, in a large arm-chair, hidden from the view of all save the lords, sat Redhall, buried in thought.

Macers in black gowns, and archers in steel caps, were visible here and there; but everywhere behind the bar was a dense crowd, whose heads were overlooking each other in close rows, like piles of cannon-shot. The whole court sat in the form of a horseshoe; and every lord's mouth, and every juryman's too, bore some resemblance to the same figure; for gloom, anger, and severity were impressed upon them all.

The bar enclosed the ends of this great horseshoe; and there, between two arquebusiers of the king's guards, sat Lady Jane Seton.

Destitute of every ornament save an amber rosary, she was plainly attired in a deep-skirted and close-bodied dress of blue silk, with hanging sleeves, each of which, from the elbow, had three rows of broad lace; and beneath these, from elbow to wrist, her round white arms were bare. A simple tri-

angular cap, of that graceful fashion which we see in the old
portraits of Anne Boleyn, covered her head. She was pale as
death, and the plain braids of her dark, almost black-brown
hair, made her seem paler still. She had become fearfully
thin and hollow-cheeked, but the character of her beauty was
rather increased than impaired by this attenuation.

There was an expression of intense sadness in her quiet
and limpid eye, and of sorrow on her lip; but there were
times when her eyes flashed and her lip quivered with surprise and contempt, or a cloud of horror would descend upon
her brow at the various proceedings of this new court, and
the bitter humiliation to which it subjected her. But now,
nearly broken in spirit, crushed, and feeling that she was for
ever degraded by the frightful accusation brought against
her, in general she was careless of what was done, or said, or
thought of her.

There was something antique in her beauty; but nothing
could be softer, purer, or more delicate than its aspect.

In silence she heard the low muttered revilings and exclamations around her; when harassed by the stern questions of the
hardhearted and the credulous, or confounded by their energy
and ferocity, their determination and their sophistry, she
became utterly silent, and sought to bend all her thoughts on
inward prayer.

A maze was before her eyes, and amid the maze were
fifteen scarlet spots, her fifteen judges; a confused murmur
was in her ears, but amid that murmur she could hear the
beating of her own heart. In its inner recesses there was but
one thought—*Roland;* and her heart only shrunk when her
chain rattled; for they had chained her.

She was a witch! . . . . .

Many a familiar face was in the crowd, yet not one deigned
to look on her with kindness or with friendship. The terrible accusation had frozen the hearts of all; thus she saw less
perhaps of sorrow than of indignation in every face; while,
generally, a silence the most profound reigned throughout the
whole assembly.

In Scotland trials for sorcery were mere formalities; the
same blind terror and insane credulity which brought forward
the accusation and hurried on the decision, led at once to the
frightful condemnation. When first indicted, Jane had some
hope of mercy, and that her perfect innocence might avail

her; for sorcery was then a new crime, and there were many who totally denied its existence; but the moment she entered the court, and looked on the faces of her judges, and saw that there were eight Hamiltons in the jury-box, she felt that her doom was written, and gave herself up for lost—as the majority of votes form the opinion of a Scottish jury.

The proceedings of the Supreme High Court of Justiciary in 1537, the year of its birth, were, in detail, widely different from what they are to-day; and such was its informality, that there was not one witness for the defence, the counsel for which based his arguments solely on the blameless life, the innocence, and conscious rectitude of the accused.

"I am innocent!" Jane would sometimes repeat to herself; "and they dare not punish me—God will not permit them!"

The clerk of the court now stood up to read the indictment, which was written on a strip of parchment:—

"Jane Seton, most falsely designated lady and of Ashkirk, thou art delated by the king's advocate for procuring the death of umquhile the queen's grace (whom the blessed Lord assoilzie!) by sorcery and incantations procured from hell; thou art accused of having a familiar spirit; of having renounced thy baptism, and having upon thee the mark by which Satan distinguishes all who have sold themselves unto his service."

"Of these crimes against the laws of God and of man, of nature and our holy Christian church, Jane Seton, art thou guilty, or art thou not guilty?" asked the abbot Mylne, sadly and solemnly.

Thrice the question had to be repeated before she was roused from her apathy to reply.

"Guiltless, father abbot—guiltless of such crimes—even as the blessed Mother of all compassion herself was guiltless," she replied, gently but energetically; "and this day I call upon her to hear the truth of my assertion; and the unhappy never seek her aid in vain."

A murmur floated above the crowd of spectators; and Jane's head sank on her breast.

Like a sharp poniard, her voice sank into the heart of Redhall. He now arose, and with a paper in his hand—a paper which he nervously folded and unfolded—prepared to speak. He looked like an animated corpse; his long flowing gown of black Parisian cloth, the sable hue of his beard and moustache, contrasted forcibly with his livid complexion. His eyes were hollow, and a ghastly agony was impressed on every lineament of his face; but attributing these appearances to his long and recent illness, the whole court, from the lord president down to Sanders Screw, the torturer, pitied his sufferings, and admired his worth and unflinching energy as an officer of state.

He dared not turn towards the prisoner, but spoke with averted eyes, which the court attributed to his gallantry and extreme delicacy of feeling. He endeavoured to condense the whole hatred of his heart against her; but love would come again, and they wrestled fiercely for the mastery. His heart swelled within his breast, and his brain became wild. He had two existences, and two hearts—one which loved, and one which hated—one that longed to possess, and another that longed to destroy her.

Then it would seem that he loved her as of old, and was prompted to avow his passion and his guilt, and, asserting her innocence, poniard himself before the court; but again his mad and murderous longing for revenge would come back upon his heart like a devouring fever, and thus he loved and thus abhorred in the same moment. Strange, wild, and inconsistent, his was the love of the devil united to the frenzy of a destroyer; he felt that it was so, and there were times when he doubted his own sanity.

The die was cast now, and a thousand eyes were bent upon him, and a thousand ears were listening. He made a tremendous effort to master his fierce emotions and open the prosecution; and being aware that there were many among the judges who doubted, and even denied the existence of witchcraft, he bent all his dangerous eloquence to prove the first position.

" My lords," said he, with a voice that, from being soft and flute-like, had now become hoarse and hollow, though it sounded like a serpent's hiss to Jane. " My lords, there may be among us those who decline to admit that witchcraft existeth in the world; albeit, divines cannot doubt it, for have not the words of God admitted that such things may be? In the eighteenth chapter of Deutcronomy, we are told that diviners, enchanters, consulters with familiar spirits, witches, necromancers, 'are an abomination unto the Lord;' and further, the twentieth chapter of Leviticus saith, 'the soul that turneth after such as have familiar spirits, and after wizards, *I will even set my face against that soul*, and will cut him off from among the people;' while the Mosaic law emphatically ordained that no witch shall be suffered to live. We need not, most reverend and learned lords, look so far back for proofs that sorcerers and charmers existed, and do exist; it must be apparent to every reasonable being that what hath once been may be again, for nothing is impossible either to God or the devil; and the ancient chronicles of Scotland, and of every other kingdom, teem with proofs of sorcery. The heathens of the olden time visited witches with the most dreadful punishments; the Persians dashed out their brains with stones; while we know that the Assyrians, Chaldeans, the Indian Gymnosophists, and the Druids of Caledonia, were addicted to the deepest sorcery. By the laws of Charlemagne, a witch who ate human flesh escaped for two hundred sous, which shows (as in the present case) that sorcery was not confined to the lower class of society.

" The emperor Manuel Comnenus punished sorcerers with the utmost rigour; and the blessed St. Patrick procured fire from heaven to destroy nine of them. St. Colme saw a wizard milk a bull, as we are informed by St. Adamnan, for the saints are constantly watching Satan, the prince of hell and promoter of mischief; and if so, how much more ought we, who are *their* servants, to watch sorcerers and witches, who are the slaves of the devil !

" The witch of Endor feared to practise her sorceries before the king, because he had put to death all who had familiar spirits; and so great was the indignation of God against the sin of sorcery, that he cut off the ten tribes of Israel because they were wedded unto its abominations. John de Fordun records, that in the days of that good knight and gallant king, William the Lion, a wizard who perverted the vision of the people, was defeated by a holy man reading even a passage from the blessed Gospels.

" Among the Romans, Publius Marcius and Pituanus were executed for this crime; as also were Publicia and Lucinia, with threescore and ten other citizens, as Valerius Maximus informs us in the third chapter of the sixth book. Hence, to deny the existence of witches, is to deny the veracity of all history, ecclesiastical as well as secular; and thus sorcery, being the greatest of all human crimes, as it includes heresy,

blasphemy, and treason against God, involves the most severe
of all human punishments—*death by fire*—for fire is the
emblem of purification.

" Picus of Mirandola, who lived in the last century, asserts
in his writings, that 'magic is not founded on truth, since it
depends upon powers that are enemies to truth ;' and further,
'that there is no one power in heaven or earth but may be
put in motion by the words of a magician ;' and he proves
that words are effectual in incantations, because God made
use of words in arranging the universe."

" My lord advocate, to the point," said the president, dryly ;
" in many parts of his writings, Francisco Picus was a rank
blasphemer."

" The prisoner at the bar is accused of procuring by sorcery,
and the aid of magic images, the death of umquhile the
queen's lamented grace, whom Heaven assoilzie! I accuse
her of this, and boldly."

" To the proof," said the abbot of Cambuskenneth, as
Redhall paused, and faltered.

" No difficult task, my lords," he resumed. " I need not
expatiate on the hereditary hatred borne to the king, the
queen and court, by the houses of Ashkirk and of Angus. Con-
sanguinity is ever a strong proof of sorcery. The countess
dowager of Ashkirk hath long sustained an evil reputation as
a dabbler in magic. If the mother be a sorceress, we hold it
in law, that the daughter must infallibly be so too. It is the
inheritance of hell, and descends, as the children of married
saints inherit a share of heaven. Arrian records that prophecy
was hereditary, like disease, and why not sorcery ?"

A murmur of assent replied.

" Hence, reared by her mother, the prisoner brought her
damnable and abstruse studies to greater perfection ; the pupil
surpassed her teacher ; and it was in *her* boudoir that this
image, which is coated over with wax and stuck full of pins,
was yesterday discovered by an officer of this high court—an
officer whose veracity and worth none will dare to gainsay."

Here Master Birrel smoothed his shock pate ; pulled up
his ruff, which was stiffened with whalebone, and looked
complacently around him.

" The good queen's gradual illness and wasting away from
the hour of her landing, was the slow but matured work of
sorcery ; and such the most learned physicians and apothegars

have declared it to be. My lords and gentlemen, here are written copies of the proofs," he added, as his clerks and scribes distributed to the bench and jury a number of written papers; but the said clerks or scribes might have saved themselves the trouble, as few of the learned lords, and not one of the intelligent jury, could either read or write. Neither had yet become fashionable or necessary accomplishments. "There you will find," continued the lord advocate, "that the queen's grace was first bewitched at the ball in Holyrood, where the Lady Seton induced others to dance a measure diabolique, which is well known to be in use among the witches of France; and as they danced, so the queen's illness increased with wondrous rapidity. That night her majesty kindly gave the prisoner her hand to kiss; then lo, again, the power of hell! the kiss burned into her heart, and she sank into a deadly faint. In both kiss and dance, my lords, we will prove there was sorcery, as the abbot of Kinloss assured me at the time. We all know how much Satan hath achieved by the agency of dancing, on looking back to the fits and visions of the Convulsionists, who in 1373 appeared at Aix-la-Chapelle. There is a certain mountain of the Harz chain in Almainie, where, on the 1st of May, every year, all the witches and wizards of the earth rendezvous to dance on *Valpurgis night*, as they name it. Now, *La Volta*, the hell-dance, was the ancient measure of the orgia, the feasts of Bacchus, a god of the pagans—a demon who loved wine. It came from Italy to Spain; from Spain to France; from France to Scotland.

"To the second proof. The prisoner with others visited the booth of Master Mossman, jeweller to the king's majesty; and there, placing on her head the queen's new crown (a notable piece of Douglas presumption), said certain words, to the effect that *she would never live to wear it, for her days were numbered*, and these ominous words we have here six witnesses to prove. Oh, my lords, did they not clearly and prophetically indicate a foreknowledge of the queen's death, obtained by the assistance of that familiar spirit who resided with her in the quality of page? Lastly, this image, half roasted and perforated by ninety-nine pins, and marked with a crown and the letters M. B., for Magdalene Bourbon. My lords and gentlemen, can other proof be wanting?"

Here he held up to view, between a pair of small iron tongs, a little wooden figure, about eight inches long, having on its head a crown.

"Mother of God!" muttered the people, crossing themselves with horror at these accumulated proofs.

"That death may be produced by wasting images, I could adduce a thousand instances; but less will suffice. In the year 980, our own King Duff, who pined under a grievous illness in Murrayshire, was rescued from death when the witch was burned and her images broken. The severe illness of Charles VI. of France was caused by sorcery, and the witch was burnt; so was another, who, in conjunction with the devil, forged a deed in favour of Robert of Artois. The powers of inflicting and of allaying diseases were peculiar to sorcerers; the mother allayed—the daughter inflicted. Solomon could allay disease by incantations, and Phyrrus, king of Epirus, did so by one touch of his great toe. Magic water may have been thrown on the queen's person; for we know that a few drops from Chosopis, the enchanted river of the Persians, brought death to all on whom they fell. As the fire scorched and wasted this image, even so did the poor queen waste and sink. Observe, my lords, it is formed of *pine*."

"The pine was consecrated, by the heathens of old, to Pluto, King of Demons," said Lord Auldhame.

"And wherever the unhappy queen endured the most severe pains,—in her head, in her heart, or the region of the stomach, *there* we find the greatest number of torturing pins. There are seven in each eye, and, like three, *seven* is a mystical number. I have but one remark more, my lords. This image was originally that of one of the three kings of Cologne; it has been abstracted from the rood screen of St. Giles's. and made to serve for that of her umquhile majesty Queen Magdalene."

"Sacrilege! sacrilege!" cried the crowd of listeners; "blasphemy and heresy!——"

"All of which assuredly require the most severe penalty your lordships can inflict—death at the stake!" and as the lord advocate sat down, pale and exhausted by his long harangue, and by the wild misanthropy of his desperate soul, the horror waxed strong in the hearts of his hearers.

"Holy Mary!" exclaimed the lord president, raising his hands and eyes to the oak ceiling, "can this woman, this being abandoned of God and of man, be a daughter of that gallant race, every chief of which has bled for Scotland and its king? Oh, what a wondrous—what a vast amount of sin is here!"

Master Robert Galbraith and Master Henry Spittal, the most able of the ten advocates, spoke in the defence of the accused long and ably, but all their arguments were overborne by the sophistry and eloquence of Redhall, and by the cloud of witnesses for the prosecution, which proceeded with such rapidity, that they were soon silenced, and sat down completely baffled. Then a long and anxious pause succeeded.

Father St. Bernard was in despair.

A senator now spoke; he was the rector of Ashkirk.

"My lords," said he, "in all that I have this day heard, there is much that perplexes me sorely; for it seemeth that the same faculties which were *miracles* when exercised by the saints, we style *sorceries* when assumed by others. St. Servan of Lochleven converted water into wine, and from the bosom of the arid earth a fountain sprang at the voice of St. Patrick. St. Baldred of the Bass used as a boat that rock which we may still see fixed in the sea near his island; the wooden altar of St. Bryde of Douglas sprouted and put forth leaves at her holy touch; the robe of St. Colme procured rain in Iona; and, in the winter time, St. Blaise could strike fire with his fingers——"

Here a stern glance from the Abbot Mylne cut him short, and he paused.

"The blessed saints of whom thou speakest, my lord, wrought those wonders by the aid of Heaven alone, and not by the agency of a black spirit. Of late, the devil hath frequently appeared at the preachings of the Reformers as a black cat, and why may he not appear elsewhere as a black boy?' said the president.

"True, most reverend and learned lord," rejoined the meagre little abbot of Kinloss, "need I remind your lordships how my predecessor, Abbot Ralph, now in company of the saints, when holding a chapter of the Cistercians at Kinloss, A.D. 121*, beheld the devil, yea, as surely as my name is Robin Reid, beheld him, in the shape of an Ethiopian, enter by a window; but, on being exorcised in good Latin, he vanished in smoke."*

* See John de Fordun's "Scotichronicon."

s

"True, true," continued Redhall, incoherently; "and by a devilishly devised compact with this familiar, she assigned her soul to Satan for the powers given——"

"Proof?" said the doubting rector of Ashkirk; "where is this contract?"

"In the archives of hell—therefore, how can we produce it?"

The judge sat down silenced, and a cold smile flitted over the face of Redhall, whose usually impassible front the Cumæan sybil herself could not have read; but he looked anxiously at the abbot of Cambuskenneth.

"Would that I knew what is passing in thy bald head, thou shaven dotard!" thought he.

"Familiar spirits are usually black," said the president; "the vile imposter, Mahomet, had one in the shape of a black cock, which, when it crew, set all the cocks in the world crowing; and the Lord Hugh of Zester had a black demon named *Gudeshovel*, who dug for him his goblin hall beneath the surface of the earth. The unhappy prisoner having persisted in denying her guilt, I require a slight application of the torture, and an examination for the devil's mark, that the ends of justice may be duly satisfied."

Redhall, who had been but half prepared for this, felt his heart die within him, and he made a convulsive start.

"The torture! the torture! Oh, rather let me die! Holy abbot—my lords—I ask you not for pardon, because I am innocent. I think not of vengeance, because I am a woman —and though an earl's daughter and an earl's sister, a poor and helpless one—but I implore death, because ye have dishonoured me by these accusations and by these bonds—cruelly and falsely dishonoured me. Put me to death, but not to the torture; for oh, I am weak, very weak, and will tell you anything. Let me die! let me die! Oh, save me, Sir Adam Otterburn—oh yes, everything—thou who hast done it all, save me from these frightful men!"

As Birrel and Sanders Screw approached the shrinking girl, with their stolid visages and huge hands, though half suffocated by sobs, she gave a low, wild cry of agony and horror, and closing her eyes, became perfectly passive. The judges looked on unmoved; a thrill pervaded the hearts of the people, and Redhall felt the perspiration trickle over his brow, though his blood ran cold through his veins.

" Oh, Roland, Roland! my love! my love! I am dying now," said Jane, in a low voice (that was heard by Redhall alone), as she was lifted from her seat.

Redhall's momentary pity died ; he sat down with one of his freezing smiles—such smiles as can only be given by one who has alike outlived the hopes of his heart and the feelings of humanity.

" *The torture,*" repeated the lord president.

Redhall dipped his pen mechanically in the inkstand, and Dobbie uncovered the rack; then, as every man respired more freely, a low, but unintentional hiss seemed to pervade the hall.

CHAPTER XXXVI.

THE RACK—THE DEVIL'S MARK.

" If on the rack you strain our bursting sinews;
If from the bleeding trunk you lop our limbs;
Or with slow fires protract the hours of pain,
We must abide it all."—*Boadicea.*

As yet neither the boot nor thumb screws had been adopted by the Scottish courts; the ancient rack alone was the instrument of torture, and now it stood before the eyes of the startled people in all its naked and mysterious horror. Though totally repugnant to the fundamental laws of Scotland, which are based on those of Rome, the practice of obtaining confessions by torture in the Privy Council and High Court of Justiciary was not discontinued until a hundred and sixty years after the date of our history, in the reign of William III., who, whatever he was in South Britain, will ever be remembered in the north as one who was merciless as a Mohawk.

The rack, which Dobbie had uncovered, was a large frame of oak, raised three feet from the floor, like a long, narrow bed without spars, but having two rings at the head and two at the foot. The aspect of this engine, with all its accompanying blocks, pulleys, chains, and handspikes in the sockets of the windlass, froze Father St. Bernard with horror. He crossed himself, beat his breast, and closed his eyes.

Old and withered, with a long beard and a hollow-jawed sardonic visage, with leering eyes, a fangless mouth, and bandy legs, Sanders Screw, the torturer and headsman—the presiding genius over this infernal machine—looked like an overgrown imp, as, with his concurrents, he hurried agilely from ring to ring, and from rope to rope, putting the whole in working order.

"*Agnus Dei!*" muttered the old priest, who, in a little volume which he wrote, has transmitted an account of these things to us; "all this for one frail body! May Heaven make it without feeling, even as the hearts of those around us."

Powerless and unresisting, Jane was borne between Sanders Screw and Nichol Birrel towards the rack, and placed within its frame. Birrel remembered Roland Vipont and Douglasdale; and, trembling with joy and revenge, made himself more than usually active. The costume of Screw and his two concurrents had something strikingly horrible in it; their doublets were scarlet—the judicial colour in Scotland—but their brawny arms were bared to the elbow; and they wore dirty leather aprons, extending from their necks to their knees. Lady Jane's garments swept the floor, and her long hair, which became unbound as her triangular cap fell off, floated over the shoulder of Screw as he adjusted her in the frame. Then a shudder came over her as the rings and cords were secured to her ankles and wrists, her beautiful arms being extended at full length above her head, revealing the exquisite rounding of her bust and waist. The whole arrangement did not occupy a moment.

While in this frightful and humiliating position, with her head supported in the hands of Screw's apprentice, and her blue silk skirt drooping on the floor, Redhall dared not look towards her, but sat down beside the rack, and bent his bloodshot eyes upon the blank sheet of paper, whereon the coming confession was to be written. He trembled excessively. On the other side was the physician, who attended all such *questioning*—John of the Silvermills—clad in deep mourning, like all the courtiers and dependents of the king, with a white St Andrew's cross on his black velvet mantle, and having a large pouch at his girdle, wherein were various revivifying drugs and essences.

Gently, but unceremoniously, the greater part of Jane's attire had been loosened by the rapid application of a pair of scissors.

"Now then, the devil's mark," said the lord president,

shading his eyes with his hand, and peering forward over his desk.

Nichol Birrel, sworn pricker of the High Court, now approached with his needle, and ruthlessly uncovered the whole neck, shoulders, and bosom of the unhappy girl. Her skin was dazzlingly white, and shone like polished ivory in the sunlight which streamed through the deep mullions of the windows above her in many hazy flakes.

"Oh!" she murmured, and shuddered, while the hot, bitter tears were seen to ooze from her closed eyelids. An icy sweat burst over Redhall, to behold that beautiful figure extended, almost nude, before so many unpitying and so many voluptuous eyes. His agony was frightful. He could have screamed aloud; and, to prevent himself doing so, buried his fingers in his breast beneath his robe. And there she lay, with a form that might have passed for Venus—one so delicate by nature and nurture, with her slender wrists and round white ankles enclosed by strong iron bands, and her uncovered bosom submitted to the eyes of so many men, and the rough paws of the ruffian Birrel.

There were a few generous hearts in the crowd who cried "*shame!*" and more than one gallant hand sought the hilt of a sword.

A pink spot, like a little rose-leaf, was discovered between her bosom and her waist, and to this the pricker, after making the sign of the cross and other preparations, applied his *brod*, or needle, which was three inches long, and, to the horror and astonishment of all, it sank up to the very handle in the mark, without Lady Seton wincing once, or seeming even aware that she was touched by the instrument.

Again and again the operation was repeated, and the pity of the generous few became blended with the fear and repugnance of the many.

"The mark of hell—the signet of Satan is always thus," said the Lord Kinloss; "for it is lost to all sensation, and deadened to the touch of every instrument—it is bloodless."

The long sharp needle of Birrel was pure and bright, as well it might be; for it was constructed like a theatrical poniard, to *retire* into the handle with the slightest pressure.

Blank dismay was impressed on every face.

Thrice Redhall asked her, in a hoarse and hollow voice, to confess, and thrice she gazed at him wildly, but made no reply; for the powers of life seemed already to have forsaken her. He then made a signal to Sanders Screw, and turned away his head.

Sanders, with his wrinkled and fibrous hands, grasped the handspikes of the windlass as a seaman would previous to starting an anchor. Then, with the whole weight and strength of his meagre body, the wretch suddenly depressed them, and every joint of the unhappy being cracked in its socket.

Father St. Bernard muffled his head in his cowl, to shut out the fearful sound.

She uttered a cry, the horror of which contrasted strangely with the sweetness and melody of her voice. Redhall felt as if he could have expired; and, in unison with her, he uttered a groan so painful and full of despair, that it must have startled all, had it not been blended with the cry of Jane.

"Mother of God! Mother of God! I will confess—I will confess! Oh, Roland, Roland!"

At these words Redhall bent his head towards the floor, for he felt that he had the face of a Nero, the eyes of a fiend, and he gave another of his horrible smiles. The name of Roland recalled his hatred, and that hatred triumphed over terror and compunction, as ferocity did over feebleness. The bars were a little relaxed, but she was not loosed until the following questions were answered:—

"Jane Seton," said Redhall, in a calm voice, and with an equally calm visage, for, being master of himself, his whole aspect was now as still as if the stormy passions which convulsed his heart were dead; "Jane Seton, dost thou confess to the damnable, the treasonable, and blasphemous sin of compassing and procuring, by sorcery and idols, the death of umquhile the queen's grace, of good memorie?"

"Oh, have mercy upon me!" she murmured.

"Dost thou confess it?"

"Yes,"

"Attend, clerks of court. Thou dost confess to having a familiar imp in the shape of a black page, who became the father of thy little devils?"

"Yes."

"Um—um—*coitus cum diabolo*," muttered a clerk of court, writing.

"How many?"

"I know not."

"Another proof of deep sorcery," said the lord president, "for the witches of Germany have been known to have twelve imps at a birth."

"And thou didst suckle these uncounted devils at the mark on thy bosom?"

"Yes, yes; oh, hast thou no pity?"

"Thou false heretic, apostate, liar, and renouncer of thy baptism, thou dost confess to having read English books, containing the dark and damnable heresies of——"

"This belongs to another court," said the abbot Mylne. "My Lord Advocate, we have no jurisdiction here in ecclesiastical matters. Surely, my lords, no further proofs are required?"

The capped or cowled heads of the fourteen lords shook or nodded an assent, and, at a word from Redhall Jane was unbound and replaced on her seat; where, with a pale, distorted face, and half insane aspect, she gazed about her, with terrified eyes, between the dishevelled masses of her hair. Her hands, weak, trembling, and almost dislocated, endeavoured to restore the disorder of her dress, but failed in their office.

The physician kindly parted her hair, and drew her disordered dress over her uncovered shoulders.

"Unhappy lady," he whispered, putting something between her lips, "take this comfit—it renders one almost invulnerable to pain; though it be not such as those to which the divine Artesius owed his eternal youth and health. But it is the essence of a wondrous herb; for whatever God planteth, hath its good or bad qualities."

Without hearing him, intent only on retracting her rack-extorted confession, she gathered her hair back from her pallid face with trembling hands, and arose, but only to sink powerlessly on her seat, for her limbs now refused to sustain her, as her tongue refused to speak; for though her bloodless lips were moving, they uttered no sound. Forced by the torture, a bright streak of pink was oozing from her nostrils.

Again she essayed to speak, but now the jury, without being charged, and without retiring—for such were not then the customs—by the voice of their chancellor, unanimously declared her guilty; and after a brief muttering and bending together of cowled heads, the abbot of Cambuskenneth proceeded at once to pass the sentence.

Taking off his black monastic cap, he raised his eyes, and was heard muttering something. "In nomine Patris, et Filii, et Spiritus Sancti, et benedictæ Nostræ Dominæ Sanctissimæ Mariæ . Thou false sorceress," he said, suddenly resuming his cap and raising his voice,—"thou heretic, blasphemer of thy God, and renouncer of thy baptism, for the crimes committed and this day doubly proved against thee by witnesses and from confession, I adjudge thee to be taken to the Castle-hill of Edinburgh at twelve o'clock on the night of the feast of St. Margaret the martyr, five days from hence, and there to be burned at a stake, until thou art consumed to ashes, which shall be scattered to the four winds of Heaven, AND THIS I PRONOUNCE FOR DOOM !"

The priestly president ended his sentence by extinguishing the candle which stood at his right hand—an emblem of death, or that hope was gone for ever. Thereupon, Dobbie the Doomster, clad in sackcloth braided with white cord, and having a white cross and skull sewn on his back and breast, approached, and laid a hand upon her shoulder, signifying that she was now *his* peculiar charge.

Those lords who were priests waved a benediction to the people, so much did they (by mere force of habit) mingle religious with civil ceremony ; then the whole bench arose, and the macer shouldered his mace ; but at that moment the clash of swords was heard, and a violent uproar arose at the door of the Exchequer Hall.

CHAPTER XXXVII.

THE GAGE OF BATTLE.

" In an evil hour I left her,
    Left her ! more I need not say ;
Since in my absence came another
    Lover, all my peace to slay.
I a captive, he a freeman,
    Ah ! our fates how different ;
Since your arm hath made me captive,
    See how justly I lament.
                    CALDERSON'S *Constant Prince*

ABOVE the clang of steel and the trampling of feet, a voice was heard that thrilled Jane to the heart ; and though feeble, aided by the iron railing of the bar, she suddenly arose, with her hands outstretched and her beautiful eyes bent towards the doorway, where the pike-points were glittering above the heads of the crowd. Love and despair gave to her aspect a courage and sublimity which vividly impressed the hearts of all. Between the thick stone mullions and grotesque tracery of a tall gothic window, and through the painted glass, the forenoon sun shone bright and joyously, lighting up her features with a radiance and beauty, the more remarkable by the fantastic prisms of the oriel, and she stood like a beautiful Pythoness.

As she turned away, Redhall ventured to gaze upon her, which he had not yet dared to do; for he felt that he trembled whenever her glance fell on him. She was but the spectre of what she was, and it was he that had made that havoc! A beautiful though hectic colour had momentarily replaced her frightful pallor, but he knew the emotion that caused it. The old whirlwind of passion arose in his heart, and he sank into a chair.

The clank of armour, the noise and swaying to and fro of the crowd continued.

"A rescue!" said the president, and all his brother senators drew towards him, and grew pale.

"Nay, think not of it, my lord," said one, the Knight of Auldhame, loosening his sword in its sheath; "for those lances of Sir Andrew Preston are more than guard enough."

At that moment Roland Vipont, master of the king's ordnance, broke through the mass of people, and approached the bench, with his armour rattling and his spurs clanking as he walked. He was cap-à-pie, with his visor up, and his plume was covered by the dust of a long summer march. With his sword drawn in one hand, and his gauntlet in the other, he appeared before the startled tribunal.

Ghastly and pale with fury and fatigue, he looked grimly at the bench beneath the steel bars of his aventayle; and with an air which he alone, above all the Scottish noblesse possessed, confronted them like one valiant Trojan in a Grecian camp.

"Father Abbot, my Lord President, justice—I sue for justice!" said he.

"And how darest thou come hither in armour to seek it?" demanded the president, with kindling eyes.

"Armour is my garb, because I am a knight and the king's soldier; besides, I dare do whatever becometh a Scottish man," replied Vipont; "and I this day stand before you to demand justice at the sword's point!"

"It has already been given!"

"Priest and judge though thou art, I tell thee thou liest! And here I lay down the gage of battle in accordance with the laws of Scotland, of justice, and of chivalry, binding myself to maintain with the edge of this good sword, and by the aid of the blessed God, on foot or on horseback, in the lists of Edinburgh, or at the Gallowlee of Leith, that Lady Jane Seton is pure and innocent of the crimes alleged against her —pure as when Heaven created her, and that all men who uphold the contrary lie—foully lie! Here lies my glove!" and he hurled the steel gauntlet on the table with a clash which made the clerks of the court start from their seats with dismay; for, like all limbs of the law, they had a mortal aversion to cold iron in every shape.

There was a momentary pause; and Redhall, who gazed with gloating eyes upon the lover's agony, felt half-inclined to take up the gage, for notwithstanding his unruly passions and studied vengeance, he was both brave and rash; but the stern voice of the president arrested him, saying—

"Sir Roland Vipont, this claim for the ordeal of battle comes too late, and cannot be admitted. She has fully and amply confessed; besides, this man hath found the mark of hell upon her bosom!"

"Her bosom—this man—John Dargavel!" exclaimed Roland, startled on perceiving the person whom he had compelled to swallow his own poison.

"Nay—no John Dargavel, but a reputable officer of court," said the president, who felt some compassion for the agony expressed in the young man's face.

"A villain, who excited the lieges to rebellion in Douglas-dale, and to a resistance of the royal standard, which occasioned me the killing and wounding of a dozen brave soldiers."

"We have had enough of this," said the president, impatiently; "the poor youth is so blind with passion, that he would not know a hawk from the heronshaw. Break up the court. Away, sir! torture hath been applied, and the ends of justice are satisfied."

"Torture—justice!" reiterated Roland, in a voice like a shriek, and looking with terror at Jane, who stretched her feeble arms imploringly towards him. "Lord, Lord, look down upon me, and preserve my senses. Oh, have ye dared—— Cowards and slaves! is it justice by rack and torture to wrench confession from the lips of a poor and helpless woman ? Smooth-fronted villains, is there not one among ye who will dare to take up my gage? Sir William of Balwearie, Sir John of Lundie, Sir Adam Otterburn of Auldhame, do you hear me ?"

Not one of the seven lay senators moved.

"Truly, thou art either a madman or a hero!" said the old president, gazing on the armed knight with admiration; "but doom hath been pronounced, and the sorceress must die!"

"Die!" repeated Roland, with a fierce smile. "And coldly thou sayest this? Oh, lord abbot! dastard judge! dost forget that thou growest old, and a day cometh when thou too shalt die, and be called to account for this misused authority. Art thou a god to create, that thou darest thus coolly to destroy; not like a gallant soldier in the heat of battle—but coldly, calmly, and without anger? But I see it all now; and though this moment be my last, I will avenge Jane Seton on Redhall—the angel on the demon! See how the pale coward is before the brave man! Art thou blanched, Sir Adam, with fear, with fasting, or remorse? Wretch and villain! who makest use of the laws to cloak thine own infamous projects of lust, ambition, and revenge; thus in face of thy deluded compeers, the just God gives thee over to me—at last—at last I have thee!"

And rushing upon the lord advocate with his long sword drawn back for a deadly thrust, he had infallibly run him through the body, had not two of the provost's guard resolutely interposed their halberts, the heads of which he hewed off by one blow.

"Oh, the fule!" said the host of the *Cross and Gillstoup*, who was among the crowd. "My thirty crowns! I may whistle on my thumb for them noo!"

A cry of mingled fear and admiration arose from the people; it drowned poor Jane's far wilder one of terror; and she made frantic efforts to free herself from the arquebusiers, and to succour or die with her brave lover, who, on being pinned against the wall with more than twenty long pikes, was soon beaten down, pinioned and disarmed.

As he fell, Jane thought they had killed him, and uttered a cry of despair; all her energies, so briefly recovered, immediately forsook her; the light left her eyes; her heart forgot to beat. She became perfectly insensible, and was re-conveyed to the Castle of Edinburgh in a litter, under the care of Father St. Bernard and John the physician.

" It matters not, this poor victory!" said Roland, with a bitter smile; " it matters not, Redhall. I will unmask thee yet, thou subtle villain, and show our too-credulous king the true aspect of the viper he has nourished so long."

" Guards! away with him—to ward!" cried the advocate, furiously, as he signed a hastily-written warrant: and in one hour from that time Roland found himself committed to the care of Sir James Riddel of Cranstoun-Riddel, on a charge of high treason, and attempting to murder in open court Sir Adam Otterburn of Redhall.

The excitement in the city was great.

The whole garrison of Sir James stood to their arms, and buckled on their harness; the brass culverins of the Spur were loaded; the gates were closed, and bridges drawn up; while a crowd composed of thousands covered the south and north sides of the Castle-hill up even unto the very ramparts of the hornwork, nor dispersed until long after the lingering sun of July had set behind the hills of Dunblane.

CHAPTER XXXVIII.

THE EARL'S DARING.

Dione, then : Thy wrongs with patience bear;
And share those griefs inferior powers must share ;
Unnumbered woes mankind from us sustain,
And men with woes afflict the gods again."

The Iliad, Book V.

A FEW chapters back we left the Earl of Ashkirk alone upon the solitary beach near the cavern, on the morning of that day which beheld his unhappy sister for the first time an inmate of the Castle of Edinburgh.

His more bitter feelings of hostility to James had been soothed, for the monarch possessed the charm of the Stuart race—that charm which won the hearts of all whom they addressed; but, being still unforgiven, Lord Ashkirk felt himself an outlaw, with the axe of the doomster hanging over his head, while he had to suspect a spy or a foeman in every man he met.

With his eyes fixed on the island castle where his mother and Sybil Douglas of Kilspindie were imprisoned,—with all his thoughts centred there, and bent on visiting and freeing them from the thraldom and captivity of a Hamilton, he walked along the sandy shore, revolving a thousand rash but gallant plans and projects.

He was buried in deep thought, and gradually his head sank upon his breast.

A draught of water from a spring, a bannock and a piece of cheese received at a cottage where he tarried, and, in the hospitable fashion of the olden time, asked for it without shame and obtained it with a welcome, sufficed him for food; and, retracing his steps, he wandered westward up the margin of the broad river, until he reached the little kirktown of Wester-Kinghorn (which now bears another name), lying behind the Burnt-island, nestling under the brow of hills that are upheld by basaltic columns, whose summits have been scorched by volcanic fire, and whose rifted sides have repelled the waves of the antediluvian world.

On the high and rocky island, which, though it has now become a promontory, was then completely surrounded by the sea at high water, stood a tower belonging to the Duries of Durie.

Crossing the sandy neck or isthmus while the tide was low, the earl concealed himself among the copsewood which covered the island on the eastward, from whence he had a view of Inchkeith, distant about three miles, reddened by the setting sun which covered with a golden tint the calm, broad waters of the Firth.*

The wood was in full foliage, and cast a pleasant shade upon the rocks, which were spotted with grey lichens or covered with verdant moss. Here passed the day; and evening came, with silence and darkness, for even the stillness of that lonely isle became more still. The wild bees and the buzzing flies forsook the cups of the closing flowers for their homes in the hollows of the old pine-tree; the notes of the mavis and merle died away; the deer came no more to drink of the stream that trickled from the rocks, and the foliage of the isle became moist with the falling dew.

* Firth, from *Fiord;* not *Frith,* from *Fretum,* as Dr. Johnson erroneously supposed.

As if in contrast to the storm of the previous evening, the night came on clear, cloudless, starry, and beautiful.

Avoiding that side of the isle which was overlooked by the Duries' castle of Ross-end, the earl sought the beach, where a few fisher-boats were moored to rings in the rocks of a lonely creek.

The place was deserted, and not an eye beheld him. His resolutions and execution were brief: selecting the smallest, he sprang on board, cast off the painter, and seizing a pair of oars, each one of which would have required an ordinary man to handle it, he pulled away from the shore with a strength and activity that the sturdiest of our fisher-wights might have viewed with satisfaction and envy. Though as accomplished a knight as ever rode to battle, the earl was somewhat of a seaman, for his father's castle in Forfarshire looked down on Lunan Bay.

He was master of the little bark both by sail and oar; and knowing somewhat of the dangerous navigation of that stately river, avoiding those perilous rocks known as the Gunnel, on gaining the mid-stream he set the brown lug-sail, which the unsuspecting proprietor had prepared for the little fishing voyage of the morrow, and, favoured by the ebb-tide, the current, and a soft west wind, bore with the speed of a sea-gull straight down towards Inchkeith.

If the wind freshened, he had a thousand chances to one of being swept helplessly out into the German Ocean ; but the bold earl never thought of that.

Alone in the middle of the broad and rapid Firth, its aspect seemed to him magnificent, as the deep red light that lingered behind the western Ochills tinged all its waves with a purple hue ; but their foam became a shower of silver, and white as winter frost, when it broke against the shining cliffs, whereon rose the castle at the west end of the island.

As the earl had resolved on freeing his mother and Sybil from their captivity, his natural boldness prevented him from seeing any difficulty in achieving this project, though he was alone in the enterprise, armed only with his poniard and an old sword which he had picked up in the brawl of the preceding night, and though the castle was commanded by Sir James Hamilton of Barncleugh, with a small but chosen party of soldiers.

" If a Seton could fear, I should certainly be afraid now,"

said the earl, on seeing how the waves burst in foam on all
sides of the Inch—one moment sinking low, to show the
reefs, which rose like jagged teeth above them, and the next
dashing in torrents against the black volcanic bluffs. "Tut!
by the pope! what a mouthful of salt-water!" he added, as
the spray was blown in his face, when he dashed his boat
through the breakers, and then, running along the lee of the
shore, struck his sail and slowly crept near the little creek,
which there forms the only landing-place; for on the east
rushes the whole current of the Firth, and on the west breaks
the thundering force of the German Sea.

The night had now come on, and solemn stillness reigned
upon the isle.

The gates of the square tower which crowned its highest
summit were closed; but here and there a red ray glimmered
from the deep windows of its dusky mass.

"One of these lights," thought the earl, as he gazed upward, "may shine on my dear Sybil's dark glossy hair and
snow-white brow."

The tide was low, and he ran the boat into a little cavern
which lay near the creek; it was, in reality, but the top of a
deep chasm in the rocks, having a clear sandy bottom, where
he could distinctly perceive the layers of dark pebbles, of bright
shells, and waving sea-weed, far down below, when the clear
moon rose above the Lammermuir, to shed its radiance on
the heaving water.

Resolving to wait till midnight, when all the inhabitants
of the town most probably would be asleep, and when, with
more security, he could make a reconnaissance of the isle and
the barbican wall, the earl guided his boat into the narrow
little fissure, which is one of many that perforate the island.
While endeavouring to prevent its jarring on the flinty rocks,
he was greatly alarmed by perceiving a human figure spring
off a shelf of the volcanic wall, and plunge heavily into the
deep dark water of the chasm, which penetrated, he knew not
how far, into the heart of the island, but which, as it receded,
became more appalling by its utter obscurity and subterranean
character.

Incident to the age, rather than the man, the earl's supernatural fears of kelpies, gnomes, and water-spirits, now became
altogether secondary to the dread of having been discovered
by some human denizen of the place. He felt for his poniard,

and paused. Behind him yawned the pointed arch of the cavern, with the distant sea-beach shining in the moonlight; before him lay rocks and water buried in darkness. He lingered, oar in hand, scarcely daring to breathe, but heard only the ripple of the rising tide as it chafed on the walls of the chasm.

Suddenly, another sound smote his ear, that as of a diver rising to the surface; then came a hard breathing on the water, and the regulated plashing as of some one swimming away into that very obscurity which the earl's eyes ached with regarding, but failed to penetrate. His hair bristled, and his heart quailed with momentary terror of a spirit, or evil thing; but from that very terror he gathered a courage, and, by his oar and hands, feeling the rocks on each side, shot further in his sharp-prowed boat, intent on overtaking the swimmer, and discovering whether it was a man or devil; but he had not gone twenty yards when the chasm terminated in a sheer wall of rock; and again he paused to listen. The dash of the water had ceased.

He thought he heard other sounds, like those of footsteps clambering up the rock; but feared he was mistaken, for all became immediately still, and he heard only the murmur of the water as it boiled among the reefs without.

"Tush!" thought he, reddening with shame at his own alarm; "it has only been some poor seal or sea-dog basking on the rocks in the summer moonlight. By midnight the moon will be in the west—till then let me sleep, for these last two nights I have never closed an eye;" and looping a rope round a pinnacle of rock, he securely moored the boat, and reclined within it to sleep.

Such was the effect of the weariness oppressing him, that in three minutes he was buried in profound slumber, rocked by the motion of the boat, which gently rose and fell on the undulations of the water; for though around the isle the swell was heavy, the waves being broken by the jutting of the rocks at the cavern mouth, they rolled gently and smoothly into its dark recesses.

Now while the earl all unconsciously was sleeping, this little cavern of the sea was filling fast; for as the rising tide or the German Ocean met the downward current of the Forth, the water rose rapidly against the impending walls.

Ashkirk knew not how long he slept, when he was suddenly

awakened by an unusual sound, and, on attempting to rise, struck his head with violence against the stone roof of the cave, close up to which his boat had floated on the rising tide.

His situation was fraught with danger and horror.

Moored fast to a point of rock now far beyond his reach, the boat was wedged between the top of the cavern and the surface of the swollen water, leaving him thus imprisoned, coffined, as it were, in utter darkness, and with the deadly fear that the whole of this now submarine grot would be covered by the gurgling tide, in which case he would assuredly be drowned, "and die the death (as he thought) of a rat in a drain."

The partial gleam of moonlight which had illuminated the mouth of this frightful trap had now passed away, and the darkness within and around it seemed palpable and opaque. He could no longer discern where the entrance lay, and his heart sank in the fear that the water had risen over it. He now heard the wavelets rippling, with a thousand hollow echoes, in the fissures and recesses, and gurgling with a sucking sound as they filled each in succession, and rose towards the gunwale of his boat, which had become perfectly immovable.

And the tide was still rising!

He found that he could not survive ten minutes longer. Already the air was stifling, and the necessity of making one desperate struggle for life became immediately apparent. Lying almost on his back, he groped breathlessly around him, and discovered a vacant shelf of rock upon his right. Clambering within it, he found with joy that it led to an inner and upper cavern. He had scarcely left the boat when, with a hoarse gurgle, the tide rushed in and filled it.

As he ascended, a faint red light now flickered on the dark, stony walls of this slimy retreat; then, indeed, the heart of the gallant earl began to tremble, as his dread of supernatural beings returned. He remembered the strange figure which had disappeared so suddenly into the lower cavern when he first entered it. Again the terror of the water-kelpie came vividly upon him; for, in that time, all Scotsmen feared that evil denizen of their native seas and lakes.

Though dark, damp, and slimy, it was evident to the earl that the water did not usually rise so far as this upper retreat; and as the light reddened and increased around him, it re vealed the solid masses of whinstone rock which composed the enormous walls of this subterranean vault. Here and there were columns of basalt, or perpendicular lava, with masses of sparkling spar, pitchstone, and porphyry. Still this strange and crimson light brightened and wavered, dying and growing again, till, overcome by dread of dwarfs and fairies, or spirits still more fell, several seconds elapsed before the earl removed his hand from his eyes, and looked steadily around him.

At the upper end of the grotto, which measured somewhere about twenty feet square, there burned a fire of wood, green bushes, and crackling sea-grass; and thereat was seated—neither a witch brewing hell-kail, nor a wizard working spells; neither a stunted dwarf forging fairy trinkets, nor some fair water-spirit rising in her naked beauty from a silver shell, but simply a man roasting one of those wild rabbits with which the island has in all ages abounded, and who, with his breath, was blowing aside the smoke, which curled to the upper air through a chasm in the roof.

Lord Ashkirk paused irresolutely; for, in advancing, he might fall upon an enemy, and in retiring, he would inevitably fall into the water, which murmured angrily in the cavern below. The whole aspect of this subterranean cook was wild and strange; and though he stooped immediately over the red embers that gleamed on a shelf of basalt, the intruder failed to discover his features.

Suddenly, something familiar in the attitude flashed upon his memory.

" Sabrino !" he exclaimed, and approached him.

Sabrino—for this mysterious personage was no other—turned round, and bounded backward with a terror which was ludicrously expressed by the blue aspect of his usually sable visage, his dilated yellow eyes and expansive mouth, in the recesses of which he rolled about the voiceless fragment of his mutilated tongue.

" O—ah !" he stuttered, capering with terror, " O—ah—ees a-mee !"

" Now, by St. Mary ! I thought thee the devil himself roasting some poor man's child. Why art thou not attending my mother in that rascally old tower above us? How camest thou to be hiding thus, and in a condition so dilapidated? But, first of all, how is my Lady Sybil—tush ! I waste my time in questioning thee, poor pagan, who art incapable of Christian speech."

As Sabrino's whole vocabulary consisted of a few guttural sounds, a vast number of contortions of visage and shark-like grins, which were seldom very intelligible to any one save the countess or Lady Jane, who had acquired a knowledge of his meaning by habit, an answer to the earl's three questions was not to be expected. After his first terror and the extravagance of his after-joy had subsided, his story, if he could have told it, might have been related in a few words.

The blow inflicted by the oar had neither killed nor stunned him; for, luckily, that portion of his frame whereon it fell, namely, his head, was stronger, by nature, than a casque of steel; thus, he merely sank to come up again a few yards distant; but he dared neither to swim after the boat, nor return to the tower where his mistress was imprisoned, and from which he had been so unceremoniously repulsed. Full of hatred and fear of the white men among whom his evil fortune had cast him, the unhappy black page had found this shelter when pursuing a rabbit by moonlight among the rocks. Externally, a thick clump of whin-bushes concealed the fissure that gave admittance to this upper grotto, where, for fourteen days, Sabrino had lurked, coming forth only at night to pick up fuel and shell-fish, crabs, mussels, whelks, and other *debris* of the ocean on the beach, and to catch the wild rabbits as they slept among the long reedy grass in the moonlight.

During the day he remained close in his retreat; for he knew well that Sir James Hamilton's men in the tower would have thought as little of shooting him, by bow or arquebuse, as of winging a Solan goose.

In these fourteen days, much of the original savageism of the African's aspect and disposition had returned. He looked wild, haggard, and strange, as his glassy eyeballs, and the gold earrings with which the countess had adorned his large ears, glittered in the light of the embers. On his thick woolly head was a cap or crown, which he had woven of seaweed, and ornamented with the crabs' claws and the cockleshells of his late repasts; his once gay doublet of white satin slashed with scarlet silk and laced with gold, his tight white hose and trunk breeches, together with the metallic collar of thrall, which had the Countess Margaret's arms and cipher engraved thereon, were all wofully changed in aspect, the former being torn to rags, and the latter encrusted with salt by the saline atmosphere of the Firth.

All this and much more the poor mute endeavoured to explain by signs, which were totally unintelligible to the Earl of Ashkirk; who, however, understood one point of the narrative, the necessity of remaining closely concealed.

As Sabrino, to avoid discovery, had to cook all his viands in the night, another rabbit was put to the spit before his fire, on which he threw some of the driftwood and dried seaweed procured from the creek; and there can be little doubt that the glow of this subterranean fire, appearing at times through the fissure in the rocks that bounded the western side of the little valley, formed the gleams of fairy light, which were the source of such alarm to the countess.

Her outlawed son made a hearty meal, which passed for both supper and breakfast, as by the time it was concluded Sabrino had carefully extinguished his fire, for morning had dawned, and the beams of the rising sun shone far into the lower cavern, glittering on its wet walls, and casting their reflection on its slimy recesses. The tide, which in full flow completely filled it, had now ebbed; but there were many fathoms of water, dark and deep, in the chasm where the earl's boat lay floating, swamped and brimful to the gunwale; and the task of baling it with his bonnet, for lack of another vessel, was a long and protracted one.

"Now, my friend Sabrino," said he, "dost thou know what has brought me to this rascally island?"

A knowing leer glittered in the shining eyes of Sabrino; and pointing to the tower, he kissed his hand, laid it on his heart, and then pointed to the water.

"Thou art right: to take my black-eyed Sybil from that villanous prison-house. By my faith, thou wouldst make a glorious lover! what a bright leer thou gavest! I would give a hundred golden unicorns to find a sable Venus for thee, my poor Sabrino; and who knoweth, but through the kind offices of the prior of Torphichen and other knights of Rhodes, I may do so. Now, dost thou know in what part of yonder tower Lady Sybil Douglas and the good lady my mother dwell?" asked the earl, pointing to the castle of the Inch, from the whin-bushes which screened the entrance to their hiding-place, and faced the little valley overlooked by the island fortress, and the winding path which ascended to it. "Not those chambers which overhang the ocean, I hope?" he added, anxiously.

Sabrino nodded his head sorrowfully.

"Ah! twenty furies! dost thou say so? How shall I ever reach them, unless I become a hoodie-crow or a Solan goose? Do they ever walk in the valley?"

Sabrino nodded again.

"Close to these rocks—eh?"

Sabrino shook his woolly head.

"Are they guarded? The devil! thou noddest thy head again. Indeed, this wary old trooper, Barncleugh, keeps a sure watch over them. By Satan's horns! I may mar his wardship yet. Do he or they know that thou art here?"

Another shake of the head replied in the negative.

"Sabrino, my dark-complexioned friend, listen and look; open thy huge eyes, prick up thy capacious ears, and attend to me. To-night I will scale that castle wall, and thou shalt assist me."

"Ees."

"I have observed that the windows on that side are not barred, because they overlook the water. Thou wilt clamber, and not be afraid?"

"Ees—ees," replied the negro, capering about.

"But we may be shot by the arquebuses of the watchmen."

"O—ah!" howled Sabrino, scratching his woolly head.

"But do not let that affright thee, my Ethiopian; for it hath been the hap of better men before us. An unlucky cannon slew King James II. at Roxburgh, at the very moment he was passing a jest with my gallant grandsire. What matters it whether we are shot now, or die quietly twenty years after this, for in the twenty-first year time would be all the same with us, at least so far as I am concerned personally; but I have it imperatively upon my mind to send certain Hamiltons to the other world before me, ere I can give up the ghost in peace."

The eyes of the negro gleamed, and he laid his hand on his dagger.

"How readily thou snuffest blood, my sable devil. I doubt not thou gottest it with thy mother's milk; for, among the knights of Torphichen, I have heard it said, that in the faraway land from whence thou camest, a child receives its first

food on a spear, even as our fierce clansmen in the north give
the young Celt his first food on the point of his father's
claymore. Well, then, listen. Thou seest the wall of yonder
barbican, all grey, weatherbeaten, and tufted with grass; well,
where that wall joins the tower, I will ascend, and so reach
the windows of their apartment. Thou starest. Ah, my
friend, thou knowest not my capabilities in the climbing way.
I have done as much before for the mere love of life, and
shall I not do thrice as much again for the love of Sybil
Douglas, who is dearer to me than a thousand lives?"

The negro clapped his hands, lolled out the fragment of his
tongue, and danced about to the jangle of his long earrings,
which clanked on his metallic collar.

Being naturally at all times of a sociable and convivial turn,
the young earl, to while away the time, talked constantly to
the poor mute, gravely and with drollery by turns, amusing
himself with his childish wonder and savage simplicity, for
they served to pass the otherwise dreary day; and gladly
Ashkirk beheld the sun sink, and the hour for more active
employment draw near.

CHAPTER XXXIX.

THE EARL'S SUCCESS.

> " You will quickly find
> I'll reach its gates, although, volcano-like,
> With thickest clouds it strikes the bright sun blind,
> And lightnings flash, and bolts around me strike."
>
> CALDERON.

DURING the whole of that day, from his secret hiding-place,
the earl watched the little green valley that lies in the bosom
of the island, and the narrow winding path that ascended
from it to the round gateway in the barbican wall of the
tower. The latter was an exact square of considerable height,
surrounded at the summit by a heavy battlement, having
little tourelles at the angles, a row of those brass cannon then
known in Scotland as *chalmers*, and a staff, from which was
displayed the blue national standard, with the white cross
of St. Andrew. But the anxious earl watched fruitlessly;
for on this day, neither at the windows, on the ramparts, on
the pathway, nor in the valley, did the countess or Sybil
appear.

About mid-day, Sir James Hamilton of Barncleugh, the governor of the little stronghold, came forth, and at the gate sat down to his daily employment of playing chess with his seneschal, and drinking Rochelle, while a few of his soldiers solaced themselves by a game with quoits in the valley below, where, as Sabrino endeavoured to acquaint the earl, the same men had played at the same game, at the same time, every day since he had been on the island; for so passed the time in this little isolated and monotonous place; and nothing ever disturbed the perfect equanimity of its governor (who was content to vegetate like a fungus or a mussel on the rocks), save when the Leith provision-boats brought some waggish rumour that his lady, who was a dame of the tabourette at Holyrood, intended to join him—the very idea of which made the bluff old knight tremble in his wide trunk hose.

So close were the quoit players to the place of the earl's concealment, that more than once he shrunk back with alarm, expecting instant discovery, when any of them overshot the mark, and hurled his iron discus to the very verge of the dark whins which shrouded the mouth of the cavern. This group of men continued to play with ardour until sunset; for of this game (which was famous of old among the ancients) the Scots in all ages, as in the present day, have been passionately fond.

While the earl, lover-like, was wasting his time in gazing at the tower which contained Sybil, the black page sat near him, cross-legged, engaged in knotting a ladder from a coil of rope he had found in the boat, and formed it very ingeniously by loops equidistant on each side of the shaft of a stout boat-hook, solacing himself the while by a deep guttural croaking, which he meant for a song, and grinning from ear to ear with delight as his work progressed.

As the sun set behind the Ochills, a culverin was fired from the high carved poop of the Admiral Sir Robert Barton's ship, and St. Andrew's cross was hauled down from the bartizan; the governor and his little garrison retired to supper, the gates of the tower were closed, and then a perfect stillness reigned throughout the island, which exhibited no sign of life, save when a seagull flew screaming round the tower above, or a wild rabbit shot like an evil spirit across the darkening valley below.

The night came on calm, still, and solemn, and the stars
were reflected on the broad blue bosom of the Forth.   The
moon seemed to linger long behind the distant Lammermuirs;
but the myriad of stars that dotted the canopy above shed a
clear white light on the magnificent river, the bordering hills,
and all its rocky isles.   Here and there a red spark, twinkling afar off, marked where a town or hamlet lay, for thickly
were they scattered along its fertile shores.

The blue waves were rolling in silver light against the
black rocks and volcanic columns of the isle, as the earl
guided his boat from its place of concealment, and moored it
by the beach; for on this night he had resolved to attempt
one of those rash and bold essays of which his life was one
continued and exciting succession.   With anxious and longing eyes he gazed at the square and lofty tower which stood
in dark outline between him and the west, where, above the
distant chain of the Ochill mountains, a red light lingered
like the last flame of a dying conflagration.

It marked where the sun had set.

"Now," said the earl, as he sprang ashore, "thank heaven,
Sabrino, I have bidden adieu to thy dark and dirty fox-
hole!"

Armed with his sword and poniard, and carrying with him
a stout rope and the boat-hook, which, like the boat itself
(acting under the law of necessity), he had appropriated to
himself, the adventurous earl, accompanied by his sable follower, stole up the dark valley, across which fell the sombre
shadow of the tower (for though rising, the moon was not yet
visible), and crept softly close to the rampart of the barbican.

From thence they piloted their way along the base of the
wall, until they reached an angle that overhung the water,
which, at the frightful depth of a hundred and sixty feet
below, was chafing in foam against the foot of the cliffs,
beetling on the very verge of which the tower was founded.
According to Sabrino, the windows of the apartments occupied by Sybil Douglas and the countess overlooked this comfortable abyss.

To pass the corner of the wall which overhung the precipice
was the most dangerous part of the adventure; and, observing that his leader paused with perspiration on his brow and
perplexity in his heart, the negro pulled the skirt of his
doublet, and made a motion indicative of advancing himself.

"My trusty imp!" said the earl. "where a Seton lingers,

it will never do for thee to take the lead; and yet, without the wings of a crow or the claws of a cat, I know not how the devil I shall pass this hairbreadth precipice!"

While Ashkirk was speaking, Sabrino, who on many a night before this had scrambled like a squirrel over every part of the island, shot past, and, with his arms embracing the corner of the wall, achieved the feat, and with a guttural laugh held out his hands to assist the earl round.

"Thou art certainly a son of our old friend with the horns; but, by my faith, fall or not, I follow thee!" and grasping the hand of the agile African, with one stride the earl was beside him.

Then he found himself upon a shelf of rock scarcely eighteen inches broad, with the waves of the Firth hissing in foam far down below—so far, that their angry boom was but faintly heard, while the scared seagulls and gigantic Solan geese, flapping their wings like thunder, flew out of their eyries, plunging and screaming in the abyss beneath.

About three miles off, the lights of Leith were faintly glimmering through that haze which often shrouds its shores.

Though eminent for courage in a gallant age, the earl felt his heart grow sick for a moment at his perilous position. At his back was the wall of the keep, some seventy feet in height; and twenty feet from where he stood was a large window secured by two bars of iron in the shape of a cross; and there Sabrino indicated, by a multitude of signs, contortions, and guttural sounds, the countess resided.

"I have thrown a lance six ells long, at a smaller mark than that window," said the earl; "and I must be blinder than a bat to miss it; but as thou knowest, Sabrino, the business just now is not to hit the window, but to click the boat-hook to the bars. Ah, plague! if we should only break the glass, and the window be, after all, that of Sir James Hamilton, or some of his fellows! my blood runs cold at the thought; they could pop at us so leisurely with their hand-culverins; and I assure thee, I have no wish to be shot like a poor pigeon here."

As the earl spoke, he secured one end of the rope to the ladder which had been formed of loops on the shaft of the boat-hook, and tied the other round his waist; he then, with all the force that his dangerous footing permitted him to exert, shot up the hook towards the window; but missing it, was nearly thrown over the cliff by the jerk of its descent.

" Courage!" said he, grasping it again; " I am only twenty feet from thee, my dear Sybil."

Again he threw, and with joy beheld the steel hook attach itself to the iron cross-bar of the window. Then he waited breathlessly to hear if the noise caused any alarm; for there was as much chance of a moustached soldier appearing at the window as of Sybil Douglas presenting her fair face and startled eyes. All remained still but the screaming of the sea-birds around them, the dash of the breakers below, and the dull hum of the rising wind as it swept along the Firth. Then fearlessly the brave earl began his ascent. On the strength of the rope, the hook, or the shaft, he never bestowed a thought; but solely intent on seeing his mother and Sybil, clambered eagerly but carefully up the rough wall, which was grey and weatherbeaten by the saline atmosphere and ocean storms of many a century, and against which the ladder swung frightfully to and fro, until he reached the window, grasped its massive cross-bar, and gained a comparatively secure seat on its deep, broad sill.

He peered in, and listened, as well as the thick panes of coarse and encrusted glass, which filled the window, would permit, and between the yellow damask curtains saw a plainly-furnished sleeping apartment, in which Sybil and his mother were kneeling at prayer, before retiring. Their rosaries were at their wrists, and they knelt before one of those little altars which then formed a part of every Scottish household; as they do in Catholic countries still. It was somewhat like a cabinet, and had a figure of the Madonna, bearing in her arms the little infant Jesus. Upon her head was a wreath of freshly-gathered flowers, and before her burned two little wax-tapers, which had been consecrated at the last candle-mass by the abbot of Inchcolm.

The earl waited until their orisons were over; and while they prayed his heart swelled within him at their unaffected piety; for his memory went back to other days, when, in their secluded home at Ashkirk, in Angus, he had knelt by his mother's side, and first learned to lisp the very prayers she was now repeating. An emotion of shame came over him, on reflecting that in the wandering life he had led, and especially during his exile at the court of the libertine Henry VIII. of England, he had neglected every office of religion. He observed that his mother had become paler and thinner, and that her hair seemed to be silvered with white; but that might have been the effect of fancy, or of the dim light of the apartment.

Sybil had lost somewhat of her rich bloom; but her dark eyes were bright as ever. Her black hair flowed from under her triangular cap, and hung like a silky veil over her shoulders, the curve of which, as she knelt with her head bent forward, was eminently beautiful. The edge of each large ringlet, the pearls of her cap, and the top of her smooth forehead, were all tipped with pale light by the tapers. She wore, a long dress of purple satin, with an open neck; and in the light and shadow its folds seemed to glitter with many prismatic hues. It is impossible to say whether it was the brilliant and piquant expression, the noble features, and pure complexion of Sybil's face that made her adorable, but, taken together, these attributes of the old Douglas race made her singularly so.

The moment their orisons were over, the old countess arose to the full extent of her great stature; and though aged, being unbent, her figure was remarkably elegant, its height being increased by her shoes—the "cork-heeled shoon" of our old national ballad—and after solemnly crossing herself three several times, she extinguished the tapers on the altar, and kissed Sybil with all the affection of a mother.

The sole light in the chamber now came from two wax-candles, which were held in the outstretched arms of a grotesque figure of Florentine workmanship, placed on the dressing-table at the farther end, and immediately opposite the window where the earl had perched himself.

CHAPTER XL.

SYBIL.

"Come, my Antonia, come,
I'll lead thee to the blissful land of love,—
I'll lead thee to the pinnacle of joys,
Where round thy path the fairest flowers of earth
Shall bloom in radiant beauty to reward
Thy noble deed—come, dearest."—THEODORE KÖRNER.

A GUTTURAL laugh announced to the earl that Sabrino had also ascended the ladder, and was rejoicing at the sight of his mistress.

"Hold fast! by my faith, thou hast the hands and feet of a marmoset. Hush! I would hear them talk a little," said the noble, adjusting himself upon his giddy perch. "By Jove! we are like a couple of crows up here—thou like the black, and I like a white one."

"Ees," grinned Sabrino, whose whole vocabulary was nearly comprised in that sound.

The moment their orisons were over, Sybil went to the opposite window, and, withdrawing the curtains, gazed steadfastly towards the eastern end of the little valley.

"Dost thou see it again, bairn—that ill-omened light?" asked the countess, approaching.

"Yes; oh, yes!" replied Sybil, with a voice of surprise and fear; "brighter to-night than ever before."

"Then it must be either a corpse-licht, that burneth on the grass, to mark where a slain man sleeps, or a fairy-candle, at the rock where the whin-bushes grow. Corpse-lichts burn blue, and fairy-candles are siller white."

"But this burns redly, and it brightens fast!"

"By the Lord!" said the earl, with alarm, "in our hurry to-night thou hast forgotten to extinguish our fire, master Sabrino; and we have widened the aperture at the chasm. Mass! if the knaves of watchmen see it, we shall be discovered and taken!"

Sabrino turned skyblue in the dark at this terrible suggestion.

"There is a knowe among the hazelwoods near our castle of Ashkirk, where the gude neibours dwell; and ever and aye on St. John's night, a light of siller white shines among the grass that grows beneath the thick dark trees. Now it chanced that, on the eve of that blessed festival, in 1510 (oh, waly! only three years before dreich Flodden-field, and good King James's death), Hughie o' the Haugh, a poor cottar-body, who dwelt at the glenfoot, was coming home from the next burrow-toun with a bag of barley on his horse's back, and trudging, staff in hand, behind, lamenting sorely at the tidings he had that day heard at the market-cross; for brother Macgridius, of the blessed Order of Redemption, had seen his son, a puir sailor lad, taken prisoner by the cruel pagans at Barbary, who demanded a hundred pieces of gold for his ransom. Hughie could as easily have raised the Bass Rock as a hundred pieces of gold; and he

went homewards, with his bonnet owre his eyen, groaning in
great anguish of mind. Oblivious of all but the loss of his
only son, poor old Hughie followed his horse, which knew
right well the drove-road that led to his thatched stable, at
the back of the auld farm toun ; when suddenly, at the fairy
knowe, the animal pricked up its ears, trembled, and stopped,
as a wee diminutive mannie, not two feet high, and wearing
an enormous broad blue bonnet, and a long beard that reached
to his middle, rose off the stone dyke, and bade Hughie hail.

"'Gude e'en, Carle Hughie,' said he ; 'how went the
markets ?' he added, with an eldritch laugh.

"'Sorrowfully for me,' replied the other, wiping his eyes
with the neuk of his plaid.

"'Wherefore, Hughie, wherefore, ye silly auld carle ?'
quoth the little man.

" ' Because I come back with a light purse and a sorrowfu'
and heavy heart,' replied the poor cottar, peering under his
bonnet, and terrified at the wee figure ; for he knew it was one
of those unco creatures whom it was dangerous to seek, and
still more dangerous to avoid or to offend.

" ' I am sorely in want of barley, carle,' said the mannikin,
stroking his long white beard ; 'ye must sell me that load,
and at mine ain price, too.'

" ' I lack siller, gude sir, as sorely as ye can lack the
barley,' urged the poor crofter, who feared that the payment
might be fairy-pennies or pebble-stones.

" ' I never was hard on a puir man yet,' replied the little
mannie, testily ; ' and I have dealt wi' your race, Hughie,
for many a generation. When grain is plenty I buy it ; for
I tell ye, carle, that a time of sad and sair scarcity for puir
Scotland is fast coming. So, here! I ken what ye are
graning for, ye greedy body,' quoth the creature, plunging
each of his hands into the enormous pockets of his doublet,
'here are a hundred pieces of good red gold; ransom your
son, and give me a help wi' the barley pock ; my back hath
borne a load like that, and mair.'

" With fear and joy mingled, Hughie received the gold,
and transferred the bag of barley from the back of his horse
to that of the little man, of whom it left no part visible, save
his bandy legs, his walking staff, and the end of his long
white beard.

" ' Gude e'en to you, Carle Hughie ; a safe voyage hame

to you son,' said the awesome buyer, and manfully striking his staff into the ground, he trudged up the steep knowe, and disappeared below the dark trees.

"Hughie hastened back to brother Macgridius, and, with joy, paid him the hundred pieces of gold for his son's redemption from slavery; and not without many a fear that before his eyes the coins would turn into birch leaves or cockleshells; but that was impossible, for they were ilka ane our gude Scottish gold, but six hundred years old, for they bore the name of king Constantine IV., who was slain at the battle of Cramond."

"And Hughie's son was released?" said Sybil.

"Yea, child, and is now master gunner of Sir Robert Barton s ship at Leith."

With his legs dangling over the surf, and being in imminent danger of drowning, it may easily be supposed that the carl listened to this fairy legend with the utmost impatience; but while his mother spoke, and Sybil listened with the utmost good faith and reliance (for in those days, as at this hour, in some parts of Scotland, one might as well have doubted their own existence as that of fairies and other spirits of good or evil), the carl had gently raised the heavy and massive sash of the window, slid into the room, and concealed himself behind the thick damask curtains, his heart beating the while with the mingled desire of rushing forward to embrace his mother and Sybil, and a fear that their alarm might be communicated to the inhabitants of the tower, many of whom had not yet retired to rest.

"Look, look, Sybil!" exclaimed the countess, "the whins are on fire. Surely that is no fairy light!"

As she spoke, a watchman on the tower-head sounded his horn.

"Hark! the castle is alarmed!" said Sybil.

The earl saw that not a moment was to be lost now. Their fire in the cavern had by some means communicated itself to the whin-bushes at the entrance; an alarm had thus been given, and immediate action became necessary.

"Sybil," said he, "Sybil——"

"Just Heaven! my son's voice!" exclaimed the countess, becoming deadly pale, and feeling in her bosom for her case of reliques. "It is a spirit—a warning! It is a spirit!"

"Ten devils, lady mother! do not cry out!" implored the

earl, gradually emerging from his hiding-place; "I am not yet a spirit, thank Heaven, and have no wish to be one."

"Then, oh, Archibald, how came you here?" she exclaimed, throwing her arms around him.

"By the window," he replied, embracing Sybil in return; "by the window, as you may see."

"And Sabrino, my poor Sabrino!"

The black sank upon his knees to kiss her hands, and then danced about the room, performing the most extravagant capers to the sound of his long clanking earrings.

"By my soul, mother, the times are sorely changed with the Setons, when my father's son comes to visit thee and his betrothed wife like a rascally stoutriever by the window instead of the door—in the night instead of the day.

"The window!" they repeated, and became speechless for a moment, as they thought of the precipice, and the water at its foot.

"Faith, very few, I believe, would have dared what Sabrino and I have dared and done—but it was for thee, mother, and thee, my life, my love, my dear Sybil!" said Ashkirk, kissing her olive cheek.

"My brave Archibald, did the power of sorcery or of Providence bring thee to this prison island?"

"Neither, lady mother, but a smart boat, which, in another hour, shall convey you hence, with a fair breeze and a flowing sail."

"But how?"

"I know not yet, for we have to leave this tower, and baffle the old bear, its governor, the Laird of Barncleugh."

"My son, here have we dwelt for more than two weary weeks, and never a letter nor message hath come from thee or Roland Vipont."

"Vipont is on the king's service in Douglasdale, and for fourteen days I have been a prisoner in the house of Redhall; for the other two I have been vagabondizing."

"And Jane," said Sybil, "your sister Jane?"

"Is safe, I trust; but whether with Marion Logan, at Restalrig, or with my old friend Josina, the fair prioress of St. Catherine, I cannot for the life of me say. Now, pretty rogue, at what art thou laughing?"

"At thy figure, lord earl; 'tis like the satyrs on some old tapestry; thou art quite a wild man."

"True, cousin; I am scarcely fitted for appearance at Falkland or Holyrood, or in the Hall of the Three Estates, unless it were, as it may too soon be, at the bar. But ah, Sybil, my dear Sybil, what pleasure the sound of your voice gives me! 'tis like the dream of——Hark! what an uproar! the burning whins have alarmed old Barncleugh and all his fellows. Come now, Sabrino, my man of the earrings, a truce to these mad capers—dost thou hear me?"

Sabrino stopped a fandango which he was performing on his head and hands, and pricked up his enormous ears.

"Quick with our rope ladder, for thou, my mother, and Sybil too, must descend from this window on the dark side of the tower; it is not more than fifteen feet from the ground, I think.

"But the barbican gate?" said Sybil.

"I will unlock it with the point of my sword," replied the fiery earl, as a savage gleam shot from his eyes.

"Nay, nay," said the countess, crossing her hands, and standing very erect, "I cannot think of flying thus; the king has placed me here, and the king must release me."

"What frenzy is this? Besotted by his French marriage, the king hath become a fool. Quick, Lady Ashkirk, we have not a moment to lose. Hark! the whole tower is silent now, for its inmates are away down in the valley, seeking the source of that sudden fire. Oh, if the knaves should discover my boat! Quick!—are you a coward, my mother—the widow of my father?"

"A coward never came of the line of Kilspindie, and a coward had never slept in your father's bosom, Lord Archibald," replied the tall matron, proudly, and with asperity, as her eyes filled with tears. "Thou knowest not, my son, how life sometimes rises in value with the unfortunate; but it is neither the love of life nor the fear of death that restrain me now, but a shame to fly, like a thief in the night, from the wardship of either king or clown."

"Now, by the faith of Seton! these are pleasant remarks to me, who have been skulking like a thief and a vagabond too, for the last few years—a creditable occupation for an earl! If thou stayest, here will I stay too," said Ashkirk, and seating himself, he folded his arms; "if Barncleugh find me, thou knowest my doom, for I shall die the death of an outlaw and traitor. By my soul! 'tis outrageous, this!"

"Thou art right," replied the old lady, trembling with sudden alarm; "I thought not of that. Quick, then! Old as I am, thou shalt see that now, as in the days of James IV., of gude memorie, I am a true daughter of old Archibald Greysteel."

"We have lost ten good minutes already," replied the earl, lowering his rope ladder from the small window, which, luckily, was ungrated, being within the barbican. Fortunately a gusty wind had risen, and the moon, which was partially obscured by passing clouds, having verged far to the south-east, threw the sombre shadow of the tower over that part of the court into which the fugitives were about to descend. The little castle was almost deserted, the iron gate of the barbican stood wide open, and the barking of dogs and hallooing of men ascended from below, where Barncleugh, with ten or fifteen of his followers, searched the valley for the source of that nocturnal fire which, on this occasion, had become so palpable, and caused such alarm.

"I will descend first, and hold steady the foot of the ladder; and do thou, Sabrino, my gallant imp, hold fast its top," said the earl, as, with his drawn sword in his teeth, he slid in a moment to the ground; "come, dearest Sybil, do thou set my mother an example."

With Sabrino's assistance, the young lady got out upon the ladder, which she clutched with a death-grasp, while the wind expanded her dress, and blew all her long black hair about her face.

"Oh, cousin Ashkirk!" she exclaimed, in great terror.

"Oh, cousin Sybil!" replied the earl, jestingly, in the same tone, to reassure her; "I will swear that thou hast the handsomest ankles and the handsomest leg in all the Lothians."

This intimation made her come down very quickly, and the earl received her in his arms with joy.

"Now, my lady mother, quick, bestir thee," said he, in a low voice. But terror seized him when a cry from his mother replied, and the explosion of a petronel followed; then Sabrino sprang from the chamber, and descended the ladder with the rapidity of light, and with his poniard in his hand.

There was blood on its blade!

A servant of Barncleugh had rushed in, and, surprising them, had fired his petronel at the negro, who, springing

at him like a tiger-cat, inflicted a deadly wound with his
poniard.

"Away, Sybil! come away! We have not a moment now to
lose!" said the earl.

"But your mother, your poor mother!" she urged.

"Her own folly has done it all; those ten minutes had
freed her; but she must be left for the present;" and, almost
dragging Sybil, he led her out of the barbican and down the
valley, keeping carefully on its shadowy side, which, fortunately, lay towards the beach.

CHAPTER XLI.

A HAMILTON! A HAMILTON!

" Oh, stay at home, my only son,
　Oh, stay at home with me!
For secretly I am forewarned
　Of ills awaiting thee!
Last night I heard the deid bell sound,
　When all were fast asleep;
And aye it rung, and aye it sung,
　Till all my flesh did creep."
　　　　　　　　THE ETTRICK SHEPHERD.

UNOBSERVED, they reached the verge of the beach, and were
about to descend, when Sabrino suddenly grasped the arm of
the earl.

He turned.

The negro had his poniard in his right hand, and placed a
finger of his left on his lips, in token of silence; there was a
savage gleam in his shining eyes.

"Well, Sabrino, what dost thou see now?"

Sabrino pointed, and, a few yards below, the earl saw a
man, having in his hand a drawn sword, which glittered in
the moonlight. That he was a gentleman was evident by his
dress—a plum-coloured doublet, orange hose, a blue velvet
mantle, and waving feather. He was ascending straight from
the little creek, where the boat was moored to a fragment of
rock, and had, beyond a doubt, discovered it.

"My lord!" said Sybil, breathlessly; "'tis Sir James of
Barnclcugh himself."

"Oho! I have not met this worthy laird since we broke the

pikemen of Arran at Linlithgow brig. He owes me more than one sword cut; and I do not like debtors of that kind."

"Oh! if possible, avoid him."

"My dear Sybil!——"

"Death will come of it!"

"A little prick with a poniard will do him no harm."

"But while you fight, his people will come upon us. Now, dear Archibald, pray——"

"I am not in the sweetest of tempers just now: and— soho! thou Hamilton! clear the pathway, or I will trounce thee soundly."

"Who are *you*?" asked Sir James, standing on his guard, right in the centre of the path that led to the boat; "and what seek you here, sirrah?—stand and answer."

"I sought Sybil Douglas, Sir James."

"What do I hear—the Earl of Ashkirk! Now, by the soul of Arran! thou leavest not this island but in a coffin. Pardon me, my young lady of Kilspindie," said the old governor, courteously raising his blue velvet bonnet to Sybil; "pardon me, but this rash gallant must pay the penalty of coming uninvited here. Hallo! *a Hamilton! a Hamilton!*"

"Dishonour dog your heels, base Barncleugh! and may that accursed slogan never be heard but in shame and defeat!" exclaimed the earl, infuriated to find him thus crying aloud to summon his men, who were scattered over the island, and many of whom were visible in the moonlight, and not far off. "To the boat, Sybil, and leave me to deal with this rough tilter! To the boat; see to it, Sabrino. Sir James Hamilton, I have fought fifteen times, and three of my adversaries are dead; thou shalt make the sixteenth combatant I have encountered, and the fourth I shall have slain; and, as God be my judge, unwillingly. Come on!"

Both drew their daggers, and stood with their swords on guard.

In the sixteenth century, fencing in Scotland was very different from what it is to-day—a pastime for boys. It was then the indispensable accomplishment of the soldier and gentleman, for every gentleman was then a soldier. Long, straight, and heavy, the swords were double-edged; consequently, there were as many cuts as thrusts; and being furnished with long arm-pit daggers, the left hands of the duellists alternately acted offensively and defensively, and very often gave the finishing blow, when the sword of one adversary had beaten down the other's guard, and the combatants came to closer quarters.

Alarmed lest the voice of Barncleugh should have reached his people, excited by the imminent danger of his position, and by the instinctive feudal hatred of Sir James Hamilton, the earl attacked him with the utmost fury, assailing him with point and edge; and warily the older swordsman received him, warding the cuts with his rapier, and parrying the thrusts with his poniard. The steel rang and flashed like blue fire in the bright moonlight; and a shower of red sparks flew from either weapon as their keen edges met, and made the arm of each combatant tingle up to the shoulder blade.

Somewhat older fashioned, and more stiff than the earl, the knight of Barncleugh was unable, like the former, to lengthen and shorten himself—one moment to spring agilely to the right, and the next to make a furious assault on the left; or, in avoiding a breast-high thrust, to lie so far back that his dagger-hand rested on the turf. Firm and erect, the old laird stood like a tower; and the whole of his skill (which was not little) lay in his sharp and unerring eye, his strong but pliant wrist.

Meanwhile, Sabrino had placed Sybil in the boat, and standing in the water, which came up to his armpits, held the bow to the edge of the rock, that the earl might readily leap on board.

The result of a combat between two such well-matched swordsmen was a number of mutually inflicted cuts and scratches, which exasperated them both. But their animosity had different incentives—Barncleugh fought for honour alone; but the earl fought for his honour, life, liberty, and possession of Sybil Douglas; a cry from whom, together with a distant "Hallo" informed him that the conflict was observed by several of Barncleugh's soldiers, who were hurrying down the steep pathway that led to the creek. This made the earl fall on with such fury, that the calmer Barncleugh ran his sword through his doublet (and grazed his ribs) up to the very hilt.

Imagining that he was run through the body and slain, the earl seized the guard of Barncleugh's sword, to retain it in his body, and closing up with his own sword shortened in his hand, buried the point in the breast of Barncleugh, whose plum-coloured doublet was covered with blood in a moment. Then hurling him to the earth, he sprang wildly on board the boat, with one sword in his hand, and another, to all appearance, in his body.

At the same moment, a loud "Hallo!" again rang in his ears —a rapid explosion followed, and the balls of three arquebuses whistled past his head. Thinking only of Sybil, he pushed off the boat, forgetting altogether the poor black page, whose tongue was unable to cry either for pity or succour; and thus Sabrino was left behind again.

Raising himself on his left hand, while with his right he endeavoured to staunch the blood that flowed from his wound, Sir James Hamilton cried hoarsely and feebly—

"To your arquebuses again, ye knaves—again! Shoot, and shoot surely! See, 'tis the black devil again!—there—there—in the water! To your arquebuses—shoot, shoot, with a wannion upon you!"

The three arquebusiers stuck their forks in the sand, and levelled their heavy fire-arms over them. Again two large bullets whistled after the earl, and one dashed the spray about the black woolly head of Sabrino, which was visible on the moonlighted water; but he dived like a duck and disappeared. The reports of these large fire-arms rang with a hundred reverberations among the cliffs and caverns of the isle, and in the fissured rocks of the Longcraig (a reef which guards it on the east), until they died away on the winds that blew freshly down the river from the west.

"To the boat! to the boat!—follow, and shoot! *A Hamilton! a Hamilton!*" cried Barncleugh, as he sank back choked in blood.

"Seton, and *Set on!*" replied the earl, with the punning slogan of his house; "for, by St. Andrew, there is one Hamilton less in the world!" and with savage glee he plucked from his doublet, and flung back to the shore, Sir James's sword.

Then snatching his oars, he placed his feet firmly against the stretchers in the bottom of the boat, and intent only on leaving the island as far behind as possible, pulled with all strength away from its rocky shores.

After some delay, Barncleugh's followers unmoored their boat, which, by a chain and padlock, was secured to an iron ring; and then pushed off, two plying their arquebuses, while four plied their oars. Away they came, with a shout that

floated far over the still water; but by this time the earl was
nearly half a mile from the island, and, acting under a natural
reaction of feelings, Sybil waved her handkerchief, in token of
the triumph and defiance which had replaced her previous
terror.

Lustily pulled the brave earl, and even Sybil would have
put her dimpled hands to the oars to assist him, had she not
soon required both to grasp the seat beside him, as their little
boat rose like a cork on the heavy ground-swell that rolls
between the island and the shores of Lothian.

The wind was rising.

It blew freshly down the Firth, and as the tide was ebbing
now, a strong current ran seaward—a current against which
the solitary rower struggled in vain; for in fifteen minutes he
found they were swept far below the island.

He saw the four oars of his pursuers flashing in the moonlight, and the glitter of steel announced that they were well
armed; while every successive gust of wind that swept over
the curling water brought nearer and nearer their triumphant
shout; and he could see how, at times, they paused, and complacently looked over their shoulders to contemplate the
distance as it lessened by their efforts.

And it was lessening fast!

The earl thought of Sybil, and of what her feelings would
be if he was taken, and of what she and his mother would
experience if he was brought back to the island a breathless
corpse. These anxieties received an additional impulse by the
flash of an arquebuse from the pursuing boat; and the earl
saw that the bullet skipped over the waves far ahead of him.

There was now but one alternative, and he did not hesitate
to adopt it.

Stepping the little mast, he hoisted the lugsail, squared it
to the western breeze, grasped the tiller, while Sybil threw her
arms around him; and now their boat, sharp-prowed and
clinker-built, like all the Scottish fisher craft, favoured by the
wind, by the ebbing tide, and the fast flowing river, flew like
a gull down the widening Firth; and then a shout of anger
announced that the followers of Barncleugh were left far
behind.

*   *   *   *   *

Grasped by a watchman of the tower, when in the very act
of attempting to descend, the Countess of Ashkirk, as we have

related, had been left behind; but she saw from her window the flash of steel on the beach; she heard the shouts and outcries of the Hamiltons, and prayed and trembled for her son. She saw the two boats which shot off from the island, on the bright surface of the glittering river, which was all shining like a mirror, save where a flitting cloud obscured it. She had seen these boats lessening in the distance; and again on her knees she implored St. Bryde of Douglas to watch over the safety and escape of her son, vowing to endow in her name a yearly mass and an altar in the great church of St. Giles.

The countess knew not that her "brave rash bairn," as she called him, had achieved both his safety and escape, until Sir James Hamilton was carried into the tower bleeding profusely, and almost dying. Now it was that the fierce feudal hatred in which she had been nurtured, and in which she had reared her own son, jarred with her natural kindliness and pity; and it was with a strange, and, as she often thought, unchristian sentiment of joy and triumph, mingling with her tenderness and compassion, she prepared lint and bandages, with some of her favourite salves and recipes, for the wounded castellan, whose sword-thrust she proceeded to probe and dress.

The moment Sir James's wound (which was a deep, but not dangerous stab in the breast) was dressed, she hurried to the tower-head, and looked towards the east, but neither of the boats were visible. The moon had become obscured, the rising wind howled drearily through the embrasures of the battlement, and the dusky shadow of a dark cloud rested upon that part of the Firth where the boat of the earl had last been visible.

The heart of Lady Ashkirk became oppressed by vague terrors; and after praying as only the people of the olden time could pray, when faith was strong in the land, and superstition was stronger, she returned to the bedside of her patient; and such was her care and skill, that in three days the hardy old knight was again seated at his little tripod table by the tower gate, with the ocean below, and the gulls around him, drinking his peg tankard of spiced Rochelle, and playing chess with the seneschal of the establishment, who knew his duty too well ever to attempt to win a game; thus that easy-tempered personage allowed himself to be defeated ten times a-day, if nine victories did not satisfy the old knight, his master and antagonist.

CHAPTER XLII.

DAVID'S TOWER—THE PHYSICIAN.

"Ah, no more can gladden me
　　Sunny shores or dark projections,
　　Where in emulous reflections
　Blend the rival land and sea;
　Where alike in charms and powers,
　　Where the woods and waves are meeting—
　　Flowers with foam are seen competing—
　Sparkling with the snow-white showers."
　　　　　　　　　　　　CALDERON'S *Constant Prince.*

IN the reign of James V. the Castle of Edinburgh was composed of numerous round and square bastel-houses, which,
connected by curtain walls, surrounded the summit of the
rock, and were built in various ages by successive princes, and
presented the various cadences of architecture, from the strong
grim peels of Malcolm Ceanmhor to the florid Scoto-French
towers of the fourth and fifth Jameses.

The principal of these bastel-houses was named King
David's Tower.

It was erected by David II. in 1357, and therein he died
on the 7th May, thirteen years after, when planning a new
crusade. This keep was of great height and strength, and
overhung the cliff, which now looks down on the gardens of
Princes-street, two hundred feet below. One of its lofty
turrets was struck by lightning during a terrific storm, on
All Saints' Day, 1524; the shattered fragments fell into the
loch, and the electric fluid set the apartments of the queen-
dowager Margaret on fire. On its summit James V placed
thirty pieces of cannon. The larger chamber within it was
named the Lords' Hall; another was styled the New Court
Kitchen;—but its first apartments were a range of dreary
vaults; for the whole edifice was a veritable castle, with its
dungeons below and battlements above. On the latter were
a flag-staff, and an iron baile to herald foreign invasion to
the shores of Fife and Stirling; just similar to one which
still remains on Mylnes-mount below the Argyle battery.

In the same vaulted apartment wherein James V had, six
years before, confined John Scott, a miracle-monger, who pretended that the Virgin Mary could maintain him for any
length of time without food, Lady Jane Seton had been detained

since her condemnation. Though the strength of the tower was great, its walls of stone being ten feet thick, its doors of iron deep and narrow, and having other securities in the shape of high curtain walls, higher rocks, cannon, towers, and portcullises, the Master Porter of the castle (that supernatural guards might not be wanting) had painted on the chamber door a flaming red cross; and thereafter nailed on a horseshoe, a fox's face, with a bunch of rosemary and rowan-tree, all of which, he had no doubt, would do more than stone redoubts and iron doors to keep the witch in and the devil out.

Let us take a view of her as she appeared on the second day after her trial, for it was now the second, and she had but three days to live.

It was evening now, and the kirk and convent bells of the city below were floating upward to her grated window, which was open, for the season was the sultry month of July. The whole apartment was as bare and stony in its aspect as the arch of a bridge, or any of those caverns in which we have seen Lord Ashkirk hiding; for the groined arch, the low massive walls, and the floor, were all composed of squared blocks of freestone, quarried from the rocks in the neighbourhood. Its whole furniture consisted of a chair and table, the latter being composed of mere fir planks; a leather jar of water, and a bed situated within an arched recess, like a pedestalled tomb in some old church; but, being destitute of curtains and bedding, it was a mere paillasse. Everything was inferior to what was used by the king's soldiers.

A witch required little.

All shrunk from her now; even Lady Cranstoun Riddel, who had formerly been so kind, avoided her; while her husband, the governor, having before his eyes the wrath of the king and the cardinal (who was more dreaded than ten kings), also remained aloof. Thus no visitor ever disturbed her sad and solitary reflections, save the under-warder, who came hastily and stealthily to deposit her food—a coarse bannock and water tinged with a little wine—and as hurriedly withdrew, fearing to meet a glance of her eye—for witches were thought to possess eyes of evil power.

The coarse bannock, the sole food offered her, remained untasted, for it was salt and bitter; the water was her only nourishment, for assuredly it contained but little wine; as the warder, who prepared it, drank the greater part; for a sorceress, who was to be burned in three days, might do very well, he thought, without wine.

Thus agony of mind, pain of body, and lack of food had sorely reduced her. She became apathetic, and sank into a stupor so deep, that it seemed as if no change of circumstances could ever tranquillize or restore her to existence and the sunshine of life.

Her large dark eyes were dry, hot, and tearless. In their stony aspect, they seemed never to have beamed in joy, or wept in grief. Her face had the pallor, the lividity of death, and her cheeks had become frightfully hollow, while her thin lips were a vivid and unnatural scarlet. They seemed to have shrunk, and showed more than before of her teeth; and even these seemed larger and, if possible, whiter than usual. There was something dry, arid, and parched in her whole aspect— as if the fire of inward grief was consuming her. As her stooped head rested on her hand, with eye fixed and jaw relaxed, her expression, at times, grew altogether vacant.

She had on the same dress in which she had appeared before Abbot Mylne and his tribunal, and the same pretty little angular cap, below which her fine hair was simply braided. She was destitute of ornament, having been robbed or deprived of all her rings and bracelets by Sanders Screw and others, into whose hands she had been so ruthlessly consigned.

Her haggard beauty was appalling, as the calmness of her despair was unnatural. Her whole mind seemed to be unhinged.

Her cheek reclined in the hollow of her right hand, and her elbow rested on the table; her vacant gaze was fixed on the landscape, which extended to the north and westward, for her chamber had two windows, and, from the west, the cool soft wind played on her hot, white cheek, and lifted her heavy hair.

The glorious plain that from the foot of the steep Castle Rock stretches almost to the gates of busy Glasgow, was yet hazy with the humid summer mist, from amid which stood boldly forth the lordly Pentlands, with their peaks of brilliant emerald green, or heath of russet brown, and the rugged rocks of Corstorphine; while afar off, and dim in the distance, among the Highlands of Stirlingshire, rose the pale blue cone of Ben Lomond, the king of the Scottish hills, then the fastness of the fierce Buchanans.

The sun was sinking behind the Ochills, and those who have seen it so sink behind those beautiful mountains in summer, will cease to boast of Roman skies and Venetian sunsets. A thousand hills, and isles, and rocks were mirrored in the bosom of the Forth, as a flood of sunlight was poured along its winding waters, kissing the wooded shores and dancing waves, throwing into light its bold headlands and forest vistas, or into partial shade the long deep glens and forest dells, where herd and hirsel grazed, "and the wee burnie was stealing under the lang yellow brume," as a beautiful old song has it.

Rock, isle, and ship seemed floating on its bosom, amid all the sparkling colours of the sun, till it sank behind the mountains, leaving a million of radiations shooting upward behind the dark peak of Dumiat. Then the Forth turned from gold to blue, and its shores from green to purple; and then, as the hills of Fife grew dark, the Lothian woods grew darker still, and the gentle star of evening rose above Corstorphine to replace, by its mild beauty, the brighter glories of the day that had passed.

Of all this magnificent effect of scenery and of sunset, Jane saw nothing; for her eyes were turned back (as it were) within her heart, and she saw only her own thoughts. The events of the last few weeks seemed all a horrible dream—a dream from which she had yet to awaken. A chaos, incoherent and fantastic, like the time of a fever and delirium. Amid this chaos came forth the figure of Roland—Roland, who was ever uppermost in her thoughts. Where was he? What was he doing? Or what had been done with him since that frightful day when, under twenty weapons, she had seen him beaten down and slain, as she then thought, before her very eyes.

She considered, then, the doom to be endured—the punishment by fire. She remembered the burning of Sir David Straitoun and of Father Norman Gourlay, two hapless Protestants, who, on the 27th of August, three years before, had suffered martyrdom at the Rood of Greenside, below the western brow of the Calton; and those who witnessed that frightful auto-da-fé, had described how like parchment scrolls the limbs of the victims shrivelled; how their stomachs burst and fell down among the hissing embers; and how the forky flames shot up between their scorched and blackened ribs, and

were vomited forth at their open jaws and eyeless sockets, till
even the morbid crowd, hardened as they were by the daily
executions of that unhappy age, became sick and turned away
with horror.

She thought of these things; she grasped her temples and
endeavoured to pray; but the terrors of a death so awful
paralyzed her, and she could not collect her energies sufficiently to address even that God before whom she was so
shortly to appear. All she had endured, and was then enduring, seemed trifles to the sufferings that were yet to come—
the stake—the faggots!

The strong chain that secured her wrists to each other, re-
taining them a yard apart, and that yet stronger fetter which
secured her left ankle to the wall of her bed, holding her in
childlike helplessness; the frequent entrance of Sanders
Screws and his assistants, or the equally brutal warders, out-
raging and violating all her privacies by day and by night;
the desertion of her friends; her hopelessness of rescue, of
mercy, and of life, were all merged in the terrors of her coming
execution.

"Three days! three days! three days!—my God! Oh, my
God!" she exclaimed, "only three days!"

And falling on her knees, she buried her face in her hands;
but, poor being! her thoughts were too incoherent for utterance, or relief in prayer.

To one in such extreme misery, death could not in itself
be very appalling; but it was the thought of Roland, of her
mother, of her brother, of her family honour, and her own
blighted name—blighted at least for a time, by the studied
vengeance of one whom she deemed all but insane, that racked
her heart with agony; while the mode of death by which she
was to die, filled her whole soul with terror. Of its ignominy
she thought little; for she had a bright certainty that her
innocence would one day be asserted, if not by the blessed
hand of Heaven, by the good sword of her gallant lover—for
Jane Seton thought like a true Scottish woman of the sixteenth century.

While stooping over the only chair her chamber contained,
on her knees, and in the paroxysm we have described, some
one, whose entrance she had not heard, touched her on the
shoulder. She looked up with a stupefied aspect, and beheld
John of the Silvermills, with his long solemn beard, porten-

tous visage and wizard-like cap, embroidered with the emblems of the Trinity, eternity, and religion—the triangle, the circle, and the cross. He wore a long black cassock-coat, trimmed with white fur; a large pouch hung at his girdle, and he leaned on a walking-staff. He raised his high cap, and partly with respect, and partly with fear, assisted her to rise and to seat herself.

Jane had become so faint, and had sunk so much since the day of trial, that the unglutted and unmerciful authorities feared she might escape the fangs of justice, by dying before the festival of St. Margaret the Martyr—that night to which all Edinburgh, indeed all in the three Lothians, looked forward with tiptoe and morbid expectation : thus the learned and deeply read physician of the royal household, John of the Silvermills (or, as he signs his name in various documents of that age, " Jhone o' ye Sillermylne"), was ordered to attend and prescribe for her health.

" Oh, good Master Apothegar !" she exclaimed, while the tears almost started into her arid eyes at the sight of a face that was familiar, and which seemed to regard her with something akin to commiseration. "Oh, Master Doctor," she added, taking his hands in her own, "dost thou think they will destroy him too ?"

" Him—who ?" stammered the apothegar, disengaging his lean and bony fingers from her cold and clammy grasp, as gently but decidedly as he could, " who, madam ?"

" Sir Roland Vipont," replied Jane, disdaining to notice this undisguised dread or aversion, though her heart fired at it.

" Poor butterfly ! whom one more revolution of the wheel of fate will crush—thou thinkest not of thyself——"

" I think only of him, and of nothing else ; I live but for him now—'tis three days—only three days !" She added, incoherently, " What is said in the town, at the court, at the palace ? Will he be punished for defending me so boldly, so valiantly ? My dear Roland—three days—oh, who is like thee ? None—and none will ever be like thee !"

" I will recast his horoscope, for I know, lady, the star of his nativity. This night it will be in Azebone, the head of the sixteenth mansion, and by its digression I will judge me of his fate. It will require a long and careful calculation, lady," said the deacon of the apothegars, shaking his long beard, solemnly, " and yet, gramercy me ! I have known as

mickle foreseen by coscinomancy, which meaneth divination
by a sieve; but *that*, as thou knowest, is altogether beneath
one like me, who knoweth the difference of sublimities and
the distance of the stars."

"Oh, Roland—Roland!" murmured Jane (who understood
not a word of all this), as she pressed her trembling hands
upon her heart, "I love thee now with the love of the unfortunate; and that, indeed, is a strong love, for by few are the
unfortunate loved in return."

"Thy pulse is quick and low," said the physician, placing
his bony fingers on her white and slender wrist, which was
fretted and chafed by the detestable manacle that encircled
it; "thou sighest deeply, thou flushest and becomest chilly
by turns. Is thy tongue dry, and is thy brain giddy? Yes,
I know they are. By the mass, I know thou art intensely
feverish. Now the pulse flutters, and the skin becomes
moist—fever—fever—nervous fever! Didst thou take the
metheglin my servitor brought thee?"

"Yes," said Jane, mechanically.

"Ah! and were much the better thereof?"

"I really do not know."

"Ah, you must have been; 'tis a compound of wort,
herbs, honey, and spices, forming a wondrous and soothing
restorative."

"What need of a restorative, sir? In three days all will
be over."

"We know not what the womb of Time may bring forth,
lady: for, verily, it is fruitful of events."

"Oh, that Father St. Bernard was here!" thought Jane;
"how terrible this cold physician is!"

"Continue the metheglin," said her adviser, putting on his
conical cap, and resuming his staff, "and from this phial
take daily one karena, whilk meaneth, the twentienth part of
a drop——"

"Sir, thou art most kind; but remember that in three
days I shall be beyond the reach of thy skill; so farewell,
and omit not to pray for me."

"Such is life!" replied the other, dreamily. "Oh, that
my elixir were complete, and then all mankind might live for
a thousand years—even as Artesius, the godlike Artesius,
lived! A thousand learned doctors have withered up their
brains searching for this elixir; but there is not one among
them to whom Heaven hath been so propitious as myself.

Rejoice with me, lady, rejoice! for it is nearly complete! Having failed to discover an herb or mineral to finish it, I have plunged into the mazes of entomology; for there are many insects whose brains or bodies, wings or claws, possess charms of potency. Moses, Solomon, Hippocrates, and Aristotle found wondrous properties in locusts and creeping things; and Ælian, the Greek, expatiates at great length on those contained in the brains and tongues of crickets, wasps, and cantharides; and there were Democritus, Neoptolemus, Philistus, Nicander, Herodius, to say nothing of Albertus Magnus (whose book, printed at Venice in 1519, has just been sent to me by the Spanish ambassador), all of whose writings I have yet to search; and doubt not, lady, that therein I must discover that which shall complete my elixir, and make my poor little laboratory, at the hamlet of Silvermills, more famous by a thousand degrees, than ever was that of Claudius Galenus, the physician of Pergamus."

And with this flourish, after reiterating his directions concerning that precious decoction, which he styled metheglin, to be taken with one karena from the phial, this homœopathist of the sixteenth century withdrew, leaving the poor little captive stupefied and stunned by the energy and fustian of his conversation.

CHAPTER XLIII.

DAVID'S TOWER—THE PRIEST.

> " There's but one part to play; shame has done hers,
> But execution must close up the scene;
> And for that cause these sprigs are worn by all,
> Badges of marriage, now of funeral."
> ROWLEY'S *Noble Soldier*, 1634.

As the physician retired, Father St. Bernard, Jane's confessor and daily visitor, and, of all the hundreds whom she knew, her only friend, glided softly in, and approached; for such was the terror excited by the accusations against her, that neither Marion Logan nor Alison Hume had dared to visit her; though they had sent many a message, saying, "how they wept and prayed for her," and so forth.

She raised her heavy head, and with an expression almost of joy, extended her hands towards him; but the ponderous fetters weighed them down.

The priest lifted the chain, and smiled sadly but kindly upon her.

"*Pax Domine sit semper vobiscum*," said he, making use of his invariable phrase.

"Good Father St. Bernard!" she exclaimed, "can this be the work of Heaven or of the fiend?"

"Of the fiend, daughter—canst thou doubt it?"

"I endure agony that is unutterable when thinking of Roland and of my mother. Oh, that she might hear nothing of all this! I have yet so much to suffer!——"

The old priest covered his face with the wide sleeve of his cassock, and wept, for he had still warm and acute feelings, though a long and ascetic life had somewhat blunted them and estranged him from the world.

"Can a merciful Heaven afflict me thus, father?"

"Hush, lady; whatever his miserable creatures may do, God is ever merciful and just. We know not but this visitation, terrible though it is, may be the means of averting some still greater calamity."

"Can any calamity be greater than death?"

"To the unrepentant? no. But pray, child, pray; for the Christian gathers hope from his prayers, while the poor heretic dies despairing and blaspheming."

"Good Father St. Bernard, if I could have been base—if I could have stooped, and been coward enough to abandon my poor Roland, and wed this frantic, this furious persecutor, all this misery might not have happened. It is a frightful alternative—a terrible reflection!"

"My good child, fear nothing and regret nothing. Think of St. Theckla, and of all she endured for shunning the love of one she detested; and now let the bright example of her whom St. Isidore of Pelusium styled the protomartyr of her sex, and the most glorious ornament of the apostolic age, be as a star and a beacon to thee. Shall I tell thee her story, as an old monk of Culross told it to me?"

Jane bowed her head, in token of assent.

"She was the pupil of St. Paul," said the prebendary, gathering energy as he spoke, "and, amid pagans, grew in holiness like a flower in the desert. Men called her beautiful, but she was good as she was beautiful, and gentle as she was good. A young noble of Lycaonia loved her; but the love of God, sayeth St. Gregory of Nyssa, burned too strongly in her bosom to admit of a human passion. She repelled his love, and, by the practice of every austerity, overcame all earthly affections, and subdued her passions in such wise that she became dead to the world, living upon it, but not in it— as a beautiful spirit, but one having no kindred feelings to those around her. The most endearing caresses, the most ardent protestations, the most brilliant flatteries and gorgeous presents failed to win her love to this young noble; and lo! from tender persuasions he betook himself to the most terrible threats; and thereupon, abandoning the stately house of her father, with its Grecian luxuries, its chambers of marble, with gilded ceilings and silken carpets, its Tyrian hangings, precious sculpture, and vessels of fine gold; abandoning home, friends, country, everything, she retired into the recesses of a forest to pray for Greece, and to commune with the God of the Christians amid silence and solitude; for such was the blessed example of the apostles.

" But there her lover, the young Lycaonian, discovered her; and, full of wrath and vengeance, accused her of certain heinous crimes before the magistrates of Isauria, who sentenced her to be torn limb from limb and devoured by wild beasts, in the public amphitheatre of the city. The day of doom arrived; and, naked in the vast arena, with no other covering than her innocence, and her long flowing hair that almost enveloped her, this tender being was exposed to twice ten thousand eyes. Undaunted in heart and high in soul, she stood calmly awaiting her fate from the fangs of those wild animals, whom goads of steel had urged to frantic madness, and whose deep, hoarse bellowing filled even the morbid multitude with dismay.

" The iron gates were withdrawn, and the mighty assemblage were awed and frozen into silence, when three enormous lions and three gigantic panthers, with manes erect and eyes of fire, bounded into the wide arena, where the helpless virgin stood in all her purity and resignation. With a simultaneous howl they rushed upon her; but lo! the mighty hand of Heaven was there! The lions forgot their ferocity, and the panthers the rage of their hunger; and gentle as lambs they crouched before St. Theckla, and grovelled in the dust to lick her snow-white feet.

" The vast multitude, their cruel magistrates, and the more cruel Lycaonian lord, were overcome at the sight of this

x

wondrous miracle, and permitted her to depart in peace; and she died, at an extreme old age, in Seleucia, where, above her grave, may yet be seen the church of the first Christian emperors."

Jane listened attentively, and with the utmost good faith, to this legend. It was one of the many miraculous tales which then formed the staple subjects for the discourses of the old clergy on Sundays and festival days.

" I thank you for this bright example," said she, " but I am altogether unlike St. Theckla, for I am not above an earthly passion; and none know how dearly and how truly I love him to whom I am betrothed. Just Heaven! I have all that last frightful day yet vivid in my memory. The court, so calm, so orderly, so formal, so satisfied with themselves, and so full of morbid curiosity; the spectators' countless eyes; the judges, so serious and so solemn; their ten sworn advocates, so silent and so dreamy ; and those cold-eyed clerks of court who gazed at me from time to time so stolidly, and with a self-satisfied air—at me, a poor helpless creature, abandoned to them, overwhelmed with desperation, and blind with fear and sorrow."

" Would that I could die for thee, Lady Jane. I am but a poor old prebendary ; the years of my life are many, though the days of my joy have been few—few indeed. I would leave no one to weep for, and have none that would weep for me. I have long been sick of the world; I have nothing in it now to regret, and, save thyself, know none that would regret old Father St. Bernard, unless I add a few aged almspeople, my poor penitents. My time in it cannot be long now, and willingly would I give my life for thine, if such a thing might be. Oh, my child, thou so nobly born, so carefully nurtured, so innocent and so gentle, the most guileless and most docile of my penitents ! Oh, this vile man, this Redhall, is a fiend ! a monster !" exclaimed the priest, suddenly giving way to unwonted passion; "may the heaviest curses of God fall upon him ! May he inherit the leprosy of Gehazi, and the despair of Judas ! May the earth swallow him up, like Dathan and Abiram ! May he sorrow like Cain, and may the wrath of God ever be upon him for the misery his unbridled passions, his blind vengeance and savage hate, hath caused unto thee !"

" Alas ! good Father St. Bernard," said the gentle being,

terrified by the old man's energy, " ought we not rather to pray for him?"

" Thou art right, my daughter, and thy resignation shames me!" replied the priest, whose indignation had, for the moment, borne away his better feelings. "Right, right—we are commanded to pray for those who persecute and despitefully use us. Thou good soul!" he added, signing the cross upon her brow, "may the angel of all purity watch over thee, for thou, in thy goodness of heart, art more like unto the angels than mortals."

" But, oh! that mode of death—by fire—by fire! It is so frightful!"

" The good should fear nothing. The hand which tempers the wind to the shorn lamb, may temper the flames to thee."

She covered her face in her hands, and began to weep. Her tears relieved her.

" And I must really die—so young! Oh, Roland, Roland."

" Child, thou thinkest more of him than of the will of Heaven. There is a sin in this."

" Heaven's will be done, father. I am not a heroine.'

" Its ways are inscrutable," replied the priest, looking upward.

" Hast thou not even once seen Roland, father ?"

" Roland, again !"

" Pardon me, but I cannot help it. I fear his name will be the last on my lips—his image the last in my heart. Oh, forgive me this ; but I cannot help it."

" They have accused him of treason."

" But there is hope of mercy for him, surely ?"

" The proud are ever ungrateful; and say, who can count on the gratitude of kings ? They may forget; but God never forgets."

" Another day has come and gone—a bright one it has been to all the world but poor Roland and me ; the air so soft, so bright, so balmy ; the leaves so green, the water so blue, the flowers so fresh and smiling. Can all my griefs be possible ? Another day, and another—and where shall I be then?"

" This is the very selfishness of grief. Dost think that thou and Roland Vipont are the only two unhappy persons in the world ?"

The night was far advanced before Father St. Bernard left

her ; and before that time, his conversation had proved so soothing, that in less than an hour after he was gone, she committed her aching head to the pillow of the hard pai-llasse, which we have before described as being in a stone recess of the apartment, and sank into a deep, but quiet slumber.

CHAPTER XLIV.

DAVID'S TOWER—THE LOVER.

> " I kist with ane sigh the ringlet fair,
> That I shred frae my Marie's golden hair,
> And I thought that I never would see her mair.
> And when I try it to rest on my bed,
> The visions of night surrounded my head.
> But had I the wings of a dove to flee,
> They had nae parted my Marie and me."
>
> HENRY SCOUGALL, 1674.

IN another chamber of that vast bastille-house, and at the north-west corner thereof, which overhung the hollow where the church of St. Cuthbert lay, and the marsh that bounded the western end of the loch, sat Roland Vipont.

The furniture and appurtenances of his apartment, without being very magnificent, were certainly better by many degrees than those afforded to his unhappy betrothed ; but then it must be remembered that she was accused of sorcery, while he had merely committed high treason ; and like hamesucken, or rising in arms, high treason was but a trivial action among the Scots of 1537

He was not allowed to visit Jane Seton; the chamber to which the warrant of Redhall had consigned him was one of the strongest in the fortress ; and Sir James Riddel was an-swerable for his body, dead or alive, when demanded, under a penalty of ten thousand merks.

Deprived of everything in the shape of weapons, even to his spurs, the lover sat with his arms folded on his breast, his chin (which exhibited an untrimmed beard) resting on his breast, his brows knit, and his eyes full of fire, revolving, as he had been for the last two days and a sleepless night, and re-revolving in anger and grief, a myriad of futile projects.

"Gloomy as death, and desolate as hell,"

his thoughts were too impetuous and incoherent to take any permanent or useful form; but when his eyes rested on the enormous iron grating which secured his window, or endeavoured to fathom the tremendous abyss that yawned below— that abyss where the loch was rolling, every hope died within him, and he became sick; while the recollection made him become frantic, that, though he remained inert, secured and shut up within a few feet of him there breathed, suffered, and wept one whom he loved to adoration.

All his recent adventures in Douglasdale—the storming of Fleming the farmer's barmkyn—the poisoning of Nicholas Birrel—the horrors of his return—the trial—his defiance of the court—his challenge, and its rejection, had all passed away from his memory, which retained but one episode, one vision—Jane, as she appeared before that cruel and determined tribunal—so pale, so ghastly, so helpless, and so beautiful.

The recollection was a frightful one.

"And the king, he who loved me so well," thought he; "has he too forgotten me? James Stuart—James Stuart! the Douglases have said truly, thou art ungrateful; and more truly and more wisely hath the good old countess said unto me a hundred times, 'Put not your trust in princes.' Who now thinks of the ancient wealth and valour of the Viponts? —who of their courage and patriotism? The honour of their name lies buried in the church of St. Colme, and beneath the moss that clusters on Aberdour—my patrimony gifted many a year ago to the grasping house of Morton. How unhappy am I! My whole life has been a struggle between poverty and pride, earning by wounds, and blood, and toil, hardly and severely, at sword's point, every penny that clinked in my pouch; for I have been a soldier of fortune, or misfortune rather, from my boyhood to the present hour. But have I not had some bright moments too? Ah, yes—yes! those I have passed with Jane—with my dear Jeanie; but they have been like the meteors that have shot over a dark winter sky; they are passed now, and a double gloom remains behind."

His apartment had two windows, one which opened to the west, and another to the north; and through both shone the last flush of the red sunset.

Now two voices beneath the west window, by attracting his attention, interrupted his sad thoughts, and he listened.

The speakers were in familiar conversation; but there was something so hateful in their tones, that his heart trembled with rage as he recognised them; and, impelled alike by hatred and a fearful curiosity, he drew near to listen.

In an angle of the ramparts, where the curtain wall joined a corner of the tower, the two gossips were seated on the stock of a large brass culverin: they were Nichol Birrel and Sanders Screw.

The yellow, livid visage, matted hair, and enormously thick beard of the former, and the shrivelled legs, nutcracker visage of the latter, were distinctly visible in the clear summer twilight; and there was a broad grin on the face of each as they conversed on a subject which, as it was pecuniary, interested them both in a high degree.

"Twenty merks and fifteen mak five-and-thirty merks," said Birrel, counting on his huge misshapen fingers.

"Ay," responded Screw, with another wide grin, as he held a piece of paper up to the light, which came from the west.

"The deil!" said Birrel, "ye dinna mean to pretend that ye can *read*, friend Sanders?"

"No, but I ken ilka item off by heart."

"Let me hear, then."

"First," said Sanders, pointing with a finger to the crumpled paper, which he ogled with the corners of his bleared eyes, as he indicated each item in succession, "first: 'Accompt of the haill expenses for ye burning of Lady Jane Seton, umquhile of Ashkirk, at ye staik, Saint Margaret's Day, fifteen hundred and thirty-seven——' "

"Weel?"

"Hoolie, man!" responded Sanders, scratching his head. "'*Item;* for one staick of aik tree, a penny.

"'*Item;* for twelve bundles o' faggots, saxpence.

"'*Item;* for three barrels o' tar and tallow, ten shillings.

"'*Item;* for greased flax and gunpowder, sax shillings.

"'*Item;* for an iron chain to bind her to the staik, twenty Flemish rydars.

"'*Item;* for a pair o' steel branks and one padlock, to Jhone, the lorimar, at ye Tron, aucht shillings of our Scots monie. *Summa*——' "

"Hech! ye'll hae gude profit off a' this; for I ken ye saved as mickle tar, flax, and faggots frae the burning and worrying o' fat Father Macgridius as will put ye owre this job, and mair."

"Never *you* heed that," replied Sanders, pawkily; "how mickle got ye for the brodding o' her?"

" Sax pund Scots."

" Sax pund! my certie, think o' that! Witch pricking is profitable wark."

" Had ye seen Friar Gourlay," said Dobbie, with a leer, as he came up and joined them, "by my faith! *he* burned brawly when the cardinal had him harled to the Calton and worrit for his foul heresies. We put a tarred frock on him, sewit owre wi' bags o' grease and powder, and piled the weel oiled faggots knee-deep about him. We then fastened up his body to the stake by three iron cask-hoops that held him erect as a lance, and the fire bleezed round him like a war beacon. His yell and skirls were awsome to hear; but the smoke and the heat soon chokit him; and then, when the breeze blew the fire aside, we saw him standing upright and stark in the middle o't. Then his belly fell out, and the flames shot up between his birselled ribs and out at his scouthered jaws, his eyen and ear-holes! By my soul! gossip Birrel and gossip Screw, it was an awsome sicht, and one to be haud in memorie!" Even Dobbie, connoisseur as he was in these matters, shuddered at the recollection of this extra-judicial atrocity.

"But come," said Birrel, "there is St. Cuthburt's bell striking ten, and we have muckle to do wi' this dame ere morning peeps."

The trio then knocked at the iron gate of David's Tower, to which they were admitted.

Roland had heard but a part of their frightful conversation; it was beyond the power of human endurance to listen to all those wretches said. He rushed into the farthest corner of his apartment, covered his ears with his hands, and wept and groaned aloud in the utter impotency of his rage and grief. But how much wilder would that rage and grief have been, had he known that they were all gone to visit his hapless mistress, for the double purpose of performing some of those additional tortures to which those accused of sorcery were usually subjected, by order of the supreme tribunal in Scotland, and at the same time to accomplish another cruel plan of Sir Adam Otterburn's device.

CHAPTER XLV.

THE BOON.

" Now is't a deed of mercy brings thee here,—
Of mercy to a suffering fellow man,
Or is't his rank that summons all thy pity,
And lends thy tongue its load of eloquence ?"—Old Play.

On leaving King David's Tower, Father St. Bernard passed
through the Spur, by the Castle Port, and descended the
Castlehill-street into the city.

The bells tolled the hour of nine in the Maison Dieu, at
the head of Bell's Wynd, as he passed it, and he saw the
lights gleaming in the chapel of this edifice, which stood on
the south side of the High-street.

The vast height of its buildings cast a dusky shade over
this thoroughfare; and the steep narrow closes which diverged
on each side from it were almost buried in obscurity. In
each of the small round archways, which gave admittance to
these deep and ghostly alleys, when the night advanced an
oil lamp was lighted, a remarkable improvement at this early
period, when neither London nor Paris could boast of such
an advance in civilization, for which our citizens were solely
indebted to their good King James V

Finding that Edinburgh was becoming a place of resort
from all parts of the kingdom, in 1532, the monarch so far
influenced the town council, that the High-street was well
paved with large stones, quarried among the craigs of Salisbury. Many of the more ancient tenements were removed,
renovated, or made more ornamental; while, as before stated,
the citizens had to hang out lanterns to light the narrow
thoroughfares; but as these were made of horn and were fed
with oil, they shed but a dim and wavering radiance on the
enormous stone bastilles and overhanging Flemish fronts,
which are still the leading features of the old grey city of the
Stuarts and Alexanders.

The watching was performed by the burghers. Every man
within the barriers being on guard every fourth night; thus
the whole citizens had to perform military service in rotation,
armed as infantry soldiers of the period, with helmet, corslet
and steel gloves, arquebuse and dagger, or with sword, pole-
axe, and partizan. The citizens of Edinburgh enjoyed the

distinction of wearing "quhite hatts," *i.e.*, helmets of burnished steel; and the whole were arrayed under their baillies four times in the year at a general weapon-show. But to return.

The prebendary descended the Blackfriars Wynd, at the foot whereof projected the turret which still indicates the cardinal's dwelling. Grasped by the teeth of a grotesque stone monster, a lantern hung above the doorway, and lighted a large stone panel, whereon were carved and gilded the armorial bearings of Bethune of Balfour, overshadowed by the cardinal's tasselled hat. Here the poor priest paused for a moment, and muttered a fervent prayer for the success of his merciful errand, and then he tirled the pin, timidly at first, but boldly afterwards.

After a brief reconnoissance being made of his person through the vizzying hole, the door was opened by one of the cardinal's guards, who wore the arms of the archbishopric on the breast of his purple doublet.

"Is his eminence at home?"

"Yea, father," replied the pikeman, falling back a pace, with a profound salute.

"Please to announce that Father St. Bernard of St. Giles's craves the honour of speaking with him alone."

"Deliver this message to my young Lord Lindesay," said the pikeman to another of the guard, who had overheard the request; and in less than a minute that young noble, who was the betrothed of Beaton's daughter, and who acted as his page and equerry, appeared, bonnet in hand.

"His eminence desires me to say, that Father St. Bernard is welcome at all times," said he.

Ascending the narrow stone stair of this antique mansion, and preceded by young Lindesay, whose crimson velvet mantle and peach-coloured doublet were covered with glittering embroidery, the prebend, on passing through an opening in a gorgeous arras, found himself in presence of the primate of all Scotland, the legate of Paul III.

Brilliantly lighted by candles of perfumed wax, which burned in rose-coloured globes of Venetian glass, the chamber, in which we had the honour of introducing the reader to the foe of Henry VIII., and the terror of the Calvinists, to the eye of the poor priest, formed a striking contrast to his own humble dormitory at St. Giles's; but he was not a man to permit such thoughts to dwell an instant in his mind; and dismissing them at once, he knelt before the cardinal's chair, to kiss the white hand which that great and luxurious prince of the church extended graciously towards him.

He was seated in a large and easy chair of stuffed velvet; his feet were encased in slippers of morocco, red as his stockings, and rested on a gilded footstool. Two vases of Italian glass, exquisitely carved, and glittering with the golden-coloured and purple wine they contained, together with two silver baskets, one full of honied biscuits and the other of grapes, showed that his eminence had been solacing his solitary hour; for a gittern that lay on a chair announced that his daughter, the Lady Margaret, had just retired, and the young Lord Lindesay, having no occasion to remain, followed her; thus the priest found himself alone with the cardinal, before whom all his confidence vanished; for, despite his conscious rectitude of heart and goodness of intention, in presence of the second man in Scotland, the poor prebend became timid as a child.

" Welcome, Father St. Bernard!" said the cardinal, pointing to a seat near his own : " you look pale and fatigued. Here are red and white Italian wines, and these are better than our ordinary Rochelle or Bordeaux. To which shall I have the pleasure of assisting you ? and then we will to business after; for I am certain thou hast come to me on business; no one," continued the studious cardinal, closing a book he had been reading, "no one, save my Lord Lindesay, comes near David Beaton for mere friendship, I find. Red wine or white ?"

" Either, please your eminence—the flask that is next you."

Reassured by the frank manner of the cardinal, and by the luscious *Greco* that moistened his tongue, which had been parched and dry, St. Bernard was about to speak, when the cardinal again addressed him.

" Dost thou come with new tidings of this Calvinistic heresy, which spreadeth, even as foul leprosy, over Scotland; or," he added, re-opening his volume, which was *The Franciscan*, of George Buchanan, " or comest thou merely here, as this arch-heretic sayeth, to exhibit—

* The greasy shaven head,
A gloomy friar, with flowing gown outspread !
The twisted girdle, and the hat's broad brim,
The opened shoe dressed out in monkish trim;

Below the garb, where we so oft will find
A brutal tyrant, whom no law can bind;
The robber, who oppression's armour wields,
The sensual glutton, to excess who yields,
To deck the husband's brow, the night will spend;
The faithless lover, and deceitful friend!
His modest face, though false, worn as a cloak,
To gull the plebeian, and delude the flock;
Ten hundred thousand crimes, wild, dark, and deep,
He hides beneath the clothing of the sheep!'

Holy mother of God!" exclaimed the cardinal (who had read this passage ironically and emphatically), as he flung the volume to the farthest end of the apartment, "and thou permittest this wretch to encumber the earth! Holy St. Francis of Assisium! thou whose life was a miracle of humility; who, in a glorious vision, beheld our Saviour hanging on his cross; and thou hast permitted the heretic dog, who writes thus of thy clergy, again to escape me!"

"I heard that he had broken forth from your eminence's archiepiscopal castle of St. Andrew's some months ago."

"True,—while my guards (the drunken rascals!) slept; but I should have made them answer for him body for body. Truly, the college of St. Barbe hath reason to be proud of its professor, this learned Buchanan, for there he is at present teaching grammar and the humanities; and now I hear that the Earl of Cassilis (whom I know to be an arch-heretic, traitor, and corresponder with Henry of England) is about to secure him from me in his castle of Culzean, as a tutor for his son, the Lord Gilbert Kennedy. By the cross, he is a rare tutor! But let this lord beware; for though he is brother of Quentin Kennedy, that good abbot of Crossraguell, whose pieties are those of a saint, the people of Scotland shall see whether a cardinal's hat or an earl's coronet will weigh the heavier in the scales of justice and of Heaven."

The cardinal was both exasperated and satirical. Father St. Bernard found that he had chosen an unfortunate time to prefer his request, and while he was rallying all his thoughts to introduce a more pleasing topic of conversation than that broached by the cardinal, the latter said, suddenly, but in a milder tone:

"And now, my good old friend, St. Bernard, what dost thou wish me to do for thee?"

"May it please your eminence to grant me your patience and pardon."

The cardinal put one leg over the other, laid his hand upon

the wine-cup, and nodded, as much as to say—" Good : I see the reverend father has some request to make of me."

" My Lord Cardinal, dost thou remember the 30th of August, 1534 ?"

" The 30th of August, 1534 !" repeated the cardinal, pondering.

" That 30th of August, when I implored your eminence not to pass through Fife to St. Andrew's."

" I do," said the cardinal, becoming suddenly animated, " for there were certain mysterious circumstances—but what of that now ? 'tis three years ago."

" My lord, I know not whether that which I am about to reveal be a sin, or whether, by so doing, I am breaking the irrevocable seal of confession ; the man who told what I am about to relate, made afterwards a public confession, when he was expiring in the streets of Kinghorn, but of all the crowd around him, I alone understood to what he referred—unhappy being !"

" Go on," said the cardinal, sipping his wine, " I am already all ears and impatience."

" On the evening of the 26th of August, just the day before Straitoun and Gourlay were burned for heresy at Greenside, I was seated in the public confessional at St. Giles's, when a man entered in great agony of mind, and knelt down before me. This man, my lord, was one whom the secret orations of the Reformers and the mal-influence of his chief, for he was a follower of old Sir John Melville of Raith, had partly led astray from the fold of the true faith. He was James Melville, the gudeman of Pitargie. The blessed hand of God was in it ! Like a dark cloud, remorse had descended upon this lost one, and he informed me, that with sixteen others he had sworn to slay your eminence as you passed along the road to St. Andrew's on the morrow ; and that this ambuscade of assassins was to be in waiting near the tower of Seafield, to the eastward of Kinghorn. In vain did I command him not to criminate others ; but he told me, that your deadliest enemies, John Leslie of Parkhill, Peter Carmichael of Kilmadie, Sir James Kirkaldy of the Grange, the Melvilles of Raith and of Carnbee, the Lord Rothes, and the Laird of Kinfawns would be there. That Henry of England was in the plot, and had offered them magnificent bribes ; and that one of his ships lay cruizing at the East Neuk, to secure for these seventeen conspirators a safe retreat to his own dominions, whither they were to bring your eminence's scarlet cope, drenched in blood, as a token that the deed was done, that their lust of vengeance had been sated, and that thou, like another Becket, had fallen beneath their swords.

" As the conscience-stricken assassin proceeded, I became frozen with horror. With groans and with tears he concluded his dark narrative, and beating his breast, implored me to make what use of his confession I pleased, but at all risks to save your eminence. To warn you was impossible, for the confessional sealed my. lips ! And I saw you—you, the greatest hope of our sinking church, and the chief pillar of the Scottish throne, its bulwark against English aggression, and Henry's grasping and heretical spirit, about to fall ! Your eminence was to be shot by arquebuses, after leaving the ferryboat at Kinghorn. After long and deep thought, the penitent begged that I would use all my little influence to detain your eminence for two hours upon your journey, and you may, perhaps, remember——"

" Thy coming to me on the second day after the *auto-da-fé* at Greenside, and imploring me to delay by two hours my journey into Fife," said the cardinal, as he arose and took in his the hands of the priest. " Thou good and venerable man ! I remember well thy diffidence, confusion, and timidity ; thy fear of being ridiculed and thy dread of offending me ; and how I railed and stormed at thy superstitious presentiment, as I now remember with regret I named it ! Well ?"

" At twelve o'clock, on the 30th of August, the knights and gentlemen I have named, with others, to the number of sixteen persons, all fleetly mounted and well armed with arquebuses and wheel-lock calivers, posted themselves among the copsewood that overhang certain thick hedge-rows, which lies between Kinghorn and Sir Henry Moultray's tower at Seafield. The king of England's ship, with all her sails set, was verging near the shore, while a Scottish flag, to mask her nation and purpose, was displayed from her mainmast head. The conspirators loaded their firearms with poisoned balls, and carefully blew their matches as the bells of St. Leonard's tower tolled twelve. It was the time at which these assassins, who were posted eight on each side of the way, expected your eminence.

" The twelfth stroke of the hour was scarcely given, when

they perceived a man, attired exactly like your eminence, in a baretta, cope, and stockings of scarlet, come riding up the narrow horseway, between the dark green hedgerows——"

"What is it thou tellest me? My wraith!"

The priest smiled.

" The seeming cardinal came on, riding fast, as if in advance of his followers! when, lo! sixteen arquebuses and calivers flashed from the screens of thick hawthorn and dark green holly, and prone to the earth fell horse and man, wallowing in their blood."

"*Agnus Dei!*"

"With a shout, the assassins rushed forward to imbrue their hands yet further in blood, and found that they had slain—not David Beaton the cardinal, but one of themselves —Raith's own kinsman, James Melville, the gudeman of Pitargie! He was carried to Kinghorn, and there, as I have said, he died. Without informing me of his project, further than to delay you, he had thus been guilty of self-immolation, as having no other method of punishing his own crime and saving your eminence. And so you were saved. I delayed you at the pier of Leith for two hours, and at the very moment you embarked, the mock cardinal was shot on the shore of Fife. On returning, your eminence was pleased to remember kindly my warning and presentiment, as you still named it: then, my lord, you promised me, that if ever I wished a boon that was in your power, I should consider it as already granted."

" True—true, my good friend, my reverend brother, I remember it all."

"You spoke of many a deanery, and many a rectory that were vacant in Angus, Mearn, and Buchan; but I still find myself the poor prebend in the parish kirk of St. Giles——"

"Yes, yes—I feel that I have been ungrateful, and thou justly upbraidest me," said the cardinal, hastily opening a portfolio, "there is the Benedictine Priory of St. Mary, at Fyvie, the superior of which——"

"Nay, Lord Cardinal, nay! Our Lady forbid I should ever presume to upbraid thee. I am but too glad that among the maze of more important matters my service has been forgotten! and thus that I can still appear as a creditor, and request the fulfilment of your promise."

" Full of shame for having so long forgotten it, I swear to grant whatever you ask, that may lie in my power to bestow."

"Oh, my Lord Cardinal, I seek nothing for myself," said the poor priest, glancing (like Sterne's Franciscan) at the sleeve of his threadbare garment; "my wants are few, though my years are many, and I have neither desire nor ambition, but in the service of our Master who is in Heaven."

The old man paused, and the great prince of the church, surrounded by wealth and luxury, grasping all but regal power, and loaded by the rank and riches of his Scottish, his French, and Italian titles, felt how great was the gulf between himself and this humble but purer follower of the apostles.

"If in my power," said he, "thy boon is granted."

"I seek the pardon of my poor penitent," replied St. Bernard, clasping his hands : "I seek the pardon of Lady Jane Seton."

The cardinal started.

"Impossible !" he replied, "for the life of this woman is not in my hands."

"But it is in the hands of the king ; and being so, is, I may say, also in thine, my lord. Thou alone canst save her, for, selfish in his grief, our good king has abandoned everything to his ministers."

"Forgiveness for her—a Seton—the daughter of a Douglas, and the grandchild of old Greysteel ! Friar, thou ravest ! the thing is not to be thought of ; besides, from all my lord advocate has told me, she must have been deeply guilty."

"Oh, good my lord cardinal, dost thou, in the greatness of thy mind, conceive that such a crime as sorcery may be ?"

"I do not—I believe too implicitly in the power of God to yield so much to that of his fallen angel ; and I believe, that as Calvinism spreads in Scotland, so will this new terror of sorcery I have not studied the trial, but shall do so to-night, and with care."

"A thousand grateful thanks."

"Immersed as I am among the affairs of this troublesome state (for its chancellorship costs me dear), and sworn as I am to extinguish by fire and sword the heresies of Calvin, which are spreading like a wildfire among our Scottish towns and glens, I can afford but little time for the consideration of minor matters, such as this trial. Thou art, indeed, an auld farrand buckie," added the cardinal, with a smile ; "and well hast thou played thy cards ; so rest assured, that if David Beaton can save thy penitent, with justice—*she is saved.*"

Father St. Bernard's heart was too full to reply : he raised his mild eyes to the ceiling, and crossed his wrinkled hands upon his breast.

"On Sunday first, I am to say a solemn mass for Queen Magdalene in my cathedral church at St. Andrew's," resumed the cardinal. "Sorely I regret that poor girl's death; but dost thou know that the Scottish church had much to fear from her; for, reared and educated as she had been by her almost heretic aunt, the Queen of Navarre, she was inclined to view too leniently this clamour raised by the heretics for liberty of conscience, as they are pleased to term their abominable creed—a creed by which they make our blessed Gospels like the bagpipe, on which every man may play a tune of his own devising. On my way to St. Andrew's, I will visit the king at Falkland, and this time, rest assured, my reverend friend, my promise shall not be forgotten."

"Oh, my lord!" murmured the now happy old man; "your eminence overwhelms me."

"There is now little time to lose. Young Balquhan and twenty arquebusiers of the king's guard must accompany me, in addition to the pikemen of my own; and the moment the pardon or order of release (if I deem her worthy of it, and receive it) is expede, Leslie shall return with it on the spur to Sir James of Cranstoun-Riddel;" and, as a sign that the interview was over, the cardinal, with an air of elegance and grace, which he possessed above all the courtiers of his time, gave the priest his jewelled hand to kiss, and thankfully and reverently this good old man, who was enough to be his father, kneeled down and kissed it.

"A thousand blessings on your eminence! *Dominus vobiscum*," said the priest.

"*Dominus vobiscum, et cum spiritu tuo*," said the cardinal, and stretched out his hand to a silver bell, which he rang.

Hurrying out from an inner chamber, Lord Lindesay drew back the arras which covered the doorway.

Then, as the priest with a joyous heart was about to retire, he was appalled by the spectral figure of Redhall (who had the private *entrée* of the cardinal's apartments at all hours), standing close behind the thick, heavy tapestry.

He started hurriedly forward, and the friar saw but too well that he had not only been listening, but had overheard, perhaps, the whole of their conversation.

His aspect was fearful; remorse, terror, and despair had

wrought their worst upon him. His jaws had become haggard and his visage pallid; but the priest thought that he
read a gleam of hatred and rage in his eyes as he passed him.

"If he has been listening, and should undo all I have
done!" thought St. Bernard, breathlessly, as he hurried down
into the dark Wynd of the Blackfriars; "but his eminence
has promised, and blessed be him, my poor little child is
saved !"

Full of joy, and feeling as if a mountain had been removed
from him, the good old prebend knelt down in the dark and
deserted street, and baring his bald head, returned thanks to
Heaven and his patron saint for having inclined the lord
chancellor to hear favourably the prayer he had just preferred.

CHAPTER XLVI.

THIRST !

> " 'Twas thou, O love ! whose dreaded shafts control,
> The hind's rude heart, and tear the hero's soul;
> Thou ruthless power, with bloodshed never cloyed,
> 'Twas thou thy lovely votary destroyed:
> Thy thirst still burning for a deeper woe,
> In vain for thee the tears of beauty flow."
>
> *The Lusiad of* CAMOENS.

AWARE that he had been seen by the friar in the act of listening, the lord advocate decided in a moment upon the course
to pursue. He resolved that the promised pardon should
never reach Edinburgh; but being too wary to make any
reference to the conversation he had just heard, after simply
giving the great cardinal a paper concerning an annual subsidy from the clergy, which was to be presented to James V
at Falkland on the morrow, he retired, and hastened to his
own house in the Canongate, where, with the utmost impatience, he awaited the return of Nichol Birrel, whom, with
Dobbie and Sanders Screw, he had sent on a devilishly contrived mission to the Castle of Edinburgh, whither we shall
return to observe them.

From his window Roland had seen them enter David's
Tower by the iron gate at the bottom of the stair, by which
they ascended straight to the chamber where Jane Seton was
confined.

After the priest had left her, the latter had become more
Y

calm, though St. Bernard had not held out to her the faintes|
hope of mercy or compassion from those powers which ha|
abandoned her to die, or of rescue from that once terribl|
faction to which her family belonged—that faction now s|
scattered, crushed, and broken.

In her prison this sad and lonely being had watched th|
woods and water darkening far below her; had watched th|
stars as one by one they sparkled out upon the night; an|
she envied the airy freedom of the passing clouds as the|
rolled through the sky—the blue twilight sky of a still an|
beautiful summer gloaming. In masses of fleecy white o|
pale gold, as they were tinted by the rising moon, they sailed
on the soft west wind in a thousand changing forms.

The very weariness of long grief overcame her, and she lay
down on the humble pallet afforded her by the orders of the
castellan, to sleep—for she had not slumbered during many
nights, and on this night, like her thirst, her fatigue was
excessive.

Her couch was a mere paillasse, with a pillow; for in everything she was made to feel painfully that she was the—condemned witch !

The bread given her during the two past days had been
unusually salt and bitter; she endured great thirst; but the
warder had removed the humble vessel that contained the
water for her use, and now, without a drop to moisten her
parched lips, she lay down to sleep. Her bread had been
purposely salted to excess, and thus, having been many hours
without a drop of water, her sufferings were greatly increased ;
and when she slept there arose before her visions of streams
pouring in white foam, of verdant banks or moss-green rocks,
of fountains that gushed and sparkled in marble basins, which
most tantalizingly receded or vanished when joyfully she
attempted to drink of them. At other times her kind old
mother or Roland Vipont, with their well-remembered smiles
of love, approached her with cups of water or of wine ; but
these dear forms faded away when the longed-for beverage
touched her lips; and then she started and awoke to solace
herself with her bitter tears—the only solace of which the
cruel authorities could not deprive her.

She slept lightly, as a bird sleeps on its perch ; but not so
lightly as to hear her prison door opened by the Messrs.
Birrel, Dobbie, and Screw, whose faces were made more vil-

lanous and sinister by the yellow rays of an oil-lamp, which darted upwards upon them. Birrel's visage, square and mastiff in aspect, livid in colour, and surrounded by a forest of sable hair above and below; Dobbie, with the eyes and moustaches of a cat; and Sanders Screw, though utterly destitute of any such appendages to his mouth, exhibiting in his nut-cracker jaws and bleared eyes a sardonic grin of cruelty and intoxication.

He carried a large Flemish jar, which, strange to say, was brimful of pure cold *water*.

Birrel raised his lamp, the lurid flame of which made yet more livid his yellow visage and ruffian eyes; and its sickly rays fell on the face of Jane; but the calm and divine smile that played upon her thin and parted lips, failed to scare from their purpose these demons, hardened as they were in every species of judicial cruelty.

Jane was dreaming of her lover, and in her self-embodied thoughts originated that beautiful smile.

Softly, but soundly, after all she had endured, this poor victim of superstition and revenge was sleeping now, and dreaming fondly and joyously—for in a dream every sensation is a thousand times more acute than it could be in reality—dreaming of that long life which was denied her, on this earth at least; she felt on her cheek the kiss of her young and gallant lover; she saw his waving plume and his doublet of cloth-of-gold; his voice was in her ear, and it murmured of his faith and love, that, like her own, would never die.

Her lips unclosed—an exclamation of rapture would have escaped her, when Birrel's iron fingers grasped her tender arm—and she awoke with a start and a cry of despair.

" Gude e'en to ye, cummer Jean," said he, insolently; "byde ye wauken, or fare ye waur; for gif ye sleep, *see*, madam the sorceress," and he shook before her eyes the steel brod, or needle, which was the badge of his hateful office.

Seated upon one side of her bed, Jane recoiled from these men, who regarded her with eyes that to her seemed as those of rattlesnakes, for they were pitiless in heart, and merciless as the waves of the sea.

We know not if we possess the power to describe the passages of that night in the vaulted chamber of David's Tower.

In the days of the witch-mania in Scotland it was the

custom, at the desire of the lord president of the college of justice, of the lord advocate, of the sheriff, or baillie of barony or regality, or whoever had tried and condemned a sorceress to subject her (even after trial) to a further ordeal; for no persecution, even unto the last hour, was deemed too severe for those unhappy beings who were accused of the imaginary crime of selling their souls to Satan, and thus irrevocably dooming themselves to a punishment that was everlasting.

Two of the most favourite modes of prolonged torture were, to prevent the prisoner from sleeping by every device that the most infernal ingenuity could suggest, and to feed them on bread salted most liberally, to produce an intense thirst, to assuage which the least drop of water was denied them.

Under this treatment many became insane, for the kirk sessions carried it to the most ferocious excess in the seventeenth century.

On being awakened, and partially recovering from her terror, Jane's first sensation was an inordinate desire for water; her thirst was excessive. Her tongue was parched and painful, for her food during the two past days had been coarse dry wheaten bannocks, rendered bitter by the plentiful supply of salt used in their composition. She had been too much accustomed to the most cruel and unceremonious intrusions, to express her keen sense of the present one, otherwise than by her flashing eyes and dilated nostrils, for her heart swelled with indignation; but, on perceiving the jar in the hands of Sanders Screw, her first thought was to satisfy her thirst, and she implored them to give her a cup of water.

At this plaintive request, a grin spread over the weasel visage of Screw and the cat-like eyes of Dobbie, while Birrel, who was somewhat intoxicated, replied with his habitual tone of insolence—

"By my faith, cummer Jean, ye shall be thirstier and drouthier than even was I in Douglasdale, ere a drop rins ower your craig."

Screw set down the jar, placing himself between it and their victim. The lamp was also placed on the floor, and seating themselves around it, Dobbie produced from his wide trunk hose of buckram a pack of dirty and dog-eared cards. Each worthy official then placed beside him a flask of usquebaugh, the cards were dealt round, and the campaign of the night commenced with an old game at which the three might play, and Birrel could cheat to his heart's content, notwithstanding that Dobbie knew the backs as well as the front, of his favourite pack of cards.

For a time Jane gazed at them with the same startled and dismayed expression that the sudden appearance of three reptiles might have excited; and again she begged a cup of water, for her thirst (which had been increasing the live-long day, and to which her salted food, the drugs of the physician, and the grief that preyed upon her, all alike conduced) had now attained a degree of torture and intensity which hitherto she could not have conceived.

Her entreaties were replied to with laughter; and it seemed as if the sight of the liberal draughts imbibed by the trio from their flasks increased the desire of the poor captive; but her prayers and tears were unheeded, and noisily the game went on.

Two hours passed thus!

The players had drained their flasks, and amid much cursing, quarrelling and vociferation, the loose change had rapidly passed from hand to hand, until the whole, amounting to somewhere about ten crowns, a few fleur-de-lis groats, and white pennies of James III., were lodged in the pouch of Birrel, who trimmed the lamp with his fingers, and offered a brass bodle to each of his companions that the game might begin anew; but, as the cards were being redealt, he perceived that, despite their brutal uproar, overcome by weariness and torture of mind and body, the unhappy girl had again fallen into an uneasy slumber.

Upon this the brodder arose with a growl, and drawing his needle from its sheath, gave her a severe puncture in the arm. The pain of this made her again, with a shriek, start up wildly from her sitting posture; and, uncovering her snow-white arm to the elbow, she found that blood was flowing from the deep incision.

With her imploring eyes full of horror, she turned towards Birrel and endeavoured to speak, but her tongue, which clove to the roof of her mouth, failed, at first, to articulate a syllable; and her lips were hard and dry.

"Did I not tell ye quhat ye micht expect gif ye dared to sleep," said Birrel, savagely.

She made a gasping effort to speak.

" Water !" she said, in a husky whisper, " water !—a singl
drop, for the love of God !"

" Oho !" grinned Screw, " the saut bannocks are now tellin
tales !"

He held the Flemish jar of polished pewter before her eye;
and shook the limpid water till it sparkled in the light.

" The haill o' this is for you, dame Seton," said Birre|
" but there is a sma' bit ceremony to be gone through first.'

" Water ! water !" moaned Jane, in a whispering voice
feeling as if her throat was scorched, and her dry, parche(
tongue was swollen to twice its usual size. " Oh, man, man!'
she added, clasping her hands, " I will pray for you—I wil
bless you in my last hour, with my whole heart, and with m;
whole soul, for one drop, a single drop of water !"

There never was a villain so bad as to be without one re-
deeming trait; thus, even Dobbie the doomster had his; anc
now the piteous tone of Jane's husky voice, her pallid face
her entreating and bloodshot eyes, had stirred some secret
chord of human sympathy in the recesses of his usually iror
heart. He poured a little water into a cup, and approachec
her. Jane's eyes flashed with thankfulness and joy; but
Birrel dashed away the cup with one hand, and laid the other
on his poniard.

Jane uttered a tremulous cry of despair.

" Then false coof and half-witted staümrel !" exclaimed the
witchfinder; " is it thus ye obey the orders of Redhall, who
is our master ? Look ye, good mistress, subscribe this paper
and we leave you wi' the water-stoup, to drink and to sleep
till your heart is contented. But refuse, and woe be unto ye!
For here sit we doon to watch by turns, to keep ye, waking
and sleepless, with thirst unslackened, till *the hour of doom*.
and so, my Lady Seton, ye have the option; sign and drink,
or refuse and suffer."

With one hand he held before her the large and brimming
jar; with the other he displayed a paper whereon something
was written.

Within the deep jar the water seemed cold and pure, limpid
and refreshing; while her thirst was agonizing, and her
whole frame felt as if scorched by an internal fire. Her brain
was whirling, a sickness was coming over her, and human
endurance could withstand the temptation no longer.

For a moment she reflected that it was impossible for any

avowal, verbal or written, to make her more utterly miserable or degraded than her sentence had already made her, and aware that nothing now could change the current of her fate save the royal pardon, of which she had not the shadow of a hope, she could only articulate—

" A pen, a pen !—the water !—the water ! I am dying—dying of thirst !"

Promptly Birrel produced a pen, which he dipped in a portable inkstand.

She took it with a trembling hand and paused.

He temptingly poured some of the sparkling water on the floor. A gleam passed over her eyes, and in a moment she placed her name, *Jane Seton*, to the paper, vainly endeavouring. as she did so, to see what the lines written above her signature contained ; but there was a mist before her eyes, and now they failed her. She threw away the pen with a shriek, and stretched out her hands towards the vessel of water.

" What would ye think, now, if I spilled it all on the flagstones ?" said Birrel, with a grin, as he withheld the jar.

At this cruel threat she could only clasp her hands, and gaze at him in silence.

After enjoying her agony for a few moments, he handed her the jar, from which she drank greedily and thirstily.

" Hechhow !" said Birrel, with a triumphant growl, " now ye drink, cummer, as I drank of the Douglasburn, at the foot of the Cairntable," and, extinguishing their lamp, the three wretches retired, and she was left to her own terrible thoughts.

Again and again she drank of the water, but the thrill of delight its coolness and freshness afforded her soon passed away ; and setting down the vessel carefully, she gazed at it, and then burst into a passion of tears.

The paper she had signed, what could it mean ?

At that moment the clock of St. Cuthbert's church. which stood in the hollow far down below the Castle, on the west, struck slowly and solemnly the hour of four, and this sound, as it ascended to her ear, recalled her to other thoughts.

The morning was shining through the rusty grating of her window—the morning of another day. She thought bitterly of the paper she had signed ; and deploring her lack of strength and resolution, buried her face in her pillow, and gave way at last to a wild paroxysm of despair.

CHAPTER XLVII.

WHAT THE PAPER CONTAINED.

" Oh, misery!
While I was dragged by an insidious band
Of pyrates—savage bloodhounds—into bondage.
But, witness, heaven! witness, ye midnight hours,
That heard my ceaseless groans, how her dear image
Grew to my very heart!"—*The Desart Island*, 1760.

SLEEPLESS, and with the horrible conversation of Birrel and
Dobbie still tingling in his ears, Roland passed the night in
that frame of mind we have endeavoured to describe, though
it can be better conceived.

The morning dawned, and the thick gratings of the windows appeared in strong relief against the saffron sky, and
sounds of life arose from the waking city below   The bright
sun was gilding the vane of St. Giles, the spire of the Dominicans, the square tower of St. Mary-in-the-Fields, and the
lofty summits of the town, while, like a golden snake, the
Forth was seen winding afar between the wooded mountains
of the west.

With arms folded, his head sunk upon his breast, and his
hollow eyes fixed dreamily on the floor, Roland was immersed in a chaos of gloomy thoughts, when a noise occasioned
by a hand raising a window opposite startled him. He looked
up, and a letter fell at his feet.

He clutched and tore it open.

" Jane! from Jane—from my dear Jane?" he exclaimed,
huskily, and pressed her signature to his lips.   " It is signed
by herself (how well I know that dear signature!) but another has written it—St. Bernard, perhaps.   Ah, my God!
she is too ill to write, and they separate me from her.   Jane
—Jane!"

Now Sir Roland Vipont, though a poor gentleman and
soldier of fortune of the sixteenth century, knew enough of
scholarcraft (which, like every other craft, was not held then
in much repute) to enable him to decipher the letter of Jane
Seton, or rather that letter which, by the order of Redhall,
Birrel had compelled her to sign by the bribe alternately
offered and withheld—a draught of cold water.

For a time there was an envious mist before the hot dry

eyes of Roland Vipont; and thrice he had to pause before he so far recovered his energies as to be able to read this epistle, which had been thus delivered to him by the hand of a friend, as he did not doubt. Literally, it ran as follows:

" MINE OWN SWEET HEART, SIR ROLAND,

" Abandoned now by my evil Mentor, and inspired by the blessed saints, who know all things, uninfluenced by any man, and of mine own free will, I hereby confess, certify, and make known unto you, that I have indeed been guilty of the sorcery and witchcraft of which I am accused; and that queen Magdalene died by the same magic and power of enchantment which forced thee to love me. Thus. the strong regard thou bearest me is in no way attributable to any beauty, manner, or apparent goodness, with which nature hath gifted me; but solely to my diabolical arts and sorceries. At this thou wilt be sorely grieved, but cannot be surprised, mine own sweet heart, when thou thinkest of the myriad infernal deeds that are permitted by Heaven and brought about by the instigation of Satan, to whom I have borne more than one brood of imps. I saw that thou wert simple, guileless, good, and brave; and thus were fitted to fall easily into my snares, where many have fallen before thee; but Heaven, by revealing my sins, hath saved thee in time. And I do further confess that I am a false traitor, a dyvour heretic and renouncer of my baptism. Written for me, by a learned clerk, at the Castle of Edinburgh, the 17th day of July, in the year of God I^m V^c xxxvii.

" JANE SETON."

"My Jane! my Jane! oh, this is hell's own work!" exclaimed the unhappy young man; who became stricken with terror at avowals which were so startling and so well calculated to make a deep impression on any man, and on any mind of his time, when a belief in the power of the devil was so strong. " This agony, and not the love I bear thee, is the work of sorcery. It is a forgery—I will never believe it; and yet her signature is there! and after trial, when torture, shame, and agony were past, what could bring forth an avowal such as this? Oh, what but remorse for deceiving one who had loved thee so well! The mother of fiends! she so good, so charitable, so religious, who never missed a mass or festival.

I shudder and laugh at the same moment! A sorceress—
Jane . . . . where is the Jane I loved—the good and
gentle? She confront the terrors of hell—the touch of
Satan?—impossible—frenzy and folly; and yet, and yet. and
yet my brain is turned, and I feel as if a serpent had thrust
its head into my heart."

Thus thought Roland, incoherently.

All the implicit trust of a lover, and the blind chivalric
devotion of a true gentleman of the year 1537, failed to bear
up Vipont against the chilling superstition which then overshadowed every mind and everything, and which tinges the
writings of the most subtle casuists and philosophers of those
days; and assuredly one could not expect much deep casuistry
or philosophy either to be exhibited by Roland, whose school
had been the camp, and whose playground in boyhood had
been the corpse-strewn battle-fields of France and Italy. It
was an age of fairy spells and magic charms, mysterious omens,
and gliding spectres—of ten thousand deadly and now forgotten terrors; and we must enter fully into the feelings of
the age to appreciate or conceive the frightful effect this un-
sought for and unexpected avowal of supernatural crime produced upon the mind of Roland Vipont.

His first impulse was to stigmatize the letter as the most
deliberate of forgeries, to rend it into a hundred fragments,
and to scatter them from the window on the waters of the
loch below; but the memory of the words those fragments
contained, and their terrible import, remained as if written
with fire upon his soul, and wherever he turned he saw them
palpably before him; thus, at times, the most cruel doubts
were added to his former despair.

He felt that his mental agony was rapidly becoming too
great for endurance; and he shrunk, as it were, back within
himself with terror at the idea that he might become insane.

The pride of his strong and gallant heart—a heart that
had never quailed amid the boom of cannon and the shock of
spears, the rush of charging squadrons and the clang of
descending swords—was now bowed down; and covering his
face with his hand, he wept like a child, and with that deep
and deathlike agony that can only be known by the strong
man when forced to find a refuge and relief in tears.

Redhall, that tiger-heart, had calculated well and deeply.
The sight of those tears, produced by the letter he had so

cruelly and so subtly contrived, would have been as balm to his heart, and as "marrow to his bones;" for he laughed aloud when Nichol Birrel, by dawn of day, related, in exaggerated terms, the agony of Vipont, which he had neither the means of observing or ascertaining; for he had simply, by the assistance of a ladder, dropped the letter into his apartment, and hurried away.

"The measure of my vengeance against this man is now almost full!" said he; "woe be to him who would lessen it! To have destroyed her while this Vipont believed in her innocence would have left that vengeance but half sated. Now have I fairly robbed her of her honour and her very soul—at least, in the eyes of this gilded moth, who loves her, as I know, even to adoration; but not more than I do—oh, no!—not more than I, who am her destroyer, and on whose hands her blood will lie. Oh, Jane!   . ."

His head fell forward on his breast.

"But harkye, Birrel," said he, suddenly recovering; "to-day the cardinal goes to Falkland, to seek her pardon from the king; and this pardon (if granted) young Leslie of Balquhan is to convey straight to Sir James Riddel, at our castle here. Now mark me, Nichol Birrel, and mark me well, this pardon must be brought to *me*, and to me alone. 'Tis an insult of this meddling cardinal to send it to Cranstoun-Riddel, the castellan, while I am lord advocate. This very day, after morning mass, his eminence and this holiday lieutenant of the guards, set out for Falkland. Do thou, with Trotter and fifteen, or as many good horsemen as you can muster, follow, and watch well for Leslie's return. Be more wary than you were in Douglasdale, or what avail your promises of service? Between this and Falkland there is many a mile of lonely muirland, where blows may be struck, or bones broken, and where a slain man may sleep undiscovered till the judgment-day—see to it! This Leslie is in your hands, as Vipont was before. A hundred French crowns if thou bringest me the pardon. Stay!—there is the Laird of Clatto, who hath a plea before the lords; tell him, that if he wishes well to his case, *a certain horseman* must not pass the Lomond-hill; there are the Lindesays of Kirkforthar and Bandon, who are the sworn foemen of the House of Balquhan. I know thy skill and cunning—ride and rouse them! Ride and raise all the Howe of Fife on the king's messenger; and here is **my** thumb on't, Nichol Birrel, my three best crofts at Redhall shall be thine of a free gift, heritably and irredeemably, to thee and thine heirs for ever."

In one hour from that time this indefatigable ruffian had Tam Trotter and fifteen other horsemen completely armed, with helmets and cuirasses, gorgets, and gloves of steel, swords, lances, and petronels, awaiting his orders (and the cardinal's departure) in the stable yard of Redhall's lodging in the Canongate.

CHAPTER XLVIII.

THE CROSS AND GILLSTOUP.

" But the curtain of twilight o'ershadows the shore,
And deepens the tint on the blue Lammermuir;
The tints on Corstorphine have paled in their fire,
But sunset still lingers with gold on its spire;
The Roseberry forests are hooded in grey,
And night, like his heir, treads impatient on day—
And now, gentle stranger, if such be thy mood,
Go welcome the moonlight in sweet Holyrood."

ON the night, with which our last chapters have been chiefly occupied, at the identical time when Father St. Bernard was concerting with the cardinal, *anent* procuring a pardon for Lady Jane, two other kind friends were elsewhere concerting the escape of her lover—but planning it like soldiers, by escalade and at point of the sword.

In the course of the present history we have, more than once, referred to a certain flourishing tavern, named *The Cross and Gillstoup*, which, in those days, displayed its signboard to the public eye on the south side of the then somewhat suburban street, the Canongate.

Though the host of this establishment was vitally interested in the freedom of the master of king James's ordnance, in so far that he owed him the sum of thirty crowns for wine, it was not deemed advisable to take him into the conspiracy. In a little chamber of this tavern, vaulted, like all the first stories in old Edinburgh, having a sanded floor, a plain wooden table, and fir chairs of capacious dimensions, a little figure of the Madonna in a corner, beneath which was a begging-box, belonging to the Franciscans, inscribed, " Help y* puir, as ye wald God dit you," sat Sir John Forrester, captain of the king's arquebusiers, and Leslie of Balquhan, his lieutenant;

though it was past the hour of nine, when, by the laws of
James I., no man was to be found in a tavern after that hour
rang from the burgh bell, under a penalty of warding in the
Tolbooth, or paying "the king's chamberlane fiyftie schil-
linges."

Being gentlemen, and moreover officers of the guard, these
two cavaliers considered themselves above such vulgar rules,
and were quietly sitting down to supper. Their bonnets and
mantles, their unbuckled swords and daggers, lay on a side
bench; each had a knife and platter of delft ware, with a
silver-rimmed drinking-horn, before him; and between them
stood a savoury powt pie, with a great pewter jug of wine,
the said pewter jug being polished to the brightness of a
mirror; and Leslie used it as such, to point up his moustaches; for the hostess of *The Cross and Gillstoup* prided
herself particularly on the brightness of her pots and kettles
—and then, be it remembered, pewter was a luxury.

Seated at another table in the background, but helped
liberally from the before-mentioned powt pie and the gallant
pewter jug, old Lintstock, the ex-cannonier, with his steel
cap and Jedwood axe laid beside him, his white hair glistening in the light of three long candles, and his eye looking
very fierce and red, was eating his supper with a stern and
disconsolate but nevertheless very determined aspect; for he
had thoroughly resolved on doing something desperate, though
he had not exactly made up his mind as to what that desperate thing should be. Ever since his master's arrest the
forlorn old soldier had been protected by Sir John Forrester,
who remarked, as they proceeded to supper—

" A whole day has passed, and yet, Leslie, we have resolved
on nothing; and now our resolutions must needs be sharp
and sure, for high and overstrained in their newfangled
notions of civil authority, the abbot Mylne and Redhall will
come swoop down like a pair of ravenous hawks on poor
Vipont, for his escapade on that devilish day of Lady Jane's
trial."

" I am aware of that."

"Then why did you not come sooner?"

" Sooner? Why, Sir John, I have never had time to cross
myself to-day."

" Busy—thou?"

" Oh, I had a score of matters to attend to. First, I had

to buy me a pot of rouge at the Tron for Madame de Montreuil, who complains that her complexion hath gone since
the late queen's death ; then I had to escort the Countess of
Glencairn and little Mademoiselle de Brissac, who must needs
go on a pilgrimage to the chapel of St. James ; then I had
to get a pint of wine at Leith to refresh me ; then I had to
write a song for Marion Logan, and to ride to John of the
Silvermills, anent some matters for bonny Alison Hume."

" I knew not that she was ailing."

" Nay, 'twas only to get some almond paste for her dainty
hands, and oil of roses for her hair."

" Plague on thee and them! Canst think of such cursed
trifles when our best friends are in such deadly peril ?"

" Now really, Corstorphine," said Leslie, as he spread the
white linen serviette over his red satin trunk breeches ; " is
the whole world to stand still because Roland Vipont is laid
by the heels ? Or dost thou think that the king will bring
to death, or even to trial, so brave a fellow as our captain of
his ordnance ?"

" The devil ! thou talkest as if brave fellows were scarce in
Scotland. But the Lady Seton, her chances of life——"

" Are small indeed ; but let us only have our Vipont free of
Cranstoun-Riddel, on horseback beside us, with his helmet
on, and his sword drawn, and we shall carry the lady off in
face of all Edinburgh ! What care we for the burgher guard,
or the lances of the provost !"

" The king——"

" Will love a deed so bold, and so much after his own
heart."

" If we were to fail ?"

" 'Tis but dying like bold fellows in our corslets."

" Thy hand, my brave Leslie, for thou art an honour to
thy name," replied Sir John Forrester, with admiration.

" Poor Marion Logan has quite spoiled her fine eyes by
crying for three days and nights consecutively about her
friend."

Here something between a sob and a growl proceeded from
the corner, where Lintstock was gulping down his supper and
his sorrows together.

" Why, Lintstock, my old Cyclop," said Leslie, " thou art
looking grave as a German lanzknecht. Tuts! cheer up ; thy
master will soon be out of David's Tower ; and then, let Sir
Adam of Redhall look to himself."

" Ay, Balquhan, but let him look well to himself before that cometh to pass!"

" How, old Tartar! wouldst thou give the king's advocate a sliver with thine axe?"

" I will hew him to the brisket for having dared to look at my master's lemane! By St. John! if any man dare look aboon his rosettes, when passing my master's next lady-love at kirk or market——"

" Oho!" said Sir John Forrester, hastily; " thou seemest better acquainted with this matter than most of us. But be wary, carle, thy head may run under a noose. Some more pie?"

" If it please ye, sir."

" If it pleases thee, rather. Eat well, my old cormorant; for it hath been a fast with thee since thy master's arrest. Now, Leslie, to return to what we were talking of. I know of no other means of procuring admittance to Vipont's prison but in disguise. If Father St. Bernard would lend me his cassock——"

" Thou art too tall by eight inches. I know my Lady Cranstoun-Riddel's little tire-woman," said Leslie, winking, and clanking his gold spurs.

" I' faith! a nice little dame, with black eyes and pretty teeth."

" But a saucy darnstocking, spoiled at court by the pages and archers."

" Through her something might be achieved though."

" Is she particular?"

" Not at all! If she would only conceal me in her room for one night——"

" Once there, rogue, thou wouldst forget all about poor Vipont, thy mission, and the coil of stout rope wherewith thou proposest to line thy trunk breeches."

Here the noise of a window being raised behind them made Leslie turn his head.

" What is that? Mother of God! what is *that?*" he exclaimed, in alarm, with his sword half drawn, on seeing a black visage, with shining eyeballs, a row of sharp white teeth, and two black paws, appear between the lifted sash and the window-sill.

Forrester started, and Lintstock snatched up his axe.

The head grinned and bowed, and waved its black paws with a grotesque air of respect and deprecation.

" By my soul! 'tis Lady Ashkirk's ill-omened page!" said
the captain, bursting into a fit of laughter.

" How—the evil spirit, anent which we have heard so
much of late?"

" Nay, no evil spirit, but a poor denizen of those countries
which lie beneath the sun. Sir Robert Barton, the admiral,
swears they are half men and half marmosets; but Father
St. Bernard told me they were the descendants of Cain. I
am not afraid of *it*—nay, not I," said the tall knight of Corstorphine, as he drew on his military gloves, and—but not
without some repugnance—seized the hands of Sabrino, and
drew him into the room.

The poor black boy, whose aspect was now deplorable, fell
on his knees, and poured forth his thanks in frightful mutterings, that seemed to come from the bottom of his throat, and
lolled out the fragment of his tongue in a way that produced
a striking effect on old Lintstock, and, to say the least of it,
was very unearthly. The old cannonier clenched his axe in
one hand, his wine-pot in the other, and recoiled as from a
snake.

" Lintstock," said Forrester, " thou hast seen this creature
before; dost understand its gibberish?"

" It is thanking you, as I think, sir; but it looks gey
wolfish-like at the last of the powt pie."

" Right, Lintstock," said Leslie, placing the dish before
Sabrino. The famished negro gave him a glance of intense
thankfulness, and straightway plunged his black fingers into
the pie, of which he ate voraciously.

After the night of the earl's adventure on the island, of the
countess's baffled flight, the duel with Sir James Hamilton,
and of Ashkirk's disappearance with Sybil in the boat, Sabrino,
who had escaped all the arquebuse shots by ducking in the
water and clinging to the weed-covered rocks, next day
found himself under dangerous circumstances, for the cavern
which had formed his hiding-place being now discovered and
searched, he had no longer any place of concealment; thus
hunger and the danger of death made him resolve to put in
practice a plan he had frequently conceived, but had not yet
dared to execute.

At certain periods a large boat came regularly from Leith
in the morning with provisions for the garrison, and generally
returned in the evening. An opportunity soon occurred, and

Sabrino, diving under the counter of this barge at the very moment it left the creek of the Inch, lashed himself (with a fragment of rope) to the iron pintles which fastened the rudder to the sternpost. In the summer atmosphere of a warm July, the water of the majestic Forth was calm and warm, and the motion was pleasant and easy as the oarsmen shot their lightened boat across its broad and glassy surface, on which the setting sun was shining. Though half choked at times by the salt spray that flew from the oars, beneath the counter, where he hung, Sabrino, with unflinching resolution, endured the danger of being towed for three miles, and was glad to find that the dusk had fairly set in before the boat was moored to the old wooden pier which then terminated the ancient harbour under the rampart of the round tower.

Poor Sabrino knew that all the white men feared and hated him; but he knew not that he was regarded as little less than the devil himself—for such he had been considered and declared to be by the wise and learned of the College of Justice. Avoiding every person, he had the sense to thread his way into the city by some secret passage, and went straight to the mansion of the Ashkirk family. It was silent and deserted, for the spiders were already spinning their cobwebs on the lock of its iron gate. Failing also to find Sir Roland Vipont, and fearing to encounter others, the unhappy mute had instinctively sought the tavern, where in palmier and more privileged days he had so frequently brought him messages from his mistress.

Sabrino knew well the approaches to the place, and entering the Horse Wynd, cleared at a bound the wall of the kailyard, and, reaching the window of the old familiar room, obtained egress,—not from Roland Vipont, as he had expected, but by the assistance of Sir John Forrester, as we have just related.

" Drink," said that frank and stately soldier, handing to the wet, weary, and famished being a cup of wine, when he had eaten to his satisfaction; " but now, what in the fiend's name shall we do with thee? I would not for all my mains and mills at Corstorphine thou wert found by Redhall living under my protection; and yet 'twere a foul shame to drive thee forth, the more so as all men's hands and voices are against '' ''

Sabrino understood Sir John, and hung his head sorrowfully.

"Nay, poor devil," he added, kindly, "thou shalt byde with me, and I bite my glove at all who dare say nay."

"Could we not paint him, or dye him, or scrub him well with hot water, so that, in colour, at least, he might be like other men?"

"We shall see," replied the captain of the arquebuses; "I will talk with my old confessor about it—he knows everything. But it hath such capacious eyes, and such a nose!"

"By Jove! its face is like a Highland buckler!" added the other; and they paused to regard Sabrino with all the curiosity a new species of animal would have excited.

"Sir John Forrester," said Lintstock, "I ken weel that this creature can clamber like a squirrel; and gif we show him the tower wherein my puir maister girns and granes for his luve and his liberty, I warrant he'll sune rax to the window. Put a saw between his teeth, a coil o' stout rope on his back, and I warrant me we shall hae Sir Roland Vipont beside us in three hours after."

"Thou art right, Lintstock," said Leslie, while Sabrino, on hearing himself referred to, looked fixedly at the one-eyed gunner; "this creature's black hide hath brought thy brave master and his fair mistress into sore trouble, and I know of none who ought to exert his energies more than he in their service. It is agreed; we shall show him the rock, the tower, the window, and that by daybreak to-morrow."

Sabrino understood them perfectly, while he gazed at them with the painful and speechless anxiety which his face depicted at times so powerfully; and, anxious to express his gratitude, his eyes shone, while he grinned and nodded, saying—

"Ees—ees—ees!" laid his hands repeatedly on his breast, and placed the hand of Sir John Forrester on his woolly head, in token that he was their liege and true man.

At that moment a loud knock was heard at the door.

"Under the table, Sabrino—hide, hide," said Leslie; "I would not for my helmet full of gold pieces, thou wert seen with us—quick!"

Sabrino dived below the table, and again the knock was heard.

"Who is there without?—come in," said Sir John.

Carrying in his hand his bonnet, which was adorned by a long white feather, a graceful young man, attired in the most gorgeous and extreme of the fashion of that age, a doublet of peach-coloured velvet, sewn with seed pearls, and stiff with silver lace, a Genoese mantle of blue velvet, and trunks and hose of the palest yellow satin, appeared.

" My Lord David Lindesay !", said the two officers of the guard, as they started from their seats.

" A message from the cardinal," said the young lord, who was soon to become the primate's son-in-law. " His eminence sets out to-morrow for Falkland Palace, to visit the king, and begs the favour of some twenty arquebusiers, under your guidance, Laird of Balquhan, as the roads are neither safe nor sure at this time."

Leslie looked at his captain.

" Half the guard are at Falkland already, under the other lieutenant, the Laird of Bute," replied Forrester ; " but my friend Balquhan will be at the disposal of his eminence to-morrow with twenty arquebusiers. At what time do you mount and ride ?"

" After morning prayer," said the young lord : " you know how unsafe the country is around Falkland—for his eminence, at least."

" True ; the Kirkaldies of Grange, the Melvilles of Raith, and the Seatons of Clatto, are no friends of his."

After a few more words of course, and tasting their wine, the heir of the princely line of Crawford bowed and retired.

" A hundred devils !" said Leslie, as he buckled on his sword. " This duty will prevent me assisting in the escape of our poor Vipont."

" It matters not, my true Leslie, for I alone will see to that. But how, a-God's name, am I to get our sable friend conveyed to my quarters in the palace ? If our fat host of the *Cross and Gillstoup* should see him, all will be over with him."

After some consideration to preclude his being seen, and avoid the dangerous surmises consequent thereto, it was arranged that Sabrino should retire in the same manner as he had entered—by the window, which he immediately did.

Thereafter, having met the captain and lieutenant of the guard at the low wall which then bordered the west side of the Horse Wynd at the foot of the Canongate, Leslie muffled him up to the eyes in his velvet mantle, and he was taken past the guards, pages, &c., into the inmost court of the palace, where Forrester concealed him in an apartment, the key of w

CHAPTER XLIX

THE CASTAWAYS.

" 'Tis very certain the desire of life
    Prolongs it: this is obvious to physicians,
When patients, neither plagued with friends nor wife,
    Survive through very desperate conditions,
Because they still can hope, nor shines the knife,
    Near shears of Atropus before their visions:
Despair of all recovery spoils longevity,
And makes men's miseries of alarming brevity."—BYRON.

WE have related how the Earl of Ashkirk, as the only means of avoiding death or recapture, had spread the lug-sail of his boat to the western breeze, and was borne down the Firth of Forth.

The gale was freshening, and it blew the white foam from the waves, as they rose and fell, and rose again in rapid succession, as if to meet the sharp prow of the boat, which shot through them like an arrow through a wreath of smoke. The boat of the Inch was left behind; for unwilling to run the risk of being carried out to sea, its crew gave up the pursuit in despair. The earl laughed in triumph, and to his breast folded Sybil, who was trembling with terror at the world of water that whirled around them.

Dim and distant, the hills of Fife and Lothian seemed soon to be afar off; the isle the fugitives had left seemed also sinking fast, and little trace of the shore remained, after the moon sank behind the peaks of Stirlingshire. The earl now attempted to turn shoreward; but in a moment found the impossibility of making the least headway against the strong and increasing wind, the ebbing tide, and the fierce current of the mighty Firth, which had there expanded to an ocean.

" The shore—the shore now. Oh, good, my dear earl, turn towards the shore!" implored Sybil, in great terror, as she clung to her companion.

" It is impossible! Against such a wind as this, I should merely have our boat upset, and this, dearest Sybil, would not be very pleasant."

" Mercy! we shall be swept out into the homeless ocean!" she continued, with increasing fear, as the boat rose suddenly up, or surged as swiftly down into a deep, dark, and watery hollow, while the heaving of the waves increased every moment.

"Nay, now, Sybil, afraid!—thou a Douglas of Kilspindie? I will never believe it. Let us bear right on towards the bonny Bay of Aberlady, which will soon receive us, and lo! we shall find ourselves just under your father's castle of Kilspindie."

"Better are we here," replied Sybil, with a kindling eye: "know you not that, like Tantallon, it is garrisoned by a party of Hamiltons?"

"Now, God's malison be on this tribe, for they have come out of their native Clydesdale to spread even as locusts over all the Lowlands."

"But there is many a crofter at Kilspindie, and many a stout fisherman at Aberlady, who will shelter us for the love they bear our grandsire Sir Archibald Douglas, and for the sake of the old race. They are all leal men and true to the Douglas name."

"I have sufficiently perforated one Hamilton to-night, and have no wish to come to handyblows with another, especially while having thee, my little lady, to protect."

"And dost thou think, cousin Archibald, that I can neither fire a petronel, or unwind a pistolette, as my aunt, your mother, doth?"

"Nay, Sybil, thou wouldst surely shut fast those black eyes of thine, when the wheel whirled and the sulphuret sprung; for thou hast seen less of blood and blows, of men unhorsed and armour riven, than the countess, my mother; for thou never sawest the Douglas banner in its glory, in the days of James IV., as she tells us many a time and oft. Why, bethink thee, Sybil, two hundred gentlemen, Douglases, all dubbed knights of name, and wearing spurs of gold, were found lying slain on Flodden field—that fatal field where bold King James, with ten thousand of the Scottish noblesse, fought till going down of the sun, against six-and-twenty thousand Englishmen."

The earl spoke of these and other things to draw Sybil's attention from their present danger; but the wind was still increasing, and he had thrice lessened the sail since leaving Inchkeith; the moon was gone, the waves were becoming gloomy, and though Sybil was too much accustomed to boating to be sick, she trembled at the increasing tumult of the Firth, and shuddered in the cold night wind that blew over it, for the plaid in which the earl enveloped her failed as a protection against the chill ocean atmosphere. This plaid—a plain Border maud of black and white cheque, he had long worn as the best of disguises, for it was a warm and ample, though a coarse and humble garment.

For a full hour the boat beat fruitlessly against the wind, which now blew off the land, and again the earl was forced to run her before it, to avoid being swamped by the fierce and foam-headed waves, that careered ahead and astern of her; and now the dark, shadowy outline of Gulane Hill came out of the dusky vapour that rested on the face of the water to the east. Aware that the little sandy Bay of Aberlady lay below it, he trimmed the lessened sail and grasped the tiller, in the hope of beaching the boat upon its level shore; but, lo! the envious wind veered suddenly a few points more to the south, and blew directly off the coast, and with such sudden fury, that the boat was nearly overset.

Instantly securing the tiller by a rope, the earl rushed to the lug-sail to take in its last reef, and fearing to be dashed on the rocks that fringe the coast, he was now compelled to pass the wished-for haven, and lie still further off, with his prow turned towards the pathless waste of the German Sea. Then, but only when he thought of Sybil and what she was suffering from cold and terror, did his brave heart sink with apprehension. Muffled completely in the plaid, she endeavoured to shut out the sight of the black tumbling waves and their foam-flecked summits, the sound of the moaning wind and the creaking of the labouring boat, but every instant the noise increased, and every shower of spray that flew over her was heavier than the last. She prayed with fervour; and the impetuous earl, who was rather inclined to swear, both at the sea and wind, more than once, amid the wild discord of the waves, heard her small soft voice raised in prayer to God, and to St. Bryde of Douglas, the patron of her race, the virgin of Kil-dara.

The castle of Kilspindie, with its great square tower and sandy shore, the beautiful Bay of Aberlady, with its sheltered village, were now astern; and nothing was seen but the bluff headland of Gulane-ness, with the white foam rising like smoke against its tremendous front of rocks.

Wan gleams of uncertain light shot over the desolate

estuary; the whole prospect was dreary and alarming. Strong, active, and determined, Lord Ashkirk might have reached the shore by swimming, but Sybil——

He struck his sail almost in despair, and now bent all his unwearying energy to bale out his little craft; for she was filling fast, and he fully expected to be swamped by every mountain-like wave, that with its monstrous head curling aloft, and snowy with foam—a foam rendered yet more terrible by the gloom and obscurity around it—rolled on towards the rocks of Gulane-ness, drenching the labouring skiff in its passage, and threatening to engulf it in an abyss for ever.

He was without fear for himself; but when he beheld Sybil crouching down beside him, his heart filled with anxiety and dread, with suspense and remorse; and he reflected that were the catastrophe, which he dreaded and expected every moment, to happen—he thrust away the thought as too horrible to contemplate, and baled on with renewed energy, pausing only to kiss the upturned brow of Sybil, or press her trembling hands. They were becoming very cold.

A thousand thoughts of home and friends, of love and life, came vividly on her mind; and Sybil reflected that she was happy even on yonder closely guarded island, when she contrasted the security and hope it afforded with the danger and hopelessness of their present predicament.

Day began to dawn in the east, and with joy poor Sybil hailed it; for though helpless and feeble, she had seen and admired the unwearying energy of her lover, in keeping the boat *alive* in such a frightful sea. His exertions were almost superhuman, for *her* existence depended upon them.

They were now past that tremendous promontory.

Uninfluenced by its bold abutment, the waves were more smooth; and again the earl spread his sail, and made another vain attempt to gain the southern shore.

A sickly yellow glow spread over the east, as the sun arose from the ocean enveloped in watery clouds; the wind had not yet spent its fury; the whole aspect of the sky and water was dark and dreary The summit of the land was veiled in mist; its shore was fringed with rocks, on which the surf was beating; and from these rocks the wind blew fierce and strong. No vessel was in sight; and not a living thing was visible but the startled seamews and kitty-wakes, the gannets and cormorants, that were whirled past them, screaming on the wind, which often dashed them into the bosom of the up-heaved water.

"Now Heaven be thy protection, my Sybil!" exclaimed the earl, as he sank exhausted beside her; "for I can do no more."

Worn out by toil, and exhausted also by loss of blood from a flesh wound received from the sword of Barncleugh, and still more overcome by his frantic and unaided exertions during so many hours to trim the boat and keep her floating, he now found himself conquered, and completely overcome. He was pale as death, his hands trembled, his eyes were blood-shot, and the blood that trickled from his nostrils declared painfully how far he had overtasked his strength.

"God protect thee, Sybil!" he repeated, as he pressed his trembling lips to her brow; "God protect thee, for all my poor strength has failed me now."

He burst into tears, from excess of weakness; but this was the emotion of a moment only; he smiled sadly, and encir-cling Sybil with his arms endeavoured to warm her.

Again he gathered courage, and setting a few feet of sail, grasped the tiller, and strove fruitlessly to keep the boat to the wind; but filling fast with every wave, she laboured heavily; and now the tumult of the water increased; for right ahead rose Ibris, Fidra, the Lamb, and Craigleith, four little rugged isles that lie at the very mouth of the Firth. On Fidra stood a little chapel, and amid its ruins (which are yet visible) a myriad of gulls and gannets build their nests, and thick as gnats in the sunshine the sea birds were flying around its rocks on the stormy wind.

These four isles are but enormous masses of basalt; and against them the Firth and ocean poured their adverse tides in ridges of foam; then seeing the utter futility of attempt-ing, in such a gale, to weather them, the earl let slip his sail, and with a crack like the report of a musket, the braces flew through the blocks, and the nut-brown canvas vanished into the air.

He now resigned the boat to its fate, and expected every moment to see it dashed upon the isle of Ibris, or swept through the little channel that lay between it and the shore, and through which a strong current was running.

By a miracle they passed these isles, and were swept to the seaward.

"A ship! a ship! dear Archibald—look, my lord—a ship!"
exclaimed Sybil, as, with an expression of the most extravagant joy, she threw her arm towards it—"a rescue from the
jaws of death!"

Eagerly the earl raised his drooping head; and lo! a stately
merchant ship, with her large foresail set, but her topsails
and square spritsail close reefed, was standing northward
across the Firth from the harbour of North Berwick. Ashkirk
waved his grey plaid, and in a few minutes, by the altered
course of the vessel, it was evident they had been observed by
the mariners, who were seen crowding the high forecastle, the
still higher poop, and low waist, which was profusely covered
with religious emblems, and she had a large blue Scottish
cross painted in the centre of each of her sails.

"If it should be a ship of the king—one of Barton's fleet!"
muttered the earl; who, before her appearance, had been entertaining visions of founding a chapel to St. Bryde of Douglas,
on the bleak rocks of Fidra, if they escaped from their present
perils.

On came the ship, looming largely, with the water plashing under her gilded bows, which rose and fell on the heaving
water.

Manned by eight stout mariners, a boat shot off towards
the castaways, and in a short time the half-lifeless Sybil and
the earl, scarcely less exhausted, were conveyed on board
the strange ship, which proved to be the *Saint Adrian*, a
large vessel belonging to the monks of the May, who in those
days possessed many trading barks, and trafficked largely with
the Hanse Towns, Flanders, and the Baltic. Once safely on
board, the necessity of caution prevailed over the earl's piety,
and concealing the rank of Sybil and himself under feigned
names, he merely stated that they had been accidentally
blown off the coast.

A run of a few hours brought the ship to the Isle of May,
whose cliffs of dark green rock, with the seafowl floating in
clouds above them, rise precipitously on the east, and descend
to foam-beaten reefs on the west.

On this verdant island stood a chapel dedicated to St. Adrian,
who had been murdered there in his hermitage, by the pagan
Danes, in the year 870; near it stood a priory belonging to
St. Mary of Pittenween, the monks of which received the
rescued fugitives with every hospitality; and there necessity

compelled them to reside for several weeks ; for in that remote place there was seldom any intercourse with the main land.

Of all that was passing in the capital Sybil and her lover were happily ignorant.

Communication between places was slow in those days, and continued to be so for many a generation after. Even a hundred and fifty years later, the abdication of James VII. from the British throne was not known in some parts of Scotland until four months after the usurper had installed himself in his Palace of St. James.

CHAPTER L.

FALKLAND.

> ' Where Ceres gilds the fertile plain,
> And richly waves the yellow grain ;
> And Lomond hill wi' misty showers
> Aft weets auld Falkland's royal towers."
>
> RICHARD GALL.

AT the foot of the beautiful Lomond hills, lie the town and palace of Falkland—a palace now, alas! like Scotland's ancient royalty, among the things that were.

Many old trees in the neighbourhood, the remnant of the ancient royal forest of Falkland, still impart to the fragment of the palace an air both melancholy and venerable ; for it is but a fragment that survives, and makes one think with sorrow and anger of that remorseless system of absorption which is laying Scotland bare, and, year by year, sweeps southward some portion of her money and vitality. A day is coming, perhaps, when Holyrood, the last and least beautiful of our Scottish palaces, may be abandoned like the rest, if not to some ignoble purpose, at least to ruin and decay. The fine old pile of Falkland was successively engrafted on the ancient tower of the Thanes of Fife, by the third, fourth. and fifth Jameses, until it formed a quadrangle, one side of which alone survives the decay consequent to its desertion, and the neglect with which every feature of Scotland's ancient state is treated by the partial and (so far as *she* is concerned) penurious government to which she yearly hands over the six millions of her revenue.

Lying under the northern brow of a mountain. and so

situated as to be concealed from the sun during a considerable portion of the winter, Falkland is a quaint-looking place, removed from any great thoroughfare, and still inhabited by a primitive race of weavers, who have, generation after generation, followed the same trade as their fathers. Their dwellings are thatched; each cottar has his kailyard; and, with much of our old Scottish simplicity and contentment, they jog through life as their "forbears" did before them; and it is no uncommon thing to hear the older burghers quoting the learned sayings, and relating the quaint doings of his Majesty James VI., as if he still kept court amongst them.

Lying at the foot of the steep eastern Lomond, with its vanes and carved pinnacles overtopping the foliage of its old green copsewood, the ruined palace of Falkland, when seen from a little distance, resembles an ancient Scoto-French chateau, and the white smoke of its burgh-town (now diminished to a village), as it curls from the green foliage that fringes the glen, makes rustic and beautiful this solitary place, which was the scene of many a sorrow and many a joy to the illustrious line of our ancient kings.

The blending of the solid Palladian with the lightness of Gothic architecture, imparts to the fragment of the palace now remaining a singularly pleasing effect. On each floor of the most ancient portion there are six windows, divided by stone mullions, beautifully moulded, and between them are buttresses formed by foliaged columns and Tuscan entablatures, which support inverted trusses covered with the most elaborate carving. Designed by the same unfortunate architect who planned the Tower of James V at Holyrood, the western front is in the castellated style, and exhibits two finely proportioned round towers, between which is the lofty archway forming the entrance to what was once the grand quadrangle. In former times, this arch was closed at night by strong gates, and was defended by loopholes in the towers which flank it. Medallions in exquisite relief, the frequent initials, crests, and arms of James V and Mary of Guise and Lorraine, the gallant thistle with its imperial crown, deep panels with many a coat armorial, grotesque waterspouts and gothic pinnacles, with many an elaborate niche and beautiful statue, all combine to show that Falkland, if not the largest, was one of the most beautiful of Scotland's ancient palaces.

The gay cardinal had tarried on his way from Edinburgh,

having made a little detour round the Moss of Kirkforthar to visit a certain fair dame, who is still known in Fifeshire tradition as the Lady Vane; thus it was the forenoon of the 24th July, before he approached Falkland; and on the next night Jane Seton was—to die.

Matters of state, rather than her safety, had drawn the cardinal to Falkland. An ambassador was coming from England, and against that ambassador he had resolved to bias the mind of James V

Despite his ecclesiastical severity, and despite all that has been urged against the character of this determined prelate— our Scottish Wolsey—we must assert fearlessly, that he was as true a Scotsman as ever breathed: and *that* should go far to redeem his errors in the present day, when Scottish spirit and Scottish patriotism are somewhat scarce commodities. Beaton was the sternest, the most active and distinguished ecclesiastic of his time. The Protestant faith recoiled before him, and its defender "by the grace of God," Henry VIII. of England, laid fruitlessly many plots for his death by assassination; but Beaton's master mind circumvented them all. He was too sagacious, and perhaps too worldly, to be superstitious, even at that time; and whatever may have been his errors and his failings (and these, God wot, were not few), his steady maintenance of our Scottish honour and independence should ensure him some little credit, even in the present age. It cannot be denied that he viewed the tenets of the Calvinists with contempt, for he considered them as the natural enemies of Scotland, of her church, and of himself; hence his indomitable attachment to that church which he considered the only true path to Heaven, and whose tenets he upheld by death and fire, and sealed by his own blood.

Cardinal Beaton had a grave, firm, warm, and confident mode of expression, which was never used without producing a due effect on the frank and manly James V., who admired his lofty spirit, his keen perception in the field and cabinet, the vastness and profundity of his political projects; his staunch maintenance of the national dignity against English aggression, his avowed hostility to Henry VIII., which, with his bold and reflective character, together with his merciless persecution of all schismatics, combined to make him the first man in Scotland, and the most formidable prince of the church in Europe.

The summit of the steep and lofty Easter Lomond, which rises abruptly up from Falkland, was veiled in mist, but below the sunbeams glanced along its sides of dark brown heath, as the cardinal's train rode through the stately park of the palace. It was a glorious summer day; that morning a shower had fallen, and everything looked fresh and beautiful; the Rose-loch, with its flowery islets, where the snowy swan and dusky ouzel built their nests among the water-lilies, was glittering with light; and the old woods of Falkland and Drumdreel rustled their heavy foliage in the gentle wind.

James V sat in the recess of a mullioned window, and gazed listlessly at the summer landscape, which included the whole strath of Eden, the fertile and magnificent Howe of Fife, from Cupar to Strathmiglo, spread before him, bright with verdure and glittering with sunlight; but James was caressing a little dog that had belonged to his Magdalene. A ribbon encircled its neck; and, though worn and faded, he would not permit it to be removed, " for," as he said, " her dear pretty hands had tied it there." Again and again James looked sadly at the ribbon, and thus he saw neither the vast landscape nor the cardinal's glittering train, which (headed by Leslie of Balquhan) swept round the palace on the soft sward, and entered the quadrangle.

James was in deep mourning for the queen. His doublet, trunk breeches, hose, and rosettes were of black satin, lightly laced. His mantle was of black velvet, with a cross of white silk sewn thereon. All the ornaments of the apartment had been removed, save a large crucifix, which stood on the ebony table, and a portrait of his grandfather James III., whose golden locks made him the original of " the yellow-haired laddie," a song and air composed for him by his favourite musician Rodgers. The walls were covered with rich French tapestry, exhibiting landscapes embroidered with green and gold. The furniture was all of the darkest walnut wood, elaborately carved in the fashion of James III., and inlaid with mosaics from Florence—the thistle and the fleur-de-lis studded with their golden leaves the oak beams and deep panels of the ceiling.

Moulded, and cusped with stone, the gothic windows were filled with lozenged panes in leaden frames, stained with arms and devices; and the curtains which shaded them were of Venetian brocade.

Absorbed in his grief, the king for some time past had

abandoned all his favourite amusements—horses, hounds, hawks, music, and masquerading, had all been forgotten; for the livelong day he sat alone and brooded over the memory of Magdalene of France. This lethargy communicated itself to the court. The dogs lay sleeping in the yard; the hooded hawks winked and nodded on their perches; the royal standard hung still and unwaven on the gateway; the swans seemed to sleep on the loch; and the arquebusier at the archway leaned on the boll of his weapon, and dozed, while the pages, who had been playing with quoits in the park, slept on the sunny benches before the gate.

The approaching train electrified the inhabitants of the palace.

" The cardinal himself, or may the devil take me!'' cried little Lord Claud Hamilton, the king's favourite page, a saucy boy of sixteen, with a long feather in his cap, and a precocious moustache on his upper lip, as he sprang off the bench, and all the pages rushed into the palace to announce the intelligence.

The dogs barked, and the hawks screamed and flapped their wings.

The arquebusier shouldered his arquebuse, and turned out the guard; the arms rattled on the pavement; the drum beat; and the whole palace of Falkland was aroused like that of the sleeping beauty in the wood.

CHAPTER LI.

THE KING AND THE CARDINAL.

" Ne'er should be a vassal banished,
    Without time to plead his cause;
Ne'er should king his people's rights
    Trample on, or break the laws;
Ne'er should he his liegemen punish,
    More than to their crimes is due;
Let they rise into rebellion—
    That day sorely would he rue."

Rodrigo of Bivar.

" His eminence the cardinal, may it please your majesty.'' said the little Lord Claud, announcing the visitor. Setting down the lap-dog, King James started from his seat, and, without any further preamble, the tall and stately figure of

Beaton approached him. James knelt for a moment to receive his blessing, and then pressed his hand in silence.

The poor king looked paler, thinner, and sadder than when the cardinal had seen him last in Holyrood, beside that grave over which a nation mourned; but this did not prevent the perfect courtier from saying—

" I rejoice to see your majesty looking so well."

" It is not merely to flatter you have disturbed my sad retirement," said James, with one of his old smiles; " but welcome heartily, Lord Cardinal; I have longed to converse with you anent many things."

The little dog whined, and the king took it again in his hands to caress it, while the page withdrew, and the cardinal seated himself. " Here are splendour and magnificence," thought he, " saloons full of guards, and chambers full of courtiers, pages, lacqueys, wealth, and rank—but where is happiness?"

" My lord," said James, " I have many questions to ask you concerning my poor Vipont, the trial of the Lady Seton, and her mad brother's invasion of Inchkeith single-handed. Faith! he is quite a devil of a fellow! But first tell me what rumour is this, of cannonading in the river Forth, which reached me this morning."

" Oh, it was merely Monseigneur Claude d'Annebault, admiral of France, who has brought the new ambassador, escorted by eight frigates, which have anchored off the Beacon rock at Leith, where they saluted the Scottish flag, and the ships of Sir Robert Barton replied by their culverins."

" France," said James, sadly; " and this ambassador?"

" Will pay his respects to your majesty to-morrow."

" By my soul, I thought it was the Lord Howard with the fleet of my uncle Henry; and that he had come to blows with stout Sir Robert."

" A new ambassador from England is also coming hither."

" Ah!—and concerning what?"

" A league with Henry. Need I implore your majesty," said the cardinal, in the most impressive tones of his persuasive voice, " need I implore you to beware! He comes to crave an interview, that Henry may instil into your heart his own hatred of France and heresy to God."

" Hatred to the France of my Magdalene—the France of Scotland's old alliance! Nay, my Lord Cardinal, I need no warnings. There is a grasping and aggressive spirit in England, of which Scotland should beware ; but can my heretic uncle imagine that he will induce me to bring about here the same change of religion that he, by a single word, has wrought in England ?"

"He cannot; but he thinks that England will never be thoroughly Protestant, or at least opposed to Rome, while Scotland remains Catholic and true; thus his whole soul is bent on breaking that continental alliance which aggravates. as he thinks, our old and just hostility to his people."

"Is not the alliance broken ? My poor little Magdalene !"

"Thou hast most unwisely and unjustly permitted Sir David Lindesay of the Mount, George Buchanan, and others, to satirize the bishops and orders of clergy : yet, in the name of the latter, I have this day approached your majesty, to offer an annual subsidy of fifty thousand crowns from the rents of the kirk, to enable you to defend yourself more ably against England and her allies the Portuguese."

"This is well! the crowns are right welcome."

"An ambassador——"

"What—another ?"

"Is coming from Rome, with a consecrated sword, which with his own sacred hands his Holiness has whetted on the altar-stone of St. Peter—yea, whetted against the English people and their king, whose fleet is now out on the high seas to intercept the envoy and his gift."

"Indeed !"

"Thou seest how far these English will dare."

"If the ambassador is taken before Barton can reach the Downs, then, d—n England—we'll go to war with her! and here into your hands I commit the books written by Henry, and brought hither by the Welsh bishop of St. David's, wherein he defends so boldly the principles of Luther."

"Good ; I shall burn them on the first *occasion*, before my gate at St. Andrew's," replied the cardinal, as he threw them outside the chamber door to his page who waited in the gallery.

"With thy advice I broke off the meeting which Henry proposed at York ; so we may now prepare for war in earnest —a wa' that will pour forth our Scottish blood like water; but on the plains of our hereditary foe. The Scottish people should be ever like a drawn sword—the king being the hilt, his subjects the blade."

" Gladly will I head the army," said the cardinal, whose eyes sparkled.

" Nay," replied James, dryly, and with a smile; " should war be resolved on, I shall lead the army in person, as my predecessors have always done. What say the laws of the church on prelates leading armies ?"

" It is forbidden by the canons of John VIII."

" Sir Oliver Sinclair of Ravensheugh is a brave serviteur of the crown, and he may be my lieutenant-general."

" Sire, Sir Oliver of Ravensheugh is a mere laird, and no lord will follow him to the field. But we are well prepared for any emergency. The Earl of Buchan commands on the eastern marches, the Lord Sanquhar on the west; and the Lord Yester commands the middle. Their paid bands of horse and foot are ever on the alert. Our ships of war are not so numerous as they soon shall be; but they fully equal those of England in every respect, for the *Unicorn*, the *Salamander*,* the *Morischer*, and the *Great Lion*, are each as large, if not larger, than the boasted *Harry*. Then we have the little frigate taken by Sir Robert Barton from the Admiral Howard, in Yarmouth Roads."

'The *Mary Willoughbie ?*"

" Mounting twenty culverins, besides arquebuses and crossbows; and we have six others on the stocks at the New Haven. Including those which came from France," continued the cardinal, consulting his note-book, " we have one hundred and fifty pieces of cannon in our arsenal; and Scotland was never better prepared for war than at the present hour—nay, not even in the days of James IV "

" For which I thank the ability of your eminence," replied James, who cordially disliked his uncle Henry. " My father, James IV., entered England, whenever he chose, at the head of an army; but I, unfortunate ! have a stiff-necked people, who, much as they love me, will not fight unless their parliament tells them to do so ; and, worse than all, cardinal, the people--hate thee !"

" Faith, sire, they are ready to hate any one—the rabble."

" Impatient of thy power and princely offices, they think the royal authority will soon sink to nothing beneath the shadow of so great a minister. But what matters it ? I long

---

* These two were burnt by the English, in 1544.

A A

for war, because I am weary of life; while thou longest for it, simply because thou hatest the English. Lord cardinal, I am come of a doomed race," said James, with a shudder, as the vague terror that his house was fated to fall with himself came upon him, and a gloom spread over his manly brow. " I remember me of a prophecy that was made by a weird woman of Strathgryffe to Allan the great steward, 'that never one of his race should comb a grey head;' and fearfully hath that prophecy been verified!"

The eyes of the good king filled.

" Come my time when it may," he continued, " I know that my dear Scottish subjects will remember me long. Cardinal, my people call me *king of the puir*, and I am prouder of that .title than the thorny crown the Alexanders, the Constantines, and the Bruces have left me. The blessings of the poor and the lowly attend me when I walk abroad, without guards, without retinue, without arms. *I hate the nobles*, for they are ever ready to barter their country and their God for foreign gold: and Scotland's nobles will one day be Scotland's destruction. Pardon this honest vanity; but I feel that to reign in the hearts of my people is a great and glorious thing. There are many kings in Europe, but not one is called the father of his poor but James Stuart of Scotland. I am ever among them. I visit the highways and the byways, the gloomy streets, the miserable garrets, and the famished cottages where pestilence, or poverty, or tyranny have been. I know where misery is, or wrongs are endured. Disguised as a beggar, I discover them; as a king and a gentleman I alleviate or avenge them. The hard hands I have shaken, and the humble hearts I have gladdened, will serve me to the last gasp; and the ingleside where a king has sat and supped his kail with the gudeman, or toyed with his bairns, will long be remembered in tradition when the king and the clown are blended in one common dust. Thus I feel with joy that I shall go down to my grave at Holyrood with the blessings of my people, and shall be remembered long in the land, which my father bequeathed me from the Field of Flodden."

The king paused; and the cardinal, remembering his pledge to Father St. Bernard, deemed this the best opportunity for opening the trenches.

" Sire, this is a good and holy frame of mind," said he,

"and I sometimes see the truth of what Buchanan teaches (heretic and republican though he is) that impulses to good or evil are common to all ranks of men, and in these respects all men are equal."

" Cardinal, all men are equal, too, in the grave. Were a beggar laid beside me at Holyrood, he would be as great as me, and I no greater than he."

The cardinal could scarcely repress a gesture of impatience.

" I fear me," said he, " that the solitude of Falkland oppresses your majesty's mind ?"

" It is in solitude that God speaks most to man; and I, oh cardinal, have been in solitude since my poor Magdalene was lost," replied James, kindly caressing the little dog.

" She is not lost, but gone before."

" Cardinal," said James, looking up with his hazel eyes full of tears, " I pray for her daily."

" One act of mercy performed in her name and memory, will do more for the soul of Magdalene than a thousand prayers."

The king looked earnestly, perhaps suspiciously, in the dark and majestic face of Beaton, and said,—

" Your eminence actually means this ?"

" Most solemnly !"

" Then what is this act of mercy ?"

" A pardon for the Lady Jane Seton."

James's bright eyes flashed with fire, and he twisted his brown moustache with anger.

" Now, by the Holy Communion, this is too much; a pardon for the destroyer of Magdalene of France—for this daughter of a Douglas, and sought in this tower of Falkland, the very chamber where her sire the Lord John of Ashkirk, and her grandsire Sir Archibald of Kilspindie, detained me once a prisoner, with a guard of some five hundred Douglases, from whose surveillance I had to fly like a thief in the night! Lord cardinal, it is impossible."

It was seldom that James refused him a favour, and his eminence was piqued.

" There is but one day now, and I beseech your majesty to consider well."

" I *have* considered well. The Countess of Arran and I talked over the matter for three hours yesterday."

" The Countess of Arran !" muttered the cardinal; " women

—women! there is ever mischief where they are concerned. It would have been well had they been altogether omitted in the great plan of human society."

" And to lessen this evil to the public thou keepest a dozen of them shut up in the tower at Creich, all fair and jolly damosels," said the king, with something of his old raillery; " truly, lord cardinal, my subjects of Fife are much indebted to thee."

" I assure your majesty," said the cardinal, with increasing pique, " that to the best of my knowledge the whole trial and accusation hath been the prompting of revenge in Sir Adam Otterburn of Redhall."

" Of my lord advocate? Impossible! why, the man is virtuous as Scipio, and upright as Brutus."

" But in their excessive zeal, the judges have wrongly construed the depositions. I implore you to reflect; her death will make an irreparable breach between the races of Stuart and Douglas. War alone will not make a monarch illustrious. The splendour of valour and chivalry dazzles for a time; but a noble action lives in the memory of the people for ever."

" True; but beware, lest I deem thee a follower of Angus."

" I follow a Master who is greater than all the princes of the earth," replied the stately prelate, warming; " and the opinions of the poor worms that crawl on its surface are nothing to me."

" Is this the fag-end of some old sermon?"

" Sire, thou mockest me, and I have not deserved it of thee," said the cardinal, rising with dignity; " but let not the ambassadors of foreign princes see thy weakness, and how thou carriest thy vengeance even against a helpless woman. Was it for such an act as this, that Francis the Magnanimous sent thee the collar of St. Michael; that the great Emperor Charles, the victor of sixty battles, sent thee the Golden Fleece; and English Henry, his noble Order of the Garter? I trow not. Glory and virtue cannot exist without mercy— the first is but the shadow of the other two. In this case, close thy heart against hatred, and thou wilt soon become merciful, even to these hated Setons and Douglases. Sire, sire, to thy many good actions add but this one more."

" Cardinal, thou pleadest well; but sayest nothing of my gallant Vipont, my comrade in many a hairbrained French adventure. I would have given my best horse and hound—

even Bawtie, to have seen him confronting Abbot Mylne and his fourteen black caps ! But the sorceries, the vile sorceries of his lady——''

" Are about as true as the miracles of Mahomet."

" How ! Did she not confess them to the whole bench ?''

" True," replied the cardinal, with a smile; "when her tender limbs were being rent asunder by the rack."

" The rack ! the rack ! Oh, was it only on the rack she confessed these things ?''

" As thou, sire, or I would have done, under similar circumstances."

The king seemed thunderstruck.

" A pen ! a pen ! though a Seton, and a Douglas's daughter, too, I forgive her—she is saved."

A few hours after this, when the sun was setting on the East Lomond, Lewis Leslie of Balquhan, mounted on a fleet horse, with the pardon, signed, sealed, and secured in a pouch that hung at his waist-belt, was galloping through the parks of Falkland, on his way to the capital.

CHAPTER LII.

THE LAIRD OF CLATTO.

" Farewell Falkland, the fortress of Fyfe,
  Thy polite park, under the Lawmound law;
Sumtyme in thee I led a lusty lyfe,
  The fallow deer to see thaim raik on raw,
  Court men to cum to thee, they stand grait aw,
Sayand thy burgh bene of all burrowis baill,
Because in thee, they never gat gude aill."
Complaynt of the Papingo.

By the machinations of Redhall, and the subtle ability of Birrel, his messenger, there lay many a deadly barrier, and many a sharp sword, between the gallant Leslie and the city of Edinburgh.

The last rays of the sun had vanished from the furzy sides and green summit of the East Lomond, once called the Hill of the Goats, in the language of the Celtic Scots, when he quitted the park of Falkland, and struck into an ancient horseway, which, under the shadow of many a venerable oaktree, led him towards Kirkforthar; and soon the hill of Clatto became visible as it rose about five miles distant on his left.

At that very time a party of horsemen, well armed with lances, two-handed swords, and daggers, and wearing steel caps, with jacks of mail, rode round by the edge of a great and dreary peat-moss, which then lay at the base of Clatto Hill; and passing the old chapel of Kirkforthar, concealed themselves in a thicket of beech-trees, near an ancient mill, some moss-grown fragments of which are still remaining in the highway. There two of their number dismounted, and borrowing a couple of shovels from a neighbouring cottage, with the utmost deliberation, after carefully removing the green turf, proceeded to dig a *grave*.

Of these horsemen, fifteen were Redhall's own vassals, led, not by Birrel, for that arch-conspirator had reserved unto himself another part in this cruel and cowardly drama, but by Tam Trotter and Dobbie, both of whom felt their personal importance and dignity increased to an unlimited extent by this command; and Dobbie's cat-like visage wore a comical expression of martial ferocity, as it peeped out of the depths of a vast helmet of the sixteenth century.

The other horsemen were led by John Seaton of Clatto, the representative of a family which had long been infamous for its lawless acts and readiness to perform any outrage. The ruins of their tower are still to be seen at the south-east end of Lathrisk, as the parish was then named.

The old road from Cupar to Kinghorn passed through a gorge, called Clatto Den, and in the face of the mountain which overhung that narrow bridlepath there lay a cavern, the mouth of which was concealed, but whose recesses afforded a subterranean communication with the vaults of the strong tower above; and there the bandit family of Clatto were wont to rush out and butcher those unsuspecting persons who rashly passed through the den alone, either by night or by day. James IV., when travelling with two esquires, had narrowly escaped assassination there; but cutting a passage through, escaped, leaving one of his assailants minus a hand. In his ignorance of the owner's free propensities, the king took shelter in the tower, when finding that Seaton's sixth son was maimed, the guilt of the family came to light; the secret passage to the tower was discovered; the old ruffian laird and all his sons were hanged, save John the youngest, who, being then a child, escaped to figure on the present occasion.

Justice was more severely administered under James V ; thus, the exchequer of the Laird of Clatto being somewhat low, the accoutrements of his fourteen horsemen were rather dilapidated and rusty ; but, like their riders, the horses of his troop were fresh, strong, sinewy, and active. Having a plea anent meithes and marches with the Boswells of Dovan, the promise of a decision in his favour had drawn him from his lair on the dark errand of Redhall.

The cavern that lay below his tower is now concealed, by the impending side of the den having fallen down a few years ago, and choked up the entrance ; but the peasantry still point to the place with fear and abhorrence.

Rendered thirsty by a six miles' trot from the tower of Clatto, John Seaton, while his men were coolly digging a grave, went boldly to the mill of Kirkforthar and demanded a cup of ale, upon which the miller gave it submissively, and without asking a question, for he knew that it was as much as the lives of his whole family were worth, to ask on what errand the Laird of Clatto was abroad in the gloaming.

" Harkee, miller," said he, with a grin, exhibiting (between his bushy moustaches and beard, which almost concealed the cheek-plates of his open helmet) a set of those sharp white teeth, which bespeak a strong healthy fellow, who is often hungry but always happy : " Harkee, carle miller ; haud fast your yett, steek close your een and lugs, and steek them ticht, for the next twa hoors ; and tak' ye tent to hear nocht else, but ablins the splash o' your milnwheel, till the mune glints abune the moss."

" Langer, gif it please ye, laird," replied the poor miller, trembling.

" Ou, that will be lang enow ; but tak' tent o' my words ; hear ye nocht, and see ye nocht ; or I may come doon by the Mossend some braw nicht, and the mill o' Kirkforthar will be toom o' a tenant in the morning ; keep close by your ingle cheek, carle, for the chields o' Clatto winna thole steering."

And carefully wiping a few drops of ale from his cuirass, which was magnificently cut, worked, and inlaid with the most rare damascene work, he left the low thatched mill, and sprang on horseback.

Meanwhile Leslie was galloping by the northern base of the East Lomond. His horse was a strong and active roadster, which he had received from the king's master-stabler.

Fortunately he had taken the precaution to retain his armour, which was a ribbed Italian suit, studded with gilded nails, and on the globose cuirass of which his coat of arms were engraved. His gauntlets were overlapping plates, without finger-scales, thus, with the ample steel hilt of the sword, forming a double protection for the right hand. His arms were a long straight rapier and dagger, and at the bow of his demipique saddle he had a pair of firelock dagues, or pistols. The latter every gentleman carried when travelling; and the former were as necessary to a cavalier of the time as his feather or spurs.

His horse having lost a shoe, the delay caused by the necessity of having this loss repaired by a roadside Vulcan made the evening dusk before he approached the mill of Kirkforthar. The summer moon shone brightly in the blue sky, and clearly and strongly the outlines of wood and mountain rose against it.

On Leslie's right rose the steep Lomond; and on his left extended the vast moss, amid the wilderness of which many a deep pool of water lay gleaming in the moonlight. The district was desolate and wild; but no idea of danger or of molestation occurred to the mind of the solitary horseman, who rapidly approached the mill of Kirkforthar, where the dark foliage of some old beech-trees overshadowed both sides of the way; and where, save the cry of the cushat-dove, all was still as death. A red spark that glimmered among the trees, alone indicated where the mill lay.

Leslie checked the speed of his horse, as the road plunged down into this obscurity, which he had no sooner penetrated, than he found his course arrested by two bands of horsemen, who wheeled round their ranks from each side of the road, barring their passage by their levelled lances and uplifted swords. Well was it for Leslie that his fiery horse made a demi-volte, giving him time both to escape their weapons and unsheath his own.

"Make ye way, sirs! I am on the king's service!" he exclaimed, still backing his horse, but disdaining to fly. "Plague! the sheriff of Fife has surely bad deputies! But, whoever you are, rascals, the life of Balquhan for the best life among ye!"

And dashing spurs into his horse, he broke through the whole band like a whirlwind, thrusting one through the body, bearing down another, unhorsing a third with his foot; and passing unhurt through the hedge of steel around him, left

John of Clatto and his ruffians to deposit one of their own number in the grave they had dug so carefully in the thicket near the mill.

He heard behind a storm of oaths and outcries, mingled with the clash of arms, and the rush of galloping hoofs, as the horsemen broke tumultuously out of the wooded hollow, and poured along the highway, in fierce pursuit of him. Heedless of their taunts and shouts, Leslie spurred on : he had now been made aware that there were those upon the road whose interest it was to intercept him. On, on he went by the skirts of the desolate and moonlighted moss, and his anxiety was not lessened by the reflection that he had to pass by the Tower of Bandon, whose proprietor was his enemy; and in a few minutes he saw the square outline of this fortalice, with its angular turrets and grated windows, rising above the roadway, among a group of old ash-trees.

The pursuers were close behind.

Leslie was almost tempted to turn towards the moss; but to one so ignorant of its paths, such a measure might prove a certain death, while the risk was scarcely less in keeping near the barony of Bandon. Half-a-mile before him, on the open muirland, he saw several men on horseback, and his practised eye soon discovered that they were twelve in number, and armed, for the moonbeams were reflected from twelve helmets. Then his heart became filled with rage; for though he knew not why his path was thus beset, he knew that if he were slain, and the pardon was not delivered by a certain hour in Edinburgh, the unhappy Jane Seton, the promised bride of his friend, would assuredly be led forth to perish by a shameful and frightful death.

Many of the troop from which he had escaped, not less than twelve, perhaps, were scarcely a hundred yards behind him; now he saw as many more in front, and his forebodings told him they were the Lindesays of Bandon. At Balbirnie there stood an ancient cross, erected by a gentleman of the neighbourhood who had slain another at that place; and this cross (which is still standing) Leslie knew would afford him a sanctuary, if his pursuers were old Catholics; but he remembered that the Reformation had made vast progress in Fife, and that its proselytes would not hesitate to violate any sanctuary; so, instead of pressing onward to gain this bourne, supposing that the direct road might be beset still further

on, he turned abruptly to the left, and plunged down a narrow
strath, which led, as he was aware, towards the village of
Markinch and the strong castle of the Lundies of Balgonie.

A shout burst from the horsemen on the muir, on finding
that he thus avoided them ; and, joining with those who came
from Kirkforthar, they all urged their horses to the utmost
speed to intercept the gallant messenger. Many a dague
and petronel were fired after him, and he heard the balls, as
they whistled sharply past his ear, crash among the branches
of the wayside trees, or sink into the flinty road ; but after
some twenty or thirty shots, the firing ceased, as the troopers
rode in such haste that they had not time to reload their
firearms. On, on came horses and men at headlong speed,
rushing, a troop of evil spirits, along the moon-lighted strath ;
now dashing through coppice and underwood, then splashing
through a brawling mountain burn ; now sweeping noiselessly
over the yielding moss and heather muirland, and anon breast-
ing gallantly up the pasture braes : but Leslie, being mounted
on one of King James's best horses, fresh from its stall at
Falkland, though he did not leave his pursuers altogether
behind, was yet enabled to keep a considerable distance
between them and himself.

And now, upon a little eminence, the village of Markinch, with
its venerable square steeple of the eleventh century, arose before
him, and near it he fortunately left almost the half of his pursuers, floundering up to their girths in the deep and dangerous
marsh which encircled the village on every side save one.
Here to halt was vain ; for the unscrupulous Lairds of Clatto
and Bandon had men enough to sack and destroy the whole
kirk-hamlet ; so forward pressed the fugitive, intent on reaching the castle of Balgonie, or the ancient mansion of the
Beatons of Balfour, where the archbishop of St. Andrew's
and his nephew, the great cardinal, were born. On, on yet !
and he soon found himself among the woods of the Leven ;
dark and thick, old and stately, the beeches were in the full
foliage of July, and the dense old Scottish firs intertwined
their wiry branches with them : and now the river, broad,
deep, and hoarse, in the full fury of its summer flood, swollen
by a night of rain, lay rolling in foam before him ; and upon
its opposite bank rose, from a wooded eminence, the strong
and lofty donjon tower of that time-honoured, but now ex-
tinct race, the brave old Lundies of Balgonie.

Glittering in the moonlight, like a silver torrent, the beautiful Leven swept out of the far and dark obscurity of its foliaged dell, and in its crystal depths (save where the foam-bells floated) the sombre outline of the castle, with its turrets, and the steep knowe on which it stood, with all its waving trees, were reflected in the deep and downward shadows.

There were not less than twenty mounted spearmen still upon his track, and, lo! a deep, fierce current lay foaming in his front. On a level sward, Leslie paused with irresolution, and before plunging into the stream, surveyed it, but surveyed in vain to find a ford.

He looked back. The hill he had descended was covered with whins and scattered trees; and there, far in advance of their comrades, came four horsemen, who were now close upon him. With a fervent, almost a ferocious prayer to Heaven, he drew his sword and awaited them, for at the first glance he discerned that one of the four was his enemy Bandon, who, to breathe his panting horse, advanced leisurely at a trot before his three immediate followers.

"Guid e'en to thee, my light-heeled Leslie," said he, with a sardonic grin; "thou hast gien us a fast ride and a far one!"

"Beware, Bandon; I ride this night on the king's service."

"I ken that well."

"And still thou darest to molest me?"

"Yea, would I, though ye rode on the errand of the king of hell instead of that of the King of Scotland. Have at thee—for thou art a Leslie of Balquhan!"

"Beware, I tell thee, beware! My life is not my own to-night," cried Leslie, guarding the impending stroke of Linde-say's uplifted sword; "beware thee, till to-morrow only. I am the bearer of a royal pardon to Edinburgh."

"To thy grave alone thou bearest it!" cried the other, furiously.

Leslie parried the blow, and then replying by a thrust at the throat of his antagonist, before withdrawing his sword, bestowed a backhanded stroke at another horseman, who had covered him with his brass petronel, a stroke which rendered his better arm useless. Another deadly thrust relieved him of a second enemy, and then he had but two to deal with.

Round and round him they both rode in circles, but by point and edge he met their cuts and thrusts; till observing that Bandon was close to the edge of the stream, he suddenly

put spurs to his horse, and charging him with the utmost
fury, by a blow of his foot forced him right over the bank,
where his horse fell upon him, and with its rider sank into
the river. There Lindesay became entangled beneath the
animal, which snorted, kicked, and plunged so violently,
that he was swept unresistingly away with the current and
drowned. Next morning the miller of Balgonie, on finding
his machinery stopped and the dam running over, was horri-
fied to see a horse and its rider, in armour, lying drowned
and jammed under the great wooden wheel of his mill.

A volley of petronels from the bank above Leslie left him
no time for further defence or reflection ; and with a shout of
defiance he leaped his horse boldly into the stream, and, regardless of the bullets which plunged into the water incessantly, exerted every energy to gain the opposite bank, using
his hands and knees, half swimming, to relieve the animal of
his burden (which was not a light one, the rider being in
armour) : keeping its dilated nostrils above water, and yielding a little to the current, he ultimately crossed, successfully
and securely.

With flattened ears and upraised head, the broad-chested
steed breasted gallantly the foaming water, and snorted with
satisfaction on feeling the firm ground at the opposite side,
where Leslie uttered a shout of triumph as he scrambled up
the bank, and thus by one bold effort found himself free.

Oaths and cries of rage resounded among the woods behind,
and many a trooper urged his horse towards the brink, but
their hearts failed them, and not one dared to cross the deep
and rapid Leven, by which their intended victim had been
saved and their leader swept away before their eyes. The
lieutenant of the king's guard now leisurely examined the
knees of his horse and the girths of his saddle ; looked to
his sword-belt and spur-leathers ; recharged his petronels,
and glanced at the pouch which contained the pardon of
Jane Seton. He then wiped his sword and remounted.

Reflecting that the river was now between him and his
enemies, that he was several miles out of the direct road, and
that (except the ducking) he was not in the least the worse
either of the ride or the combat, he resolved, instead of seeking shelter either at the place of Balfour or the castle of
Balgonic, to push onwards to Kinghorn.

The ramparts of this stronghold, which are eighty feet in

height, were glimmering in the moonbeams, above the tossing foliage, as he descended into the hollow which lies to the south of it, and then turned westward, little thinking that the ferocious Laird of Clatto, with Dobbie, Tam Trotter, and some fifteen horsemen, in anticipation of such a measure, had long before wheeled off to the right, and were pushing on the spur towards the Kinghorn road to intercept him.

CHAPTER LIII.

THE FIGHT AT INVERTEIL.

" Let us hasten to receive them,
Placing in the foremost ranks,
Those who bear the arquebuses ;
Let the horsemen next advance,
With the customary splendour
Of the harness and the lance."—CALDERON.

WITH a heart divided between emotions of rage and exultation, the fugitive messenger rode towards Kinghorn.

The aspect of the tract of country he crossed is very different now from what it was in those days. Many places that are bare pasture lands were then covered by dense thickets of natural wood ; other places, that are now fertile and arable, were covered with broom and whins of such gigantic size that horsemen might have been concealed among them ; while all the straths and glens were filled with the water which then flowed through innumerable mosses and marshes. Streams, which were then impassable rivers, have now, by the drainage of the land and other agricultural improvements, shrunk to mere burns or mountain runnels ; while those which were then burns and trouting streams, have in many instances totally disappeared ; and waters, such as those of the Boathouse bridge in Linlithgowshire and the Eden in Fifeshire, which had ferry-boats plying upon them, are now scarcely deeper or broader than a wayside drain. Thus, when, to save time and the trouble of riding round in search of fords or bridges, the brave Leslie, all heavily armed as he was in Italian plate, boldly swam the winding Loctie and the Ore, near the Spittalcots, he performed two gallant feats, for *then* those waters foamed in deep, broad currents between torn and rugged banks, with a breadth and force very different from what they exhibit in the present day, even during the fury of a winter speat.

But before he had entered on the moss and moor that lay between the Ore and an old mansion named the Temple Hall, which then belonged to the knights of Torphichen, the waning moon was disappearing behind the hills, and shed a cold, pale light on the dreary waste that spread before the solitary rider.

Having lost all traces of the ancient drove-road, which had guided him thus far, Leslie walked his horse forward with caution, to avoid the peat-bogs and pitfalls that now surrounded him; while, impelled either by the dreariness of the solitude on which he was entering, or by some vague presentiment of danger, he narrowly observed every bush and hillock as he approached, and listened for any passing sound.

The moon seemed to rest on the summit of the distant hills, the solid outline of which rose blackly against the blue sky. Light clouds were floating across her surface; but a clear white light was shed along the countless ridges of the muir—the moss-covered roots of an old primeval forest—which resembled the waves of a motionless sea.

A sharp, low whistle on his left, and somewhat in advance of him, made Leslie look in that direction; and he saw the moonbeams reflected back from something bright, that too evidently was not moss-water, but polished steel; while two or three light puffs of smoke curled upward, showing where the matches of petronels were being blown for active service.

The moss was full of armed men!

" Fool that I was not to byde me at Balgonie !" thought Leslie, as he put spurs to his jaded horse, and quickened its speed to a hand-gallop. By his devious route he had now ridden fully twenty miles, over a frightful tract of country, full of steep hills and rocky glens, deep morasses, brawling torrents, and hills covered with forest and brushwood; he had forded three swollen rivers, and thus, like himself, his horse was already becoming exhausted.

" Hollo, Balquhan !" cried a mocking voice; " whither so fast ? Is your lady-love sick, or is your house on fire ?"

A shout of derisive laughter, together with the explosion of four long petronels, followed this remark; and Leslie became aware, from the sudden bound and snort of pain given by his horse, as it shot away like the wind, that the poor animal was wounded; one bullet had penetrated its near flank, and another had grazed its ears.

" The devil! 'tis quite an arquebusade! But I am getting used to such music to-night," thought Leslie, as he gave a wistful glance at the Temple Hall, which was not far off. All property which belonged to the Knights of St. John in Scotland afforded a safe sanctuary from debt and danger, and did so until a recent period; but Leslie knew too well that his present pursuers would violate the holiest shrine between Cape Wrath and the English frontier to reach him; and that he had nothing to trust to but the blade of his sword and the heels of his horse; for by the number of ambuscades, prepared in every direction, it became evident that his enemies, whoever they might be, were bent on his destruction.

Tall lances and bright helmets flashed in the moonlight, as the dark forms of many a horse and man arose from behind the heather knowes and clumps of moss and whin to join the chace; and Leslie found that again the ferocious John of Clatto, with all his band, was riding on his trail.

Though the balls which had wounded his horse caused a great effusion of blood, they acted as spurs of fear and pain to accelerate its speed; and Leslie soon heard the shouts, the clank of arms, and the rush of galloping hoofs growing fainter and fainter with every bound that his fierce strong charger made. The banks of the Ore, the desolate muir, and the grey Temple Hall soon vanished in the distance; and he saw the spire of Kirkaldy, and its long and straggling town, rising on the left, from the low flat shore of the Firth, which lay beyond it, glimmering in the last light of the moon, and bringing forward, as from a brilliant background, the innumerable roofs and gables, clustered chimneys, and turretted edifices of the venerable burgh. Near him rose the hill and castle of Raith, where Sir John Melville, the great Reformer, dwelt; and nearer still, embosomed among summer woods, lay the Abbotshall, a seat of the abbot of Dunfermline, the site of which is still indicated by an old stupendous yew that grew before its gate. Right in the fugitive's front lay the broad green links of Kirkaldy, and the glittering estuary, with the black rocky promontory of Kinghorn jutting boldly into its waters.

The strength of his horse was failing fast; its eyes were blinded, and its head was drenched in the blood flowing from its wounded ears; and he felt certain that, to turn from his straightforward course, to seek shelter in the neighbouring town, would only serve to exhaust it more. He knew well that the brave animal was dying beneath him, for with every convulsive bound of its foam-covered haunches, the blood-gouts gushed forth upon the sandy turf.

Balwearic, in older times the birthplace of the wizard, Michael Scott, was left behind; and now the hoarse brawl of the Teil—a flooded torrent—rang before him. He gave his horse the reins, and furiously applying the spurs, keeping his head back and his bridle-hand low, as he urged it to the flying leap. Lightly it rose into the air, cleared the stream, with all its banks of rock and bed of stones, but reached the opposite side only to die; for the noble horse sank down with its forehead on the turf, and after making more than one fruitless effort to rise, rolled heavily over, stretched out its legs convulsively, and with that mournful cry which few hear, but a horse alone can give, expired.

At that moment, with brandished swords and panting steeds, six horsemen appeared on the opposite bank; and the exhausted Leslie knew that nothing now remained for him but to sell his life as dearly as possible.

He was now but two miles from Kinghorn, and after all his exertions, he felt how hard it was to die; and reflected that, with his life, the pardon of poor Jane Seton would be futile, or forfeited, as she would inevitably be put to death before additional tidings of the king's favour came from Falkland. The very excess of his bitterness gave him a superhuman courage, and alone, on foot, he resolved to confront them all; but in doing so, to use every stratagem.

With the rapidity of thought, and unseen by them, he threw himself close beside his dead horse, the body of which was greeted by a shout of fierce exultation.

"Awa and on!" cried John of Clatto; "for gif ance he wins the burgh o' Kinghorn, the tulzie will be owre, and I sall tyne my plea anent the meithes and marches. On, on, ye fashious fules; hae your naigs nae mair mettle than the mules o' monks?"

Leslie grasped his drawn sword with both hands, and as the Laird of Clatto leaped the Teil, with one fierce back-handed stroke hamstrung his horse the moment its hind heels alighted near him.

With a tremendous curse, this ferocious rider with his steed tumbled prone to the earth; and as they fell, Leslie sprang up, and by the same daring manœuvre, unhorsed another, and slew him as he fell. Then rushing to the summit of the bank, that he might have all the advantage the acclivity could afford him, he stood resolutely on his guard. The rest of the band were yet far off, and by their leisurely trot it was evident that their horses were breathless and blown. "John of Clatto!" exclaimed Leslie, as he engaged that person furiously, each swaying his sword with both hands on the hilt; "thou unhanged thief and son of a thief! now—now shalt thou receive the coward's reward."

"Fause coof!" retorted the other, with one of his ferocious laughs, as with a deadly coolness and activity he dealt his thrusts, while the force of his parries announced that his eye was sure, and his wrist was of iron, as he hewed away with his long and trenchant sword; "Coward? ha! ha! 'tis a name never kent by a son o' auld Symon o' Clatto. Strike weel and surely, my bauld Balquhan, for by God and Macgriddel, I sall handsell thy braw harness in thy hettest bluid."

"Dog! it hath been handselled by the swords of better men!" exclaimed the furious Leslie, as by a single sweeping stroke his heavy sword beat down the guard of his adversary, breaking his blade like a withered reed, and, cleaving his helmet through the very cone, killed him on the spot. A curse was half uttered by its quivering lips, as the body fell backwards over the bank, and lay half merged in the water of the Teil. With his great natural courage exasperated to a terrible pitch by the knowledge that he must inevitably perish at the hands of these cowards, Leslie fiercely met the horsemen as they leaped the stream, and in succession fell sword in hand upon him. A shower of blows rang upon his tempered helmet, his eyes swam, and, amid a cloud of fire, it seemed as if a myriad of men and horses had assailed him, and as if as many swords were ringing in his ears, and flashing before his eyes.

He was soon beaten to the earth, and several men sprang from their horses to despatch him, when the shots of two petronels were heard, and two assailants sank heavily, dagger in hand, beside him, tearing up the grass with their hands and teeth in the agonies of death. A rush of horses followed, and Leslie found himself free!

Clatto's men had fled; and a young cavalier stood before him richly clad, with three tall feathers in his bonnet; he was mounted on a superb black horse, and in each hand had a petronel, from the barrels of which the smoke was curling. The drawn swords of his six mounted attendants were gleaming in the bright twilight of the July morning, for day was already glimmering over the far horizon of the German Sea. The features of this deliverer were noble, but delicate ; his eyebrows and closely-clipped moustaches were coal-black, his lips were red, and cut like those of a woman, but his large dark eyes sparkled with courage and animation.

"Now, by Heaven, 'tis our loving cousin and clansman, Balquhan!" he exclaimed ; for in those days, "when old simplicity was in its prime," every man of the same name in Scotland was designated *loving cousin.*

" Sir Norman Leslie," said the lieutenant of the guard, as with thankfulness and respect he greeted the gallant Master of Rothes, the son and heir of the earl, his chief, " thou hast saved me from a cruel and bitter death ! what do I owe thee ?"

" Two brass bullets at a similar juncture."

" May it never happen !" said the young baron, to which the master replied with a reckless laugh, in which his followers joined.

" Balquhan," said he, " this gentleman is your cousin—my uncle, John of Parkhill.   Here are three men and two hamstrung horses lying on the grass !   By St. Mary ! my true Leslie, thou hast this night handled the sword as if it had been thine own invention."

" Anent what hath all this been ?" asked John Leslie of Parkhill, an elderly gentleman, sheathing his sword.

" Heaven only knows, sir," replied Leslie, as he caught the bridle of a riderless horse, and leaping into the saddle began to examine the petronels that were attached to it.

" They seem to have found you a rough jouster !"

" I am riding on the king's service, with a pardon for the Lady Seton."

" The Lady Seton !" they all repeated, in varying tones of astonishment and satisfaction.

" Yes, sirs, I am bound for Edinburgh, and have been thrice beset by horsemen, and thrice have swum a river, the Leven, the Ore, and the Lochtie !"

" Sheriff of Fife, what say you to this ?" said Parkhill to Norman Leslie.

" That it shall be looked to, and that sharply," replied the young Master of Rothes, as he replaced his pistols in the holsters ; "a harmless rider, a messenger of mercy on God's own service, to be molested thus !"

" Besetting the highway—'tis a capital crime."

" Perhaps John of Clatto (for it was he) thought that messengers of mercy, or of Heaven, seldom ride in coats of mail."

" To thy spurs, Balquhan, and on !" said the master ; " the poor dame Seton will assuredly fall a victim to the malice of the Hamiltons at midnight—*this midnight*, for see, the day is dawning. They were setting the stake, and tearing the faggots, on the castle bank, as we left Edinburgh by the West Port last night."

" I go to the *King's Horn* hostel," said Balquhan ; " would I were there, for I am drenched like a water-dog, and well nigh wearied to death. Farewell."

" Take ye care, sir !" cried John of Parkhill.

" Come now, you jest, my cousin," said the lieutenant, jocularly ; " does a Leslie ever fall from his horse ?"

" I only mean, beware thee while at Kinghorn, and keep thine errand secret ; for there are several men of the house of Arran in the burgh, and their nags are stabled at the very hostel thou hast named."

" Nay, nay, uncle of mine," said the fiery Norman, " no Hamilton would arrest the pardon of any woman ; then how much less that of a lady of high name and gentle blood !"

" Nephew Norman, we know not the tricks of which the Lord Arran and his faction are capable ; and to whom shall we attribute this treble molestation of our cousin, the king's messenger ?"

" True—adieu."

" Adieu, sirs, with many fair thanks for this good service."

They separated, and Balquhan rode on, feeling in his heart that he could slay all who bore the name of Hamilton ; for the idea that Redhall was his evil genius never once occurred to him.

Those Leslies who had saved him were, nine years after, among the conspirators who slew the great cardinal in his castle at St. Andrew's, less to avenge the frightful deaths of the early martyrs, than as the hired assassins of Henry VIII.; and twenty years after, the fiery Master of Rothes died in the battle of St. Quentin, fighting valiantly at the head of thirty Scottish gens d'armes.

CHAPTER LIV.

THE KING'S HORN.

" Be yet advised, nor urge me to an outrage;
Thy power is lost—unhand me."
Edward the Black Prince.

THE clock of St. Leonard's tower struck three as Leslie entered the old burgh of Kinghorn, and rode through its steep and straggling, narrow and deserted wynds, to the hostelry with which the reader is already acquainted. Though a vast sheet of pale light was spread across the east, sunrise was nearly an hour distant, and the whole town was silent as some ruined city in a desert; every door was closed, and not a single face appeared at the rusty gratings of the street windows.

It was not until after much noise and vociferation with the drowsy peddies and stable-boys that Leslie gained admittance to the inn-yard, and from the yard obtained ingress to the mansion, where his whole aspect excited fear and suspicion. His armour was dimmed by water and rusted with dew, cut, hacked, and bloody; the straps were loose and torn; he was feverish and excited; and there was a stern determination in his bearing, as he carefully took his petronels from his saddle-bow, and, ordering the attendants to look well to his horse against the time of the ferry-boat sailing, entered the first empty chamber that offered itself.

He looked first to the pardon, which, notwithstanding his frequent immersions, was dry and secure; he looked next to the wheel-locks of his fire-arms, which he laid on his pillow ready for immediate service. Thereafter, he examined his apartment. The window was two stories from the ground, and a harrow-grating amply secured it. Like all others in that age, the door was secured by a multiplicity of bars, all of which he shot into their sockets; and thereafter piled behind them all the available furniture—a great oak almrie, a meal-girnel, four chairs, and, lastly, the table.

He then took off his armour, and found that his clothing was almost dry.

" Come, 'tis well," thought he; " save three pricks and four scratches, I am not a whit the worse, and have still six hours for sleeping and dreaming of merry Marion."

And after assuring himself that he could not be taken in flank either by trap-door or sliding-panels, this brave and wary soldier threw himself on the bed, and behind his barricades slept soundly and securely.

The ferry-boat was to sail at ten in the forenoon.

Half-an-hour before that time Leslie awoke, and sprang up quite refreshed. His first glance was at his barricade.

"Oho! I have been beset even here!" said he, on perceiving that the door had been forced, and the heavy almrie and girnel pushed about three inches inwards, by which the chairs had been overturned, thus baffling the assault, as their fall had scared the intruders.

The sun was shining brightly on the river, and the merchants were opening their booths and displaying their goods under the stone arcades of the principal wynd.

"This devilish piece of paper is likely to cost me dear. I find I must still be guarded," thought Leslie, as he minutely examined his iron trappings, stuck his petronels in his belt, and, with his sheathed sword under his arm, descended to the hall of the hostel and ordered breakfast, but without mentioning the attempt which had too evidently been made to disturb his privacy. Looking sharply around, he seated himself at the arched ingle, where a comfortable fire was blazing, and above which appeared a rude fresco painting, which represented St. Leonard, the patron of Kinghorn, surrounded by a swarm of cherubs in the forest of Limoges.

"Quick, old hag—my breakfast," said the traveller to the landlady; "let your rascals look well to my horse, or look well to themselves if they fail."

The gudewife—a slipshod and sullen-looking crone, with a nose and chin that were nearly meeting, a coif of the time of James III., and an enormous bunch of keys—being a little scared by the stern and distrustful aspect of Leslie, who sat down by the table with his helmet on, left a buxom damsel to attend on him, and retired. The young soldier found that his indignation could no way extend to her substitute; for her cheeks were blooming and her eyes sparkling with health and good-humour; she wore a very piquant, short linen jacket, short petticoat, and her brown hair tied up in a blue silk snood, after the fashion of unmarried girls in Scotland.

A fowl, from among several that were roasting on the spit, cheese, cakes, and honey, cold beef, eggs and bacon, with the addition of ale, formed then, as now, the staples for breakfast, and while it was preparing, Leslie solaced himself by whistling the *March to Harlow*, and by means of a piece of half-burned wood, decorating with an enormous pair of moustaches each of the fat little cherubim which surrounded the figure of St. Leonard; an amusement which neither the gudewife nor the diminutive gudeman, whom she seemed to rule with " a rod of iron," dared to interrupt.

" This is for thee, my rosy belle," said Leslie, kissing the plump cheek of the waiting-maid, after breakfast, " together with this French crown ; as for the rascal, thy master, and the hag, thy mistress, let them rejoice that I have not burned the house about their ears, were it but to smoke out certain Hamiltons, who, I am assured, are within it. Thou hearest me, fellow ?" added Leslie, as he passed the landlord, who, sheepishly, and bonnet in hand, was standing at the door of the house.

" I do, gude sir, but understand ye nocht."

" Nor do I you ; but wherefore was my door forced last night — this morning, I should say — eh, thou rascally Filer ?"

" I swear to ye, noble sir, that, under God, I ken nocht o't," replied the poor man, with the utmost earnestness.

" It may be so, for I see that, in thine own house, thou art but Joan Tamson's man, as the saw has it."

The landlord gave a sickly smile.

" Harkee, gudeman, is thy better-half a Hamilton ?"

" To my sorrow, I ken she is, sir," sighed the hosteller, in a whisper ; " for never one of her name enters Fife, between the East and West Neuk, without lying a week and mair at the *King's Horn*, and never a bodle will she take for the lawing, for they are a' her cousins to the hundredth degree, and will scarcely let me call my soul my ain."

" Then, which of her worthy cousins are here now ?"

" Sir John Hamilton of Kincavil," replied the gudeman, setting his teeth on edge.

" And his room ?——"

" Was the next to yours."

" Hum ! indeed ; and this Sir John extends his patronage to you, gudeman—eh ?"

" He pays like a prince, to be sure ; for he had a fancy for my gudewife in her young days."

"He is a man of taste, Kincavil!" said Leslie, smiling; "but where is my horse?"

"My son holds it at the gate."

"How, the devil! is that tall fellow thy son?"

"No," replied the little man, with a grin of bitterness; "he is the son of my wife."

As Leslie slipped another crown into the hand of the host, and was turning away, a tall, swaggering cavalier—the same whom Roland Vipont had fought with and wounded near the Water Gate, as related in a preceding chapter of this history—brushed past him somewhat unceremoniously.

"Sir John of Kincavil!" said Leslie, with angry surprise.

"Well, sir! at your service," replied the other, swelling up his rose-coloured doublet, and resting his left hand in the bowl-hilt of his long rapier, as he assumed a lofty attitude.

"Is this to be taken as an insult?"

"It is to be taken just as you please," replied the other, twirling his moustache.

"Take care, sir. I am on the king's service."

"Does that entitle you to occupy the whole doorway of the *King's Horn?*"

"We are not equally armed—you see my coat of mail."

"Oh, that matters little—behold!" said Kincavil, as he opened the collar of his doublet, and displayed below it a mail shirt of exquisite workmanship. "We are quite equal, my friend," he added, clapping Leslie with easy familiarity on the shoulder, while a number of armed men, who, by their badges, seemed to be his followers, crowded ominously round them.

"Kincavil!" said Leslie, scornfully, "the next time thou touchest me, pray do so with a hand that is gloved."

"A thousand pardons," sneered Kincavil, whose insolence was as proverbial as his deadly skill and admirable sword-manship, "I forgot thou wert *Falkland bred.*"

This was a phrase of the time to signify foppery, affectation, and refined manner. Leslie's eyes flashed with rage, but he leaped on his horse, saying—

"I know your object well, villain, to involve me in a brawl; but you will fail. Taunt me as you please, I will not draw my sword unless I am molested; and woe unto them who do so. To-morrow I will be a free man, and at noon will await you, braggart, on the sands of Leith, near the chapel of St. Nicholas, where seek me if you dare."

A shout of derisive laughter followed him; but, stifling his rage, he heard without heeding it, and in ten minutes more was on board the ferry-boat, which he endeavoured to beat across the river against a strong head-wind.

CHAPTER LV.

THE BLUEGOWN.

*" Bless your honour, noble gentleman,
Remember a poor soldier."—Auchindrane,* Act I.

WE have now the events of only one night to relate, but these events are of the most varied description.

Father St. Bernard, the kind and philanthropic old clergyman, had prayed fervently that the cardinal, among the multitude of public matters that weighed upon his master-mind, would remember his promise; and as earnestly had he implored Providence to inspire the heart of James with more than his usual mercy, that a pardon might be granted to his poor penitent, for so a confessor always termed those under his care in the olden time.

Every hour after the cardinal's departure he had sought Sir James Riddel, in the hope that tidings had arrived from Falkland: but hour after hour passed; two weary days, and two still more weary nights elapsed; but no tidings came of the pardon, and no messenger.

Could the cardinal have forgotten his promise? or had he failed in his purpose? The poor friar racked his invention with suggestions, but hope died as the evening of the fatal 25th drew on; and Father St. Bernard was forced to confess to himself that she was lost; for the hour at which the ferry-boat usually arrived at Leith was long since passed. From the rampart of David's Tower he had seen it pass the Beacon Rock and enter the harbour, and with a beating heart he waited, but Leslie never came.

He saw the people already gathering in groups and crowds to witness the frightful execution, and the old man wept as he sought the knightly governor of the fortress for the last time, and turned away hopeless.

"Thou good and pious priest!" said Sir James Riddel, touched by the old man's grief, and warmed into a betrayal of his own religious opinions, "why art thou not, as I am, a Protestant?".

" Thou good and valiant soldier! why art thou not, as thy father was before thee, a pious Catholic and true ?" asked the prebend, in the same tone, as he descended from the citadel towards the gate of King David's Tower, to visit Jane Seton for the last time. At that moment the great copper bell of the fortress, which swung at the gable of a tower called the Gunhouse, tolled the hour of nine.

She was to die at twelve.

Among all the snares laid for the destruction of Leslie, and to obtain the document he carried, Birrel had reserved unto himself the last, and, failing others (which he scarcely believed could fail), the surest, and perhaps most deadly plan for his death.

The road between Edinburgh and Leith was then a lonely, and (after dusk) unfrequented place. Between the monastery of Greenside, which lay at the foot of the Calton Hill, and almost in the very gorge that descends to the foot of Leith Wynd and the Port St. Anthony, there was not a house or edifice save a little wayside oratory ; and thus between the Loch and village of Restalrig on the east, and the old house of Roystoun, near the shore, on the west, all the country was open pasture-land, links, or muir, with here and there a small farm-cot at its boundaries, with a kailyard and oxgang of arable land, watered by the runnels that ran into the river Leith, which then was twice, and in some places four times its present breadth, covering great pieces of holm-land at Comely-bank, and the Canon-mills, where the old scaurs that overhung its margin are still visible.

The few persons who traversed Leith Loan on the 25th July, 1537, could not have failed to remark a man wearing the well-known garb of a Bluegown, one of the privileged mendicants of the charitable olden time. These received a new cassock on every anniversary of the king's birth, together with a penny for every year of his age. The Bluegowns of the Stuart times seldom received much, as the monarchs of that gallant race were generally cut off in early life by war or misfortune ; but the Bluegowns of later years, when kings have been more economical of their persons, have been wont to hail the day of his birth with joy ; and those of George III. drew more shillings Scots than ever did other beadsmen since the society was instituted.

With a black cross sewed on the breast of his long blue cassock, as an emblem of sorrow for the late queen's death, and his face concealed in his hood, the beggar, who appeared lame in his left, and also lacked the right hand, which was hidden in the folds of his ample garment, sat by the way-side; and whenever a person passed (which was very seldom) he either begged for alms in a low peevish voice, or repeated an *Ave* to show how very good and pious he was, notwith-standing the hardness and humility of his lot in life.

This beggar was no other than Nichol Birrel. The hood concealed his yellow visage, his cunning eyes, and matted beard, as the blue gown did a shirt of mail, a belt full of daggers and pistolettes, and his right hand, which grasped a dague, loaded with two brass bullets. Being certain that Leslie could not escape all the ambuscades prepared for him in Fife—where Dobbie and Trotter, with fifteen troopers from Redhall, John of Clatto, with his lawless men, Lindesay of Bandon, with *his* ruffians, and lastly, Kincavil, a deadly fencer and professed duellist, were all induced, under various insti-gations, and from various motives, to beset his path—Birrel kept but a careless watch, looking upon Leslie as one whom he had not the least expectation of seeing.

It was one of those beautiful evenings which are common to July; and, at a part of the road which afforded him a view of St. Anthony's Port, he lay on a grassy bank, where a thicket of hawthorn overhung the roadway, which was then but a narrow, deep, and rugged bridle-path.

Behind lay Lochend and the house of the Logans, perched on a rock; before him stretched the level muir and pasture-land which joined the Firth at the New Haven, which had been constructed by James IV., all an open and unenclosed prairie; and across it shone the hot rays of the sun, then sinking towards the dark peaks of the Ochil mountains. The air was close and still; there was no sound but the casual rustle of a leaf, or the "drowsy hum" of the mountain bees as they floated over the verdant grass, and the air was filled with the perfume of the fragrant hawthorn.

The whirr of the nut-brown partridge, as it rose from among the long grass; the voice of the blackbird and thrush, as they sang joyously among the gnarled branches of an aged thorn-tree; the solitude of that place, though it lay between a fortified capital and its thriving seaport, had no charm for the disguised ruffian, nor could they wile him from his deadly purpose.

Thrice that day had horsemen left the Port St. Anthony, and thrice had the assassin grasped his weapon with the fellest intent. The first was the young Lord Lindesay, and he dashed up the Loan with all his feathers waving, and embroidery glittering in the sun. He had not gone to Falkland, because the Lady Margaret Beaton remained at her father's archiepiscopal palace. The second rider was a knight of Torpichen, in his black mantle, with its white cross; and the third was Sir Andrew Preston, of Gourtoun. None of these were in armour, as Birrel knew Leslie was sure to be, so, at their approach, his hand three times relinquished the pommel-butt of his daguc. Each, as he passed, threw arms to the supposed beadsman, and disappeared in the gorge that led towards the city.

Mid-day passed, and heavily the still sultry afternoon lagged on. The Bluegown took from his wallet some bread and cheese, a roasted fowl, and flask of usquebaugh, and proceeded to dine under the bower of sweet hawthorn.

While engaged in this pleasing occupation, the sound of voices and hoofs arrested his attention; he looked up, and beheld a young lady, with several attendants on foot and on horseback, dashing straight towards him across the level muir, from the east, and continued a rapid gallop until she gained the opposite bank of the roadway, where she reigned up her horse, and looked hurriedly around.

She was a tall and stately-looking girl, with bright blue eyes, a blooming complexion, and a profusion of flaxen-coloured hair, that fell in heavy ringlets from under her scarlet velvet hood. She was richly attired; and as no one could then be completely dressed for company, for riding, or promenading, without a leather glove, with a hawk sitting thereon, she bore one on her right hand, while her left grasped the reins of her fiery and spirited horse. The bold and beautiful girl was Marion Logan of Restalrig.

A cloud rested on the usually happy aspect of her broad fair brow, and her sunny smile was gone, for her thoughts were full of the misfortunes that encircled her friend Jane Seton. Two men on foot ran after this party with all their speed; strapped over his shoulders, each had a square frame of green-painted wood, on the spars of which sat a number of hawks of various breeds, accoutred with plumed hoods, through which their fierce red eyes were glancing, and having little silver bells, which jangled with every motion. Around their necks were silver collars, whereon was engraved the legend—" Zis gudelie hawk belangis vnto ye Knicht, Schyr Robert Logan of Restalrig and zat ilk."

" Dost thou see nothing of my father ?" asked the young lady of her attendants.

" I see nocht, madam," replied an armed horseman, who wore the Logans' livery, and had their crest embroidered on the sleeve of his pyne doublet, " but this auld Blewgoon may. Harkee, puir body," he added, addressing the disguised Birrel; " saw ye oucht o' a gentleman in a suit o' plum-coloured taffeta, wi' a white ostrich feather in his bonnet ?"

" Had he a blue mantle ?"

" Yes."

" Laced wi' siller pasements ?"

" Yes—the very same."

" Riding——"

" A roan-coloured horse."

" With siller bells at his bridle ?"

" Yes—yes !"

" Well, then, I havena seen oucht o' him."

" God confound thee ! thou wordy carle, dost laugh at us ?" said a falconer, angrily, as he shook his long pole threateningly towards Birrel, whose natural insolence could not omit this opportunity of indulging itself a little.

" 'Twas an evil day this to come forth hawking," said the young lady; "the day on which my dearest friend is to die——"

" Now haud ye, Lady Marion," said the white-haired falconer, cautiously; "for ken ye not, that noble though that lady be, it's far frae being safe or wise to claim friendship wi' her at the present time. If Sir Robert turned towards the Corstorphine marshes——"

" I hope not, for they are both dangerous and deep," said the young lady, looking westward, and shading her large blue eyes with an ungloved hand, that was white as the hawthorn blossom. " God knoweth how sadly and unwillingly I came forth this day; and it was but to please him that I forsook our little oratory for the saddle. Thou knowest my father, Steenie—— ?"

" Aye, the auld knicht winna thole steerin," replied the old falconer, as he also shaded his sunburned face with a large brown hand, and scanned the glowing west.

" 'Tis very strange, Steenie—where was my father seen last ?"

"Galloping over the mains, after his favourite hawk, madam," replied a servitor, touching his bonnet.

"Mercy ! if he should have mistaken the way, and fallen into the moss of Craigcrook."

"Toots, bairn !" replied the falconer; "he kens owre well the dreich hole where, last Lammastide, we saw young Adamson o' Craigcrook gae down in the floe, baith horse and man, till even the point o' his lance vanished ; and there they lie yet !"

"Look, Steenie ; is not yonder bird a hawk ? See how it ascends from Pilrig—up and up !"

The tramp of a horse arrested their attention.

A man on horseback, who left the gate of St. Anthony, came galloping from Leith ; his armour flashed in the setting sun, and a cloud of dust rolled under the hoofs of his horse.

" In harness," said one falconer.

" He is not Sir Robert," muttered another.

"St. Mary ! how he drives his horse !" exclaimed Marion Logan.

"It is Leslie of Balquhan !" growled Birrel, ferociously, as he grasped his dague. "Now, curse be on my folly, that sent not this butterfly, with her attendant wasps, hence on a fool's errand."

The continual glitter of the rider's armour showed that he was richly accoutred, and the incredible speed at which he rode announced that he was nobly mounted. In three minutes he reined up his horse at the foot of the bank, where, with a glow of pleasure beaming in her beautiful face, Marion Logan recognised him.

"Lewis Leslie !" she exclaimed, and kissed her hand frankly to him, for he was her favoured lover.

"At your service, my dear madam," replied the officer of the arquebusiers, bowing to his very saddle. Birrel's eyes were starting from his head, as he strained his ears to listen.

" From whence ?"

" Falkland."

" Falkland ! and why so fast ?"

"Oh, rejoice, my dear Lady Marion ! I have here the king's gracious pardon for Jane Seton ; she is saved ; and one hour from this will see her free !"

The brave young cavalier shook the pouch that hung at the girdle, which Marion had embroidered for him.

"The *pouch!* d—nation wither my tongue, for it alone hath made this woman and her varlets loiter, instead of hurrying them away," said Birrel, as he limped past, and posted himself a few hundred yards farther off.

"Pardoned!—Jeanie pardoned!" said Marion, whose blue eyes sparkled with tears and joy. "Can it be? Lewis, Lewis, how much I love you at this moment! For this good news I would let you have a pretty kiss, but for all those eyes about us. Oh, what blessed tidings for us!"

"Still more blessed for her, I think, and for my brave friend Vipont too! 'Tis all the cardinal's doing; his good offices have achieved this.

"The cardinal!"

"Faith, it is thought dangerous for a woman to accept a favour at his hand. But dost think, Marion, that such a gallant man will permit such an outrage upon youth and beauty as Abbot Mylnes' sentence to be carried into effect? No, no! Long live the cardinal, say I. But what a night I have had of it, Marion! nearly fifty scoundrel horsemen have tried to intercept and cut me off."

"Hamiltons?"

"Hamiltons or hell-hounds, I know not which," replied Leslie, angrily; "but I have given more than one the Leslie's lick, and have escaped them, blessed be Heaven!"

"My brave friend! 'tis like thee."

"Lady Marion," said Steenie, the falconer, approaching; "Sir Robert is in sicht; see yonder, by the bank o' the loch. Noo he flees his goshawk at a heron," he added, as the burly old knight was seen to rein up his horse, and let the bird slip from his wrist. "So—brawly cuisten off! See, the hawk is noo aboon, and noo it stoops to the quarry!" said the venerable servitor, as he waved his broad bonnet; "it's a true bird o' my ain training. See how the sly heron turns up her belly—ah, the lang leggit devil! she seeks to use baith claws and bill; but the hawk passes—noo the hawk tak's her at the sowse, and strikes doon. No; it's these Milan bells, they're owre full i' the sound, and spoil the bird i' the mounting. See, my brave bird plumes her—noo, doon for a croon, like a bow-shot!"

The birds disappeared among the sedges.

" Farewell, Leslie," said Marion ; " on, on to the Castle, and delay not your errand of mercy. But come soon to see us ; you know well how lonely we are on the Rig yonder, and how well my father loves you. How rejoiced he will be to hear these tidings of our poor Jeanie Seton ; my faith, he will drink a deep tankard to-night, for it was but to shake off the dolours he rode forth to-day, and neither to hunt nor to hawk."

" Then, my Marion, to-morrow, at noon, I will stable my horse at Restalrig."

" We will expect you."

" My dutiful commendations to the good knight your father, and meantime, adieu !"

With eyes full of affection they kissed their hands to each other, and separated.

Whipping up her tall and fiery horse, with her veil and her long tresses floating behind, Marion, by one flying leap, made it clear the roadway and gain the summit of the opposite bank, from whence her lover saw her (followed by her attendants) cantering across the fields towards the sheet of water which her father's old manor-house still overhangs. She went at a pace which put the poor falconers, who were on foot, to their mettle ; and the young Laird of Balquhan, despite his anxiety to deliver the important paper, which had thrice nearly cost him his life, checked the speed of his charger to look after the retiring figure of her he loved.

He little knew what that brief pause and that last glance after Marion Logan were to cost him.

Birrel's heart danced with joy to see him loitering, while the young lady and her armed servants were fast retiring beyond ear-shot.

The sun had now set, and the dun blaze of light it shed from the western hills across the muir of Wardie was dying away. The whole Loan, from the round arch of St. Anthony to where it disappeared under the brow of the Calton, was deserted. The Calton then was bare, bleak and desolate, or covered by waving furze, broad-leaved fern, or dark whin ; so was the opposite bank, which sloped up to the height of eighty feet, and was crowned by the chapel and little hamlet of St. Ninian, the smoke of which was visible as it ascended into the calm air from the cottage chimneys.

This knoll was named Moultrays Hill ; and between it and

the Calton the narrow road plunged down into the gorge, where the church of the Trinity lay, passing, on the left, the Carmelite Friary of the Holy Cross at Greenside. Standing forward in strong relief from the dark shoulder of the hill, and against the blue sky, the broad boundary, the stone cross and crow-stepped gables of this edifice, were visible from a group of old elm-trees, under which Birrel posted himself. As Leslie approached, the assassin shrank under their branches, drew his hood over his face, and gave a last glance to the wheel-lock of his dague.

A leer of cruelty and malice shone in his eyes, and a horrible smile curled his square lips, as, with a limping step, he approached the centre of the path.

" Gie a plack or a bodle, sir, to help a puir carle that hasna broken a bannock these three days and mair.''

" Try the Carmelites, my good friend," replied Leslie, riding hurriedly on.

" The Virgin bless you, noble sir," continued Birrel, hobbling after him ; " mind a puir soldier of Sanct John, that lost his arm fighting under the Preceptor at the battle o' Haddenrig ?''

" An old soldier ?'' said Leslie, checking his horse; " by the three kings of Cologne, an old soldier shall never in vain seek alms of me ! Here, thou cunning carle, and say an *Ave* for me to-night ;'' he stooped to feel for a coin in the purse which hung at his sword-belt ; then Birrel drew forth the arm that appeared to be maimed, and levelled his dague full at the ear of the unsuspecting horseman ; his glistening eye glared along the burnished barrel ; the wheel revolved ; a bright flash, the sharp report, and a low groan followed.

Leslie rolled lifeless in the dust beneath his horse's hoofs, with the blood flowing from his mouth. The muzzle of the dague having been but three inches from his helmet, two brass balls had passed through his brain, and as the wretch turned him over, he saw in a moment that the hapless cavalier was far beyond the skill even of John of the Silvermills, the Scottish Galen and Avicenna of his age.

Birrel gave one ferocious glance around him to see that none were near ; he gave another at the glazing eyes turned back within their sockets, the relaxed jaw and noble features of Leslie, which in a moment had become livid and horrible, as in the pale twilight they stiffened into the ridigity of death.

From the dead youth's glittering baldrick he tore away the leathern pouch, and rending it with his dog-like teeth (for he was in too great haste to undo the. buckles), drew forth the pardon, and fled towards the city. . .   .

And there on the road the slain man lay, with the dew and the darkness descending upon him; and he felt not one and saw not the other.

Near him, and under the dark shadow of the hill, his horse was grazing quietly, as if nothing had happened.

An old and withered elm, with scarcely a leaf, but a sprout of one of those which lined the way, still remains in the middle of the street to mark the site of this catastrophe.

Slowly the moon rose above the Calton; the long shadow of the hill grew less and less as the orb soared up, until its beams fell on the white visage of the murdered man, and on his polished armour. A black pool lay near, and mingled with the dry summer dust.

The horse, with its bridle trailing, was still grazing placidly at a little distance.

Some crows were beginning to perch on the elms, or flying round the body with screaming beaks and flapping wings.

They came from an adjacent gallows on the Lea.

CHAPTER LVI.

THE TEMPTATION.

"Oh! Harpalus (thus would he say),
Unhappiest under sunne;
The cause of thine unhappy day
By love was first begunne;
As easy 'twere for to convert
The frost into a flame,
As for to turn a froward heart,
Whom thou so fain would'st frame."
Reliq. of English Poetry, 1557.

THE clock struck in the steeple of St. Giles. Jane heard it distinctly in her prison. Each note was wafted towards her as with a solemn note of lamentation, from the vast and broad mouth of the great church bell. Every stroke vibrated painfully through her heart.

It tolled *eleven!*

She had but one hour to live. One hour! and then——

C O

A loud and palpable murmur, as of many thousand voices, arose in the city; her heart for a moment died within her; she covered her face with her hand and burst out into a passionate prayer to Heaven—for she knew that, encompassed as she was by sorrow and despair, and engirdled by that strong tower, the eyes of God were upon her.

The broad flame of a torch, which was stuck in a tin sconce that hung upon the wall, cast a livid glare on the bare masonry of the vaulted chamber, on her kneeling figure, on her dark and disordered hair, on her white hands, and her whiter forehead.

"Roland, my Roland! thou believest these things of me? Oh, I could never have believed such of thee!"

A shudder passed over her, and it seemed as if her heart would burst. She had received a reply to that paper so cunningly devised by Redhall, the letter signed and addressed to Roland, when suffering under the agony of an artificial thirst; and that answer, which showed that *he* believed in her guilt, as confessed to him under her own hand, had crushed her spirit more than all the tortures, inflictions, and insults she had so unmeritedly undergone.

Signed by Roland, but written generally to his dictation by the chaplain of the fortress, an old Dominican friar, the reply was sad and sorrowful, full of regrets for her sore temptation to evil; her bitter humiliation, blended with expressions of satisfaction at her contrition; and closing with a pious hope that the sincerity of her repentance and the severity of her earthly punishments would save her from those of another life, solemnly committed her and her works to Heaven.

This unlover-like epistle, the embodying of which poor Roland, in his sorrow and confusion of mind, had left entirely to the ingenuity of the friar, appeared to Jane Seton the crowning stroke of her misfortunes. It left her nothing more to wish for, to hope for, or to bind her to the earth. Her Roland had cast her off!

For the thousandth time she drew forth the letter and gazed upon the name his hand had traced; now the paper was sorely worn and fretted by her tears. She read it over for the last time, sighed bitterly, and placed it in her bosom.

"It shall go with me to—death," she said, for, with a shudder, she reflected that by the mode of that death *even a grave* was denied her; and there was something frightful in the idea that a week, a month, or a year hence, no one could point to a stone slab or a mound of earth, and say that she whom they remembered, or loved, or regretted, lay below— for the ashes of a witch were scattered to the four winds of heaven.

"Oh, my Roland, thou hast abandoned me! but God will not abandon me!"

"Look up, Lady Jane," said a mild voice.

She raised her eyes suddenly, but without surprise or terror, for neither of these emotions could affect her now; absorbed in her own thoughts, she had not heard any one enter.

The stately figure of Redhall stood before her. He wore a court dress of black velvet, with a white cross on his mantle, as mourning for the queen. His close-clipped beard and black moustache were trimmed with their usual care, but he seemed the shadow of what he was. His grave and noble features were pale as death, and, like her own, were attenuated to excess, but by mental rather than bodily suffering (though he had endured both), and their pallor contrasted strongly with his large, dark eyes, which were so full of light, and yet were so expressive of sorrow. Every part of his dress was black, save the shoulder-belt or scarf that sustained his silver-hilted sword, and which, like the band of his bonnet, glittered with silver embroidery and precious stones, that, ever changing in the light of the torch, sparkled with a thousand prismatic hues. He held his bonnet respectfully in his left hand, and its long black feather drooped on the floor.

"Look up, Lady Jane," he repeated; and Jane arose, with horror and aversion expressed in every feature of her face.

"You have dared to come hither? Is it to gloat upon the sorrow you have made—the poor being you have devoted to destruction—a being who never harmed you? Oh, Redhall! Redhall! what a plot of hell thy plot hath been?"

"Dost thou think me cruel?"

"Cruel?" reiterated Jane; "didst thou say *cruel?*"

"Hear me, hear me! for there is but little time, as in an hour thou art to die."

"St. Giles's bell has told me that. Begone, begone! wretch, thou horror and abomination! Leave me to prayer, I implore thee! to prepare for that death thy guilt, and not mine own, deserves."

" Lady, if I am guilty, love hath made me so."

" Love !"

" Turned to hatred by vengeance and despair ! Thou didst permit me to love thee, and then destroyed the dear hopes which that permission excited. Then I hated thee and loved thee by turns; but hatred became the strongest, and I swore that never should another man wed thee. Taunted, I longed for vengeance, but on thy lover rather than on thee—yes. even as the thirsty long for water, and thou art here ! It was my destiny, perhaps, to accomplish thy death, and if so, my doom and thine must be fulfilled. Thy death ! and yet —yet I could love thee, even after all that hath passed—even loathing life as I do. To the storm of passions which so lately agitated me, a horrid calm has succeeded, and I can look back to the events of the last few weeks as one saved from shipwreck might do to the boiling ocean he has escaped. Thou lookest on me with horror ; yet knowest thou not, Jane, that God put much of human kindness in my heart, and, until I met thee, knew thee, and most fatally loved thee, I was good and gentle, save when men wronged or thwarted me. My capacities for love and hatred have but two extremes. Thee, I could have loved for ever ! Thy beauty is like that of the rose, or of the lily, born to wither, to lose form and perfume ; but my love would have endured unto death, and would have passed away but with life alone. Taunted and repulsed by thee, mocked by my friends as thy plaything, vanquished by a mischance in combat with Vipont, who can wonder that the poison of hatred entered my heart ? that it rankled there, and grew strong, distorting every object to my mind and eye ? Life lost the few pleasures it possessed. I thought of nothing but destruction, and felt that I was predestined to accomplish thy death, for I felt (he added, in the very words of the Jew) that if it would feed nothing else, it would feed my revenge —that revenge for which I lived alone ! Oh, Jane, this is all the truth, the sad, the solemn truth. Is it not frightful to think that in less than one hour thou wilt have to die ?"

" The victim of a madman—a fatalist ! Just Heaven ! will this be permitted ?"

" Heaven has left you yet one chance of life," said Redhall, as his eyes lighted up with a wild gleam, and drawing from his bosom the pardon, which had cost the gallant Leslie so dear, the pardon which was spotted with his blood, and which bore the royal signature, " *James Rex*," and a seal, the well-known private signet of the king, he held it before her startled eyes. " Be silent, and listen. Your life and death are in my hands. This is a free pardon from the king, granted yesterday at Falkland. Save thyself, not one in Edinburgh knows of its existence, and, without it, you die in half an hour. Oh, ponder well on this," he added, with eyes that eloquently expressed his sorrow, triumph, eagerness, and fear, as with one hand he grasped her, and held it before her with the other, but at arm's-length, lest she might snatch it from him. " Swear before Heaven, the Mother of all Compassion, before the Apostle John and all the saints, to accept me as thy husband; to banish Vipont from thy mind for evermore, even as he has banished thee from his, and into thy hands I commit this paper, and thou art saved. Reject me, I consume it at this torch, and thou art lost!"

He held the paper within an inch of the flaring torch.

" Sir Adam Otterburn," replied Jane, firmly, and with dignity; " I have nothing now to lose but a life that thou hast made hateful to myself, and abominable in the sight of Scotland—a name thou hast covered with such shame that even he who loved me most abhors it now. Thee! the wife of thee, thou murderer and assassin of the gallant Bombie!—thou destroyer of my honour, and the honour of my family! Oh, no!—welcome, a thousand times more welcome are the grave, the gallows, the stake—death under any form, than an alliance so detested. Out upon thee, coward, demon, and tempter!" and in the wildness of her scorn and hatred, she smote him on the mouth with her clenched hand.

" Then be it so!" replied Redhall, with a horrible laugh, as an emotion of rage rose within him. " Thou shalt die as one accursed by God and man, with the flames around thee, and the yells of an assembled city in thine ears, as the meed of thy unmerited scorn. Proud and unrelenting woman, unshriven and unabsolved, even by the fantastic rites of a church that is falling, thou shalt die, with the bitter conviction that all thy sorrow, and all thy tears, and all thy pain are futile, as the wings of the demon are over thee."

And with these terrible words he thrust the pardon into the large flame of the torch, which consumed it in a moment.

Jane uttered a wild cry as he did so; for an instant the love of life had dawned strongly in her bosom.

Again she sank on her knees in despair, and covered her face with her hands; when she looked up, Redhall was gone. He had departed so silently, that she might have deemed the whole interview a vision, but for the ashes of the pardon which were floating about her.

One small fragment, which the flame had left undevoured, lay on the floor; but there was a fiery circle within it—a circle that spread and reddened—spread—spread, until it reached the edge, where it died away in blackness, even as her momentary hope had died.

At that instant she heard footsteps approaching her chamber door, and there was the knell of death in their echoes.

CHAPTER LVII.

THE LOCH.

> " And quickly Walter seeks once more,
>   With eager steps, the ocean's shore;
>   And lingers on impatient there,
>   The appointed hour—now do and dare!
>   He eyed the high and rugged steep
>   Which overhung the foaming deep."
>
> *The Convent of Algarve.*

To avoid the vast crowds that were assembling on the Castle-hill, and before the Port of the Spur, Redhall left the fortress by the postern gate; and though the descent from thence to the foot of the cliffs on the west was steep and extremely dangerous, even in daylight, he plunged down from rock to rock, grasping the hazel-bushes and wild willows in his progress, until he reached the old and narrow horsepath which led from the King's Meuse and the tilting-ground towards the venerable kirk of St. Cuthbert the Bishop.

Breathless and exhausted by the rapidity of his descent down these pathless and precipitate rocks, and overcome by the load of agony that pressed upon his heart, he sank upon the turf, and lay there for a few minutes motionless.

Above him, the fortress and its stupendous rocks towered away into the obscurity of the midnight sky; before him, spread the ripening corn-fields, divided by thick hedgerows; and in the hollow on his left lay the kirk of St. Cuthbert, with the dim lights twinkling in its aisles, and shedding through its Gothic windows an uncertain radiance on the adjacent water; for it had then two minor altars, the great lamps before which were never extinguished until 1559. The sky was starless, and the moon had gone down enveloped in clouds. The great square tower of the church, a monastic relic of the eighth century, built by the Culdees of Lothian, stood boldly, in black outline, against the dark gauzy vapour that shrouded the north; a rising wind moaned through the marshy hollow, shaking the old woods which overshadowed the Kirkbraehead, and rippling the waters of the loch, which almost washed the castle rock.

There was a voice of reproach in that midnight wind; and from the passing clouds many a grim face seemed to peer upon the unhappy wretch, who, at the foot of the rocks, lay below the postern, listening to the fierce beating of his tortured heart.

And save its beating, and the moaning wind, all seemed deathly still around him. The Guelder roses and the wild violets filled the air with perfume, though the dew of midnight rested on their leaves.

The appearance of Jane, the expression of her eyes, and the familiar sound of her voice, had recalled his first passion in all its strength; and before it, for a time, revenge melted away like summer mist. He contemplated himself with horror; but *now* to save her, would be to cover his own name with disgrace and contumely; and to avow his master-villany and deep-laid vengeance, though it might snatch Jane from the jaws of death, would but restore her to the arms of Vipont, and afford that hated rival a triumph which could not be contemplated with calmness. The agony, the repentance, the fear, the shame, the abhorrence of himself, and the chaos of his mind, were frightful.

A flame shot across the sky.

It was but the sheet lightning of summer flashing redly behind the afar-off hills, and showing the dark woods of Coats, and of the Dean that waved between.

For a moment it illuminated the dark hollow where this repentant sinner lay, and gave him a startling shock; for he thought of the funeral pyre that was soon to blaze before the gates of the fortress which overhung him.

" Jane, oh Jane!" he cried, incoherently and aloud; " oh, thou whom I could have worshipped with the adoration of an

idolater, but whom I have destroyed with the blind fury of a
fiend! Can I not save thee without burying myself under a
mountain of disgrace as well as of misery? And for this
paltry tremor thou art left to die! thou, so beautiful, so innocent, so pure in spirit and so single in heart! The icy
sweat is again on my brow, the iron in my heart—for all thine
image is before me, as it was once, so full of smiles and pride,
of bloom and high-born loveliness, as on that night at Holyrood. . . . Thy voice is ever in my ear, thy name on my
lip! . . . Oh, misery! oh, for one hour of oblivion! . . ."

He sprang up, and slowly descending the narrow path by
the base of the castle rock, below St. Margaret's Tower, approached the loch, but without any defined object. The
stillness of its dark and almost waveless water had something
in it that attracted him involuntarily towards it.

The loch was then full and the water deep.

" Coward that I am!" he thought; " one bold plunge and
all would be over."

The temptation was a strong one: there was a rushing in
his ears, a whirling in his brain, and a fearful palsy in his
heart, which seemed to stand for a moment still; he looked
around him hurriedly, and no one seemed near.

But a single star was visible. like a watching eye, and its
rays were reflected in the motionless water under the solemn
shadow of the impending rocks.

At such a moment the human mind is like a bullet which
a hair may turn aside.

He took one step backward, and was about to make the
desperate leap, when the sound of voices and footsteps arrested
him; and, like one surprised in a guilty action, he shrunk
behind a clump of wild hazel bushes, and thus was saved from
the committal of another heavy crime.

Two men, whom he had not before observed, now appeared
on the narrow pathway below. One was mounted, clad in
half armour, and by the ostrich feather which waved in his
bonnet, appeared to be a gentleman; the other was on foot,
and led a horse by the bridle.

Redhall heard the name of *Vipont*.

It called up all his evil passions and bitter memories. It
restored him to life and energy of purpose. He put his hand
on the hilt of his sword, and listening, approached them
stealthily.

CHAPTER LVIII.

THE LAW OF THE SWORD.

" Dost thou, O traitor! thus to grace pretend,
Clad as thou art in trophies of my friend?
To his sad soul, a grateful offering go!
'Tis Pallas, Pallas gives this deadly blow.
He raised his arm aloft, and, at the word,
Deep in his bosom drove the shining sword.
The streaming blood distained his arms around,
And the disdainful soul came rushing through the wound."

Æneid, XII.

ACCORDING to the tenour of his last conversation with his unfortunate lieutenant, when they supped at the *Cross and Gillstoup*, Sir John Forrester had not forgotten the safety of their mutual friend, Vipont; and being well aware that the hostility of the king's advocate had no boundary but death, while the cruel assassination of Leslie, the scarcely less cruel visit of Redhall to Jane, and the destruction of the pardon in David's Tower were taking place, he had prepared everything for the escape of Roland from the fortress in which he was confined.

Aware that the attention of the city without, and of the garrison within the castle, of the governor, of the provost, and all the authorities, was wholly occupied by the preparations for the execution of the first sorceress to be burned in Scotland, this gallant gentleman wisely considered the hour of midnight as the most fitting time to achieve the liberty of his friend.

Aware that our agile acquaintance, Master Sabrino, could climb like a squirrel, he had been employed by Forrester as the principal agent in the adventure.

From the fields on the opposite bank of the loch Sabrino had been shown the tower and the window of the apartment wherein Roland Vipont was confined, and to that window, at nightfall, the active negro had clambered with wondrous bravery and skill; and had introduced to the tower a pair of saws formed of the sharpest steel, and a strong cord, of great length, knotted with loops for the hands and feet, by which he was to descend some twenty yards of the most dangerous part of the rocks; while Sabrino, who could cling to their perpendicular front as a fly does to the wall, was to descend without other aid than his own black paws and tenacious feet.

At the very time that Redhall approached, and in the two figures recognised the captain of the king's guard and the old servant of Roland Vipont, the latter had just removed (by the aid of his saws) the last bar from the window, and trembling with eagerness, was preparing to descend the rope-ladder which Sabrino, with a broad grin on his vast mouth and in his shining eyes, fastened to the remaining stumps of the stanchels.

Who the kind person might be that had furnished and sent the bold page with these means of escape, Roland had no means of ascertaining; for, being tongueless, poor Sabrino was mute as a fish; and of all his innumerable signs and nods, winks and unearthly chuckles, the master of the ordnance could make nothing.

A plain wooden pric-dieu formed part of the furniture of his apartment. On his knees Roland Vipont sank into it, and on a lock of Jane's hair fixed a long, a passionate, and indescribable gaze of love and sorrow, and then uttered a brief, emphatic prayer.

"Innocent or guilty, I will see her once again, or die in the attempt," said he, placing the ringlet in his bosom, and preparing to descend.

The passage of the window was easily accomplished; and reaching the base of the tower, he found himself upon a narrow ledge of rock; the chill wind rushed up past him, and voices were faintly borne with it from below. There, the cliff on which King David's Tower was built is somewhat impending, and from the broad battlements a plumb-line might, without meeting an obstacle, be dropped to the depth of nearly two hundred and fifty feet, to the pathway on which Sir John Forrester and Lintstock stood on that night. If dropped one yard beyond the rock, it would have fallen into the waters of the lake.

Roland's heart expanded in his breast; for to his active spirit, which had writhed in captivity, there was almost a relief in the new energy of action.

He descended with equal rapidity and boldness, for he was utterly regardless of life; and this very carelessness was perhaps his salvation, by affording him the means of achieving that in which the timid or the wary man would inevitably have failed. The wild wallflower, the strong docken blades, the long grass, the longer and more tenacious ivy which grew in the clefts of the rocks, or overhung their lichen-spotted brows, afforded him the means of descent after he had passed the bottom of the cord.

In the darkness and obscurity of the night, he could not have been seen even from the windows of Wallace's Tower or the Constable's Tower, but now their inmates had all deserted them; for the entire population of the castle were crowding on the battlements of the great peel, the eastern curtain, and the spur, which overlooked the place of execution, the preparations for which were being made on the south side of the Castle-hill.

He had one risk of discovery alone; for, not eighty yards from where Forrester awaited him, the pathway was crossed and defended by the Well-house Tower.

Those of our readers who may have perused our "Memorials" of the ancient fortress, may remember how frequently we had occasion to mention this now ruined ravelin.

Built over a fountain, the waters of which fed the loch, this strong square tower rose within six feet of the enormous perpendicular cliff sustaining David's Tower. A massive wall, having an archway with an iron gate and loopholes for arrows and musketry, secured the narrow path which led to St. Cuthbert's Church on one hand, and ascended the Castle-hill on the other, passing between the tower and the rock. The guard here had the treble duty of protecting the well, the private roadway, and the city wall of A.D. 1450, which enclosed the Castle-hill at its northern base. The tower was entered from the inside of this flanking wall by two doors, which, by a stair partly hewn in the rocks, led to the first and second floors. The upper was at that time always occupied by a party of arquebusiers, and the light of their guard-fire streamed redly through two narrow grated windows upon the still dark bosom of the loch, which washed the north wall, and rolled away in obscurity towards the east end of the city.

Then the wide ravine that yawned between the southern hill of the Modern Athens and the giant ridge of Auld Reikie, her *mither-town*, was an impassable gulf. Now the waters have disappeared, but the tide of life ebbs and flows in their place. A stupendous mound and a lordly bridge now cross that hollow glen where the fountain welled which David, " by consent of his earls and bishops," gifted to God and the Holy Cross, and where the queen of Robert III. held her brilliant tournaments ; and now, the red gleam of the furnace, the hiss of the steam-engine, the clink of hammers, the hum of voices, and the roar of the railway train rise up from its depth to scare the woodcock, the snipe, and the wild coot who come as of old to seek the bed where for ages the water lay.

Once only did Roland pause in his perilous descent, to assure himself that he was not seen. Dislodged by his foot, a stone gave way, and as it bounded from the rocks he heard it plash into the loch, far, far down below. There, by its margin, stood Forrester and Lintstock listening intently, and glancing silently at each other from time to time ; for, brave and adventurous though the age might be, there were bounds, even in warlike Scotland, to hardihood and adventure.

" If he should be afraid to descend !" said Sir John.

" Afraid ?" retorted Lintstock ; " I have kent him, Sir John Forrester, since he was a bairn that couldna' blaw his ain nose, and never saw fear in his face yet.—There he comes," added the old cannonier, as the stone we have just mentioned rolled over their heads and fell into the calm loch, forming a hundred circles on its dark bosom ; "there he comes—there he comes !" continued the veteran, whose solitary eye moistened with a tear as he uttered a fervent supplication to " Sancta Barbara, the virgin and martyr, patroness of all bold cannoniers and artillery " (according to the military superstition of the age), to protect his master.

In a few minutes more, both Roland and Sabrino were seen descending the dangerous path. Lintstock uttered a cry of satisfaction.

" Courage !" said Forrester, placing his hand at the side of his mouth, lest the guard at the tower might overhear, and fire on them.

In another moment Roland, breathless with his exertions, was beside them, and in the arms of his old servant, who swore and wept with joy.

His hair and beard were so disordered, that Forrester could scarcely recognise him.

" My dear friend," said Roland, sadly, "if the thanks of one to whom life is valueless are worth accepting, take them from me a thousand times, and a thousand more. Believe me, I am almost mad—I know not what I do, or what I say, or whether my words are incoherent as my thoughts."

He was frightfully pale and haggard.

"Truly, Vipont, we live in strange times—times that future men will talk of with wonder, for we participate in deeds of which our posterity will scarcely believe," replied Forrester, gravely; "but I pray you, mount and begone, for we have not a moment to lose! Instant flight ——"

"Horses and arms! by what magic hast thou divined my secret thought? Oh, my good, my kind Forrester, it is so like thee!"

"Here is your own sword—the old Italian blade you loved so well."

"I am glad thou'st brought it, for 'tis all my heritage," replied Roland, as he buckled it on, and then unsheathed the blade and waved i in the air.

"My castle in the west is at your service. Mount and ride, I implore you, Vipont; for every moment of delay is fraught with danger to us all!"

"Mount and ride, say you? Yes; but not to your castle in the west, my dear friend—no! I have sworn to see Jane Seton once again before she dies. Jane! Jane! that letter—ah! why didst thou send it, for I would rather thou hadst stabbed me with a poniard? My good sword! how great, how glorious a thing it is to be free, and to feel thee in my hand. Now can I deal death for death, blow for blow, and blood for blood! Oh, Forrester, I feel that wrong and oppression have made me a very savage."

To crush his agony, he bit his lips till the blood came, and hastily, but scrupulously examined the bridle and stirrups of the horse his friend had brought him.

Breathlessly, and with a heart full of rage, Redhall from his place of concealment had seen and overheard them.

"I have destroyed her, and shall *he* escape me?" he thought. "No, by the Power of Heaven!" and, drawing his sword, he made stealthily towards the Well-house Tower, for there was no time to give an alarm elsewhere. Thrice he essayed to gain it, but in vain! for those he wished to intercept stood right in the narrow path leading to the gateway which the tower flanked; the cliff rose up on one side like a wall, the deep water descended into darkness on the other.

"Hallo! we are watched!" cried old Lintstock, whose single eye was worth a dozen of others, and had seen this dark figure which glided near them in the gloom.

Full of rage and shame at being discovered, Redhall, who was too proud and too brave to retreat, advanced boldly, with his sword in his hand, exclaiming loudly—

"A rescue! a rescue! a rescue and escape! Ho, the guard! ho, in the name of the king! treason! and breaking ward! treason! treason!"

"*Redhall!*" cried Roland, in a choking voice.

"We are lost!" said Forrester.

Roland could utter no more; he thought that destiny had delivered his enemy over to his vengeance; and a wild tempest of holy fervour and infernal fury filled his heart. He rushed upon him like a lion, and they both engaged with blind desperation.

Their eyes were full of fire, their breasts burning with as much hatred as could possibly animate two human hearts, and much more intent on slaying each other than on protecting themselves, they hewed and thrust, cutting showers of sparks from their swords in the dark, while their blades rang like bells. They seemed to be transformed into demons by their mortal hatred.

Resolved that even if himself should be slain, his enemy should not escape, Redhall called incessantly to the guard in the adjacent tower; and Sir John Forrester, with alarm, heard the voices of the soldiers, who were part of his own corps of guards, and saw the glow of their lighted matches reddening behind the loopholes, and through the bars of the gate, as they prepared "to make service" against those who were brawling on St. Cuthbert's roadway; in other words, to fire on them.

Before this measure took place the combat was decided.

Stepping back a pace, and grasping his sword with both hands, Redhall raised the hilt above his head, and dropping the blade behind him, resolved to give a cut-down stroke, which would end the conflict and his rival's life together; but Roland, quick as lightning, on seeing his whole body unprotected, sprang forward, and ran more than two feet of his double-edged sword through his body.

A groan of rage and agony escaped from Redhall; with his left hand he grasped Roland's sword near the hilt, and fiercely writhed his body forward upon it, to shorten the distance between himself and his antagonist, in whose heart he endeavoured to bury a poniard which he grasped in his right hand, and for which he had relinquished his sword.

But seeing his deadly intention, Roland spurned him with his right foot; he staggered backward, the blood gushed forth, and at the same moment he rolled over the narrow path, and falling off the blade of the sword, sank heavily into the dark water of the loch, thus being stabbed and drowned almost at the same moment.

Roland uttered a wild laugh, leaped on horseback, and galloped madly away by the base of the castle rock.

Forrester followed at full speed, but the frantic horseman had disappeared like a spirit round the western side of the rock, and even the sound of his horse's hoofs had died away.

At that instant a volley of six arquebuses flashed redly from the parapets of the ravelin, and their bullets whistled about the ears of old Lintstock, who immediately scrambled after Sir John Forrester; but one pierced the brain of the poor page Sabrino, who fell dead on the spot.

The discovery of his body next morning caused unusual consternation in the "good town" of Edinburgh, and the expenditure of several gallons of holy water, which were sprinkled upon the livid corpse and the place where it lay; while the tidings went far and wide that "my Lady of Ashkirk's devil had been found under the castle rock."

CHAPTER LIX.

THE PLACE OF DOOM.

' But when the appointed day was come,
    No help appeared nye;
Then woeful, woeful was her heart,
    And tears stood in her eye.
And now a fyer was built of wood,
    And a stake was made of tree ;
And now Queen Elinor forth was led,
    A sorrowful sight to see."
                    Sir Aldringar, an old Ballad.

ON this night a strange sound floated upward to the Castle of Edinburgh from the city below; it was like the murmur of distant waves, or of the rising wind shaking the branches

of a forest.　This was occasioned by the crowding of the
people towards the *Place of Doom*, as it was graphically
named.

It was a dark midnight, moonless and starless; the eyes
of thousands were raised inquisitively to the black, opaque
mass of the castle rock and the zone of lofty towers which
then engirdled its summit, with their embrasured battlements
and frowning cannon.

Culprits usually suffered at a place on the south side of the
Castle-hill, where a green bank of several hundred yards
sloped steeply downward from the ramparts of the Spur, to
the north ends of the closes in the Grass-market, a broad
arena which, from its fantastic architecture, has been said
closely to resemble the Plaza of a Spanish or Italian town,
and which lies in a valley to the south of the castle.

The wall of the city, which descended at an angle of nearly
fifty degrees from the rock on which the fortress is built
until it intersected the streets beneath at the King's Meuse,
closed this sloping bank on the west.　The back of a narrow
close, which was demolished in the civil war of 1745, enclosed
it on the east, and the Spur, with its strong rampart and
twenty pieces of brass cannon, overlooked it on the north.
There were then no Castle-terrace or Western Approach to
disfigure the city on the south, and this green and verdant
bank descended smoothly and gradually downwards to the
great market-place.

The stake was placed on a small natural platform a few
yards square, the same place where Thomas Forrest, vicar of
Dollar, John Keillior, and John Beverage, two Dominican
priests, Duncan Simpson, and Sir Robert Forrest, a gentleman
of Stirlingshire, were burned for heresy in presence of the
regal court, on the night of the 2nd of March, two years
after the events we are about to relate.　This was the place
of death until the year 1631, when the Scottish government
deprived the city of it for military purposes.

The stake was a strong column of oak, roughly dressed by
a hatchet, and had rivetted upon it the *branks*, or witch's
bridle, which hung at the end of a short chain.　This instrument, which was considered so necessary in punishments by
fire, and which was soon to become so famous in Scotland,
that every burgh required one, was a circle of iron, formed of
four parts, connected by steel hinges, and adapted to encircle

the neck, like the modern *jougs*, which may sometimes be seen at kirk-doors. The chain was behind ; in front was the broad gag which entered the mouth, and pressed down the tongue to prevent the unhappy wretch, whose head was locked within it, crying aloud ; and after the execution, this diabolical invention, which was usually found among the ashes of the fire and of the skeleton, with fragments of bones and teeth adhering to it, was carefully preserved by the thrifty baillies in the council-chamber until the next "worrying," as it was termed.

Several horseloads of faggots, nicely split, and tied up in bundles, were piled three feet deep around the stake by the concurrents, or assistants of Sanders Screw, in absence of Dobbie, whom a blow from Leslie's sword had left half dead at a cottage near Inverteil ; and on these bundles they poured several buckets of tar and oil, thereafter sprinkling the whole with gunpowder and sulphur. These operations soothed the excitement and impatience of the expectant thousands, who long before the fatal hour had taken possession of the whole ground about the stake, a circle round which was kept open by the halberds of the provost, while beyond there were a party of fifty mounted spearmen under his kinsman, Sir Andrew Preston of Gourtoun, who was sheathed in complete armour. Every second trooper bore a lighted torch ; thus the mob could see with ease, and be seen.

In addition to the inhabitants of the city, nearly all those of the four municipalities, or burghs of regality, which lay without the barriers—viz., the Portsburgh, lying before the West-port ; the Canongate, without the Netherbow-port ; the Potter-row, which lay before the Kirk-of-field-port ; and the Calton, lying without St. Andrew's port, or the Craigend-gate, were collected in the spacious area of the Grassmarket, and on the steep face of the castle bank. The walls of the ravelin which crowned it on the north ; the bartizans, roofs, windows, even the chimney-heads and pediments, every ledge and part of the houses on the west ; and the ends of those which closed the ground below, were crowded with spectators. The market-place was like a sea of upturned faces, all visible in the torchlight, though far down below ; and the hum of their myriad voices, mingled with many a shrill cry or threat, the clink of steel or clatter of iron hoofs, as the armed horsemen rode to and fro keeping order among them, ascended the side of the hill, and echoed among the rocks and towers of the fortress, where the poor victim for whom they waited was kneeling at her prayers.

So great was the crowd in the market, that even the bartizans of the Greyfriars' monastery, a large building which formed part of the street, and had been built by James I. about a hundred years before, for Cornelius of Zurich and certain canons of Cologne, together with the loftier houses of the Knights of Torphichen, in the Bow, though still more distant, were covered with spectators.

Clad in thin grey cassocks girt with knotted cords, the Greyfriars ran about among the people, barefooted, and carrying little wooden boxes to receive money from the charitable and religious to pay for "masses and prayers for the soul of the poor lost heretic and sorceress,"—prayers and masses for the poor girl who was yet living. Solemn mass, as for the dead, was to have been said in the chapel of St. Margaret, the queen of Scotland, by Father St. Bernard, and the chaplain of the fortress; but the baillies, the portly deacons of the crafts and consequential councillors of the gude town, were impatient for the *deid chack*, and had ordered that, as the friars had lingered too long with Jane in her cell, and as the hour of twelve approached, and the people were impatient, they should do their office at the stake—an edict of selfishness and cruelty.

This *deid chack* was a dinner or supper (according to the hour) of which the magistrates always partook after an execution; and it was generally served up with great civic state, in a chamber which adjoined the church of St. Giles, and which in later days was the vestry of the Tolbooth kirk.

Twelve rang from the great tower of that venerable fane; and to the ears of all it seemed to do so more slowly and solemnly than usual, for such is the force of imagination. At the same moment the lurid flash of a culverin broke redly from the battlements of the Constable's Tower, and its hoarse boom pealed away over the heads of the people.

Every heart leaped, every ear tingled, every eye dilated. A rapid murmur pervaded the vast multitude, and then died away, leaving them all attention—all ear and eye; they seemed to have but one pulse, one heart, and their expectations were excited to the utmost degree when the strong iron portal of the Spur unclosed, and the procession of death appeared slowly descending the steep bank towards the stake.

First came six arquebusiers in steel caps and crimson doublets, marching in double file, with their matches smoking.

Then came Sanders Screw, dressed in flaming scarlet, with a leather apron, and his arms bared to the elbow. He bore a lighted torch, which flared luridly on his withered visage and decrepit figure. He looked like an antiquated fiend.

Then came the governor of the fortress, Sir James Riddel, walking on foot, but in half armour, attended by an esquire and two pages, one bearing his sword, the other his helmet. With him were the magistrates in their scarlet gowns, wearing their chains of gold, with their sword-bearer, macer, and halberdiers, clad in blue doublets, laced, and slashed with yellow.

Then appeared Father St. Bernard, with the Dominican who acted as the governor's chaplain. Both were walking bareheaded and in full canonicals, with their eyes fixed upon their books. St. Bernard was praying, the Dominican made the responses in a loud and audible voice. All the people immediately uncovered their heads, and the horsemen of Gourtoun lowered the points of their lances.

When Lady Jane appeared, another low murmur pervaded the people, mingled with exclamations of—

"Alake! alake! oh, waly! waly! Eh, sirs, and gude preserve us! waly! waly!" for the latter is an old Scottish exclamation expressive of the utmost commiseration.

It rose almost to a shout, then it died away, and silence sealed the lips of nearly ten thousand persons; they seemed for a time to be frozen with pity, horror, and expectation of the dire catastrophe; and so they remained with their countless eyes fixed upon her, their mouths open, their voices hushed, their breathing suspended.

Poor Jane! Amid all that living sea, around, above, and below her, she saw not the face of a friend, and yet the heads were rising and falling like the billows of a heaving ocean, as the hushed people, animated by morbid curiosity, struggled in silence to obtain a full view of her.

The lines of Nicholas Rowe are strikingly descriptive of her aspect; for as she descended to the pile—

> " Submissive, sad, and lowly was her look;
> A burning taper in her hand she bore,

And on her shoulders carelessly confused
With loose neglect her lovely tresses hung;
Upon her cheek a faintish flush was spread;
Feeble she seemed, and sorely smit with pain.
Her streaming eye bent ever on the earth,
Except when in some bitter pang of sorrow,
To heaven she seemed in fervent zeal to raise,
And begged that mercy man denied her here."

Instead of being dressed in a penitent's frock of tarred canvas, painted with flames pointing downwards, like those of the "heretics" whom the same spectators had seen burned at the Rood of Greenside, before the gate of the Carmelites, a short time before, Jane wore an ordinary tunic of blue silk, and her little velvet cap, with its triangular front, from the top of which a pendant bob-jewel sparkled on her brow,—for she had resolved to die bravely. Her rosary, formed of silver and coral beads, hung at her wrist; her missal was in one hand, a taper in the other. Her luxuriant brown hair hung over her shoulders, in sign of sorrow and repentance; she was sorely changed, and worn almost to a skeleton, but there was something almost holy in the solemn and resigned expression of her beautiful face. It was the pallor of long mental suffering, mingled with a sublime resignation to the will of God and the hard fate He designed for her at the hands of His creatures, who seemed to her so merciless.

Now, hovering between time and eternity, she seemed as one beyond the pale of life.

The fear and hatred which her name, as a rumoured sorceress, had excited in the minds of the people, died away when they beheld her. Sorrow and compassion swelled in every heart, and each man whispered to his neighbour of her youth and beauty, and the memory of that good and valiant earl her father, "who fought so well for Scotland, God rest him!"

Many wrung their hands, many wept, and more prayed for her; for if they were blunt and fiery, our Scottish sires of the olden time, and somewhat too ready with the use of their swords and dirks, they were warm-hearted and kind, as they were honest and true.

Her dignity and courage deserved their praise, for on beholding those assembled thousands, the glittering pikes of the mailed horsemen, the halberds and arquebuses, the stake with its chain, and the oiled faggots which formed that appalling pile, Jane gathered courage from her pride of birth and name, and resolved that history should never have it to record that a daughter of the house of Ashkirk blanched in the face of death—that grim foe whom its sons had so often confronted on the fields of France and England. As these thoughts fired her heart, her cheek flushed, her dark eye lighted up, she became in a moment sublime; and as the bright torches glared on her wasted and ghastly beauty, the people saw in her no longer the regicide and the sorceress, but a heroine, a martyr!

Now she knelt down by the pile, for Father St. Bernard, in a low voice, almost inaudibly tremulous, began to repeat the prayers contained in the mass usually performed for the dead on the day of decease or burial; for, as an "obdurate heretic and sorceress," Jane was not permitted to receive the last sacraments of her church in public, but the good old pre-bendary had bestowed them in secret.

Then, as this solemn service commenced, the entire as-sembled thousands sank upon their knees and bowed down their heads. Even the Reformers who were in the crowd (and there were many) could not refuse to kneel and pray at a crisis so sad and terrible, when a poor human soul was, as they thought, hovering on the brink of hell.

The horsemen of Gourtoun remained upright in their saddles, with their armour gleaming in the torchlight, which shed its uncertain glare upon the crowded bank, and on the giant fortress that towered into the clouds above it, upon the bastions and cannon of the Spur, upon the crowded win-dows and fantastic architecture of the closes, and the sea of heads that were bowed in the market-place, far down below, upon the kneeling sufferer, the silver hair, bald heads, and shining vestments of the priests beside her; while, like the murmur of a gentle wind as it passes over a full-eared corn-field, the voices of the people rose when they joined in the beautiful hymn prescribed by what was then their church,—

> " The day of wrath ! that dreadful day !
> Shall the whole world in ashes lay,
> As David and the Sybils say.
> What horror shall invade the mind,
> When the strict Judge, who would be kind,
> Shall have few venial faults to find !"

and so on to the close of the solemn chaunt,—

> " Prostrate, my contrite heart I rend,—
> My God, my Father, and my Friend.
> Do not forsake me in mine end !
> Well may they curse their second birth,
> Who rise to everlasting death.
> Thou great Creator of mankind,
> Oh, let *this soul* compassion find !"

Amid all that vast assemblage, there was one person who did not seem to join in this hymn. He had lost his bonnet ; his head was bare, and his hair, wild, matted, and disordered, waved around his head, and mingled with a beard that seemed to have been untrimmed for a fortnight. He was armed with a long sword, and rode a powerful horse, the blood of which was dripping from a pair of sharp spurs, which appeared to be hurriedly buckled on. The whole multitude were intently regarding the poor being who was about to suffer, otherwise the pale visage, fierce eyes, and wild aspect of this strange horseman must have attracted, in a marked manner, the attention of all who chanced to observe him.

He was Roland Vipont, who, with a heart full of fury, and a head full of desperate thoughts, had posted himself as near the pile as the spearmen of Sir Andrew Preston would permit.

Love and wrath, together with wounded pride, had excited his great inborn courage to a point of rashness and bravery that made him feel strong as a Hercules, bold as a lion, and fitted to encounter, without a shadow of fear or qualm of doubt, Sir Andrew of Gourtoun's fifty lances in a general mêlée.

Slowly and impressively the chapel bells of the Greyfriars, and of St. Mary in the Portsburgh, began to toll a knell for the passing soul, and the heads of the people bent lower.

" Blessed Lord," Roland heard the voice of the prebend praying ; " oh, King of Glory, deliver the souls of all the faithful departed from the flames of hell, and from the deep pit."

Jane's pale lips seemed to move as she made a response.

" Deliver them from the lion's mouth, lest hell swallow them, and lest they fall into darkness.

" Let the standard-bearer, Saint Michael, bring them unto the holy light which of old thou didst promise to Abraham and to his posterity."

" Amen !" responded the calm voice of the old Dominican.

St. Bernard shut his missal, and covered his face with the sleeve of his vestment.

As one man, the silent thousands raised their heads, and Sanders Screw shook the flame of his torch, to light it fully.

Jane arose, and gazed placidly around her.

The time had come!

Then, if it could be possible, the heart of Roland Vipont beat quicker, and he unsheathed his sword.

" Aid me, thou blessed Power, whom all these hearts have invoked! aid me for her sake! But, aid or no aid, if I am forsaken, 'tis but the soldier's death! Vipont! Vipont!" he exclaimed, and suddenly urging his horse towards the stake, he threw his left arm around Jane, and drew her across his saddle before any one had the least idea of what he meant to do; and brandishing his sword around his head, dashed the gory spurs again into the torn flanks of his horse.

Appalled by the rapidity of the action, the vast assemblage stood immovable.

Down the frightful steep towards the King's Meuse he rode with the speed of an arrow; and, as the clouds part before a thunderbolt, the horsemen gave way, and the people parted before him.

" Shut the gates of the town!" cried Sir Andrew Preston; but a roar of voices burst from the multitude, and amid that roar his voice was confounded and lost.

Fortunately the gates were open, and deserted by their warders; and thus, before the people had recovered from their astonishment, and before the troopers of Gourtoun were ordered to pursue, Roland Vipont, with his rescued prize, had cleared the Castle Wynd, the crowded market-place, and left the city's western barrier far behind him, as he spurred, like a whirlwind, towards the wood and marshes of Corstorphine, where, almost girded by a lake, and surrounded by a deep moat, the strong and stately fortress of the Forresters awaited him with open gates.

CHAPTER LX.

CONCLUSION.

" So they were wedded, and life's smoothest tide
Bore on its breast the bridegroom and the bride."—CROLY.

WITH these two lines we might fairly dismiss the hero and heroine of these volumes, without describing. or expatiating on the explanations that brought about a termination so pleasing; but it suddenly occurred to us that the reader, who had kindly accompanied us so far, might have some curiosity to learn the fate of the other actors in our drama or history, for it partakes of both.

Jane's relations accounted for the extorted letter which caused such pain to Roland; and the next messenger from Falkland announced that a pardon had actually been granted by the king, while the whole plot against her life and honour was fully revealed and made conspicuous by the secret papers and correspondence of Redhall, all of which were purchased at the sale of the effects of an eminent antiquary, lately deceased, and are preparing for publication by a Scottish literary club.

Roland and his bride lived to see the subversion of all order in the days of the Douglas wars, when he fought valiantly under the Duke of Chatelherault for his queen, like a man of truth and honour, for which he received from her own fair finger a ring of gold, which his descendants possess unto the present day.

Released from Inchkeith by order of the king, the venerable Countess of Ashkirk had soon after the happiness of procuring from Rome, through the influence of Cardinal Beaton, a dispensation, by which Sybil Douglas of Kilspindie was married to her cousin, the earl, who survived that period more than fifty years; and, during a long and useful life, was eminently distinguished for his loyalty and patriotism. The last time we heard or read of him was in 1587, when, on tidings of Mary's murder at Fotheringay arriving at Edinburgh, he appeared at Holyrood with his eight tall sons, all sheathed in black armour, to show King James VI. what he considered the most proper court mourning for the occasion.

Father St. Bernard lived to see the Reformation, which

nearly broke the old man's heart; for he thought that the end of the world was at hand. In his ninetieth year he died among the monks of St. Jerome, at the Escurial, in Spain, whither he had travelled to deposit the arm-bone of St. Giles.

Ten years after the events we have narrated, the gallant Sir John Forrester fell, fighting for his country, at the battle of Pinkey, on the 10th September, 1547. He was shot when making a brilliant charge with his own vassals against those regiments of Spanish arquebusiers, who, under Don Pedro de Gamboa, gained that battle for the Duke of Somerset.

Honest old Lintstock, the ex-gunner, instead of settling on the estate which Vipont received in free barony from the king, married the hostel, or rather the hosteller's widow, to whom he had paid his court so long; and though he became one of the wealthiest burgesses of the good town, instead of becoming either a councillor or baillie, he preferred to doze away his time by the tap-room fire, where, with other old iron-headed troopers and trampers, over a can of mum-beer, he told long and interminable stories of the battles of Flodden and Haddonrig; of sakers, of carthouns, and cannons-royale; and of blowing Englishmen, Spaniards, and Highlandmen all to rags and fritters, for he had fought against them all in his time.

The end of Dobbie the Doomster is buried in obscurity, unless we connect him in some way with the same legal functionary who is said to have drowned himself by leaping in a drunken fit from the steep pinnacle of rock which over-hangs the Loch of Duddingstone, and is now known as the *Hangman's Knowe;* but if it will comfort the reader to know the end of Birrel the Brodder, we may add that this amiable individual became unfortunately involved in the murder of Cardinal Beaton in the year 1546, and being taken with other prisoners when St. Andrew's was stormed by the admiral of the galleys, Leon, prior of Capua, he was conveyed to France, where he died, miserably chained to an oar, and scourged almost to a skeleton, in a galley at Brest.

John of the Silvermills, first deacon of the barber-chirur-geons at Edinburgh, never completed his famous elixir, which would have brought his profession to a close, and enabled us to live without an ache or an ailment for ever. This precious compound was just on the point of completion by the addi-tion of that small ingredient it had lacked so long, and for

which he had found a substitute in the blood of a certain
reptile, mentioned in the black letter " Ereptology" of Francis
Redi, when one dark night ten thousand Englishmen landed
and gave all to fire and sword in and around Edinburgh.
This was Lord Hertford's famous invasion in 1544.

Poor John's laboratory was destroyed, and for months
afterwards he was to be seen, like the ghost of himself, rending his beard, and lamenting over the ruins of his premises,
strewed with shattered retorts and broken crucibles, and
mourning heavily, like another Jeremiah, over the fall of an
imaginary Babylon.

NOTES.

I.

THE unfortunate passage in Scottish history, which afforded a hint for the foregoing romance, will be found in " Pitcairn's Criminal Trials," at considerable length, and also in a little history of the " Life of James V.," reprinted in *Miscellanea Scotica* from the edition of 1710; but as both these works may be beyond the reader's reach, we may briefly state the facts as being these.

In the year 1537, Jane Douglas, the young and beautiful widow of Lord Glammis, and sister of the Earl of Angus, together with her second husband, the Laird of Skipness, an aged priest, and others, were accused by a person named William Lyon, of endeavouring to compass the king's death by poison and sorcery.

Slighting the addresses of Lyon and many others who aspired to her hand, after the death of Lord Glammis, she had preferred Campbell of Skipness ; upon which Lyon, inflamed by rivalry and revenge, made a terrible vow, that his life should be dedicated to her destruction ; and hence came the charge, upon which she and her immediate friends were committed to the Castle of Edinburgh.

" The accuser, who had the car of the jealous king, used

all his rhetoric to aggravate the matter, that he might dis
pose him to treat them with all possible cruelty," says the
old French author of James the Fifth's life.▪ "He repre
sented that the family of Douglas had always been dangerou
and troublesome to his predecessors, himself, and his kingdom
and reminded him of the insolence of Archibald Douglas, Ear
of Angus, the prisoner's brother, in the time of his majesty'
minority—a peer whose practices were so pernicious, that by
a public decree he was banished the kingdom, as a disturbe
of the peace of his native country; and that since that time
he had become the subject of Henry, King of England."

Examined, on *the rack*, by the king's advocate, and ques
tioned mercilessly, notwithstanding her rank, delicacy, and
beauty,—for which she was renowned through all Britain,—
she was compelled to admit the alleged treason and sorcery
and James having solemnly sworn never to forgive a Douglas
she was burned alive on the Castle-hill, on the 17th July, in
presence of the citizens, and almost in view of her son and
husband, who were confined in David's Tower. There the
former remained a prisoner until 1542; but the latter, when
attempting to escape, like Roland Vipont, by means of a rope
on the night of the execution, fell, and was found next morn
ing, literally dashed to pieces, at the bottom of the rocks
Struck with remorse, James V., who was naturally a mercifu
prince, set the old friar at liberty. But it is remarkable tha
William Lyon was merely banished from Scotland; while a
quack named Makke, by whom the pretended poison, or ma
gical preparation was made up, escaped with the loss of his
ears.—See *Pinkerton, Tytler, Lesley, Arnot,* &c. &c.

II.

JOHN OF THE SILVERMILLS.

This character is purely imaginary. James IV. and James V., both great dabblers in alchemy, are said to have had a laboratory, furnace, and their appurtenances at Silvermills, a little village which took its name from these operations, and is now a district of Edinburgh. It was probably at these mills that the gold, of which great quantities were found during the reign of James V., was refined. The preface to the French life of that monarch, printed at Paris in 1612, states that he had " three hundred men employed for several summers in washing gold, of which they got above £100,000 of English money."

Lest some may suppose we have overdrawn the popular credulity of 1537, in delineating John of the Silvermills, we may mention that it is not long since a similar character existed in Scotland, and was put under the ban of an ecclesiastical court.

This individual, whose name was Andrew Dawson, lived on the Grampians, and having been unfortunate as a farmer, became a veterinary surgeon, and dealer in herbs for the cure of his own species. His mother having enjoyed the reputation of being *uncanny*, Andrew easily succeeded to this unenviable inheritance; but patients flocked to him from all quarters, and his chief mode of cure was friction, accompanied by charms muttered, or chaunted, in an unintelligible language. " His hut," says the *Dundee Courier*, " which was built by himself, like the *Black Dwarf's*, on a muir, was situated not far from a spot called the ' Fairy's

Knowe,' and was the terror of the benighted traveller."
Strange sounds were heard; unearthly lights were seen;
and the fama of unhallowed rites, together with a distemper
among the cattle, soon brought Andrew on a distinct " charge
of soreery before the Kirk Session."

This Scottish Paracelsus had treated three citations with
sovereign contempt; but he was compelled to attend on the
fourth being served at his hut; and on the appointed day
appeared before the Session an aged and infirm man. On
the minister asking him, if he " wished the sentence of ex-
communication reopened, and on what grounds ?" Andrew
pulled from his ample pouch three common quartz pebbles,
and explained that in all diseases of the *head* he had employed,
by friction, one which bore a rude resemblance to that part of
the body. In diseases of the *heart*, he used another, shaped
like that organ; and the third was for affections of the
kidneys, to which it bore a resemblance. As to his wakes
and nightly orgies, he admitted that they were meant to
impose upon the ignorant, and increase the mystery. " To
describe the shame and astonishment at this recital would
have required the pen of Scott, or the pencil of Allan."—
Dundee Courier, Dec. 25th, 1851.

He died a few months after this scene; the last instance
in Scotland of belief in sorcery, followed by kirk censure;
and his resting-place is still pointed to, with something of
fear, as " the warlock's grave." A still later instance of
popular credulity will be found mentioned in the London
Times, of the 10th January, 1852, wherein a gentleman of
Marseilles was accused of discasing a child, by sorcery and
the *evil eye*.

III.

THE THUMB.

The ancient mode of confirming any bargain or bond, for good or for evil, in Scotland, was by the pressure of wetted thumbs, an eastern custom, which is still traceable among the Moors and other tribes. It may still be found among the boys in some districts of Scotland. Doubtless the various sayings now common among the peasantry, such as, "Here's my thumb on't,"—"Ye needna fash your thumb,"—"Keep your thumb on that,"—or, "Having one *under* your thumb," &c., have arisen from this old custom. The heart-shaped stone, on which parties were wont to press their wetted thumbs, when ratifying their bargains at the Cross of Edinburgh, was presented about three years ago by the Town Council to Lord Cockburn. Prior writes,

> "Now let us *touch thumbs*, and be friends ere we part;
> Here, John, is my thumb, and here, Mat, is my heart."

Various old songs record this mystic sign of truth and fealty; one in *Orpheus Caledonius*, 1725, says,

> "Dearest maid! nay, do not fly me,
> Let your pride no more deny me;
> Never doubt your faithful Willie,
> There's *my thumb*, I'll ne'er beguile ye."

Another, in Ramsay's *Tea-table Miscellany*, 1723, has it,

> "Though kith and kin, and a' revile ye,
> There's my thumb, I'll ne'er beguile ye."

To *bite* the thumb at any one was anciently an insult in

Scotland and England, as it is still in France. Scott mentions it in the *Lay of the Last Minstrel*, when describing
the quarrel between the Laird of Hunthill and Conrad of
Wolfenstein, canto vi.,

> " Stern Rutherford right little said,
> But *bit* his glove, and shook his head," &o.

And Shakespeare, in *Romeo and Juliet*, has,

> " I will bite my thumb at them, which is a disgrace if they bear it!"

> " Dags and pistols! to bite his thumb at me !"

Innumerable other instances might be cited.

IV.

THE BRODDER.

As stated in the text, this was an indispensable legal
functionary, whose name occurs frequently in all trials for
witchcraft in Scotland. Among the expenses for burning
Margaret Denholm, is the following item:—"To Jhone
Kinked, for ye *brodding* of her, vi. lib. Scotts."—*Pit. Crim.
Trials.*

In March, 1649, the magistrates of Newcastle employed
a noted Scottish witch-pricker, to discover all those who
dabbled in sorcery within the walls of their town, " offering
him twenty shillings a-piece for all he should condemn as
witches, and a free passage thither and back " to Scotland.
A proclamation by bell summoned all persons to give infor-

mation of witchcraft. Thirty women were brought to the Town Hall, stripped nude, had a pin thrust into their flesh by this charlatan, who acquainted Lieut.-Colonel Hobson, the English commandant, that they were guilty, and that " he knew whether women were witches or no by their *look;* but when the said person was searching of a personable and goodlike woman, the Colonel said, 'surely this woman is none, and need not be tried;' but the Scotsman said she was, and therefore he would try her; and presently he ran a pin into her, and set her aside as a guilty person and child of the devil, and fell to try others whom he pronounced guilty. Lieut.-Colonel Hobson proved upon the spot the fallacy of the fellow's trial of the woman; and then the Scotsman cleared her, and said she was *not* a child of the devil." After being paid in Newcastle, this witch-finder went into North-umberland, to *prove* women at the rate of " three pounds a-piece;" but, on returning into Scotland, his villany came to light, and he was hanged, confessing " at the gallows, that he had been the death of above *two hundred and twenty women* in Scotland and England, for the gain of twenty shillings a-piece."—See *Sykes's Local Records of Newcastle.*

As mentioned in the romance, the *brod*, or steel pin, used in piercing the devil's mark. is now supposed to have been made to slip into its handle, thus giving the appearance of entering the body without producing pain—an infallible sign of sorcery.

Within two years after the publication of James the Sixth's *Demonologie*, twenty-six persons were tortured for witchcraft, at Aberdeen, and twenty-one were condemned to the flames. " It would have been considered a prodigal wasting of such a happy windfall, to have burned all these wretches at once; and accordingly," says the *Book of Bon Accord*, " by judicious management, and by bringing two or three to the stake at a time, it was contrived to delight the public with incremations on the Castle-hill for upwards of a twelvemonth."

The *last witch* in Scotland, was accused of transforming her daughter into a pony, and getting her shod by the devil, for which she was burned in 1722, near the Earl's Cross at Dornoch, in Sutherland.

Of the *last witch* in England, a curious account will be found in the *Courier*, of the 28th of February, 1834, which records one of the most gross and startling instances of superstition ever known; it concerned the enchantment of a herd of pigs in the Forest of Dean. See also the *Monmouth Merlin*, of the same date.

The Act against Witchcraft was not repealed in Scotland and England until about 1750; and not in Ireland until 1821!

THE END.

ROUTLEDGE'S SHILLING NOVELS.

By CAPTAIN MARRYAT.

In fcp. 8vo, fancy covers, 1s. each.

PETER SIMPLE.
JACOB FAITHFUL.
NEWTON FOSTER.
THE PACHA OF MANY
 TALES.
PERCIVAL KEENE.
JAPHET IN SEARCH OF
 A FATHER.
FRANK MILDMAY.

MR. MIDSHIPMAN
 EASY.
THE POACHER.
VALERIE.
THE KING'S OWN.
RATTLIN THE REEFER
THE PHANTOM SHIP.
THE DOG FIEND.

By MR. DISRAELI.

In fcp. 8vo, fancy covers, 1s. each.

HENRIETTA TEMPLE.
IXION IN HEAVEN, &c.
THE YOUNG DUKE.
VENETIA.
TANCRED.

VIVIAN GREY.
CONTARINI FLEMING.
ALROY.
CONINGSBY.
SYBIL.

GEORGE ROUTLEDGE & SONS, Broadway, Ludgate Hill.

ROUTLEDGE'S SHILLING NOVELS.

By J. FENIMORE COOPER.

In fcp. 8vo, fancy covers, 1s. each.

THE PILOT.
THE PIONEERS.
THE DEERSLAYER.
LIONEL LINCOLN.
THE BRAVO.
THE TWO ADMIRALS.
THE WATERWITCH.
WYANDOTTE.
MILES WALLINGFORD.
THE PRAIRIE.
THE HEATHCOTES.
PRECAUTION.
MARK'S REEF.
THE LAST OF THE MOHICANS.
THE SPY.
THE PATHFINDER.
THE RED ROVER.
THE HEIDENMAUER.
SATANSTOE.
AFLOAT AND ASHORE.
EVE EFFINGHAM.
THE HEADSMAN.
HOMEWARD BOUND.
THE SEA LIONS.
OAK OPENINGS.
NED MYERS.

GEORGE ROUTLEDGE & SONS, Broadway, Ludgate Hill.

ROUTLEDGE'S SHILLING NOVELS.

By W. HARRISON AINSWORTH.

WINDSOR CASTLE.

THE MISER'S DAUGHTER.

THE TOWER OF LONDON.

CRICHTON.

JAMES THE SECOND.

OLD ST. PAUL'S.

THE FLITCH OF BACON.

GUY FAWKES.

THE LANCASHIRE WITCHES.

MERVYN CLITHEROE.

OVINGDEAN GRANGE.

ROOKWOOD.

ST. JAMES'S; OR, THE COURT OF QUEEN ANNE.

THE SPENDTHRIT.

THE STAR CHAMBER.

AURIOL.

JACK SHEPPARD.

GEORGE ROUTLEDGE & SONS, Broadway, Ludgate Hill.

ROUTLEDGE'S SHILLING NOVELS.

By G. P. R. JAMES.

In fcp. 8vo, fancy covers, 1s. each.

THE BRIGAND.

DARNLEY.

THE WOODMAN.

MORLEY ERNSTEIN.

THE GIPSY.

HENRY OF GUISE.

ATTILA.

ARABELLA STUART.

AGINCOURT.

RUSSELL; OR, THE RYE HOUSE PLOT.

THE KING'S HIGHWAY.

THE CASTLE OF EHRENSTEIN.

THE STEPMOTHER.

FOREST DAYS; OR, ROBIN HOOD.

THE HUGUENOT.

THE MAN AT ARMS,

A WHIM AND ITS CONSEQUENCES.

HENRY MASTERTON.

THE CONVICT.

MARY OF BURGUNDY.

MARGARET GRAHAM.

GOWRIE; OR, THE KING'S PLOT.

DELAWARE.

DARK SCENES OF HISTORY.

THE ROBBER.

ONE IN A THOUSAND.

THE SMUGGLER.

RICHELIEU.

DE LORME.

ARRAH NEIL.

BEAUCHAMP.

CASTELNEAU.

THE FALSE HEIR.

THE FORGERY.

THE GENTLEMAN OF THE OLD SCHOOL.

HEIDELBERG.

THE JACQUERIE.

MY AUNT PONTYPOOL.

ROSE D'ALBRET.

SIR THEODORE BROUGHTON.

CHARLES TYRRELL.

JOHN MARSTON HALL.

PHILIP AUGUSTUS.

THE BLACK EAGLE.

LEONORA D'ORCO.

THE OLD DOMINION.

GEORGE ROUTLEDGE & SONS, Broadway, Ludgate Hill.

4

ILLUSTRATED BOOKS.

Price 21s. each, or morocco, 31s. 6d., unless otherwise expressed.

ELEGANTLY PRINTED IN FCAP. QUARTO, ON TINTED PAPER, WITH DESIGNS BY THE FIRST ARTISTS, ENGRAVED BY DALZIELS, CLOTH ELEGANT, GILT AND GILT EDGES.

Home Thoughts and Home Scenes.

The Poems by Jean Ingelow, the Hon. Mrs. Norton, &c. Illustrated with large Pictures by A. B. HOUGHTON. Morocco, £1. 15s.

Longfellow's Poems.

A New Edition, including "The Wayside Inn," &c., with 149 Illustrations by JOHN GILBERT.

Robinson Crusoe. By DANIEL DE FOE.

With Portrait, and 100 Illustrations by J. D. WATSON.

*The Parables of our Lord.

With large Pictures by J. E. MILLAIS. Morocco, £1. 15s.

Tennyson's Poems.

Illustrated by CRESWICK, MACLISE, MULREADY, MILLAIS, C. STANFIELD, HORSLEY, &c.

*Birket Foster's Pictures of English Landscape.

With Descriptions by TOM TAYLOR, &c. Morocco, £1. 15s.

English Sacred Poetry of the 16th, 17th, 18th, and 19th Centuries.

Selected and Edited by ROBERT ARIS WILLMOTT, M.A. Illustrated by HOLMAN HUNT, WATSON, J. GILBERT, J. WOLF, &c.

Bunyan's Pilgrim's Progress. Edited by GEORGE OFFOR.

With a Portrait and 110 Illustrations by J. D. WATSON.

Eliza Cook's Poems.

With a Steel Portrait, and Illustrations by JOHN GILBERT, J. D. WATSON, H. WEIR, and J. WOLF.

---

* A few copies of the Illustrations (Proofs), printed on India paper, and mounted on imperial boards, in a portfolio, each £5. 5s.

Illustrated 21s. Books continued.

Price 5s. each, cloth gilt and gilt edges,
Illustrated by GILBERT, FOSTER, HARRISON WEIR, CORBOULD, &c.

Longfellow's Miles Standish (The Courtship of).

Wordsworth's Deserted Cottage.

Campbell's Gertrude of Wyoming.

Milton's Comus.

Beattie's Minstrel.

Longfellow's Voices of the Night, Ballads, and other Poems.

What Men have said about Woman.

A Collection of Choice Thoughts and Sentences compiled and analytically arranged by HENRY SOUTHGATE. Illustrated by J. D. WATSON. Crown 8vo, cloth extra, 7s. 6d.

Every Boy's Annual for 1865.

Edited by EDMUND ROUTLEDGE. With a Coloured Frontispiece and Title-page, and 120 Illustrations. Demy 8vo, cloth, gilt edges, 768 pages, 6s.

Golden Light.

Being Scripture Histories for the Young, from the Old and New Testament. With 80 large Illustrations by BAYES. 4to, cloth gilt, 5s.

Adventures of Young Munchausen (The).

Written and Illustrated in a Series of large Plates, by C. H. BENNETT. Super-royal 8vo, cloth, 5s. ; or, with the Plates Coloured, cloth, gilt edges, 7s. 6d.

Hans Andersen's Stories and Tales.

With 80 Illustrations, by A. W. BAYES. Imperial 16mo, cloth gilt, 5s.

The Golden Harp; or, Hymns, Rhymes, and Songs for the Young.

Elegantly printed on tinted paper in the best style, with 52 Illustrations by J. D. WATSON, DALZIEL, WOLF, &c. Square 12mo, cloth gilt, 3s. 6d.

Picture Fables. By OTTO SPECKTER.

With Rhymes by HEY. Illustrated with 100 Engravings by DALZIEL. Crown 8vo, cloth gilt and gilt edges, 3s. 6d.

Children's Songs.

By Mrs. HAWTREY. With very superior Engravings by SCOTT, finely printed in the best style. Imperial 8vo, cloth boards, 2s. 6d.

Sunday Alphabet (The).

By J. CLOTHIER. A Series of 26 Pictures by CRANE. Printed in the best style. Imperial 8vo, cloth boards, 2s. 6d.

Books for the Country. Best Editions—continued.

Wood's Common Objects of the Country.
Coleman's Woodlands, Heaths, and Hedges.
Moore's British Ferns and Allied Plants.
Coleman's British Butterflies. 200 Figures.
Atkinson's British Birds' Eggs and Nests.
Thomson's (Spencer) Wild Flowers.
Wood's Common Objects of the Microscope.
Haunts of the Wild Flowers. By ANNE PRATT.

*** Cheap Editions of all of the above are also issued in boards with plain plates, price 1s. to 2s. each.

STANDARD WORKS.

The Old Dramatists; and the Old Poets;

With Biographical Memoirs, &c.

Wycherley, Congreve, Vanbrugh, and Farquhar.
With Biographical and Critical Notices by LEIGH HUNT, and Portrait and Vignette. Royal 8vo, cloth, 15s.

Massinger and Ford.
With an Introduction by HARTLEY COLERIDGE, and Portrait and Vignette. Royal 8vo, cloth, 15s.

Ben Jonson.
With a Memoir by WILLIAM GIFFORD, and Portrait and Vignette. Royal 8vo, cloth, 16s.

Beaumont and Fletcher.
With Introduction by GEORGE DARLEY, and Portrait and Vignettes. 2 vols. royal 8vo, cloth, 32s.

John Webster.
With Life and Notes by the Rev. ALEXANDER DYCE. Royal 8vo, cloth, 10s. 6d.

Marlowe.
With a Memoir and Notes by the Rev. ALEXANDER DYCE. Royal 8vo, cloth, 12s.

Greene and Peele's Dramatic Works.
Edited by the Rev. ALEXANDER DYCE. Royal 8vo, cloth, 16s.

Spenser.
With selected Notes, Life by the Rev. H. J. TODD, M.A., Portrait, Vignette, and Glossarial Index. Royal 8vo, cloth, 10s. 6d.

The Old Dramatists and Poets—continued.

Chaucer.
With Notes and Glossary by TYRWHITT, and Portrait and Vignette. Royal 8vo, cloth, 10s. 6d.

Dryden.
With Notes by the Revs. JOSEPH and JOHN WARTON, and Portrait and Vignette. Royal 8vo, cloth, 10s. 6d.

Pope.
Including the Translations. With Notes, Life by the Rev. H. F. CARY, A.M., and Vignette. Royal 8vo, cloth, 10s. 6d.

The Dramatic Works of Sheridan Knowles.
With Portrait. Post 8vo, cloth, 7s. 6d.

The Dramatic Works of Sir Edward Bulwer Lytton.
With Frontispiece and Vignette. Fcap. 8vo, cloth, 6s.

The Poetical Works of Sir Edward Bulwer Lytton.
With Frontispiece and Vignette. Fcap. 8vo, cloth, 7s. 6d.

Routledge's British Poets. Cheap Edition.

Fcap. 8vo, cloth, gilt edges, price 3s. 6d. each; or morocco, elegant or antique, 7s. With Illustrations by BIRKET FOSTER, GILBERT, CORBOULD, WOLF, HARRISON WEIR, *&c. &c.*

COWPER'S POETICAL WORKS.
MILTON'S POETICAL WORKS.
WORDSWORTH'S POETICAL WORKS.
CRABBE'S POEMS.
SOUTHEY'S JOAN OF ARC, AND MINOR POEMS.
GOLDSMITH, JOHNSON, SHENSTONE, AND SMOLLETT.
KIRKE WHITE. By SOUTHEY.
BURNS'S POETICAL WORKS.
MOORE'S POEMS.   BYRON'S POEMS.
THOMSON, BEATTIE, &c.
POPE'S POETICAL WORKS.
GERALD MASSEY'S POEMS.
JAMES MONTGOMERY'S POEMS.
SCOTT'S POETICAL WORKS.
HERBERT'S WORKS. Edited by WILLMOTT.
ROGERS' (SAMUEL) POETICAL WORKS.
CAMPBELL'S (THOS.) POETICAL WORKS.
CHAUCER'S CANTERBURY TALES.
BLOOMFIELD'S POEMS AND REMAINS.

Also, uniform with Routledge's British Poets. Cheap Edition.

LONGFELLOW'S COMPLETE POETICAL WORKS, including " Tales of a Wayside Inn."

Routledge's British Poets. Best Edition.

Edited by the Rev. R. A. WILLMOTT, Illustrated by BIRKET FOSTER, GILBERT, CORBOULD, FRANKLIN, and HARVEY. Elegantly printed on good paper.

Fcap. 8vo, cloth, bevelled boards, gilt and gilt edges, price 5s. *each; or morocco elegant or antique, gilt edges,* 10s.

SPENSER'S FAERIE QUEENE.
CHAUCER'S CANTERBURY TALES.
KIRKE WHITE. By SOUTHEY.
SOUTHEY'S JOAN OF ARC, AND MINOR POEMS.
DRYDEN'S POETICAL WORKS.
POPE'S POETICAL WORKS. Edited by CARY.
MILTON'S POETICAL WORKS.
THOMSON, BEATTIE, AND WEST.
GOLDSMITH, JOHNSON, SHENSTONE, AND SMOLLETT,
HERBERT, WITH LIFE AND NOTES. Edited by WILLMOTT.
GRAY, PARNELL, COLLINS, GREEN, AND WARTON.
COWPER. Edited by WILLMOTT.
AKENSIDE AND DYER.
BURNS'S POETICAL WORKS. } Edited by Willmott.
FAIRFAX'S TASSO'S JERUSALEM DELIVERED.
PERCY'S RELIQUES OF ANCIENT ENGLISH POETRY.
SCOTT'S POETICAL WORKS.
MACKAY'S BALLADS AND LYRICS.
WORDSWORTH.
CRABBE.
MACKAY'S SONGS. Complete Edition.
ELIZA COOK'S POEMS.
MOORE'S POEMS.
BYRON'S POEMS.
LEIGH HUNT'S POETICAL WORKS.
ROGERS' (SAMUEL) POETICAL WORKS.
BENNETT'S (W. C.) POETICAL WORKS.
CAMPBELL'S (THOMAS) POETICAL WORKS.
BLOOMFIELD'S POEMS AND REMAINS.

Also uniform,

LONGFELLOW'S COMPLETE POETICAL WORKS, including " Tales of a Wayside Inn."
LONGFELLOW'S PROSE WORKS.

LONGFELLOW'S NEW POEMS.

In fcap. 8vo, elegantly printed on tinted paper, price 3s. 6d.

Tales of a Wayside Inn.

By HENRY WADSWORTH LONGFELLOW. With an original Steel Portrait of the Author.

ELIZA COOK'S NEW POEMS.

In fcap. 8vo, price 5s., elegantly printed on fine paper.

New Echoes and Other Poems.

By ELIZA COOK. With a Portrait

ILLUSTRATED GIFT-BOOKS.

Every Boy's Book. By Many Authors.
A complete Encyclopædia of Sports and Amusements. With 600 Illustrations. Post 8vo, cloth, 8s. 6d.

Our Garden Friends and Foes.
By the Rev. J. G. WOOD. With 200 Practical Illustrations. Crown 8vo, cloth gilt, 7s. 6d.

Miller's (Thomas) English Country Life.
With 300 Illustrations by BIRKET FOSTER, ANSDELL, HARRISON WEIR, etc. Crown 8vo, gilt and gilt edges, splendidly ornamented cover, 7s. 6d.

Homes and Haunts of the British Poets.
A New Edition. By WILLIAM HOWITT. With numerous Illustrations. One thick volume, crown 8vo, cloth gilt, 7s. 6d.

The Playbook of Metals, Mines, and Minerals.
By J. H. PEPPER, author of the "Boy's Play Book of Science." With upwards of 300 Illustrations. Post 8vo, cloth gilt, 7s. 6d.

Grimm's Household Stories.
Complete Edition. With 240 Engravings by WEHNERT. Post 8vo, cloth gilt and gilt edges, 7s. 6d.

The Arabian Nights' Entertainments.
Complete Edition. With large Illustrations by WILLIAM HARVEY. Post 8vo, cloth, gilt edges, 6s.

The Three Midshipmen.
By W. H. KINGSTON. With 29 Illustrations by JULIAN PORTCH, THOMAS, etc. Small 4to, cloth, 6s.

The Fairy Tales of the Countess D'Aulnoy.
Illustrated by JOHN GILBERT. Post 8vo, cloth, 6s.

Fairy Tales.
By CHARLES PERRAULT and others. Translated by J. R. PLANCHE. Illustrated by GODWIN, CORBOULD, and HARVEY. Post 8vo, cloth, 6s.

Don Quixote.
Translated by JARVIS. With Illustrations by JOHN GILBERT. Post 8vo, cloth, 6s.

An Illustrated Natural History.
By the Rev. J. G. WOOD. With 500 Illustrations by WILLIAM HARVEY, and 8 Designs by WOLF, WEIR, etc. Post 8vo, cloth, 6s.

The Boy's Play Book of Science.
By J. H. PEPPER. With 400 Illustrations by H. G. HINE. Post 8vo, cloth, 6s.

Entertaining Knowledge by Popular Authors.
With 100 Pictures. Crown 8vo, cloth, gilt edges, 6s.

Pleasant Tales by Popular Authors.
With 140 Pictures by Eminent Artists. Crown 8vo, cloth, gilt edges, 6s.

CLEARANCE STOCK: SOLD AT HALF THE PUBLISHED PRICE.

Eighteenpenny Volumes sold at 9d.

Adrien, Author of "*Zingra the Gipsy*"	Hobbses and Dobbses *Crayon*
Bashful Irishman	Home and the World *Mrs. Rires*
Billets and Bivouacs	Little Pedlington *John Poole*
Clement Lorimer *A. B. Reach*	My Cousin Nicholas *Barham*
Derby Ministry *Mark Rochester*	Mutiny in India
Drafts for Acceptance *Raymond*	Nan Darrell *Miss Pickering*
Duke *Mrs. Grey*	Pin Money *Mrs. Gore*
Garies (The) *Webb*	Rifle Clubs *W. H. Russell*
Gold Worshippers	Twenty Years of an African Slaver
By the Author of "*Whitefriars*"	

Two Shilling Volumes sold at 1s.

Comic Sketch Book *Poole*	Mothers and Daughters *Mrs. Gore*
Colin Clink *Hooton*	Phineas Quiddy *John Poole*
Embassies and Foreign Courts	Roving Englishman in Turkey
The Roving Englishman	Tylney Hall *Thomas Hood*
Fanny the Milliner *Rowcroft*	The Captain's Wife
Household Law *Fonblanque*	By the Author of "*Carendish*"
Jasper Lyle *Mrs. Ward*	The Ladder of Gold *Robert Bell*
Millionaire *Dudley Costello*	Soldier of Lyons *Mrs. Gore*
Maximums of Muggins *Selby*	The Unloved One *Mrs. Hofland*
Sepoy Revolt (History of the)	Up among the Pandies (sells at 2s. 6d.)
Eliza Cook's Jottings	Vicissitudes of Italy *A. L. V. Gretton*
Francesca Carrara *L. E. L.*	Waltham, fcap. 8vo *Gleig*
Longwoods of the Grange	William the Conqueror *Sir C. Napier*
Lord George Bentinck *Disraeli*	

BY W. H. PRESCOTT.

In fcap. 8vo, price 2s. each volume, boards; or cloth, 2s. 6d.

HISTORY OF THE REIGN OF FERDINAND AND ISABELLA. 2 vols.
HISTORY OF THE CONQUEST OF MEXICO. 2 vols.
HISTORY OF THE CONQUEST OF PERU. 2 vols.
HISTORY OF THE REIGN OF PHILIP THE SECOND. 3 vols.
HISTORY OF THE REIGN OF CHARLES THE FIFTH. 2 vols.
BIOGRAPHICAL AND CRITICAL ESSAYS. 1 vol.

ROUTLEDGES' HANDBOOKS.

Price Sixpence each, boards, with Illustrations.

Swimming and Skating *J. G. Wood*	The Cardplayer *G. F. Pardon*
Gymnastics *J. G. Wood*	Rowing and Sailing
Chess *G. F. Pardon*	Riding and Driving
Whist *G. F. Pardon*	Archery and Fencing
Billiards and Bagatelle *G. F. Pardon*	Brother Sam's Conundrums
Draughts and Backgammon *G.F.Pardon*	Manly Exercises, Boxing, Walking, &c.
Cricket *E. Routledge*	Croquet *E. Routledge*

LONDON: GEORGE ROUTLEDGE AND SONS.

www.ingramcontent.com/pod-product-compliance
Lightning Source LLC
Chambersburg PA
CBHW030939110726
47900CB00004B/1056